SKANDALON

A GLANCE INTO THE UNSEEN REALM
Revised Edition

CINDY SCHROPPEL

CINDY SCHROPPEL

Skandalon: A Glance Into the Unseen Realm Revised Edition

To Contact the Author:
www.sftjm.com

Acknowledgment

To Lori Vanta, one of the bravest, most valiant prayer warriors I've ever known. You fought your fight. You finished your course. Enjoy your rewards. I'll see you at the gates!

FOREWORD FOR SKANDALON

You know those people who read the foreword of a book before they dive into the author's words? Well, guess what? I'm not one of them.

This is my confession.

I know. It's positively awful to say those words and then have them printed right here on this page for all you foreword readers to see. I'm not a bad person. It's just that when I start a new book, I'm so anxious to get into the meat and bones of it that I simply don't make time for the foreword. Y'all, I had to read several just to understand how this should work!

It is not lost on me that some precious friend or mentor took great time thinking up kind, superfluous things to say about an author's work, and here I am, too impatient to give them a few minutes of my time to honor their effort. I'm so sorry, foreword writers! Please forgive me, because I understand now why you did it. Standing here in your shoes, I get why you said, yes.

I am a lover of well-crafted stories. I don't make enough room for them in my reading schedule. (*referring to when I actually make time to read*) I love to read, but most days my reading stacks consist of books on leadership, Christian living, or ministry related titles. It's what I do, and I want to be learning, growing, and teaching others until my final breath. That's why when Cindy handed me a copy of this book, I was thrilled! When was the last time I read something for the sheer fun of it? How long had it been since I got lost in a good story? At least I was hoping it was good. I didn't know because, at the time, I didn't know her, but that would quickly change.

Over those next few days, I felt like I was back in my twenties again. Back then, I stayed up for hours past my "bedtime" (*What twenty-something has a bedtime?*) reading because whatever Jeanette Oake or Frank Perretti novel I was reading, was much too riveting to put down.

Okay. So I'm a child of The Little House on The Prairie years, and yes, I did find Jeanette Oake's books riveting. However, to give a little clout to myself here, notice I did include Perretti in that little shout out. And that brings me back to this foreword.

I have been blessed to grow up as an adult, in a church fellowship that understands that *we wrestle not against flesh and blood, but against principalities, against powers, against the rulers of the darkness of this world* (Ep. 6:12). That doesn't mean we look for a demon under every rock, or that we blame the devil for every bad thing that happens. It means that we live fully aware that there are spiritual forces at work, both for and against us, and that as believers, we have the honor of partnering with the good at the peril of the bad.

This story Cindy crafted together so beautifully brings that to light in such a powerful way. It's not scary or dark, like some fiction books on this subject can be. Not at all. In fact, while reading this book, I was filled with hope. These aren't real people, but I was rooting for them like they were.

Something else I found myself doing while reading this book was praying quite a bit for people I knew who seemed to have lost their way. I prayed fervently for friends so entangled in the enemy's trap that they're blind to it, and have been for years. I prayed for myself and for places in my own life where I'd settled for convenience instead of pressing in and putting up a righteous fight. I prayed through this book more than any other I could remember, and I regularly pray through most of them (*considering the genres I listed earlier*).

This book is not just for believers. Anyone reading this foreword (*thank you very much for not being like me*) can probably understand that there is something dark at work in our world today. You have but to turn on the news to see it, or perhaps, just have a conversation with someone you know. There is more to this darkness than meets the eye, and Cindy does an incredible job of making us more aware of this truth.

You know, I probably would've gone back and read the foreword when I finished the book had there been one when I initially read it. Instead, I did something better. I told everyone about Skandalon. I talked about it incessantly. I recommended it to everyone I knew that loves to read, and to a few friends I know haven't picked up a book since it was required of them in high school or college.

It was that good! Good enough for me to share it with you here. And I guess that's why people write forewords, and why I will always, from henceforth, read the foreword before starting a new book.

By Cheryl Moses
Women's Ministry Leader
Calvary Community Church
N W Houston, Texas

1

Come to Me, all you who labor and are heavy laden,
and I will give you rest.

—Matthew 11:28

Beelzebub, the prince of demons, stood towering over the army under his vast domain of utter darkness and evil. The darkness was his abode, and he, as well as his demonic forces, could see quite well in this secret underworld. It was the womb of iniquity, the place where every evil scheme was conceived. He reveled in the fact that the power of darkness was able to hide his well-spun lies from the truth. It was the light that made him tremble, for only in it could his lies be exposed and dismantled, causing great harm to his kingdom.

Before him stood a myriad of followers, lined in military fashion, waiting for his orders, and eager to do his bidding. It was his daily ritual to stand before this noxious group to spur them on, keep them focused on the urgency of their assignments, and make adjustments to their plans where needed. He knew the word of Jehovah. He'd heard the prophecies. He knew time was short. Of course, no one knew precisely how much time he had left to vent his unabashed hatred out against Jehovah and His followers. Not even the dearly beloved Son was privy to that information. However, his time to influence humanity was coming to an end. Oh, he sensed it all right, but he did not fear, and he would never grovel at the feet of Jehovah or His beloved Son.

There was a time he'd loved and served the great Jehovah. He'd seen His power displayed in creation both of the physical world and the humans who occupied it. He, along with the holy angels, had rejoiced over the great wonder of it all. But Jehovah's demands for reverence and such single-minded worship proved to be more than he could bear. Jehovah could not, or would not, share His throne with anyone else, and it sickened Beelzebub to the core.

Jehovah himself had proclaimed that Beelzebub was the anointed Cherub. His resplendent beauty was matchless…except to One. All of the holy angels had been aware of his position and power. He'd led the heavenly choir in such majestic worship, hitting musical notes the likes no human ear has ever heard or even imagined, and no celestial being could match. That should have made him worthy of worship too. He'd convinced at least a third of the angels to bow down in worship to him. They'd recognized his giftedness and were in awe of his beauty. They were ready to give him the homage he felt he too deserved. He'd convinced them that one day they would rule and reign with him for all eternity.

Jehovah was jealous of receiving all the glory for Himself. He had labeled him a rebel, a liar and cast him out of the third heaven and onto this godforsaken earth realm where he'd made it his aim to see to it that every human would bow down and worship him and him alone. He had plenty of human followers who were devoted to him.

He would have to step up his game and ramp up his strategies against the children of Jehovah. Those shriveling idiots who chose to put their trust in a God they could not even see. How weak and ignorant they were. He was determined to destroy the faith of each and every one of them and make sure they did not reproduce after their own kind.

This army of demons cowering before him took great delight in manipulating humans to do their bidding. They were a skilled army having thousands of years of experience in their trade. Their nefarious tactics had worked well for them from century to fallen century. The human heart was so utterly predictable. Anger, greed, pride, lust, envy, and jealousy, as well as a multitude of other sins, have all found their place of habitation in the heart of man since he'd first succeeded in instigating the fall of Adam and Eve in the garden of Jehovah.

In the heart of every man and woman was the deep-seated desire to worship him, and he'd see to it that they had every opportunity to do so. Even if they worshipped themselves, lusting after power and preeminence, it was all the same to him. It was still a means to keep them from faithfully following and being blindly obedient to Jehovah.

Zoe scrambled around the house muttering to herself while searching for her keys. "Oh, not again! Jeez, help me find my keys, Lord." The baby had obviously gotten a hold of them and misplaced them. "Ahh…there they are." She pulled the keys out from between the couch cushions where the baby had been playing the night before. She then lifted up a casual offering of thanks. "Thanks, Lord!"

She yelled into the direction of Michael's office. "Good-bye, we're leaving." Michael, who was seated at the desk in his office didn't have a chance to respond. She whisked Emma up into her arms, grabbed her diaper bag while at the same time doing a mental inventory to be sure that everything the baby needed for the day was inside of it before rushing out the door in her usual hurried state.

After strapping her thirteen-month-old daughter into her car seat, she hurried into the driver side of her silver Lexus and made her way down the winding driveway and off for another day at work, running late as usual. She hated rushing. Checking her appearance in the rear-view mirror, she caught a glimpse of her baby. *It can't possibly be healthy for Emma.* "Thank God it's Friday." She spoke the words aloud as she pulled out of her subdivision.

Her job as a receptionist at Dream Maker's Employment Agency wasn't a great job, but it earned a paycheck and helped her and Michael pay the bills. She often, though she'd never tell Michael, wished they'd heeded the wisdom of Michael's parents to buy a home in which they could afford to maintain all of their expenses on Michael's salary alone.

At the beginning of their marriage, they had made a wise purchase of a cute little two-bedroom fourteen-hundred-square-foot townhome in the Village. It wasn't brand new, but it was in a great area of town. She and Michael had enjoyed the time they'd spent together making repairs and decorating their modest home. At the time, it had seemed to be more than adequate to meet their needs. They had plenty of room and were proud to entertain friends and have church members over for fellowship or Bible studies.

They'd both agreed to live there for at least five years to build up equity in hopes that they could make a profit when they were ready to start a family and purchase a larger home. But she had to admit; she'd become green with envy when Kira and Brad Parker, their best friends, bought their brand new three-thousand-square-foot home in the new, gated community of Windgate Terrace just north of downtown Houston. Suddenly, their modest townhome seemed small and out of date. After having their church cell group at the Parker's, she was almost embarrassed to have the group meet at her home any longer. So despite warnings from Michael's parents, they'd purchased her dream home in Windgate Terrace just two streets away from the Parkers.

As much as she loved the new house, they'd failed to consider the endless expenses that go along with a home of that size in an upscale neighborhood. They had an electric bill that often equaled the mortgage on the townhouse, outrageous subdivision dues and a water bill that was sky-high due to their pool. Unfortunately, between work and taking care of Emma, they barely had time to clean the pool, much less get in it.

Just two months into the new home, Zoe realized she was pregnant. In all of the hustle and bustle of moving and decorating, she'd forgotten to take her birth control pills once or twice. They'd agreed to be in the house at least two years before starting a family in order to recoup some of their expenses and put a little money aside. Though Michael had appeared to be excited about the pregnancy, she wasn't aware of the many sleepless nights he'd spent worrying about how they were going to make ends meet.

It'd always been her desire to be a stay-at-home mom, but the strain on their finances demanded that she continue to work through her pregnancy, and even after Emma was born. She hated dropping her precious baby girl off at the daycare. It grieved her that she wasn't there for all of Emma's "firsts." Her very first steps were taken at the daycare. Ms. Tina, Emma's caregiver, had told her all about it, and even filmed it on her smartphone and texted it to her while she was at work. Though Ms. Tina had undoubtedly meant well, she'd sat at her desk and cried while repeatedly viewing the video. It just wasn't the same as being there to see with her own eyes the wonder of her precious baby taking her first steps.

Well, there was no use crying over spilled milk. Today was Friday, and tomorrow she could spend quality time with Emma and Michael. They could enjoy a family day at home since they didn't have the finances to go anywhere or do anything.

She wondered how the Parkers were able to manage their finances so well. She didn't think Brad, a self-employed landscaper made much more than Michael. Yet Kira was able to stay home with their two children, Simon and Rebekah. They never appeared to worry about money.

Michael, a self-employed contract computer programmer, made a decent salary when he was working. For the most part, he stayed pretty busy, but there were seasons when he could go several weeks in-between jobs. Unfortunately, they hadn't learned to save up for those seasons and often fell behind on their bills because of it. They were always playing catch-up with their finances, living paycheck to paycheck; and she hated it.

Her salary wasn't much, but without her job, there would be no medical insurance. It paid for daycare and her car note as well as for any extras they were able to afford. The Lexus was a major splurge, but she'd argued with Michael that if she were going to get up every day and fight the traffic for an hour each way into downtown, she deserved to do it in style and comfort.

Financial worries were foreign to her. The word budget had never been in her vocabulary. Her dad was a prominent corporate lawyer, a member of Golden Heights Country Club, and well known in their city. He'd provided well for her when she was growing up. He occasionally offered to help them out, but Michael was proud and didn't want to be dependent on her father. Still, her daddy would often slip her a couple hundred here and there so that she could continue to dress the way she was accustomed and see to it that Emma never went without. But that was just between her and her dad. She didn't want Michael to feel like he couldn't provide for her and Emma. Michael rarely noticed her new clothes, and when he did, her response was always the same little white lie. "I've had this hanging in my closet forever."

Admittedly, most of their financial mess was her fault. She was well aware that Michael, like her father, couldn't say no to her, and she often pushed him to make rash decisions, knowing that he wouldn't deny her what she desired if she sweet-talked and pleaded with him enough. She supposed she had some of her father's lawyer genes in her too because she could make her case when she wanted something, wearing Michael down until he gave in. He would have been content to stay in the townhouse, but she'd pleaded with him for the house in Windgate Terrace. She had dangled the idea before him of an extra room that could be used for an office, pointing out that it would be a tax write-off. She'd made sure to emphasize the large patio, deck, and backyard that would be great for entertaining as well as for children when they came along, not foreseeing that it would be much sooner than later. But the icing on the cake was the man cave. She'd seen how blown away Michael had been at Brad's sport-themed room, and she'd promised to make his even more spectacular. She could not be satisfied until she got what she wanted.

She had no one else to blame but her selfish desires, so off to work she went after dropping Emma off at the daycare into Ms. Tina's loving arms.

Ramiah waited in the corner of the living room as Zoe searched for her keys. As soon as she lifted up a short prayer petitioning God to assist her, he nudged her into the direction of the couch by whispering into her spirit a simple thought. "*Wasn't the baby playing with them on the couch last night?*"

Ramiah was thankful that Zoe had prayed for such an insignificant need. If only she spent more time in prayer petitioning God for His abundant promises, it would enable him to assist her more often. He was grateful that the Almighty would assign him to guard His most-prized possession. When Zoe was conceived, he'd been given charge over her. Since the day she came forth from her mother's womb, he'd never left her side. He stood vigil over her as she slept at night and dutifully followed her every move throughout the day.

Zoe's father and stepmom had never been churchgoers, however, she had a maternal grandmother who was a devoted worshipper of the Almighty. She'd prayed daily for God to protect her granddaughter and draw her into a relationship with Him through His Son. As a child, Zoe would attend church without the accompaniment of her father or stepmom at the small First Assembly of God located several blocks away from her house. Occasionally, she would spend the weekend with her grandma and attend church with her. Though she'd enjoyed her grandma's church, she'd loved the praise band at the First Assembly over the hymns at her grandma's church.

Ramiah would accompany her to church and observe her listening to her Sunday school teachers with a hungry heart and entering into the worship service. She would sing the praise songs at the top of her lungs, clapping her hands in perfect rhythm, and beaming from ear to ear with joy. When Zoe was ten, he was there praising, along with a host of other angels, as she made the decision to make Jesus her Savior.

It was he who had prodded her to go on the youth retreat at Pine Country when she was sixteen, which was where she'd met Michael who'd been interning as a camp counselor. He knew that it was the Almighty's plan for the two of them to meet, and he'd done everything he could to assist in the connection, making sure Zoe was in the right places at the right times.

God, in all of His wisdom, chose Michael for Zoe. They were very different in so many ways, yet the Almighty knew that they'd be perfect for each other. Michael was shy and quiet. His often serious demeanor was balanced out by Zoe's effervescent, outgoing personality. He was raised in a pastor's home filled with faith and love while hers was filled with greed and jealousy. But they had two things in common, their faith in God and their love for each other.

Michael loved God with all of his heart. He'd made the decision to give his life to Christ at the age of seven. Though he was very young, Michael understood what it meant to become a Christian and had surrendered his life over to the Lord. His greatest desire was to be a pastor just like his father.

He'd determined to honor God and remain a virgin until the day he married the woman God had chosen for him. Oh, he'd been tempted on many occasions. The enemy had often sought to entice him. "Since you know she's the one for you, you might as well have sex together." But His love for God was strong, and by His grace, he'd been able to resist the temptation every time. Deuel had fought the battle against the enemy so Michael could stand against the war raging between his body and spirit.

Michael was Deuel's charge, which often united Ramiah and Deuel in their combat for both Michael and Zoe against Beelzebub, the enemy of their souls. They kept a relentless vigil, loved and protected them, helped them to make divine connections, and always sought the guidance of God for them.

Michael sat staring at the program on his computer screen. With Zoe and Emma now gone, the house was silent. Finding it difficult to focus, he'd been working on the same line of his program for the last hour with no real progress. The weight of the finances was heavy upon him, and he was concerned that there would not be enough money to pay the bills coming due at the end of the month. For the first time, Michael had even thought about holding back their tithe. *Surely God would understand the predicament we're in.* He felt himself slipping into a familiar funk.

Michael and Zoe had been married five and a half years. She was the love of his life. He adored everything about her. He'd known the moment they'd met at summer camp that she was the one God had fashioned for him. Her blond hair, sparkling blue eyes, cute little figure and infectious personality had instantly won his heart over. They'd fallen, almost immediately, head-over-heels in love during that memorable summer, and their affection for each other had only grown when they'd returned home. Though he'd lived a good fifty-minute drive from her house, they had devoted all of their free time to each other on the weekends and talked on the phone for hours at a time every day and, often, well into the night.

Though his parents adored Zoe, her father tolerated Michael. He thought Michael and his family were too radical in their religious beliefs. Amos Richards, Zoe's father, also wished that Michael had better aspirations for his future and disapproved of his lack of an Ivy League education.

They married as soon as he'd graduated from computer tech school. Michael was twenty-two, and Zoe had turned twenty a month before they'd married. They were kids with a fairy-tale idea that their love for each other and faith in God would be enough to help them overcome any obstacles they would ever face as a couple.

Though he did not regret their marriage or Emma coming much sooner than he'd planned, reality was making it clear to him that love and faith were not enough to carry them to that place of happily ever after. If they were going to make it financially, he would have to heed the wisdom of God a whole lot more and his wife's determined pleading a little less.

He and Zoe had begun to argue regularly about finances. They'd had a very heated argument the night before, and she'd gone to bed angry. She was never content with what they had but always wanted more than he was able to give to her, and she couldn't understand why it bothered him that she'd run to her daddy to meet her needs when he wasn't able to.

Though he enjoyed the challenge of his work as a contract programmer and the freedom of working from home, he felt the call of God on his life to pastor a church. Unfortunately, he had no choice but to continue working at secular employment because it paid much more than most pastors' salaries. For the time being, he was trying to remain content with being the assistant youth pastor at his church.

He felt blessed to be a part of New Zion Fellowship, the church they attended. Pastor Steve, though relatively young, was very learned in the Scriptures and a captivating speaker. He was gifted in presenting the word of God in such a way that anyone could understand it. He was humble, loving and caring and the type of pastor who was accessible and easy to get to know. It had been apparent to Michael the first time they'd attended New Zion that Steve was to be their pastor. With his father's church forty minutes away from their new home, it made it difficult for them to attend except for on special occasions. He'd also wanted to experience being in a church other than his father's since it was all he'd ever known.

Michael enjoyed and even looked forward to his study and prayer time with God every day. Nothing could compare to the times when God would speak and make His presence real. He loved when the word came alive, and he received nuggets of revelation as he studied. On several occasions, he'd heard God's audible voice, which drove him to seek Him that much more. However, he knew that he'd slipped in his spiritual walk, and was not happy as he reflected on some of the ways he'd allowed the world to creep into their home. Television shows that had once been considered off-limits from watching due to the language, sex scenes, and violence were now recorded if there was a possibility they might miss them. He and Zoe rarely prayed together anymore. When they were dating, they had made it their habit to pray together on the phone before hanging up each night. Life kept them both so busy that it had somehow crowded out what had once been so important to them. And then there was the debt, which kept him filled with anxiety every month when the bills were due. It was the cause of the knot in his stomach and the oppression he was experiencing this morning.

He heard the Holy Spirit gently whisper into his spirit as he sat at the desk staring at his computer. *"Come to Me, all you who labor and are heavy laden, and I will give you rest."*

Michael felt the urge to pray. He realized this financial burden was more than he could bear, and though he felt responsible, he knew he needed the Lord's help. "Father, I've made a mess of our finances. I've made poor financial choices, and I realize that Zoe and I have not sought You on many of them. I'm ashamed, and I ask You to forgive me. Help me, as the spiritual leader of my home, to make right decisions. Give me wisdom and direction. I desperately need Your help and Your grace. Show me what to do to get us out of this bind. Father, please give me a desire to seek You above all that the world has to offer. I ask you to draw Zoe into a deeper relationship with You. I don't see that fire in her anymore. I ask all of this in Jesus's mighty name. Amen."

He was unaware that Deuel, his guardian angel, had one hand on his shoulder for strength while he raised his powerful sword high in his right hand, ready to thwart any enemy opposition assigned against Michael as he prayed. If he could have seen and heard in the spiritual realm, Michael would have also known that a host of angels were immediately dispatched to bring forth the answers to his prayer.

Michael felt as if an elephant had been lifted off of his chest. Peace washed over him. He would have prayed sooner, but he felt to blame because he had such a difficult time standing up to Zoe. He wanted to give her everything she wanted and needed. He'd always feared he might lose her once she realized that he'd probably never be able to lavish her with the lifestyle her father had made her accustomed to.

He knew, however, that he couldn't blame Zoe for the mess they were in. It was his responsibility as her husband and spiritual leader to use the wisdom he'd learned from the scriptures as well as the example of good stewardship his father had mirrored to him. If he were honest with himself, he'd have to admit that when he first saw the house, he had wanted it just as much as Zoe. It was nice having an office in the house instead of working at the kitchen table, and, he had to concede, his man cave was pretty sweet.

However, if they were going to keep this house, he would have to learn to say no to Zoe when it needed to be said. "Lord, help me."

Beelzebub began his address to the sea of demons arrayed before him. It was the same message he'd spoken over the countless eons to his workers of iniquity with only a slightly different twist as the evolution of technology had afforded them incalculable opportunities and effective methods to entice man to sin.

"It is imperative that we secure the gates of Hades. We know that to lose our battle against Jehovah and His hosts must not even be considered, for the loss to us would have eternal consequences. You are all aware of Jehovah's plans. He's determined that your end will be the lake of fire. But I, your wise master, will not let that fate befall you as long as you listen to me and follow my instructions precisely. We have made great strides against the kingdom of light. We can, and must, win this battle against the forces of Jehovah. You need only to remain my faithful, loyal followers and heed my advice, and we will see the victory." The hideous crowd cheered uncontrollably. Panting like a pack of ravenous dogs, they hung onto every word spoken by their prince of lies.

Spurred by their enthusiasm, he continued his mantra. "We know that humans are weak creatures who can be easily ensnared. By a simple whisper in their ear, they will readily follow the power of your suggestions. You need only listen when they speak and watch their habits and routines so that you can discern the bait best suited to entrap them."

"Don't preoccupy yourselves so much with those who've chosen to worship me nor with those who have set themselves up as gods of their own lives. They are not a threat to our kingdom as long as they remain entrenched in their lifestyle of destruction. Most of them are so deceived they'll never find their way to Jehovah as long as you keep the saints from praying for them. Beware, it only takes one devoted, praying child of Jehovah to untangle them from the web of deceit we've so painstakingly woven." The demons wagged their heads in a show of delirious agreement.

"Those who are religious because it satisfies their guilty souls are not a major concern to us either. Leave them to their rituals and pious prayers. They're not bothering us. It's those pesky praying Christians you must target." Venom spewed from his mouth. "Target the ones who claim to be devoted followers of Jehovah. Seek to destroy those who've sworn allegiance to Him and grovel at His feet. It's their hearts that I desire to corrupt with every fiery dart hell can throw at them." Again, an uncontrollable cheer went up. An immense hatred, the likes of which no human has ever experienced, filled the atmosphere.

"Keep them so preoccupied with their lives that they'll be too distracted to seek after their God. Busyness will lead them to spiritual barrenness. Make sure their jobs, families, children's activities, and their hobbies are so demanding of their time that they have none left at the end of the day for worship of Jehovah. I don't even mind if they follow after godly well-meaning pursuits as long as they stay too busy to pray."

"Convince them that there is more than one way to their God and that to think otherwise is hateful and narrow-minded. Utilize the perceived freedom of other religions to draw and entice them away from the truth of their God. Persuade them that to truly walk in love, they must embrace the beliefs of others, and that to do so pleases Jehovah."

"Bait them into sexual sin through the use of multimedia that now spans the globe. I am the prince of the power of the airwaves and have been using it to my advantage for years. Continue using the mediums of television, Internet, and radio to break down the biblical idea of the family—that marriage should be solely between a man and a woman till death do them part. Persuade them that homosexuality is normal and accepted by Jehovah and that those who practice this lifestyle were merely born that way. Entice them to commit adultery and introduce them to their lovers through social media to which they've become addicted like a drug." Those before him knew the power of media and the damage it could do against Jehovah's kingdom. Many had worked themselves into such a frenzy of excitement, hooting, and hollering their adoration of the one they worshipped that Beelzebub had to quiet the rabble before he could continue.

"Since the invention of television, we have used it to occupy their time with endless hours of mindless entertainment as well as corrupting their beliefs and feeding their lusts. I revel in the fact that we have duped their children into using it for the play of their graphically violent and often deliciously vulgar games, which enforce the sins of promiscuity, hate, rage, and murder. What an excellent medium of destruction this invention is to us. Keep them mesmerized by it!"

"Draw them to lust after money and captivate them with an overwhelming craving for the latest gadgets and inventions, the largest houses, and the finest cars. I want materialism to be their god. Sow seeds of lust for food, drugs, and alcohol, making them entirely dependent on something other than their beloved Jehovah."

"At all cost, you must keep them from walking in love with their fellow man. Utilize the weapons of accusation, offense, bitterness, and unforgiveness. It will hinder their prayer life and give you entrance to cause great havoc in their lives. Jehovah cannot bear unforgiveness." A smile spread across his diabolical face, the mere thought of making Jehovah unhappy brought immense pleasure. "Fear will diminish their faith. A fearful Christian is a faithless, powerless Christian." The word Christian was like poison on his lips. "Your assaults against them must be so strategic and well-timed that they become insurmountable in their eyes. Even the smallest of their problems must appear like a mountain before them so that they get their eyes off their God."

Rage and loathing spewed forth from the prince of darkness as he proceeded with his sermon. "But above all, discourage them from speaking the truth of God's word in faith, for when they do, your assignments against them are broken. His word has power that even I cannot stand against. When the word dwells in their hearts, and they speak it from their mouths, we have lost the battle. Angelic hosts are summoned into action when they pray and declare the word. Induce them to talk about how sick and broke they are. Coax them to speak words of defeat, failure, and fear. Persuade them to talk about their problems so that they loom before them like an impenetrable fortress." The imps chattered agreement. The one thing they feared the most was the word of Jehovah spoken in faith. There were no weapons strong enough to fight against it. An uncontrollable shudder went through his being. "Remember, even the strongest and fiercest of demons tremble at the name of Jesus. Confuse their understanding so that they do not grasp the power of that name nor utter it from their lips. Do you want to cower down to that name?" The very thought disgusted him. They stood before him paralyzed with fear. "No! Then you must use your wiles to coax them to use the name of Jehovah and His Son as a curse word for that derails it of its power in their life."

"Your mission is to steal, kill, and destroy everything and anyone that is dear and precious to them. You have many weapons in your arsenal, and you've had years of experience in your trade."

"Some of you are dispatched to geographic locations and rulers while others are assigned to individuals. Whatever your assignment, do it well, for the welfare of our kingdom depends on every one of you. And never underestimate the power of a human who has the understanding of his covenant relationship with Jehovah."

Satisfied with himself and his speech, he let out a roar like that of a ferocious lion before disappearing into the darkness, leaving his minions to go forth to do his bidding against his adversaries.

Those set over countries, rulers, and authorities quickly departed with their legions following to defend their acquired domain against the heavenly forces. Many of them conspired to plot large-scale systematic attacks against churches, ministry leaders, evangelists, and intercessors. Others collaborated on their strategies against single individuals to ensure that they were successful in their efforts against Christianity. They understood the power of unity and the need to work together to accomplish their destructive goals.

2

I will never leave you nor forsake you.
—Hebrews 13:5

Zoe woke up Saturday morning feeling drained. She and Michael had stayed up late. He'd been busy working in his office while she'd been in bed playing games on her iPad and browsing through Pinterest. Pinterest, a popular and addictive website, was like crack to a woman's soul and it was her guilty pleasure. Glancing at her cell phone docked on the nightstand, she realized that it was already nine forty-five in the morning. She hopped out of bed and headed in search of Michael and Emma.

"Michael, why did you let me sleep so late?" Strolling into the living room, she caught sight of her husband and child.

Michael looked up at her from his recliner and smiled. Emma was sitting on his lap, dressed in footed pajamas, her hair tousled, a book in her hands and milk dripping down her chin. Cheerios were spewed across the coffee table, and a sippy cup half-filled with milk was turned over on its side. Her chubby little hands were filled with cereal, ready to be shoved into her mouth as soon as her chunky cheeks were emptied of their current contents.

"Emma was crying in her crib, and you obviously didn't hear her, so I decided to let Mommy sleep in this morning while I spent some time with my baby girl. We've been eating and playing, and now we're reading. She has a poopy diaper though, and I saved that for you."

Zoe made a face at him and giggled. "Gee thanks, babe!"

She scooped Emma up into her arms and showered her plump little face with kisses until the baby squealed with frustration, pushing Zoe's face away from hers.

"Come on, munchkin. We can't expect Daddy to be perfect, can we?" She carried her chattering toddler into the nursery.

As often happened, she was overcome with love for her daughter and reflected on how grateful she was for the precious life squirming before her on the changing table. Gazing at her beautiful little girl, she knew every square inch of her pudgy face. She'd kissed it a million times. She loved the deep dimples etched on either side of her cheeks, a gift from her daddy's gene pool. Her blond hair with tight ringlet curls spilled onto the changing table as her inquisitive blue eyes stared back at Zoe.

"How much does your mommy love you?" She rubbed her nose against Emma's in an Eskimo kiss. It was a rhetorical question she frequently asked her toddler and always followed it up with the repeated response. "As much as the water in the ocean and the sand by the sea, that's how much my mommy loves me." Grandma Abby had told her that her mom had always recited the same little rhyme to her when she was a baby, though Zoe had been too young to remember.

Zoe's mom had died from cervical cancer when she was only four, leaving her father, a young, upcoming lawyer to raise his daughter single-handedly. He'd doted on her and did the best he could, but his hectic career and travel necessitated the hiring of a live-in nanny to take care of her.

Barbara had pretended to adore Zoe when she'd first came to the Richard's home. However, it wasn't long before she'd had her sights on her handsome employer and his six-figure income. Ten years younger than Amos and extremely attractive, she used her female prowess to gain his affections. Zoe, awakening from a bad dream, had run into her father's bedroom one night to find Barbara sleeping in her daddy's bed. Before long, Amos, being lonely and infatuated with her beauty and quick wit, asked her to marry him thinking he'd also found the perfect mom for Zoe.

Barbara began to display her resentment toward Zoe early on in the marriage. She was jealous of any affection Amos showed toward his daughter and was very demanding, desiring his full attention be on her. It was often the cause of many heated discussions in their home.

Zoe remembered overhearing a conversation between her father and stepmom one night as she lay in her bed. Amos begged Barbara to be a little more understanding and compassionate toward Zoe citing how desperately she needed the love of a mother. Barbara had responded with anger in her voice. "I feel like you always put her before me. How can you expect me to love her like she were my own when I didn't give birth to her?" Zoe's heart had been crushed.

When Amos wasn't home, Barbara made life difficult for young Zoe, often restricting her to her room, yelling and cursing at her and giving her chores that were far beyond her ability to perform and then punishing her when she was unable to do so. She tried her best to please Barbara, but her best was never good enough. When she failed to live up to her expectations, she was often threatened with being sent to live with her grandma, a fate that she would have embraced except she couldn't bear the thought of separation from her dad.

Amos, intoxicated by Barbara's charm and beauty, tolerated her tantrums and attitude toward his daughter. He did everything within his power to make her happy, hoping she'd change. He'd bought her a beautiful home in the exclusive neighborhood of Golden Heights. They were members of the country club where she golfed, swam, and played tennis. She had the finest cars and shopped at high-end stores and boutiques. He'd even taken his young wife to Paris on their first anniversary. But he would not deny his daughter the love and attention he knew she needed and his wife resented. Therefore, the early years of their marriage were marred by turbulence.

Within two years of the already strained marriage, Amos John Richards Jr. was born. Barbara had hoped Amos would be so enamored with having a son named after him that he'd spend less time and affection on his daughter. Though he adored little John, Amos felt guilty for the pain and loneliness he'd often see in his daughter's eyes, making him want to spoil her with gifts and affection even more.

Zoe adored her little brother from the moment she'd laid eyes on him. Her stepmom had not wanted her at the hospital when he was born, claiming that she might carry in germs and cause baby John to get sick. Amos saw through her pretense of worry but, to keep the peace, abided by her wishes. As John grew older, her stepmom enjoyed making a dramatic presentation over the gifts she'd bring home for her son from her frequent shopping excursions, though she never bought anything for Zoe. Although it infuriated Amos, he made up for the ill-treatment of Zoe by spoiling her profusely.

Barbara refused to take her shopping, complaining that she was too picky, so Zoe and Amos shopped together for her clothes, often including Grandma Abby to ensure she was dressing appropriately for a girl her age. Even though Grandma Abby was her maternal grandmother, Amos made sure Zoe remained close to her. Some of her favorite memories were of the times the three of them spent together.

Grandma Abby tried to teach Zoe the importance of forgiveness. When Zoe would relate stories of Barbara's abuse and blatant partiality toward John, Grandma never wavered in her response. "Zoe, we'll just have to pray harder for her. Jesus loves her as much as He loves you or me and wouldn't want us to hate her or wish evil upon her." Zoe would return home determined to love and forgive Barbara until the next offense, which usually occurred as soon as she stepped across the threshold of Barbara's domain.

As Zoe dressed Emma, she remembered the two things she'd promised her baby on the night she was born. First, that she'd never die and leave her in the hands of a wicked stepmom, and second, she would make it her goal in life to make sure Emma always knew how very much she was loved.

"*I will never leave you or forsake you.*" Zoe paid little attention to the still small voice she heard in her spirit.

"Mommy will always love and protect you. I'll always be here for you, my sweet baby girl." She picked Emma up from the changing table and squeezed her tightly.

Zoe returned to the living room with Emma toddling behind her. Michael met her with a cup of coffee in his hand. "I'm going to go into my office and pray for a while if that's okay with you." He kissed her on the lips and handed her the cup. "Do we have any plans for the day?"

"No, I have a few errands to run after Emma wakes from her morning nap. Do you want to go with us?"

"No. I think I might do some yard work. I noticed yesterday the grass is getting high, and we don't want to get another nasty letter from the homeowner's association."

He kissed her again before retreating to his office for his daily quiet time with the Lord. He felt uneasy in his spirit due to a disturbing dream he'd had the night before about Emma.

In the dream, he'd looked into her crib and reached to cover her with her blanket. He remembered thinking how innocent she looked and sensed the need to protect her. He'd turned to get something…maybe another blanket to cover her or perhaps her pacifier…He couldn't remember…but when he turned back to the crib; she was gone. Panicking, he frantically searched her room but couldn't find her. He was startled awake by the sound of her crying in the distance, quickly realizing he was hearing her through the baby monitor on Zoe's nightstand. Fear gripped him for an instant as he jumped out of bed to check on her, only to find her sitting in the crib sucking on her pacifier and holding her favorite stuffed bear.

He questioned God as he reflected on the dream. "Father, what did that dream mean?" He waited for a moment but heard nothing in his spirit to indicate that God was answering his question, so he proceeded to pray for the people and needs that were on his heart. He prayed for protection for his little family and asked God to watch over them.

His prayer time was always followed by a time of reading in the Bible and his daily devotional. His Bible reading for the day was in Isaiah chapter forty-three. He paused as he read the second verse: "When you pass through the waters, I will be with you; and through the rivers, they shall not overflow you. When you walk through the fire, you shall not be burned, nor shall the flame scorch you."

A quickening in his spirit made him aware that God was speaking to him through this verse, although he wasn't sure why or what He might be saying to him. He reread it several times and then continued with his reading. It didn't surprise him at all to see the same scripture passage in the text of his daily devotional. He had a sense of foreboding and was sure that God was warning him. *Lord, what are You warning me about, and what do You want me to do about it?* Before finishing his devotional time, he wrote the scripture in his journal along with a detailed description of the dream.

Deuel, with his massive eight-foot-nine-inch frame, stood guard over

Michael as he prayed and read his Bible. He loved that Michael always read the Bible out loud, knowing it made his spirit man grow stronger as the spoken word increased his faith. As Michael asked God to watch over the family, Deuel took a warring stance, raising his mighty sword high in the air, ready to fend off any attack of the enemy. The Almighty had alerted Michael of impending danger. He often used dreams to warn individuals just as he'd warned Joseph in a dream of the enemy's plan to harm baby Jesus.

He would do his best to secure the hedge about Michael and his loved ones. Ramiah and Hanniel, Emma's angel, would have to be on the alert against the enemy as well. He could do his part as long as his charge prayed diligently and did not dismiss the forewarning. Doors were often left open to the enemy because dreams and prophetic words were dismissed or forgotten.

Hanniel stood, a devoted sentinel silently watching over Emma as she slept in her crib. The Almighty had placed her into his care. If only both of her parents understood their responsibility to be diligent in prayer for their child and speak God's promises over her. He wished all saints realized that it was the word of God that enabled angels to work on their behalf.

"Bless the Lord, you His angels, who excel in strength, who do His word, heeding the voice of His word." He could only be heard in the unseen realm where God, the angels, and demons, as well as those humans who were sensitive to the Spirit, were able to hear his booming proclamation.

Through the ages, Hanniel had often heard people blame and curse God because bad things happened to those they loved. They didn't understand that angels were present and available to protect them, yet because of their prayerlessness, the heavenly hosts were restrained from battling the enemy on their behalf. They also didn't comprehend the power of agreement available to them when they united their prayers with other believers.

"How could one chase a thousand, and two put ten thousand to flight." He paused a moment before continuing. "Again, I say to you that if two of you agree on earth concerning anything that they ask, it will be done for them by My Father in heaven."

"Amen! All glory to God, the Almighty. The only wise God, the Great King above all the earth." The sound of a multitude of angels joined him in ecstatic praise.

Although Michael prayed daily for his family, Zoe was not as faithful. She'd lift up a prayer when she felt like it was warranted, but she lacked the discipline in her life to spend quality time before the Almighty on a daily basis. Hanniel knew that the enemy preyed on such as these, and unfortunately, it hindered his efforts at protecting the life of the one he was sent to guard since she was unable to intercede for herself.

After putting Emma down for her morning nap, the thought came to Zoe that maybe she too should spend some time in prayer since Michael was still in his office. Her Bible sat idly on the nightstand beside her bed, untouched and gathering dust, often unread for weeks at a time. She couldn't remember the last time she'd read her devotional. However, there were clothes to be washed, morning dishes in the sink, and she wanted to get her shower before Emma woke from her nap. Besides, it was easier for Michael, their spiritual leader, to find the time to pray. He worked from home and kept his own schedule. *Surely, he prays enough for the both of us.* She knew the thought was just an excuse, but she also felt that God understood how busy she was as a working mom and loved her nonetheless.

She showered and dressed for the day and still had time to spend on Pinterest before Emma woke from her nap. Michael was still in his office, so she knocked before opening the door to inform him that she and Emma were leaving to run errands.

"Hey, sorry to interrupt your prayer time. Emma's up, and we're going to take off for the store. You staying here?"

"Yea, ya'll go ahead. I'm gonna mow and get some things done around here. My girls sure look beautiful today. Come give Daddy a kiss, baby girl." Emma eagerly toddled into Michael's extended arms.

Zoe walked over and kissed him good-bye. "Text me if you need anything. Tell Daddy bye-bye." She took the baby from him and slung her up on her hip.

"Zoe, we are running short on the budget this month, so, please be careful how much you spend."

She gave him a dirty look before snapping a reply. "Michael, I'm always careful. I can't help how much groceries cost. Maybe you need to go with me so you can see for yourself."

Michael sighed. "I know…I'm just saying be careful, baby. Don't get upset."

Perturbed, she'd already slammed the door shut before he got the last sentence out of his mouth. *I get so dang tired of him bugging me about how much money I spend.*

The rest of their day was spent running errands, doing chores, and taking turns watching after Emma. After the baby was bathed and put to bed that evening, they settled on the couch to watch two movies Zoe had rented. Both had an R rating, and Michael, having read the reviews, complained that he didn't think they should be watching movies with violence and sex scenes, not to mention filthy language including the blasphemous use of the Lord's name. But both were award-winning movies with great storylines, Zoe had argued, and several of their friends at church had even recommended them.

"It's cheap entertainment. At least we're saving money by not going out." Zoe hated that she had to defend herself.

Michael, not wanting to upset her again, had agreed.

It was well past one in the morning when they finally went to sleep; their bodies tangled together after a time of intimacy.

Zoe woke up Sunday morning and informed Michael that she had a headache and planned on skipping church for the day. She saw the anger and disappointment in his eyes. However, she reasoned, she was tired and wanted to stay home with the baby. *After all, Michael won't be the one who'll have to get out of a nice comfy bed bright and early in the morning to rush off to work. I don't have the luxury of working from home and keeping my own hours.* Deep down inside, she knew her reasoning was unfair since Michael was usually up and in his office long before she got out of bed.

She was furious with Michael for storming out the door without even so much as a good-bye. *He's acting unreasonable and immature. Surely he understands I work hard during the week, take care of Emma when I'm home, and keep the house clean, though he does help with that. I'm entitled to a little downtime once in a while. It's not like I skip church all the time.* She determined that she'd punish him with the silent treatment when he returned.

She spent much of the morning on the floor in Emma's play area, entertaining the baby and relishing every moment she was able to spend with her. After putting Emma down for her nap, she plopped on the couch, opened her laptop, and logged onto Facebook. She hadn't been on it for a few days and noticed several instant messages, two friend requests as well as a ton of news feed to catch up on. To her surprise, one of the friend requests was from Zachary Thomas. He had been her first love at the early age of fourteen, and they'd gone together for a year and a half, beginning her freshman year in high school. He was arguably the cutest guy in her school, star of the football team, and she'd been infatuated with him. She'd secretly dreamed they would one day marry until she caught him kissing Alexis Brennan behind the bleachers during a basketball game.

Zoe couldn't contain her surprise. "What? Talk about a blast from the past!" It'd been a little over seven years since she'd last seen Zachary at their high school graduation ceremony. He was even better looking than she'd remembered and had apparently done well for himself as a private pilot for an oil company. In his profile picture, taken at some beach, he resembled a GQ model, leaning up against a cobalt blue BMW convertible wearing a pair of faded denim jeans. His shirtless body revealed his muscular, tanned bare chest, and his perfect-teethed smile seemed to be tantalizing the person on the other end of the camera as he ran his fingers through his thick wavy brown hair. Interested in finding out what he'd been up to, she accepted his friend requests and curiously went to his page to check out more of his photos. There was nothing to indicate whether he was single or married, but scrolling through his pictures, she didn't see any images of children, though there were plenty of beautiful women, some scantily clad. There were also numerous pictures of Zach, some in his pilot uniform, which, she noted, made him look incredibly handsome. For a split second, she allowed herself to daydream of being in the arms of this drop-dead gorgeous and obviously successful man. A tinge of guilt gripped her, but she quickly waved it off. "Good grief. It would be rude not to accept his friend request."

After replying to her instant messages and looking over the recent feed of mostly gossip, ads, and encouraging sayings posted by friends and family, she snapped her laptop shut. At least an hour and a half had passed. Emma was now awake and crying in her crib, so she padded upstairs to get her. But she couldn't get the pictures of Zach out of her mind. *Is there any real harm in befriending Zach?* She thought about asking for forgiveness since she was a married woman but quickly brushed it off. *It's just Facebook. What harm could there be in reconnecting with an old friend on Facebook?*

Abstain from fleshly lusts which war against the soul. The thought drifted into Zoe's mind like a soft summer breeze. However, she paid little attention to the whisper in her spirit.

A door flung open in the spirit realm as Zoe took the bait set before her on the computer. A slimy unseen creature cloaked in darkness slithered into the room and wrapped itself around her body while imparting thoughts into her mind. "*Oh, look at him. He has done well for himself, wouldn't you say? Wow, look at that car! That must cost a fortune. I wonder what he's been up to? Is he married? He looks amazing in that uniform. You don't have to feel guilty for thinking he looks hot. After all, you're only human. You're just looking. Who wouldn't look?*"

A seed was implanted into her soul as she accepted the thoughts spoken by Lust. It was up to her as to whether or not that seed would grow and bear fruit in her life.

Ramiah, drawn sword in hand, glared defensively at the grotesque creature. "The Lord rebuke you."

The demonic spirit taunted Ramiah. "I have a legitimate right to be here. She opened her heart to me when she entertained thoughts about him as she drooled over his pictures." He let out a ghastly laugh. "You can rebuke me all you want Ramiah, but until she prays and stands against me, I will be sure to feed her what her heart desires."

Ramiah knew the demon was right and that there was little he could do except to encourage Zoe to pray. He had no authority in this matter except what she gave him through prayer and declaration of the word. He also knew the Holy Spirit was speaking to her and prayed she'd pay close attention to His warnings.

Though filled with the Spirit of God, Zoe still had a free will. She could choose to seek first the things of the kingdom of the Almighty and be obedient to His word, or she could meditate on the things of this world and rebel against the word of God. Unfortunately, she'd chosen to meditate on the images of this young man, allowing lustful thoughts to take root in her soul though she was in a covenant relationship with Michael.

When Zoe had first met Zachary, the Almighty had made it clear to Ramiah that he would not be a good influence on her or the plans He had for her life. He had done everything he could to break up their alliance, including making sure Zoe found the young man cheating on her with one of the cheerleaders in high school.

Zoe's freedom was at stake. The enemy's goal was to bind her in chains, lead her away from the Almighty's presence, and do harm to her marriage. *"You need to pray and ask God's forgiveness for thinking about this guy."* Zoe brushed off the thought Ramiah whispered into her ear and continued to think about Zach.

Michael woke up too late to spend time in prayer. He rushed to get ready for church, had a cup of coffee, and stormed out the door without bothering to say good-bye to Zoe. Upset and embarrassed to be going to church once again without his wife, he knew he'd have to make an excuse for her absence. It was the third time she'd missed church in less than two months, and he didn't buy her explanation of a headache. Since he was involved in the youth, he felt they needed to be faithful in their attendance together on Sundays. It was bad enough that she didn't come to the youth service with him on Wednesday nights. She claimed it was because of the baby's early bath-and-bed schedule, but he knew that she didn't enjoy working with the youth. Zoe seemed to be going backward in her spiritual walk and it was beginning to disturb him. How could he ever expect to become a pastor if his wife didn't support him in the ministry nor share his excitement and hunger for the Lord? He could feel the resentment burning within him as he pulled into the parking lot of the church.

"Dude, do you really need to take up two spots?" He shouted at the unseen driver of the empty car he parked beside. He slammed his car door shut before making his way into the sanctuary. He didn't even bother trying to put on a fake smile.

"Good morning, Michael." Bob Cline, the elderly gentleman, greeted him as he held the door open for him to enter the building. "Where is that lovely wife and baby of yours today?" Bob smiled while handing him the Sunday bulletin.

"Morning, Bob. She has a headache, so she and Emma stayed home." Michael walked briskly past the man, not wanting to engage in further conversation.

Donovan Scott, the youth pastor, walked straight toward him. "Hey, buddy, what's going on? Where's Zoe?" His thick east Texas drawl grated on Michael's frayed nerves.

Michael hated when Donovan called him buddy. It made him feel like he was talking down to him. After all, he was two years older than Donovan and had been in church all of his life whereas Donovan had only been saved for six years. Michael felt like it was Donovan's way of asserting his authority over him. Though fairly good looking, Donovan was short and stocky. Zoe often said she felt like he had little man syndrome.

"Hey, Donny. She wasn't feeling good, so she stayed home with the baby." Michael was fully aware of the fact that Donovan preferred being addressed as Pastor Donovan by those working under him in the youth department.

"Well, Theresa and I will be praying for her. Hey, I was going to ask you if you could do me a favor and take over for me Wednesday night at the youth pizza party. I've got everything lined up, and all you'd have to do is order the pizza, hang with the kids, and play some games with them. The other adult leaders will be there to help too. Theresa got free tickets to a Rockets game from her boss, and we hate not to use them." Donovan smiled, confident that Michael would not turn him down.

"Sure." Michael pretended to be agreeable. Though he loved working with the youth, it chapped him that Donovan would ask him to take over the event while he was going out to enjoy a basketball game with his wife. After all, Donovan was a full-time staff member of the church and got paid to be the youth pastor. Michael was given the title of assistant youth leader but received no compensation for the work he did. He didn't mind serving, but sometimes it seemed a little unfair.

Donovan often planned events only to back out at the last minute, leaving Michael and the other leaders to carry the load. Zoe had even pointed out to him, on more than one occasion, that Donovan often delegated assignments to Michael that he didn't want to do himself.

"He never asks you to preach." Zoe had complained to him on more than one occassion. "He just wants you to handle the events and clean up after everything is finished. Ever notice how he always has something important to do and leaves it to the rest of the team to clean up? But boy he's big on touting how he's such a servant."

Michael usually shrugged off Zoe's comments and made excuses for

Donovan, but today…well, today it bugged him.

"Are you sure you don't mind? You okay? You seem upset or something. I can get someone else to do it."

"No, I don't mind." Michael felt a tinge of guilt for his uncharacteristically bad attitude. "Ya'll have a good time Wednesday. Don't worry about a thing."

"Thanks a lot, buddy. I owe you one." Donovan patted Michael on the shoulder before entering the sanctuary to take his seat beside his wife. They always sat in the front row right next to Pastor Steve and Marcie so Donovan could assist the pastor if he needed anything. He insisted on carrying Pastor Steve's Bible and water up to the pulpit just before he preached even though the pastor didn't feel it was necessary.

You owe me more than one. Michael could feel the anger growing on the inside of him as he followed Donovan into the sanctuary where the worship team had already begun playing an upbeat praise song. He strolled up to the second row directly behind Pastor Steve and his wife where he and Zoe usually sat. Pastor Steve often joked that Christians could be very religious about their seats, and if you wanted to offend someone in the church, just sit in what they felt was their unofficially assigned chairs. Today, of all days, an unfamiliar couple were sitting in his seats.

That's just great! They must be new. Exasperated, he turned and walked to the back of the sanctuary, taking a vacant chair on the third to the last row. He found it difficult to enter into worship as guilt gnawed at him. *How could I expect God to receive my worship when my attitude stinks?*

He felt trapped amidst the crowded row of saints lost in boisterous praise. His negative thoughts led him into a downward spiral of self-pity. *If I were the youth pastor, I'd never ask people to do anything that I'm not willing to do myself. Donovan uses people. And I hate the way he brown-noses his way up to Pastor Steve. You'd think Pastor could see right through him. I just don't understand why God doesn't answer my prayers about Zoe. I feel like He doesn't hear me when I cry out to Him. Even though I've been faithful to tithe, we are still in such a financial bind. Why don't I see God's promises coming to pass in my life? I should have just stayed home with Zoe and Emma today.*

Taking a seat after worship was over, he was startled as his eye caught the scripture on the cover of the Sunday bulletin. It was the same scripture in Isaiah the Lord had quickened to him the day before in his quiet time.

When you pass through the waters, I will be with you; and through the rivers, they shall not overflow you. When you walk through the fire, you shall not be burned, nor shall the flame scorch you.
Isaiah 43:2

Michael didn't hear a word of the sermon. The scripture kept whirling over and over in his mind as he tried to figure out what God was speaking to him. *Maybe He was trying to warn me about the anger and resentment I'm feeling today.* He thought about how disappointed he was in Zoe and himself for his ungodly attitude. Ashamed that he hadn't even tried to fight against his emotions or cast down negative thoughts, he left church feeling defeated instead of encouraged. Certain that God was disappointed in him, he didn't even bother asking for His help.

The well-planned attack against Michael had been fortified the night before when he'd opened his spirit to the demonic realm by watching movies filled with sex, violence, and rage. He'd been convicted of watching such filth and knew he shouldn't allow it into his home.

In the midst of such dynamic worship, spirits of Anger, Resentment, and Offense were busy enjoying their own celebration with hoots and cheers as each one of their flaming arrows hit their target with precision. They reminded Michael of Zoe's constant accusations about the youth pastor, feeding his anger. Offense, a particularly crafty spirit, incited another couple to sit in his and Zoe's regular seats fueling his already inflamed disposition to strengthen their attack. Guilt and Shame joined in on the barrage to keep Michael from crying out to God for help or forgiveness. They watched with satisfaction as their prey sunk deeper and deeper into the pit of depression and despair.

"Michael, your offense and anger cause you to focus on yourself and not on My love and care for you. Cry out to Me." Deuel heard the Spirit of God speaking to Michael as he sat sulking in church. He prayed that Michael would heed His voice.

For the time being, Guilt and Shame had successfully seen to it that Deuel was ineffective in the situation. *If only Michael would ask the Holy Spirit to help him reign in his emotions or use the word of God to cast down those vain imaginations, then I could fight against these foul spirits of darkness.* He stood with sword prepared for battle, patiently waiting for Michael to cry out to the Lord, but he never did.

Deuel had strategically set up a hedge around Michael over the years, strengthening it by Michael's consistent prayer life and confession of the word of God. However, Michael was allowing worldly influences, as well as condemnation, to create a gap in that hedge wide enough for the enemy to infiltrate.

Because he'd always been so strong in his faith and tried desperately to live a life pleasing to the Almighty, Michael had recently begun to confuse his position of righteousness as being connected with good works and right behavior. If he perceived he'd failed God in some way, he felt unworthy to go before His presence in prayer, a typical ploy of Guilt and Shame. They were working diligently to render Michael impotent in his prayer life.

Deuel knew that a major battle was brewing. He and Hanniel had spoken with Ramiah to formulate an offensive plan against Beelzebub's attack. They agreed that they would need to pray and ask the Almighty for reinforcements as they could see the storm clouds gathering over this little family.

3

For if you forgive men their trespasses,
your heavenly Father will also forgive you.
But if you do not forgive men their trespasses,
neither will your Father forgive your trespasses.
—Matthew 6:14

Grandma Abby stood hunched over the kitchen sink, watching the cars whiz past her kitchen window as she washed dishes. She'd lived in the tiny white wood-frame two-bedroom house far too many years now to count. The town had sprung up around her. What had once been a two-lane street in a small Texas town on the outskirts of Houston was now a well-traveled highway off a major Interstate. She was hemmed in by a Wal-Mart just across the busy road, a fast food restaurant to her right, and a brand new drugstore to the left of her. Only one other house remained on what used to be a quiet street.

Amos had tried, on several occasions, to get her to move closer to him and Barbara, but she'd refused. He'd generously paid off her mortgage after her daughter had passed away. Between social security and teacher's retirement, she lived comfortably. This house held so many memories of her precious daughter that she would not part with it, even if they built a mall in her front yard.

In her early seventies, Grandma Abby was an attractive, white-haired, elegantly dressed spitfire of a little woman. She loved getting dolled-up as she called it and never went to church without wearing a hat and wouldn't dream of being seen in public without lipstick. Most of the time, she felt as energetic as she had in her forties. She adored gardening, played Bingo religiously every Friday night, and was a faithful member of the First United Methodist Church. Her husband had died in a car accident when she was thirty-six, leaving her to raise her daughter single-handedly. She'd come close to remarrying once, right before Claire had been diagnosed with cancer, but the long hours spent caring for Claire had caused the relationship to dry up. Now all she had left in this world was her home, Zoe and her little family, and Amos, who was like the son she'd never had.

Zoe permeated her thoughts today. Her granddaughter had been on her mind all during the church service, so much so that she couldn't remember a word her pastor had said. She'd been awakened the night before by a frightening dream. In the dream, Zoe was being tossed about in an enormous dark funnel cloud. The cloud had carried her so far away that she could no longer hear her grandma frantically calling after her.

Her last few conversations with her granddaughter had given her the impression that Zoe might be backsliding in her faith. She was concerned that Zoe wasn't allowing Michael to be the spiritual leader of their family and continued running to her father for financial support. Abby was afraid that the cares of this world had overtaken her granddaughter's zeal for the Lord.

"Oh, most gracious Father, I don't know what's going on in Zoe's life right now, but You do. Lord, You know how much I love that girl. Please, keep her and her family in Your loving care. Protect her, Michael, and the baby. Give Your mighty angels charge over them. Guide their steps and meet all of their needs according to Your glorious riches in Christ. I plead the precious blood of Jesus over them. I ask all of these things in Your Son's precious and holy name."

With her head tilted back she looked up toward heaven. "I would have gotten down on my knees, Lord, but today they are bothering me something fierce, so please forgive me, and if You would heal them, I'd be very grateful. Amen."

Feeling confident that God would work out whatever situation her granddaughter was going through; she dried her hands, made her way slowly into the den, and parked in her favorite chair for her Sunday afternoon nap.

Pastor Steve Mize tried to make his way down the aisle to the back of the sanctuary through the mingling crowd of people. Many sought to gain his attention to compliment him on his sermon. Thanking them humbly, he made his way as quickly as possible out to the foyer. Having noticed that Michael had rushed out of the sanctuary before the altar call had been given, he hoped to catch up with him before he left the building. Disappointed that he was nowhere in sight, he made a mental note to call him later in the week.

He'd also noticed Michael and Zoe weren't in their regular seats during the service and that Michael had been alone. Since Zoe didn't serve in the nursery or Sunday school departments, he assumed she had missed church again. He was concerned for the young couple because God had laid them on his heart earlier during the week.

Pastor Steve was a gentle, caring man in his early forties. He had a genuine shepherd's heart for those who attended New Zion Fellowship. It was his love for the members as well as a dynamic preaching gift that was partially responsible for the growth of the church from only four couples meeting in his home to over five hundred in attendance in a little over six years. He was careful to base his messages solely on the word of God and listened intently to the Spirit for direction as he prepared each sermon.

New Zion was a church on fire with a healthy mixture of young and old. It was both racially and culturally diverse, attracting people from all over the city as well as outlying areas. The worship was current and exuberant.

It wasn't at all uncommon to see him preaching in a pair of blue jeans and a sports coat. People were encouraged to come dressed comfortably. He believed that God wasn't worried so much about the outward appearance as much as He was concerned about the heart of His people. And for the most part, people at New Zion were true lovers and followers of God. He worked diligently to teach them that Christianity wasn't about religion but an intimate relationship with their God.

He and his wife Marcie tried to get acquainted with every member of the church, wanting to make themselves available should they ever need counseling or encouragement. They desired that everyone would feel like they were an integral part of the body and what God was doing at New Zion Fellowship Church.

Therefore, it wasn't unusual at all for Pastor Steve to take particular notice that something didn't seem right with one of his members. He was especially fond of Michael, knowing he understood the burden that comes with being a pastor, as Michael's father was a pastor too. It honored and humbled him that Michael had chosen him to be his and Zoe's pastor knowing how much Michael looked up to his father. He saw great potential in him and believed God had a pastoral calling on the young man's life.

The church had emptied out, and he was locking the front doors when Marcie came and stood by his side in the foyer. "You sure made a quick beeline for the exit. Did you have a fire to put out?"

"No, I was looking for Michael Davis. At least, I'm hoping there's no fire. I've noticed Zoe hasn't been with him at church several times lately, and I'm concerned for the two of them. I don't know if they're having marriage problems or what. He didn't seem to be himself today. Usually, he hangs around and fellowships with everyone. But today I noticed he was up and out the door just as soon as I began the altar call. I was hoping I could still catch up with him. I'm going to try to call him this week. Don't let me forget." He took her hand as they walked to their car.

It was well past four in the afternoon when Michael arrived home. He'd called Brad Parker after church explaining that he needed someone to talk to, and they'd spent the better part of the afternoon conversing at a Starbucks.

Zoe and the baby were not at home. He'd sent her several texts during the day, but she hadn't responded, an indication that she was upset with him. *She's probably out shopping. So much for her headache.* Feeling annoyed, Michael plopped down on the couch.

While sitting on the couch, he reflected on his conversation with Brad earlier in the day. Brad was a good friend who had a heart for God, and Michael knew the conversation wouldn't go any further than between the two of them. They'd confided in each other on several other occasions. Brad was the type of friend that he could count on to tell him what he needed to hear though not necessarily what he wanted to hear.

"I just don't understand what's going on with Zoe." Michael recalled the conversation he'd had with Brad. "She doesn't seem to be hungry for the Lord anymore. I don't ever see her praying or reading her Bible. Lately, she finds excuses to keep from going to church. She knows that I want to be in full-time ministry someday and that to be a pastor, I'd need her to be involved in the ministry with me. She's knows how active my mom is in helping my dad at their church. Zoe needs to be mature and seeking after God with all of her heart. I've prayed about it, but I don't feel like God is doing anything or even hearing my prayers."

"Well, bro, all I can tell you is that you can't force someone to be spiritual. God has to draw them by His Holy Spirit. All you can do is continue to pray and be an example to her. If God has a plan for you, it includes Zoe too. You have to trust God to get her to where He needs her to be to fulfill His plan in both of your lives. Sometimes, we feel like it's our responsibility to do the Holy Spirit's work. You can't change Zoe. Just love her unconditionally and trust God to do the rest."

"And, of course, I will be praying for you guys. As a landscaper, I often have to prune plants to get them to grow thicker and fuller. I have to cut away what appear to be healthy limbs, but I know it will enable that plant to grow even stronger and healthier and be even more beautiful or fruitful. I'm saying this because I hear a scripture in my spirit for you." Pulling out his smartphone and opening the Bible app, he scrolled to John 15:1-2.

"I know you're familiar with this scripture, Michael." He looked down at his phone and began reading the passage. "I am the true vine, and My Father is the vinedresser. Every branch in Me that does not bear fruit He takes away; and every branch that bears fruit He prunes, that it may bear more fruit."

Michael looked at Brad with a puzzled expression on his face. "Why would God be talking to me about pruning? It's not me that has the problem. It's Zoe. He needs to prune her."

"Yea, but the two of you are one flesh. God sees you as one. So, if He's dealing with her, He's also dealing with you. Maybe there are aspects of your character that you do not see clearly, and God wants to prune them away." Brad took a sip of coffee before continuing. "There was a time when I was always harping on Kira about keeping the house neat. I felt like she was a slob, you know? And she was home all day homeschooling the kids. She would complain that she wanted a maid because she didn't have time, and the house was too big for her to clean on her own. It made me mad because she was the one that begged me to buy that huge house."

"I know exactly what you mean!" Michael interrupted with sarcasm dripping from his voice.

"Well, I prayed about it because I was brought up by a meticulous mom. Our house was always spotless, so that's how I expected, or rather demanded, Kira keep our home. One day in prayer, the Lord revealed to me that I was the one with the wrong attitude. I was trying to make Kira conform and be the kind of housekeeper I thought she should be based on the way my mom cleaned and kept house. I was constantly comparing her to my mom. The problem was that Kira is not my mom. When I allowed God to prune that attitude out of my heart, Kira suddenly started keeping the house neater. God did the work in her heart. We began having people over, and she wanted her house to look nicer. But the point is, I had to change first."

Brad chose his words carefully. "I hope you won't be offended when I say this, but you need to make sure your motives are right in praying for your wife's spiritual walk. It sounds to me like you want her to be spiritual so she can help you fulfill your calling. Although I understand your reasoning, your only motive for her seeking after God should be because you love her unconditionally and want her to be able to enjoy all of the blessings God has for her."

Michael looked surprised. "It never occurred to me that my motives could be wrong. All I want is for Zoe to be hungry for the Lord. I see your point. It's not that what I desire is wrong. It's that I want her to change for me and my own selfish motives."

Before leaving the coffee shop, Brad prayed for Michael and Zoe.

It wasn't difficult for Zoe to coax her dad into spending quality time with her and Emma when she'd called and explained that she was playing hooky from church. Since Barbara was attending a charity fashion show that morning, Amos had been quick to accept her invitation. She and the baby had met him for lunch before the trio went shopping. Zoe still enjoyed spending time with her dad.

Though Barbara's heart had mellowed and softened with age, Zoe would have nothing to do with her and refused to allow her to be a part of Emma's life. Her heart was bitter and unforgiving toward her stepmom, holding onto the hurts of the past as if they were lifelong friends. She had tolerated her attending her wedding to Michael only because she wanted her dad to walk her down the aisle, and Amos had refused to come without Barbara. It gave her great satisfaction to be able to make her stepmom pay for the years of rejection she'd endured. Barbara had neither been invited nor welcomed at the hospital when Emma was born, a fact that grieved both Amos and Barbara tremendously.

As usual, Amos willingly paid for the lunch and shopping excursion as it afforded him time with his daughter and granddaughter. He was smitten with Emma and couldn't get enough time with her. He only wished Zoe would allow Barbara to be a part of her life too. She had often expressed to him how truly sorry she was for the way she'd treated Zoe as a child and had tried, on more than one occasion, to speak to Zoe about it. She longed to meet her granddaughter. He shared pictures with her and had even learned how to record the baby on his phone so that he could show her videos of Emma walking and gibbering. He was caught between a rock and a hard place. He dearly loved his daughter, but his love for his wife had grown over the years too. She was a much more tender and caring individual than she'd been when she was younger, and she brought so much joy and fulfillment into his life.

After shopping, they went to a café for dessert and coffee. As he'd often done in the past; he tried to broach the issue of Zoe bringing the baby and Michael over for dinner and a visit.

"Zoe, she's tried to apologize on several occasions. She regrets the past, but she can't change it. She wants so much to meet the baby and make it up to you by being an exceptional grandma." Amos defended his wife though Zoe had already turned him down on the prospect of her ever setting foot into Barbara's house again.

"Daddy, she was horrible to me, and I don't believe she could ever change. Leopards can't change their spots. I don't want Emma to experience the rejection I felt from her. Besides, she should have thought about her actions years ago. She's reaping what she sowed."

"Zoe, I think you're acting stubborn and unreasonable. I'll be the first to admit she was hard on you when you were growing up, but she was so young back then. She's a different person. I know she'd be a wonderful grandma to Emma."

"Over my dead body." Zoe ignored the pleading in her father's voice.

"You're supposed to be a Christian. Doesn't God require you to forgive?"

Zoe could hear the anger in her father's voice. "Daddy, that's not fair. Besides, you don't even go to church, much less know anything about God." She held her hand up to signal the end of the conversation. "Now that's the end of this discussion. She is not going to meet my baby. Ever! Now, eat that chocolate cake, or I'm gonna have to eat it for you, and then I'll have to take back all these new clothes and exchange them for a larger size." She smiled coyly at him from across the table hoping her charm would defuse his anger.

Amos left Zoe and Emma feeling hopeless at the prospect of his wife and daughter ever reconciling.

Ramiah was all too familiar with the loathsome presence of Unforgiveness. He'd been hanging around Zoe for a very long time. After all, he'd soothed her broken heart on many a night in her childhood, always promising her a false comfort. Ramiah had to suffer his company and work around him because of her refusal to forgive her stepmom. He wished he could open her spiritual eyes so she could see how Unforgiveness would mockingly get in the way of the warfare that often needed to be waged on her behalf.

Unforgiveness was like a shackle wrapped securely around her heart holding her hostage and keeping her from growing in her faith walk. So many blessings the Almighty had for Zoe were withheld because of her unwillingness to send the familiar spirit packing. Unforgiveness had become such a constant companion she no longer recognized his presence nor gave him much thought.

The demon was primarily responsible for keeping Zoe from desiring to pray or read her Bible. He was successfully driving a wedge between her and the heavenly Father, Whom she'd once sought after with all her heart.

He'd also brought in Revenge to reinforce his long-established hold on her and to ensure that she remained trapped in his snare. She willingly accepted his tantalizing suggestions.

"Don't ever forget how hateful she was to you. You have the upper hand now. You can repay her for every time she was so evil and spiteful to you. Make her regret the way she treated you. You can withhold from her what she wants most.

She doesn't deserve even one minute with your precious Emma. She should have thought about her actions years ago." The demon was cunning as he spoke lies into her soul. *"After all, she is reaping what she sowed."*

All the while, Ramiah stood by listening with disgust as these demons of darkness manipulated their prey. He knew that there could be severe consequences to those who refused to give up the companionship of Unforgiveness and Revenge. He'd seen it time and again throughout the centuries, myriads of believers stumbling in their faith and going through unnecessary hardships because of entertaining the noxious suggestions of Unforgiveness. Ramiah also knew, all too well indeed, that the price required for allowing these unrelenting spirits of darkness a place was never worth it in the end.

Michael had fallen asleep on the couch and was awakened by the sound of the front door closing. Zoe quietly entered the house carrying Emma, who was sound asleep, her head resting on Zoe's shoulder.

"Hey, girls, where have you been?" He stood and went to greet her as she entered the living room. "I texted you, but you never answered."

"Shhh. The baby is asleep." Zoe gave Michael a dirty look. "I'm going to put her in her crib. Will you get the shopping bags out of the car for me?"

"Sure." Michael tried to sound cheerful. He obediently went to retrieve the bags as she carried the baby upstairs.

"Good grief!" Zoe walked into the room as he placed a mountain of bags onto the dining room table. "Did you leave anything in the stores? Please tell me your dad bought all of this."

"Really, Michael! Don't you think I'm well aware of how broke we are?" She glared at him as she began sorting through the bags.

"Zoe, calm down. I was joking. You don't have to get so angry. And, we are not broke. Things are definitely tight, but we are not broke, and you shouldn't confess that."

Michael found it difficult to control his anger. "I don't appreciate it that you run to Amos to take you on these shopping excursions. It makes me feel like you don't think I'm able to provide for ya'll. If we can't afford it, then you probably don't need to buy it."

"Well then how am I supposed to get new clothes for Emma and me? You certainly haven't put money in the budget for that. And what do you want me to say? I'm just speaking the truth. We are broke. There is never any money for anything other than this house."

"Don't go there, babe. You're the one who couldn't live without this house. Well, you got it and the bills that go with it."

Realizing that things were quickly escalating out of control, he tried to change his tone and the atmosphere in the room. "Honey, I know it has been tight, but we have to trust God for our needs. I'm tired of fighting over money."

Zoe recoiled as Michael attempted to embrace her. He knew that once she lost her temper, it was almost impossible to get her to simmer down. She would often vent her anger by giving him the dreaded silent treatment, which could last for days and had, on more than one occasion, continued for more than a week. "Zoe, please, I don't want to argue. I told you I was just joking. Why didn't you answer my texts today?"

"Because you were a jerk when you left out of here this morning." Zoe folded her arms across her chest. Her body language an indication of her increasingly foul mood. "Besides, I was with Daddy, and we were talking. It's rude to text while you're having a conversation with someone else." A fire burned in her eyes. He knew her sarcasm was a pointed dig at him because he often got upset with her for texting while he was trying to carry on a conversation with her.

"Babe, I'm sorry I was in a bad mood this morning. I just wanted you to go with me to church. You obviously didn't have a headache, or you wouldn't have gone shopping with your dad all afternoon."

"I took aspirin, and it left." She glared at him. "Besides, you slammed out of here this morning and didn't even bother saying good-bye. I couldn't help it if I had a headache. You hurt my feelings."

Softening his voice, Michael tried to smooth things over. "I know. I'm sorry. Will you forgive me?"

"Michael, right now I'm tired, and all I want to do is take a shower." She stormed out of the kitchen toward the bedroom.

"I guess you don't need me to wash your back then?" He shouted after her, knowing all too well the answer before even asking.

There was a deafening silence between the two of them for the remainder of the evening. Zoe stayed in the bedroom watching television while he spent time in his office working. Michael tried once again to apologize when they went to bed, to no avail. Before turning out the light on his nightstand, he asked her if they could at least say a prayer together and ask God to reconcile their hearts.

"No, Michael. I'm tired. I have to get up early for work, and I want to go to sleep."

Zoe laid on the edge of her side of the bed as if the touch of her husband might contaminate her. Because of His great love and mercy, the Holy Spirit whispered into her spirit. *"For if you forgive men their trespasses, your heavenly Father will also forgive you. But if you do not forgive men their trespasses, neither will your Father forgive your trespasses."*

However, as in times past, she chose to reject His voice and hold on to her pride and anger. She rolled over with her back to Michael and tossed and turned until she fell into a fitful sleep.

The enemy was satisfied with his success.

Zoe awoke during the night and couldn't go back to sleep. After tossing and turning for over an hour, she glanced at the time on her phone. It was three-thirty in the morning. She moaned as she grabbed her robe at the foot of her bed. *Great. This is gonna make for a long day tomorrow.*

Getting out of bed, she padded into the kitchen to make herself a cup of coffee. With coffee in hand, she went into the living room and curled up on the sofa, picked up her iPad, and promptly opened up to Facebook. She was surprised to see an instant message in her inbox from Zachary. Her heart fluttered unexpectedly as she began to read it.

Hey lady,

Haven't seen you in a long time. Had a difficult time looking you up until I ran into a mutual friend a week ago who told me your married name. I heard you'd gotten married but didn't know you'd had a baby. You look amazing. Your husband is a very lucky man. You've always been one of the most beautiful women I've ever known. I was married for about three months, but it didn't work out. I'm working for an oil company as a pilot for several of the executives and enjoy my job. Hope life is treating you well. Would you be interested in meeting for lunch sometime?

Zach

After reading through her news feed, she put the tablet down on the coffee table. She sipped her coffee while reflecting on Zach's message. *Oh my gosh, how in the world do I respond to that?* She found it flattering to know that he thought she was still attractive. *Maybe he just needs a friend. What would it hurt to go to lunch with him?* Zoe was unaware that, at that very moment, a battle for her soul was being waged in the spirit realm.

In the back of her mind, she knew it would be wrong and was disappointed in herself for even entertaining the idea of meeting with Zachary. She loved Michael. *I might be upset with him at the moment, but he's still the best thing that ever happened to me. How could I even think about going to lunch with Zach? Not that it would lead to anything, but if Michael found out, it would break his heart.*

A scripture popped into her mind. *"Resist the enemy, and he will flee."*

Oh, God, forgive me. What in the world am I thinking? She opened Facebook again and quickly typed a reply to Zach before she could change her mind.

Hi Zach,

I am doing great! Married to the love of my life, and we have a beautiful daughter together. I don't think it would be appropriate for us to meet for lunch, but thank you for asking. I'm so glad you're doing well.

Zoe

Grandma Abby was awakened from a deep sleep at three-thirty in the morning. She sensed the presence of God in the room. "What is it, Lord?" Her granddaughter's face came to her mind. She felt an intense urgency to get up and pray for Zoe. She quickly obeyed. Wiping the sleep out of her eyes, she grabbed her glasses off the bedside table. She went into her living room, sat down in her favorite chair, and prayed for about an hour until she felt the peace of God come upon her. Assured her prayers had been effective and that God was pleased, she went back to bed.

"Lord, what's going on with my Zoe girl?" She whispered before falling back to sleep.

Ramiah knew the Almighty had commissioned someone to pray for his charge. He'd felt a surge of strength from their prayers. It was in the power of that strength that he struck Lust fast and hard the moment Zoe cried out to God for forgiveness. Lust slinked away screeching in pain.

"You haven't seen the last of me." Lust threatened. "And when I return, I'll bring seven spirits more evil than myself. You just wait and see. You'll pay for this Ramiah." The demon disappeared as quickly as he'd made his sleazy entrance.

It wasn't the first time Lust had tried to use Zachary to entice his charge to enter into fornication. He'd used his clever wiles against her when she was young and unable to make a stand against the lies of peer pressure, telling her everyone her age was having sex and enjoying it. One winter night after a date at the movies, Zach had driven her to a dark parking lot behind an abandoned strip center. He'd convinced her that he loved her and that, if she felt the same about him, sex was the next step in their relationship. She'd given in, afraid of losing him if she didn't.

The deed had left her feeling empty, dirty, and profusely ashamed. When Zach had dropped her off at her house that night, she went straight to her bathroom, took off her clothes, and cried under a long hot shower. She was painfully aware she'd given away something precious that she would never be able to reclaim. A week later, she'd discovered Zach cheating on her.

Ramiah prayed to the Almighty that history would not repeat itself.

The aroma of freshly brewed coffee along with bacon and eggs frying coaxed Michael out of a deep sleep. Michael always woke up early so that he had plenty of time for prayer and exercise before getting his day started, a habit he'd learned from his dad, but Zoe was a late sleeper. So he was pleasantly surprised to see her standing over the stove in her thick fuzzy blue robe, hair pulled back in a ponytail, with a mug of coffee in one hand while a spatula turned an egg in the other. Startled, she jumped as he came through the archway entrance leading into the kitchen.

"Oh my gosh, you scared me to death. You made me spill my coffee." Placing her coffee mug on the counter, she grabbed a dishtowel to dry the few drops that had splashed onto the floor and then playfully tossed it toward Michael who was grinning from ear to ear, enjoying the fact that he'd startled her.

Michael bent to pick the towel up off the floor. "What are you doing up so early? It's only five o'clock."

"I couldn't sleep. I've been up since three-thirty. So I decided to make you breakfast." She grabbed his favorite mug from the cabinet and began to fill it. "Here, this is my peace offering." She handed him the freshly brewed coffee fixed just the way he liked it while kissing him on the cheek. "I'm sorry for last night, baby. I know I need to work on my temper."

Michael wrapped his arms around her and kissed her tenderly. "It's okay. I shouldn't have gotten upset with you and stormed out mad yesterday morning. I'm sorry too."

"Your eggs are gonna burn." Zoe smiled before turning her attention back to the stove. She placed three eggs on a plate along with several slices of bacon and toast before handing it to him. Thanking her, he took it into the living room to eat while watching the early morning news. She cleaned up the kitchen and prepared Emma's bag for her day at daycare.

After devouring his food, Michael brought the empty dish into the kitchen and put it in the dishwasher. "Thanks again for the breakfast, baby. That was a nice surprise." He leaned down to give her a peck on the cheek.

At six-foot-two, Michael towered over Zoe, who was barely five-feet-four. His daily workout routine of lifting weights and running kept his body lean and fit. His light hazel eyes popped against the backdrop of his tanned complexion and dark curly hair. Zoe often teased that the deep dimples etched on either side of his face were the reason she'd fallen madly in love with him. It was his smile that had caused her heart to melt like butter the first time she'd laid eyes on him. But it was his heart that made him so attractive. He was easily the sweetest, most loving man she'd ever met, with a tender heart toward God as well as others. He would give the shirt off his back to help someone in need. Everyone who met him liked him instantly.

Zoe stared longingly at her husband. *How in the world could I ever think about another man, even for an instant?* Guilt gnawed at her conscience. *I don't even deserve the one I've got.*

"I'm gonna go get ready for work." Zoe looked coyly up at Michael as she placed her hands on his neck and kissed him seductively on the lips. "Maybe today I can be on time for a change unless you wanna try to make me late." She turned and walked toward the bedroom while dropping her robe to the floor to expose her bare body.

Michael laughed as he followed after her. "Baby, I think you just might be late again today, and you can tell your boss, it's all my fault."

Dekar, one of Beelzebub's ruling demons, smacked Lust hard across the head, knocking him to the ground. "You bumbling poor excuse of a fool. You had her in the palm of your hands, and you let her go." Dekar roared with fury.

Those who were under his jurisdiction greatly feared Dekar. He was known to be incredibly hateful and easily incited to rage. Demons fought for his approval though they knew that it would always be short lived. His only real allegiance was to his leader, Beelzebub. He knew that failure on the part of those under his immediate command was a complete disappointment to his lord, something he would not tolerate.

"My lord, I did my best. I was sure that the bait I used would work perfectly, but she spoke the word of God, and her angel immediately struck me with his sword. I didn't know what to do." Lust whimpered all the while scampering backward, away from Dekar's fearsome claws. He didn't know which fate was worse, suffering at the hands of the angel Ramiah or Dekar's fierce rage.

"I had no choice but to leave her alone. But I vow to you, my lord, I haven't given up. Oh, be assured I will get her in my snare again. I give you my word. I have enlisted others to help. We have a great plan already working to destroy this family's faith. I just need a little more time."

Dekar glared at the whiny little underling. "As our master has stated before, we cannot afford to fail. And rest assured I will not be the one to go back and report to him your disgraceful shortcomings. Oh no, you useless imbecile, it will be you."

Dekar shrieked while pacing back and forth. "When these believers in Jehovah think that they have overcome the strongholds we build against them, they have a habit of sharing their victories with others and encouraging them that they too can be overcomers. Their faith grows every time they successfully use the word of their God against us. So we must be aggressive, using every weapon we can against them." He ceased his pacing and walked toward Lust, who was shuddering uncontrollably. "Decimate this woman's family, and you will destroy her faith." Hatred emanated from his eyes like burning coals as he came face to face with Lust. The stench of sulfur from his breath filled the air. "This time, you'd better make sure you succeed."

"Yessss...yes, my lord!" Lust stammered, his voice trembling with fear. "I will not fail."

4

Yea, though I walk through the valley of the shadow of death,
I will fear no evil; for You are with me.

—Psalm 23:4

Zoe was awakened early Wednesday morning as the sound of Emma crying came through the monitor on the nightstand beside her bed. She bolted out of bed and ran upstairs to her room with Michael following close behind.

"What's the matter with my munchkin?" She lifted the baby up out of her crib. As her lips brushed her baby's forehead, Zoe noticed that Emma was warm to the touch.

"Michael, I think she's running a fever."

Michael could hear the worry in her voice. "Here, let me have her." The baby slid into his arms as he reached out toward her.

"What's up, pumpkin? You want Daddy to rock you?" His heart melted as Emma looked up at him with huge tears filling her eyes. "Oh, does Daddy's baby girl feel bad?" He gently nudged her head onto his shoulder with his hand.

Zoe reached up and ran her fingers through Emma's curls. "Poor baby." She fussed over Emma before addressing Michael. "She's probably just teething, but I may need to take her to the doctor this morning. I'll give her some Tylenol to see if the fever goes away."

Michael sat down in the rocking chair positioned in the corner of the nursery and began to rock while Emma's head rested quietly on his shoulder. It wasn't long before Zoe returned with a Tylenol-spiked sippy cup.

Michael took the cup from Zoe. "Listen, why don't you go get ready for work, and I'll see if I can't get her back to sleep. If she needs to go to the doctor, I can take her."

Zoe reluctantly headed back downstairs. She hated that her baby didn't feel well and was torn between getting ready for work and comforting her child. However, she knew that if Emma were only teething, Michael could keep her home, she could go on to work, and everything would be fine. As far as she could tell, Emma showed no symptoms of anything other than a slight fever, which was more than likely the result of her baby molars coming in.

Michael spent the next half hour rocking the baby while giving her the cup Zoe had fixed for her. His gaze was fixed on her as she fell fast asleep. She was the picture of innocence and beauty. Her pink lips curled up in a petite pout. Her little blond curls framed her sweet plump cheeks and cascaded down his arm. She snuggled into his chest as he cradled her in his arms. He caressed her tiny hand, brought it to his lips and kissed it tenderly before placing her back into her crib.

"What a sweet gift from God." He carefully covered her with her favorite blanket.

Michael walked into the bedroom where Zoe was dressing for work. "She's asleep. Just leave her home with me today. I'll keep my eye on her, and if she continues to run a fever, I'll take her in to see the doctor."

"Are you sure? I know you have a deadline you are working on. I can stay home."

"No, we'll be fine. I can work on my project tonight when you get home. I wanted to clean the pool today and work in the yard, but I can do that while she naps. I kind of like the idea of spending the day with her. Just leave me a schedule of when and what to feed her."

"Thanks, babe. I really needed to be at work today. We are having a Career Builders Seminar, and I know they'd be upset if I missed. I'll get everything ready for you. Will you please text or call me throughout the day and let me know how she's doing?"

"I will." Michael drew her close to himself and held her for a moment. "But she'll be fine, I promise. Don't worry."

Emma was still asleep in her crib when Zoe was ready to leave for work. She tiptoed into the nursery to peek in on the baby. "My poor sweet munchkin." Tears ran down her cheeks as she patted the baby's back. She hated leaving Emma even though she knew Michael would take good care of her.

Michael was in the office reading his Bible when he heard Emma crying through the baby monitor. After retrieving her from her crib, changing her diaper and clothes, he brought her down for breakfast.

He delighted in her giggles as he pretended to take bites of cereal offered from chubby little hands. "You get to stay home with Daddy today, baby girl." Her little legs kicked excitedly up and down beneath her highchair as if she understood what he was saying. Wiping her sticky face and hands after breakfast, he retrieved her from the highchair and took her to the play area in the living room.

Zoe had a corner section of the living room dedicated to Emma's play time. She had a miniature kitchen complete with dishes and fake food, a toy box filled with dolls as well as every baby toy imaginable, thanks to Amos's deep pocketbook. There were enough toys to stock a small daycare, and usually by the end of the day, Emma had them strewn from one end of the living room to the other.

Seated on the couch, he attempted working from his laptop while Emma played with her toys. He was often interrupted by offers of imaginary drinks from a plastic teacup, promptings to give her baby doll a kiss and a hug, diaper changes, and snack time. He soon realized that he wasn't going to accomplish much as long as she was awake and got down on the floor to join her in her play time.

He followed Zoe's schedule to a tee and put Emma down for her nap directly after lunch. However, not wanting to go up and down the stairs, he placed the sleeping baby on a quilt he'd laid on the floor in their bedroom instead of in her crib. Assured she was asleep, he left the bedroom door cracked open, grabbed her monitor, and went outside to clean the pool and water the plants.

Since the water was still too cold to swim in, Michael had allowed several weeks to go by without cleaning the pool. Debris from a storm that had blown through the week before filled the pool and the sides were turning green from a lack of attention and too little chlorine.

He hated the pool. It, like the house, was another one of Zoe's needs. She'd grown up having a pool and claimed she couldn't bear the thought of her children growing up without one in the heat of a Texas summer. As usual, he'd given in to her pleading. Of course, he was the one who had to fight the heat and mosquitoes to keep it clean.

He'd worked up a sweat for about an hour before going back inside to peek in on the baby as well as get a drink of water. Inadvertently, he left the back door open and the baby monitor on the patio table with the intention of heading back outside.

He opened the bedroom door just enough to see that Emma was still asleep on the floor in the bedroom. *Poor baby, she must have been tired. That Tylenol just knocks her out.*

While getting a glass of water from the fridge, Michael heard his cell phone ringing in his office. He ran to answer it and recognized Pastor Steve's voice.

"Hey, Michael. How ya doin'? I tried to catch up with you after church on Sunday, but you flew out of there like a man on a mission."

Michael grinned. He always found it easy to talk with Pastor Steve. "Hey, Pastor. I'm fine. I'm babysitting today. Emma is teething and was running a little fever this morning. Zoe needed to work, so I'm being the dutiful daddy." He sat down in his desk chair, knowing that the call might be lengthy. Pastor Steve was a talker.

"Well, I'll be praying for her. Listen, I'm calling because I'm kind of concerned about Zoe. Is she doing okay? I've noticed her missing church a lot here lately. I was wondering if maybe someone had done something to offend her?"

"Oh, not at all." Michael squirmed in his chair. He knew Zoe was often easily offended. "She had a headache on Sunday. I think she just gets tired between work and taking care of the baby. But she's fine. I'm sure she'll be in church this Sunday. I appreciate you checking up on her though."

"Well, are you guys doing okay as a couple? I just sensed something might be wrong on Sunday. Are ya'll having any problems I can help with?"

"Oh no, we're fine." Michael knew his statement was only a half-truth. He and Zoe had worked out their argument, but he didn't feel the need to share any of their other problems. So he didn't mention the financial strain they were under or that he was concerned about Zoe's relationship and walk with the Lord. Most definitely, he wasn't about to tell Pastor Steve how he'd been upset Sunday morning with Donovan Scott and how he felt like Donovan often took advantage of him. He didn't want the pastor to see him as a weak, whiny Christian, who was unable to run his household and take care of his problems.

Assured that all was well, Pastor Steve proceeded to talk about plans he had for a new Bible study at the church as well as a building expansion project. He kept Michael tied to the phone for a good half hour. Michael didn't mind. He was enjoying the distraction as well as the air condition after being outside in the heat.

The angel wore a long pale grey tunic with a beautiful crimson sash tied around his waist, unlike the short white tunics and golden sash of the guardian angels. He stood a foot taller than Hanniel's nine-foot stature and carried no sword or weapon in his girdle.

"You are only to accompany her." His voice was deep and commanding though he was by no means menacing or unsympathetic.

"Am I not to try and fight for her?" Hanniel confirmed. It was never easy for a guardian to accept the death of his charge, especially when that charge was still just a child. He knew there would be others to guard, and he must obey the will of the Almighty. He also knew that to be absent from the body that housed her soul and spirit was to be present with the Almighty, a reason to rejoice indeed. However, the call of every guardian was to protect their charge at all cost, and being so familiar with humans; he knew her family would grieve her loss deeply.

"The Almighty has prepared a place for her. Precious in the sight of the Lord is the death of one of his saints." The angel departed as suddenly as he'd entered the room. Hanniel knew he would return soon. He was an angel of death. His primary purpose was to escort believers to their final destination. He, along with Hanniel, would accompany his tiny charge into the Presence.

Hanniel was thankful that a believer's ascent into their eternal existence was never one they made alone. The Son, in order to comfort the saints and alleviate their fear of death, had even spoken of this heavenly escort when He'd told the parable of the beggar being carried by angels into Abraham's bosom. For centuries upon centuries, there have been angels helping believers make the transition into their heavenly home. A home prepared for them by the Son from the foundation of the world.

Hanniel glanced down at the innocent child sleeping peacefully on the mat her father had prepared for her on the floor. It was a glorious day indeed!

After hanging up, Michael decided to check on Emma before returning outside. His heart skipped a beat when he realized the toddler, along with her favorite blanket, was missing from her pallet on the floor.

"Emma?" Michael walked throughout the downstairs calling after the toddler. "Emma, where are you, baby?" The house was silent. He checked the bathroom before going into the living room. To his absolute horror, he realized he'd left the back door open. He spotted Emma's baby blanket lying in a pink heap at the edge of the pool.

"Oh my God!" He ran outside screaming her name, nearly tripping over the back step. Fear gripped him as he spotted Emma's lifeless body floating face down by the steps in the pool. Her blond curls formed a golden halo about her little head. Her favorite baby doll floated eerily beside her.

"No!" Jumping into the pool, he scooped her up out of the water. "Oh God, oh God!" Michael cried out, his voice a mixture of a terrified scream and a heart-wrenching sob. "Emma." Sitting on the steps of the pool, he laid the baby on his lap and carefully began to perform CPR. Her body remained limp and cold. "Somebody help me!" He screamed into the air. "No! Please don't take her God!" He began to sob uncontrollably.

Coming to his senses, he gathered the lifeless body of his baby girl into his arms and ran back into the house to grab his cell phone. His hands were shaking as he dialed 911.

A female voice was on the other end of the line. "911, what is your emergency?" The operator's voice was calm and controlled. She was unable to understand Michael's hysterical screams. "911, what is your emergency?" Michael's message was still garbled.

"Sir, you are going to have to calm down and state your emergency." Her voice was firm yet filled with compassion.

"My baby." Michael wailed into the phone, his voice barely understandable. "I think she's dead." He broke into heaving sobs.

Missy Thomas had been an emergency operator for six years. It was apparent to her that the man on the other end of the phone was distraught and in a state of shock. She prayed a silent prayer asking for help to bring peace and calm into the desperate situation. From experience, she knew this call would probably not have a happy ending.

Though a chill ran down her spine, she remained composed. "Sir, how old is your baby?"

"She's thirteen months old." Michael looked down at his unresponsive child.

"Sir, I'm sorry, and I know this is difficult, but I need you to speak clearly so that I can get you the help you need. Is the baby breathing?" Missy asked when he'd calmed down enough to hear her question.

"No." His answer sounded more like a yelp than a reply.

"Can you tell me what happened?" Though she'd experienced similar scenarios on many occasions, her heart always broke for those on the other end of the line. The man's desperation and despair hit her like an arrow shooting straight through her own heart.

"She drowned in our backyard pool." The words seemed surreal as he spoke them out loud. "Oh, God, this cannot be happening!" Michael felt as if he was in the midst of a terrible nightmare.

"I'm so sorry. Can you tell me your name and address?"

"Michael Davis." His mind was foggy. He tried to collect his thoughts as he stared down at Emma. "Umm…413 Wild Wind Lane. We live in the Windgate Subdivision. Please hurry. Oh, God." Michael wailed into the phone while rocking Emma back and forth in his arms.

"Sir, I'm going to stay on the line with you. Someone should be arriving to help you shortly. Can you open the front door for them?" The operator had already typed the call information into the computer and knew that an EMS unit was dispatched and on the way, along with a police unit that had been in the vicinity.

Michael carried Emma and went to unlock the door as instructed. "The door is unlocked and open." He sat down in the open doorway, still holding his lifeless daughter.

"Sir, was the baby breathing when you found her? Have you tried doing

CPR?" Missy wanted to keep Michael busy while he waited for emergency personnel to arrive.

"No, she wasn't breathing. I tried CPR, but it didn't help. Now she's just blue and cold." Michael cried uncontrollably once again. "She's just so cold."

"What is your daughter's name?" Missy had tears streaming down her cheeks. A devout Christian, she continued to pray silently for Michael.

"Emma." He heard sirens wailing in the distance. "I think they are almost here."

"Well, stay on the line with me until they arrive."

An ambulance pulled up in front of his home. Michael saw several of his neighbors coming out of their houses, curious as to why their peaceful day was being invaded by the sound of a siren in their ordinarily quiet community.

"They're here. I'm gonna hang up now."

The paramedics rushed into the house, carrying medical equipment. Cory, a tall, thin black male pried the baby out of Michael's arms and began working on her. His partner Sandra started to intubate the baby, while he began to place an IV in her tiny arm. They worked together quickly and methodically.

"Sir, can you tell me how long the baby was in the water?" Sandra asked, never taking her eyes off of Emma.

"I'm not sure. Maybe as much as twenty minutes or so." Michael began to relay the story of being distracted by the phone call in his office. "I checked on her before the call, and she was still asleep. I think I was on the phone for about thirty minutes. I never heard her cry or get up." He placed his head in his hands as a fresh torrent of sobs racked his body. "I always keep her monitor close by, but I'd left it outside thinking I was going right back out after getting a glass of water."

With the front door still standing open, an officer entered the home. He squatted down beside the two paramedics attending the baby, his back toward Michael. They spoke in hushed whispers before he stood and walked over toward Michael now seated a few feet away on the tile floor. His clothing was soaked, and his body was shaking from cold and shock.

"Mr. Davis, my name is Officer Todd O'Neil. I'm so sorry for your situation, but I'm going to need to ask you some questions."

Michael relayed the same story to the officer that he'd told the paramedics. Officer O'Neil took careful notes.

"Is there someone I can call for you?" Officer O'Neil asked. "Maybe your wife."

Michael felt as though all of the air was suddenly sucked out of his lungs. He couldn't respond. The reality of the situation hit him like a head-on collision. He stared at the paramedics tending to his daughter as he rocked back and forth. His thoughts turned to Zoe. *How could I have let this happen? This is going to kill Zoe.*

"No, I should be the one to call her."

Officer O'Neil placed his hand on Michael's shoulder. "Sir, would you like me to pray for you?"

Michael began to weep as he shook his head in agreement. Officer O'Neil prayed.

Deuel placed his hands on Michael's shoulders. He'd witnessed Emma's ascent into the Presence. He knew this would be an extremely difficult time for his charge. Though he couldn't quite comprehend it, he was well aware that the death of a loved one was always the cause of much grief to the humans who were left behind. He, along with the other angels, viewed death as the beginning of a higher life for the child of God. Emma was experiencing the fullness of life now. Her short life on earth could never compare with the glories before her at this moment. She'd never felt fear or experienced pain in the journey. As a matter of fact, she'd never actually experienced death. She'd merely left the earthly shell her spirit had taken up residence in while on this earth.

Regardless, he wanted Michael to feel his love and strength. The Son entered the room filling it with brilliant light seen only by the angels. Deuel bowed in worship to the Lord, while a host of angels filled the room. They reverently worshipped the Son in melodious song and ministered peace into the atmosphere.

The Son cradled Michael in His arms, and Deuel watched in awe and listened intently as He, with tears in His eyes, gently whispered into Michael's grieving spirit. *"Though you walk through the valley of the shadow of death, do not fear the evil one, for I am with you. My rod and my staff will bring comfort to you."*

Unfortunately, Michael couldn't feel the Son's presence as He lovingly stroked his back nor could he see the compassion in His Savior's eyes. But he had received, by the Spirit, the word of hope the Son had spoken into his spirit. Michael was repeating it over and over again in his mind. Holding onto the word as if it was a lifesaver thrown out to a drowning man in a storm-tossed ocean.

Deuel knew the enemy would be lurking close by waiting to pounce on his charge with thoughts of self-pity, self-loathing, worldly grief, and doubts about the Almighty's faithfulness and love. Believers who'd experienced tremendous trauma and loss were extremely vulnerable to the attacks of the enemy.

Officer O'Neil escorted Michael to the front seat of the ambulance as the paramedics loaded Emma into the back of the vehicle. He shook Michael's hand and vowed to continue to pray for him and his family. He wiped tears from his eyes as he watched the ambulance speeding away, its siren howling.

He thought about how fragile life is. *Man, you can wake up to a beautiful day like today and be faced with a life-altering tragedy. I need to be more thankful for my blessings. I need to appreciate my wife and kids a little more and make sure they know how much I love them.*

"You just never know what a day may hold." Officer O'Neil shook his head as he got in behind the wheel of his cruiser. He knew he'd go home and gratefully tuck his two children into bed, while this young father was left childless. His heart ached for Michael and Zoe.

"Father, be with this family. Comfort them. My heart goes out to them. And, Lord, thank You for this day that You have so graciously given me. I forget to tell You sometimes how much I love and need You." He wiped moist eyes with the back of his hand before checking the rearview mirror and driving out of the neighborhood.

Speeding along in the ambulance, Michael knew he needed to call Zoe but was holding out hope that once they got Emma to the hospital, they'd somehow be able to revive her. He couldn't fathom telling his wife that their baby girl was gone. *She trusted me to watch Emma today, and I failed miserably. She's never going to forgive me if we lose Emma. God, please! I need a miracle. I'm*

begging You, Father. Please, don't let her be dead. Please, Lord. Tears fell in a steady stream down his cheeks.

He called Pastor Steve while in route to the hospital, knowing he needed the spiritual strength of his pastor. Michael relayed the events to him through intermittent sobs. Pastor Steve jumped into his car and sped to the hospital, even as they continued talking. He was there within minutes after the ambulance arrived. He found Michael in the waiting room leaning up against a wall and staring blankly out the window. His clothes, though wrinkled and damp had begun to dry. His hair was disheveled. It was apparent to Pastor Steve that he was in shock.

After only a short time in the emergency room, a young female doctor came out to give him the news. "Mr. Davis, I'm so sorry for your loss. We did all we could, but we were not able to revive your daughter. Can we call anyone for you? Does your wife know about the accident?"

Michael shook his head. "No, but I'll call her. I was just hoping…" His voice trailed off.

"If you will wait a moment, we'll get you a room where you can have some privacy. Is there anyone here with you?" The doctor's gentle manner and the compassion in her voice told Michael that she was genuinely concerned for him.

"My pastor is here with me." Michael motioned toward Pastor Steve. Pastor Steve walked up beside him and draped his arm over his shoulder.

Within a few minutes, they were ushered into a waiting room furnished with only a small round conference table and a well-worn plastic grey couch. The room felt sterile and cold. *This room must be reserved for people who get bad news.* The thought made Michael begin to weep again.

Pastor Steve comforted him as they sat on the couch. "I'm so sorry for your loss Michael. Would you like me to call Zoe or have Marcie pick her up from work?" It was now almost two in the afternoon, and he knew Houston's rush hour traffic would begin to back up, possibly hindering their ability to make it home before Zoe.

"No. I need to be the one to tell her. It's going to devastate her." They decided that he would take Michael home and remain there until Michael broke the news to Zoe. Michael took care of paperwork that had to be signed before they could leave the hospital. They rode together in silence with occasional sobs escaping from Michael as he stared blankly out the window.

Zoe was late leaving work. It had been one of those days. The copier had been acting up all day, and the technician arrived fifteen minutes before time for her to go home. It was her responsibility to stay and make sure the rebellious machine, which broke down almost every other week, was in working order as well as to lock up the office.

The seminar had kept her busy greeting guest, taking orders for refreshments and lunch, and handing out application packets. With such a hectic schedule, she hadn't had time to think about Emma or Michael. She assumed that if Michael had taken the baby to the doctor, he would have called or texted. She tried calling him as she left the office, but he didn't answer.

Zoe complained aloud while pulling onto the freeway. "Ugh! I hate traffic." A sea of cars and eighteen-wheelers sandwiched her in as she inched her way home. As always, she passed the time during the monotonous drive home listening to the country music playlist on her cell phone. It helped her relax, though Michael claimed it did little to edify her spiritually.

It wasn't long before she escaped the crowded freeway and entered into the peaceful beauty of her well-planned subdivision built within an already existing array of mature pine and oak trees. Several parks for the children and small lakes, as well as a magnificent golf course made the area a particularly serene setting.

She was surprised to see Pastor Steve's car blocking her entrance into the garage as she pulled into the driveway. *It's almost six o'clock. What's he doing here?* An eerie sense of dread washed over her, as she walked up the stone pathway leading to the front door.

Ramiah could see the demonic spirits closing in like sharks on a feeding frenzy. He kept his sword held high in his right hand as he escorted Zoe into the house. He was ready to strike the drooling demons waiting to pounce on his charge. It would only take one purposely directed prayer from her to send them all packing.

He had been before the face of the Almighty and knew that his charge was about to embark on a journey into deep despair. Her faith would be tested and shaken, and only those things that could not be shaken would remain. It was not the Almighty's doing, but his charge's choice to go this route, though she would never rationally or intentionally make this decision. It was more a consequence of her not making the right choices and being obedient to the loving direction of the Almighty.

5

Satan has asked for you, that he may sift you as wheat.
But I have prayed for you, that your faith should not fail.
—Luke 22:31–32

Michael sat slumped over on the loveseat in the living room. He could hear Pastor Steve in the kitchen whispering into the phone as he rearranged his schedule for Emma's impending funeral as well as to solicit Marcie's help in arranging meals and prayer support for Zoe and him. He dreaded the moment Zoe would walk through the front door. He knew this would be, by far, the worst day of her life. *How do you tell the mother of your child her baby is gone? How can I face her?* He was overcome with guilt. *It's my fault. If only I hadn't left the door open. How could I have been so careless?* He berated himself for the umpteenth time. His body shook with convulsive sobs as he bent over holding his head in his hands.

Pastor Steve's heart ached for Michael as he stood watching him from the entryway of the kitchen.

"How do people go through something like this without the love and support of the body of Christ?" He whispered to Marcie after they'd prayed together for the Davis family.

"I don't know. I can't even begin to imagine the pain and loss. Poor, sweet Michael. How awful for him to have found his baby like that. We need to be praying for them. Zoe is going to be beside herself with grief. I just can't fathom what it will do to her to come home and find that her baby is gone. Oh, dear Father, please help this couple get through this. It's so devastating."

"I feel somewhat responsible. I mean it was my phone call that distracted Michael." Steve confided in his wife, his voice choking with emotion.

"Oh, honey, it's not your fault. You had no way of knowing. Please don't beat yourself up like that."

"I know...it's hard watching Michael go through this, especially knowing I played a significant part in her death."

"Steve, I'm sure Michael doesn't blame you. He could have been on the phone with anybody. It was an accident."

"I'm so thankful Michael has a solid relationship with Christ. However, I'm concerned for Zoe. She's been kind of hit-and-miss lately at church. I've had a feeling she wasn't where she needed to be spiritually..."

Pastor Steve heard the front door opening. "Honey, I've got to go. Zoe's home. Pray hard!" He hung up the phone before she had a chance to respond.

Zoe walked in the front door expecting Emma to come toddling toward her. Instead, she saw Michael slumped on the loveseat sobbing uncontrollably. "Oh, my God, Michael what's wrong? Where is Emma?" Even as she asked the question, she knew deep down in her heart that something was dreadfully wrong. Fear gripped her as a knot formed in the pit of her stomach. She dropped down to the floor in front of Michael, her hands on his knees as she glanced questioningly at Pastor Steve, who'd walked into the living room and knelt down beside her.

Michael lifted his head, his eyes swollen from crying and his face contorted with emotion. "Zoe, I'm so sorry. I'm really sorry. I accidentally left the back door open, and Emma got out without me knowing, and she drowned in the pool. I thought she was sleeping...I..." He broke into sobs as he reached out to comfort his wife who stared blankly at him in horror and disbelief.

"Oh, God, no!" She pushed his arms away violently as she scrambled to her feet. "No! Michael, tell me you are lying or joking or…" She glanced at her pastor, her eyes wild with fear as if he might somehow make everything better and tell her that this was all a terrible misunderstanding.

Zoe crumpled in a heap to the living room floor. "Oh, God, no! My baby! Why? My baby! Oh, God, no!" She screamed hysterically over and over again. The sorrow she felt was incomparable to any pain she'd ever experienced. It reached deep down into the depths of her soul like an unseen force, planting roots that intertwined around her heart. Michael knelt down beside her and held her while they cried in each other's arms.

She sprang to her feet suddenly as if in defiance of the truth. "I want to see her. Michael, this just can't be. Please tell me it's not true. I want to see her. Where is she?" Her voice rose to a frenzied pitch as she became enraged, unable to cope with the magnitude of the loss. "Where…is…she? I want to hold her. Tell me where she is."

Michael stood and grabbed her firmly by both arms, his face only inches from hers, his voice cracking under the strain of his grief. "Baby, listen to me. She's gone. I'm sorry. I'm so sorry."

Heaving and gasping for breath, she glared at him. "Michael, how could you have let this happen? How? Why did you let my baby die? What could have possibly been more important than watching my baby?"

Pastor Steve, with tears in his eyes, reached out to Zoe in order to console and help calm her.

"No!" She pushed him out of her way and ran up the stairs into Emma's room. "Emma? Emma? Please let her be in her room."

"No." The word came out in a gut-wrenching scream, as she stood paralyzed in the doorway of the dark and barren nursery.

Michael bounded up the stairs and came up behind her as she stood over the empty crib. "Baby, I'm sorry." He reached out for her, only to be violently rejected.

"Don't you touch me. This is all your fault." With eyes wild, she screeched at Michael. She beat unrestrainedly against his chest with clenched fist before pushing him away from the crib.

She turned her attention back to the last place she'd seen her sleeping child. Everything was in its place just as it had been that morning when she'd checked on her daughter before leaving for work. Everything, except Emma.

"Oh, God." Zoe covered her mouth with her hands. "Did I tell her I love her this morning?" She stood over the empty crib and bawled. "What am I going to do without my baby girl? She was my life." Snatching Emma's favorite stuffed bear from her crib, she slumped into the antique rocker in the corner of the room. She held the pink bear to her chest and began to moan as she rocked it back and forth. "No...no, no, no! Why God?" She stared up at the ceiling. "Why? Why my baby? I hate You! I hate You!" She ranted into the darkness of the empty room. At that moment, she determined in her heart that she could no longer serve a God who would take the life of her baby especially after all she'd been through herself as a child.

Michael knelt beside the rocker and tried to take her hand. "Zoe, baby, please. We'll get through this."

Her eyes bore down at him, her heart as hard as a stone. As far as she was concerned, he was to blame. "You told me you'd take good care of her. I trusted you, Michael. How could you let this happen? How could you be so irresponsible with my baby?" She saw the hurt etched all over his face, but she didn't care. She wanted to punish him for the unbearable pain she was experiencing.

"Zoe, you can't imagine the guilt I feel right now. I don't blame you if you are upset with me. If I could take her place, I would. Please, forgive me." His voice was hoarse with emotion.

She didn't acknowledge his plea. "Have you called my daddy?"

The question took Michael by surprise. He hadn't even bothered calling his parents, much less Amos Richards. He'd been so caught up in his grief and the dread of telling Zoe the news, he'd forgotten about the rest of the family. *What will they say? Will they blame me too? Will they hate me too?* The questions flooded his mind.

"No, I haven't told anyone. I'll call our parents now. Baby, are you gonna be okay up here by yourself?" His voice was tender despite the harsh words she'd hurled at him.

"Michael, I'll never be okay, here or anywhere else. My life is over. My baby is gone. How can you ask me if I'll be okay?" Zoe heard the hatred seething out of somewhere from deep inside of her. It felt good. It gave her satisfaction, and it felt oddly comforting to lash out at her husband.

"Baby, don't say that. Your life is not over. We still have each other, and we have God. He'll see us through this. I don't know how, but I know He will." Michael spoke with every ounce of faith he could muster.

"Michael, I will never serve God again. He let this happen. He could have kept Emma from drowning. Where was he? Why would He allow this to happen to us? We go to church. We've done everything right. Why?"

"I don't know, Zoe. Honey, I understand you're angry right now. I'm angry too. But God is our only hope. He is the only way we'll get through this. He didn't cause this. It was an awful accident. Together, we have to lean upon Him with all our might."

"Oh, she must have been so scared." Zoe covered her face with her hands. "I can't bear the thought of her being all alone."

"Baby, I don't think she was alone. God promises to never leave us. He was with Emma. I'm sure of it."

"Michael, just go. I can't bear to talk about it anymore." Hatred and rage flooded her soul. She sobbed as she turned her head away from him, not wanting to see the pain she was causing him.

Michael left the room feeling broken. Dealing with the loss of his baby girl was one thing, but an old fear came creeping up in his mind. *What if I lose Zoe too?* The thought was more than he could bear.

The Almighty held Zoe in His arms as He gently rocked her. Her seething anger didn't move nor anger Him. His love for her was unconditional. He knew the deep recesses of her heart and soul. He was well acquainted with loss and deeply touched by her grief. Tears fell down His face as He wept with her. "*Weeping may endure for a night, my precious daughter. But rest assured, joy will come again.*" The Comforter ministered to her wounded spirit.

Ramiah bowed in worship. He was confident that the Almighty would never leave Zoe, though she might choose to walk away from Him for a season. No matter what declarations she made, He would wait patiently with an all-encompassing, everlasting love until she turned back again to Him.

Daniel and Shara Davis stood in the open doorway. "Hello, we're Michael's parents." Daniel extended his hand to Pastor Steve. Steve stepped aside so they could enter the house.

Daniel, a tall man in his late fifties, had hazel eyes and pronounced dimples on each side of his cheeks. Though his hair was strikingly gray, it was evident to Pastor Steve that Michael resembled his father. His wife was petite and very attractive. He kept his arm around her shoulders as if protecting her. Both were visibly shaken.

"I'm Steve Mize, Michael and Zoe's pastor." Pastor Steve introduced himself as he shook Daniel's hand and hugged Shara. "I'm so very sorry for your loss."

Shara stifled a cry as Michael came down the stairs into the living room. He fell into his parents embrace, his head resting on his father's shoulder as fresh tears gushed forth. After several moments, Daniel asked his son what had happened. Michael relayed the events of the day as Pastor Steve brought cups filled with hot coffee into the living room.

"Where is Zoe?" Shara blotted her eyes with a tissue while addressing her son.

"She's upstairs in Emma's room and won't come down. I'm hoping Amos will be able to help console her when he gets here. Mom, she blames me. I'm so afraid of losing her too." Fresh tears fell down Michael's cheeks once again.

Shara cupped Michael's face in her hands. "Oh, baby, she's just grieving. I'm sure she doesn't blame you. It was an accident. It could have happened to anyone. Do you think we should go up and try to talk with her?"

"No, I think we need to let her be until she's ready to come down. Let the Lord minister to her." Daniel placed his arm across his son's shoulders. "Listen, why don't we all gather together and pray?"

The four gathered in a circle and held hands with their heads bowed. Pastor Steve asked God to comfort the family and prayed for grace and strength for the days ahead. He knew they were going to need all the prayers they could get to make it through this trial. Secretly, he worried that this marriage might suffer significantly as a result of this loss.

"Where is my daughter?" Side-stepping Michael, Amos authoritatively pushed his way into the house. Barbara stood quietly by his side. He'd been so shaken at the news that she'd insisted on driving him over.

"She's upstairs in Emma's room." Michael pointed to the stairs.

Without even acknowledging the presence of the others in the room, he bolted up the stairs, leaving Barbara to awkwardly introduce herself to Pastor Steve. She'd met Daniel and Shara once before at Michael and Zoe's wedding.

Michael went to follow him, but Daniel grabbed his arm. "Give them a minute, son. Maybe he'll be able to help calm her down."

Amos's eyes had to adjust to the darkness as he entered the room. "Zoe, Daddy is here." He burst into tears as she jumped from the rocker into his arms.

"Oh, Daddy!" Zoe's body shook with emotion as she cried into her father's arms. "I just keep thinking about her lying in her crib like she was when I left this morning. I should have stayed home with her. I shouldn't have left her."

"Shhh, Daddy's here." Amos held her in his arms and stroked her hair as he whispered in her ear. "Shhh. It's going to be all right now. Daddy's got you."

Unforgiveness, Zoe's longtime friend, as well as Grief and Despair, entered the room on the tails of Amos. Though they kept their distance from Ramiah, they defiantly crooned into Zoe's ear. Grief and Despair, two very crafty demons, almost always worked together. They sucked the hope out of the lives of their victims and caused them to view tragedy as the end of all joy instead of an opportunity to trust in and cling to the Almighty. They would stir up both good and bad memories in the soul of their prey, playing them over and over again like a sad movie. They were merciless predators who sought to devour those who'd experienced the loss of a loved one, dragging them down into a deep, dark, bottomless pit of despondency.

"*Oh, it'll be alright. Your Daddy will get you through this. He's the only one who's always been there for you. You don't need Michael, God, or your church family.*" In perfect unison, the demons mocked Zoe. "*Look what following after your God has gotten you. Nothing! Your baby is gone. He could have easily saved her. But He didn't. You have every right to hate Michael. He killed your baby.*"

Zoe, choosing to turn away from the Almighty, opened her heart to a violent assault of the enemy. Unfortunately, her free will kept Ramiah from fighting against the barrage hurled against her. She didn't resist the enemy, nor did she cry out to the Almighty for help.

Amos and Zoe had been upstairs for over an hour before he finally coaxed the grieving mother downstairs. He'd forgotten that Barbara had accompanied him and hadn't considered the fact that her presence might bring further distress to his distraught daughter. Barbara grieved the loss of the grandchild she would never know, and she mourned for Amos. She loved him beyond words. He'd put up with her selfish immaturity in the early years of their marriage. Regrettably, by the time she'd realized how horrible she'd been, it was too late. Zoe hated her, and she certainly couldn't blame her. She felt her body stiffen in anticipation, not knowing what to expect as Zoe walked into the living room.

"What is she doing here?" Zoe seethed. The room became awkwardly silent as all eyes turned toward Barbara.

"Why are you here?" She directed the question toward Barbara. "Did you come to gloat? I'll bet you're happy I've lost my baby? You probably..."

"Zoe!" Michael snapped, stopping her mid-sentence. "She's here because she cares. Barbara cares about us and is here to support her husband. She drove Amos here. I know you are upset, but this is not the time or place to talk to her like that." He'd tried to get her to reconcile with Barbara on numerous occasions.

Zoe opened her mouth to retaliate, but Barbara spoke up, her voice filled with overwhelming compassion. "It's okay. I know how upset you are, Zoe. I'll step outside. I don't want to do anything to cause you further grief."

"No, you don't need to leave Barbara. You're a part of this family too." Zoe was stunned by the firmness of Michael's voice.

"That's great, Michael. You've killed my baby, and now you are taking up for that witch." Zoe could hear how terrible the words sounded coming out of her mouth, but she couldn't seem to help herself.

Barbara grabbed her purse, glanced apologetically at the group, turned, and walked out the front door in humiliation and defeat, unable to hold back the tears. Seated in the front seat of her Mercedes, she prayed.

"Lord, I know I was horrible to Zoe in the past. I've asked for Your forgiveness. But, Father, when will she forgive me? I know it's my fault, but it hurts so much knowing I'll never get to meet Emma this side of heaven. I pray for peace and comfort for Michael and Zoe. Oh, God, please help her as she walks through this valley of the shadow of death. In Jesus's name, I pray for You to be in the midst of this family to restore and heal our wounds."

Amos wasn't aware that Barbara had surrendered her life to Christ. He'd often referred to Christians as weak hypocrites who used God as a crutch. She was afraid of how he'd react if he knew she'd become a believer. For the past two years, she'd made excuses for her absence when she'd accompanied her neighbor to church. Her active involvement in so many charities made it easy for her to get out of the house on Sunday mornings and Wednesday nights. She felt guilty for being deceptive, but she couldn't bring herself to tell him the truth. *Maybe God is punishing me for lying to Amos all this time. The thought was accompanied by a feeling of hopelessness.*

She was startled as Amos thumped on the window. Barbara rolled down the car window. "Oh, Amos, I'm so sorry for that scene."

"Honey, it wasn't your fault. I'm sorry you had to endure that. I should have known better than to bring you here. I don't know what to do? Zoe needs me in there, but I hate leaving you sitting out here in the car. I know I should have defended you, but Zoe's so upset. I'm sorry."

Barbara reached out her hand and touched his cheek. "Don't worry about me. I'll go driving around for a while. Just call me when you're ready to be picked up."

"Are you sure?" Amos could see the pain in her eyes. "I hope you don't think I'm choosing her over you. It's just that she's so..."

"No, I don't think that. Zoe needs you. I promise I'm fine. You go back in there."

He drew her trembling hand to his mouth and kissed it. "I love you. You're my angel."

Barbara comforted Amos' concern with a deliberate smile as she backed out of the driveway.

Remembering that it was Wednesday night, she headed straight toward her church.

Pastor Steve broke the uncomfortable silence by announcing that he would be leaving. He knew that Michael and Zoe were in capable hands with Daniel and Shara. Daniel was a seasoned pastor, and though he was Michael's father and Emma's grandfather, he seemed to be handling the situation very well.

"Michael, you know how to get in touch with me if you need anything. I spoke with Marcie, and she has arranged for several families to bring food over for ya'll. The church is available for Emma's funeral, and I'd be more than honored to officiate, although I know you may want your dad to do that."

Michael's eyes told Pastor Steve that he hadn't yet thought about planning a funeral. "I guess we will need to make arrangements. I'll let you know what we decide as soon as possible. Thank you so much for everything, Pastor. I couldn't have made it through this day without you." Michael embraced Pastor Steve.

Pastor Steve walked toward Zoe, who was seated on the couch beside her father, her head leaning against Amos's shoulder. Sitting down beside her, he placed his hand gently on her arm. "Zoe, I'll be leaving now. Words cannot tell you how sorry I am for your loss. Marcie and I will be praying for you and Michael. Please know that we love ya'll and will do absolutely anything we can for you." Zoe didn't respond.

Against Michael's wishes, Amos gave Zoe one of his anti-anxiety pills. "It will help her relax and be able to sleep tonight." Amos defended his actions as Zoe swallowed the pill down without a protest.

"Zoe will have to face this loss sooner or later, and I don't want her depending on a drug to get her through it. We have hard decisions to make and a tough reality to face over the next few days and weeks. We need to lean on God to help us get through this."

Amos seethed as he responded through clenched teeth. "Where was your God when my grandbaby was drowning, Michael? Where is He now as my daughter sits here with her heart completely broken in two? Where? Why would you want to lean on a God who has allowed this to happen?"

Michael stared blankly at Amos. The questions hit him like a ton of bricks. Though his faith remained intact, he would have to spend time in prayer before he could begin to answer these questions for himself, much less respond to a grieving grandfather.

The imps danced hideously around their leader in triumph. "See, I told you we had a plan." Lust boasted to Dekar.

"We did it!" Unforgiveness chimed in. "This family is falling apart. They won't be serving Jehovah any longer."

Dekar raised his hands in a motion to silence the demons. "Never, for one minute, take for granted the power and determination of Jehovah to save one of His own. He doesn't give up on His beloved. Haven't you heard that He will leave the ninety-nine to go after one lost child? Your task is not complete. It's just beginning. You may have wounded them, but I wouldn't claim victory just yet."

"You must make them doubt the love of their God and question the validity of His word. Turn them against each other so they cannot stand united in prayer. Isolate them from other believers. I want this family destroyed. I loathe this young man. He's been a thorn in my side since the day he was born to his Bible-thumping parents. He uses the word to defeat my plans. He thinks he wants to be a pastor someday? Well, we will show him how much serving his God will cost him." He let out an eerie sound like that of a wild animal.

It was well after ten o'clock before Amos and Michael's parents left with the promise of returning the next morning to help make funeral arrangements. Shara helped Michael get Zoe into bed before departing.

Michael glanced out at the pool as he checked the backdoor locks and turned off the outside lights in preparation for the night. The house was eerily quiet. Amos's questions came racing through His mind. *Where was your God when my grandbaby was drowning?*

Michael questioned God as he sat alone in the darkness of the living room. "Lord, where were you? Why didn't you warn me? I don't understand why you allowed this to happen."

He sensed the Lord speaking to him. "*I did warn you, my son. I spoke to you in a dream. My people perish for lack of knowledge. However, I will take what the enemy meant for harm and turn it for your good. All things work together for good to those who love Me, to those who are the called according to My purpose. Hold onto this promise for the enemy desires to sift you as wheat. But I have prayed for you that your faith will not fail.*"

Michael thought back to the dream he'd had several nights before as well as the scriptural promise that God would be with him in the midst of the fire. He knew God had spoken to him, and though it didn't erase the unbearable pain he was feeling, God's voice was like a healing balm soothing his aching soul.

6

And God will wipe away every tear from their eyes;
there shall be no more death, nor sorrow, nor crying.
There shall be no more pain, for the former things have passed away.
—Revelation 21:4

The next few days passed in a frenzy of activity. The doorbell continually rang as friends and family brought food to the house. The refrigerator and countertops were piled high with casseroles, desserts, sandwiches, fresh fruit, and jugs of sweet tea. Beautiful flowers, plants, and cards arrived on a recurrent basis, causing the Davis home to take on the aroma and essence of a floral shop. The fragrance of lilies, carnations, and roses wafted throughout the downstairs. Michael was grateful for the love and support they were receiving though Zoe seemed to be oblivious to it all, spending most of her time in bed or the rocking chair in Emma's nursery.

Michael, with the help of his parents, made the funeral arrangements and picked out a tiny pink casket for Emma's burial. He was distraught as he left the funeral home flanked by his mother and father on either side of him.

"This is the hardest thing I've ever had to do in my life." Not only was he dealing with the loss of his child, but Michael also felt alienated by Zoe. Her distance served to nurture the feelings of fear growing inside of him like a cancer.

Zoe had refused to go with Michael to the funeral home. However, she chose the yellow dress Emma would be buried in and demanded that her favorite stuffed bear and pink blanket accompany her baby.

Zoe was also insistent on a closed casket. "I don't want to see my baby lying in a casket. I want to remember her the way she was when she was alive."

Though Michael thought an open casket would help others receive closure; he didn't want to do anything to further upset his wife.

Emma's funeral went by in a blur. For the most part, Michael couldn't recall who had attended. He remembered the overwhelming love and sympathy he'd seen on the faces of those who'd come to give their condolences.

Zoe, dressed in a simple black dress with lace sleeves, wearing no makeup and her blond hair pulled back in a tight ponytail, sat beside her dad at the funeral. He hovered over her like a mother hen. Grandma Abby sat on the opposite side though she'd made it clear to Zoe that she should be sitting next to her husband. Zoe refused to sit beside Michael or hold his hand as they walked in procession behind the casket. It was apparent to Michael, as well as to those present that she was distancing herself from everyone except Amos.

Pastor Steve, using Revelation chapter twenty-one verse four preached a wonderful message of hope for the day when every tear would be wiped away, and sorrow and sighing would be no more. He spoke about the Holy Spirit being a comforter, a very present help in a time of need, and reminded them of God's promise to turn tragedy into triumph. He asked everyone to continue to remember Zoe and Michael with a call or card of encouragement throughout the coming weeks and months. He reminded them that life would go on for everyone present, but for the young couple and their family, the days ahead would be the most challenging days of their lives.

Michael was grateful for the love and support of his parents. Shara stayed in the guest bedroom upstairs, and Daniel would come by almost every day to see how he and Zoe were doing. Shara helped Michael move all of the toys from the play area in the living room to the guest room closet, hoping it would help Zoe to cope a little better with Emma's absence. Zoe had insisted on Emma's room remaining untouched.

Amos's presence was constant as well. He made Michael feel as if he were a visitor in his own home and made it clear that he blamed him for his daughter's broken heart and shattered emotions. He took charge, barking orders and making decisions for Zoe that should have been left up to her husband. Zoe went along with whatever Amos decided for her, ignoring Michael's opinions or desires. Though he would express his disappointment to his mom and dad, he would not stand up to Amos for fear of upsetting Zoe.

Zoe's cold silence drove a wedge between the two of them, and Michael didn't know how to break through the wall of grief, anger, and depression she was steadily building around her heart. Except for Amos, she shut out the rest of the world as she grieved for Emma. Though she never cried, or at least he didn't see her crying; her stoic gaze told him she was hurting beyond what she was able to express.

Taking Zoe to his doctor, Amos had seen to it that she received prescriptions for anxiety and depression, disregarding Michael's protest. Zoe adamantly defended her father, arguing that she didn't think she could manage without the pills.

Life became a melancholy rhythm for Zoe. She knew her emotions were on a downhill spiral but didn't know how, or even care, to regain control.

Amos was her rock. She knew it should have been Michael, but every time she looked at him, she was reminded of her baby's absence due to his irresponsibility. She loathed his weakness. He didn't fight for her but instead, allowed her dad run over him in his own house. *My love for him died the day he let Emma drown in that pool, and I can't resurrect it any more than I can my baby girl.* Zoe indulged the negative thoughts, giving them access to her soul.

The house she'd once desperately desired was now a tomb for the living dead. Every room held memories of Emma. Unbeknownst to Michael, she planned on moving out as soon as possible and was even contemplating divorce. Amos, at her request, was searching for her an apartment and had promised her a job within his firm so that she wouldn't have to return to Dream Makers Employment Agency.

She'd become dependent upon the medication she was taking. It helped steady her nerves and took the edge off the constant nagging grief. Plagued with recurring nightmares of Emma crying out for her, she relived the loss over and over again each night. She'd wake up drenched in sweat, her pillow wet with tears she'd cried in her sleep. At Amos's urging, she'd been to his psychiatrist who'd prescribed sleeping pills. With the help of the medication, sleep came quickly, but she'd find it impossible to go back to sleep after one of the nightmares. She would eventually make her way to the rocker in Emma's room in the early hours of the morning.

It was only in that rocker and the shadow of night that the tears would flow without reserve, like a dam being allowed to release its swollen waters. The darkness reminded her that she was alone once again, without her mom and now without her baby girl.

Her mother-in-law had offered to locate a Christ-centered grief support group for her. Zoe rejected the offer while snapping at Shara. "A grief support group would only be a constant reminder of Emma's absence." She was relieved when Shara announced her plans to return home and leave the couple to grieve on their own. Though she'd meant well, Zoe felt like Shara had mothered her to the point of suffocation and was thankful to have her space back so she could be left alone and move on with her life.

Zoe's anger toward God spewed out upon all who came in contact with her. She resented the fact that Michael still defended Him, unapologetically nixed anyone's offer of prayer and did nothing to disguise her disdain at the mention of His name. As far as she was concerned, He didn't care about her. Therefore she refused to care about Him.

The band of demons rejoiced. Their prisoner, confined securely in their snare, wasn't struggling against their dark suggestions by taking control over her thought life, nor did she lift up a single prayer. And though others were praying for her, she remained imprisoned by her own stubborn will. She rejected truth, which could have brought immediate freedom and a quick end to their destructive schemes.

Pharmacia, an extremely dangerous demon adept at drawing his prey into the world of drug addiction had joined their ranks as well as Rebellion. Beautiful in appearance though his power was not to be underestimated, the spirit of Divorce was also working to ensure the success of the kingdom of darkness. Divorce was successful at deceiving humans to believe that the grass is greener on the other side of the fence; a greater love is just outside of their grasp and they deserve happiness instead of the joyless, wretched existence they are living.

Amos, being unsaved and unaware of the spiritual battle being waged against his daughter innocently heeded their voices, relaying to Zoe everything they told him to say like a dutiful slave.

Even Ramiah was powerless to stand against them since Zoe wasn't praying, casting down the lies whispered into her spirit or standing on scripture. The Almighty, from the beginning of man's creation, had given humans the right to choose whom they would serve. Ramiah knew that he was not allowed to intervene in Zoe's free will.

As far as they were concerned, she was as good as defeated. However, they knew Ramiah would continue to try and protect his charge, so they plotted to draw her even deeper into their web of deceit.

Dekar commended them and declared that Beelzebub, their supreme prince would be pleased with their strategies.

Pastor Steve sat in his office preparing his Sunday sermon. His thoughts kept drifting to Michael and Zoe. It had been almost three weeks since the Davis couple had lost their baby. He couldn't help but feel partially responsible. They'd been on his heart every day since the accident.

He and Marcie prayed diligently for them, but it was evident the enemy was working overtime on poor Zoe. She'd recoiled at the mention of prayer the last time he'd visited their house, unashamedly announcing that they could pray all they wanted, but she was going to her room. It had grieved him. Marcie tried contacting her, but Zoe would not answer or return her calls.

Michael was struggling to hold his marriage together and had confided in him that though they still shared the same bed, she wouldn't allow him to touch her. She made it very clear that she blamed him, as well as God, for Emma's death. She'd abandoned her faith. *How will she make it through this trial without leaning upon the loving arms of her Savior?* The thought disturbed him.

He and Marcie had decided to fast one day a week for the couple and pray for the restoration of all the enemy had stolen. They knew there was exponential power in united prayer and fasting.

"Amos, you need to allow them to work this out together. I don't think it's healthy for Zoe to depend solely on you. She needs Michael. She needs to forgive him. After all, it was an accident." Barbara desperately wanted to encourage her husband to trust in God to heal his daughter's broken heart but couldn't since she wasn't ready for him to know about her faith in Christ.

"Honey, I appreciate that you are concerned for her, but she's my daughter, and I know what's best for her. She needs me now more than ever. She doesn't think she can continue living in that house, and I will see to it that she doesn't have to if she doesn't want to. I need to protect her right now. I'm afraid of what she might do to herself."

"They can get counseling. And if you would encourage her to go, Zoe would probably do it. She does whatever you tell her." Barbara felt an overwhelming urge to fight for Zoe and Michael's marriage. "You can convince her to stay and work on the marriage. But if you help her leave him, she'll do that. Amos, Michael is good for her, and he loves her. Zoe is his life."

Amos looked at her with an angry scowl. "Well, if he weren't so irresponsible, his baby would be alive, and my daughter's life wouldn't be in shambles. How can I trust him with her happiness? He couldn't even watch his daughter for one day for god's sake."

Though wincing at the harshness of his voice, she remained persistent. "Honey, it was an accident. How can you blame him? You know Michael loved his daughter just as much as you love Zoe. Accidents happen!"

Barbara could see that the enemy was using her husband as a pawn to help break apart Michael and Zoe's marriage. There was no winning an argument with Amos Richards. She'd seen him at work in the courtroom on many occasions. At this point, she'd said all she could, however, she would continue to pray and trust the Lord to work in Zoe's life, despite Amos's interference.

7

Therefore what God has joined together,
let not man separate.

—*Mark 10:9*

Zoe could no longer hold back the tears as she finished packing the last of her belongings. Michael had argued passionately with her when she'd told him she was leaving, trying desperately to convince her to stay.

"Zoe, you can't leave. We made a covenant agreement before God. We committed to love and cherish each other through good times and the bad times. I can't believe you're going to give up on our marriage so easily?"

"I'm sorry, Michael. I can't spend one more day in this house. It's been almost two months since Emma died, and I've tried to stay here with you, but I can't pretend, to you or anyone else, that everything is going to be okay. I'm suffocating in this house. I need this separation."

"Baby, I'll sell the house. I'll move anywhere you want to move. We can get a hotel room tonight until I can rent us an apartment. But I will not give up on our marriage. I know you blame me for Emma's death, and I'm so sorry. I can't turn back the clock or change what happened. But I promise I'll spend the rest of my life loving you and trying to make it up to you. We can have another baby together."

Zoe fumed as she looked at Michael with hate-filled eyes. "You can't make everything better by having another baby. It's not like getting another puppy. Emma was my daughter! We can't simply replace her with another child. She was my life."

"Baby, I know that. I didn't mean we could replace Emma. She was my daughter too Zoe. I loved her just as much as you did. I just meant we could still have a family together. We can have a fresh start."

"Michael, it's not just this house that bothers me. It's you! I'm sorry. I wish I didn't feel this way, but I can't help it."

"You could if you'd turn back to God. Zoe, you can't run from everything, and you certainly can't run from God. He'll help us get through this. Don't you think I'm hurting too? If it weren't for Him, I don't know how I could face each day. Every day I'm reminded that my negligence costs my baby her life. But I know God forgives me, and He'll help me through it as long as I lean on Him. He loves you and will help you too, but you have to let Him."

Zoe stood against the kitchen counter with her arms defiantly crossed over her chest. "That's great, Michael! You let me know how that works out for you, but I can't lean on Him. He could have saved her!" She screamed through angry tears. "I just can't get around that fact. He could have saved her, and He didn't. Why? Didn't He love me enough to save her? He took my mom. Why did He have to take my baby too?" Crumpling to the tile floor, she began to sob uncontrollably.

"Zoe." Michael's voice was tender as he knelt down beside her, reaching out to comfort her. Her body stiffened at his touch. "Baby, I don't know why He didn't intervene. But I know His love for us never fails. I know He's promised to comfort and carry us through this. We have to trust Him. Remember the story of Job in the Bible? Even though he lost everything, he still trusted God. In the end, he saw the goodness of God. That's the God I choose to continue to believe in."

"Well, I can't do that." She glared at him with steely eyes. Her voice was as cold as ice.

"So you are willing to throw it all away? Our marriage, our life together, and your relationship with God mean nothing to you anymore? I just can't believe that, Zoe. I think you are going to wake up one day and regret this decision. You're allowing your dad to influence you. If you didn't have his help, I don't think you'd be leaving."

"Don't go blaming Daddy. You've always resented him helping us out financially. He's all I have now, and I need him."

"No, he's not all you have. You have me, your husband!" He thumped his hand on his chest. "I'm the one God holds responsible for taking care of you, not your dad. I think he's happy you want to separate. He's never thought I was good enough for you." He felt a resolve rise within himself. "Well, I can promise you and Amos this, Zoe—I will fight for you with everything that is in me. I will pray and stand and believe God for this marriage to be completely restored. I won't give up."

His voice was shaking with emotion as he got up and stood looking down at her. "I'll always be here for you when you are ready to come back. I'll be the one praying for you when you lay your head down each night and when you rise each day. You will always be on my mind. No one else will hold the place in my heart that's meant for you. I love you with an everlasting, unconditional love, and that will not change whether you leave or stay."

Zoe resisted the tug on her heart and the prick in her conscience as she remembered a familiar scripture passage. Assuming she'd thought of it on her own, she chose to ignore it. She reasoned within herself that she needed to stick to the plans that had already been made. Her father had gone through the trouble of securing a beautiful high-rise apartment for her near the Galleria, and when she was ready, he'd gotten her a receptionist job at his law firm.

"I'm sorry, Michael. I wish I didn't feel this way, but I do. I have to move on."

Ramiah heard the Spirit of God speaking to Zoe.

"*Therefore what God has joined together, let not man separate.*"

Because she'd hardened her heart to the Spirit's gentle whisperings, she disregarded His voice.

Ramiah knew he'd have to wait patiently as the Spirit gently worked on his wounded charge. As long as she remained a willing vessel for the spirits of darkness attacking her soul, there was little he could do to defend her against the attacks that continually bombarded her.

However, of this Ramiah was certain, God was well able to keep those who belonged to Him. "He has already won the victory." Ramiah spontaneously began to sing a song of exuberant worship. "He has won the victory, and He is undefeated. He is the King. He is Lord of all. Every knee will bow before

His throne."

Ramiah could hear the angels around the throne singing as they bowed in homage to their King. A multitude in heaven joined in with him to rejoice.

He recalled the words of Jesus in His prayer for His disciples. "My Father, who has given them to Me, is greater than all; and no one can snatch them out of My Father's hand." The angel smiled.

Indeed, God has won the victory. It is written!

Sitting in his father's office, Michael recalled being a young boy quietly reading or coloring in the same chair while his father studied behind his desk. He remembered the feeling of being so small, his feet barely touching the floor and eyes straining to see his dad over the top of the massive oak desk. He felt a lot like that little boy as he listened to the wise counsel of his father. Today, it was a mountain of despair blocking his vision as he told his father of Zoe's plans to leave and confessed his fear of losing her for good.

"Son, you'll have to trust God as He deals with Zoe's heart. She's hurting beyond our comprehension. I have a feeling that she needs this time alone to heal. I believe God has a work to do on the two of you individually." Though candid, Daniel's voice was tender and soothing.

"What do you mean?" Michael looked puzzled.

"Your mom and I have discussed this privately, but I wasn't sure if I should say anything to you. Remember the night Emma died and how Zoe responded with so much anger toward her stepmom?"

He continued without giving Michael a chance to respond. "We both feel like Zoe has a deep root of bitterness and unforgiveness toward Barbara, which has allowed the enemy a major entrance into her life. The Bible says, 'My people perish for a lack of knowledge.' I firmly believe that one way God's people perish is from a lack of understanding about the traps the enemy sets for us. He can cause great havoc in our lives, and even loss when we aren't aware of his schemes. The word warns us against giving him a foothold and that he is always looking for prey to devour."

"Listen to what the word says about bitterness." Picking up the Bible from the corner of his desk, he opened it to Hebrews chapter twelve. He began reading verses fourteen and fifteen to Michael.

"'Pursue peace with all people, and holiness, without which no one will see the Lord: looking carefully lest anyone fall short of the grace of God; lest any root of bitterness springing up cause trouble, and by this many become defiled.' This passage makes it clear that bitterness is an opening for the enemy to bring trouble into our life."

"Are you saying that God caused Emma's death as a result of Zoe's bitterness toward Barbara?"

"God is a giver, not a taker. He gives us His love, His life, His provision. The enemy is the taker. The word of God is like a key. We can use that key to open up God's provision and blessings in our lives. Or we can fail to use it and therefore give Satan an opportunity to bring havoc and destruction into our lives. We're the ones who've been given the key. It's ultimately up to us how we choose to use it. But first off, we must know the word and have it living in our hearts. We're repeatedly told how important it is to forgive. Jesus spoke about it often and said that we are forgiven to the extent we forgive others. When we refuse to forgive, we open the door to the enemy, and our prayers are hindered. God, because of His great love and mercy, would have been continually trying to deal with the unforgiveness and bitterness in Zoe's heart. When we refuse to listen to and obey Him, darkness is allowed to overtake us. It's not that God allows the darkness. We allow it."

Michael thought for a moment before responding. "But, Dad, I prayed for Zoe and Emma's protection every day. I prayed for the angels to protect us and pleaded the blood of Jesus over our house and over them. I can understand that Zoe might have opened the door to the enemy, but what about my prayers? Didn't they count for anything?"

"Michael, I don't have all of the answers. I know you were concerned about Zoe's walk with the Lord and that you two weren't praying together before the accident. Maybe the fact that you and Zoe weren't praying together in agreement was also an opening for the enemy." Daniel wished he had a clear word from the Lord that could comfort his son and shed light on his situation.

"I don't know. I'm just a man searching for answers too, Michael. I don't understand everything. Yes, I believe your prayers are heard and important to God, but He sees the bigger picture and…" Daniel's voice trailed off. A thought came to him that he was hesitant to share.

Michael could hear the hesitation in his father's voice "Dad, just say what's on your mind. That's why I came to you. I knew you'd be honest with me."

"A thought just came to me. From the foundation of the world, God knew the choices Zoe would make, and He allowed her the free will to choose. Her wrong choices may have cost our sweet Emma her life, but she's in heaven before the throne of God, living her eternal destiny. God promises to take the bad that happens in our lives, even when it's due to our rebellion or ignorance, and turn it for good. Yes, we are all suffering because we miss Emma, but didn't God say He'd leave the ninety-nine to go after the one lost sheep? It wasn't His will for Emma to die, but perhaps God will turn this dreadful loss for good by drawing Zoe completely back to Him. Zoe is lost in a sea of unforgiveness and bitterness, and He's going after her like the hound of heaven. Maybe it's not that your prayers weren't answered. You were praying for her walk with God, weren't you?"

Michael raised his eyebrows in a look of confusion. "So, Dad, are you saying that God took Emma's life because He was concerned for Zoe's walk? I just can't imagine that God would want someone's heart so much that He'd take the life of their child."

"No, I believe His hands were essentially bound. However, because you were praying for her walk and your marriage, He'll use this tragedy to work in both of your lives."

Michael nodded agreement. "I'm praying God will be able to draw Zoe back to Him. Before Emma died, I realized that I wanted Zoe to seek after God because I needed her to help me fulfill my call in ministry. Now, I just want her to be strong in her walk because I know it's God's desire for her. To see her struggling through this whole grieving process without Him breaks my heart."

"Son, God is also working on your faith and ability to trust Him for your marriage. Unforgiveness and bitterness are not the only doors we open to the enemy. If I were you, I'd seek Him during this time and ask Him if you've allowed any access to the enemy."

"Dad, do you think Zoe and I will get back together?" Michael hoped for a reassuring response from his father.

"I can't answer that. Your mom and I will certainly be praying for you two. I know God hates divorce, but Zoe has a part to play in this as well. She has to reach the place where she desires God's will to be done. It may take time, and there may be some challenging days ahead for both of you. However, nothing is impossible with God."

Daniel stood beside Michael, and the two embraced each other. He said a prayer for his son and daughter-in-law. Michael had tears in his eyes as he left his father's office. But, for once, these weren't tears of loss and despair, but of hope. "Nothing is impossible with God." When his father had spoken the words, the scripture exploded like fireworks, causing hope to radiate into his spirit. Michael kept repeating the scripture over and over again in his mind as he drove home.

After a strenuous day of moving and unpacking in the extreme July heat, Zoe, emotionally and physically exhausted, sat on the sofa to relax and enjoy a glass of chilled wine. She'd recently discovered that a glass or two of chardonnay in the evenings, working together with the antianxiety drugs, helped calm her frayed, tired nerves.

She grabbed her iPad off the cluttered coffee table and decided to catch up on Facebook. It'd been almost a week since she'd last been on the popular social networking site, and there were thirteen messages in her inbox as well as tons of unviewed news feed. She knew most of the messages would be condolences from friends who'd heard about Emma's death. She dreaded reading them. Though people meant well, they often asked for details. It was like pouring salt into a fresh wound every time she had to replay the tragedy to the curious and concerned. She decided not to read most of the messages.

However, a message from Zachary caught her eye and took her by surprise. She hadn't heard from him since she'd turned down his offer for lunch. She opened the message and began to read.

Zoe,

I'm very sorry to hear about the loss of your daughter. I'm sure that you are devastated. I know there is nothing I can do or say to take away your pain and heartache, but I want you to know I'm here if you need a shoulder to lean on. A mutual friend told me you were separating from your husband. I don't want to infringe on that relationship. I'm sure you have a lot to work through. Just wanted you to know I was thinking about you and that my offer still stands to take you to lunch or dinner.

Zach

Though puzzled, Zoe was touched by Zach's note. *How sweet. Who could have told him that Michael and I are separated?* Only a handful of people knew. She wrote out a quick reply.

Zach,

Thank you for your sweet message. Wondering who our mutual friend could possibly be? Not too many people knew. Right now, I need time to be alone. But, if I change my mind, I'll let you know. Thanks again for the invite and concern.

Zoe

The thought of going out to talk with someone who wouldn't thump the Bible at her was becoming somewhat appealing to Zoe. Given that most of her friends and acquaintances were Christians, they all had biblically based, well-meaning advice, that she didn't want to hear. She'd confided in her friend Kira, who'd told her, without reservation that she was making the mistake of her life by leaving Michael and reminded her that it was not God's will for them to separate. Many of her friends encouraged her to get into a grief support group. The thought made her cringe. *That's just exactly what I need…to get in with a group of depressed people who've all suffered the loss of a loved one and continue to wallow in it meeting after meeting. No, thank you.* She took another sip of wine.

"I Walk the Line," the song made famous by Johnny Cash, and which was Michael's distinct ringtone, began to play on her phone. *Note to self…I need to change his ringtone.* She decided not to answer it. "I'm not ready to talk to you, Michael." She tossed the phone onto the coffee table. "Good grief, I just moved out today." With the wine now working its magic, she snickered to herself at the choice of her own words. "Is there such a thing as good grief?" The question lingered in the air.

The beep on her phone indicated that Michael had left a message. "Ugh!" She reluctantly picked up the phone and listened to the message.

"Hey, baby. Just wanted to see if you got settled in. I've been thinking about you. I miss you already. The house feels so lonely without you. I'll be praying for you tonight. Let me know if you need any help setting up any of your furniture or hooking up the TV. I love you, Zoe. I will always love you. Well, I guess that's all. Talk to you later."

Oh, how I wish he would just let me go. She knew that he wouldn't give up easily. If only she didn't have to hurt him. Michael was the sweetest, most caring man she'd ever met. Why couldn't she forgive him? He'd once been the love of her life. How could her life have changed so quickly? "Just two months ago, we were still a family, happy and in love." The incredulous thought whispered out loud brought her to tears.

Not wanting to dwell on the situation, she bounded up from the couch and decided to get back to her unpacking. *I need some music to get me going.* As soon as the thought entered her mind, she found the playlist of her favorite country music tunes that Michael had loaded onto her phone. She began to play them, turning the music up loud. The up-tempo songs filled her apartment and the second glass of wine served to mellow her mind to the point where she forgot about Michael and her sorrow as she worked feverishly to get her new apartment in order.

Before going to bed that night, she surveyed the fruits of her labor. Her new luxury high-rise was beginning to look more like a home. Her home. *A home without Michael or Emma.* Hot tears burned her eyes as the thought came flooding into her mind. She took a sleeping pill as she'd done every night since Emma's death, hoping to fall asleep quickly.

"*A home without Michael or Emma.*" Confusion whispered in Zoe's ear while pretending to rub his eyes with his fist and mimicking bawling noises. He'd been recruited into the band of demons assigned to destroy her. His primary goal was to make her miserable, causing her to vacillate between the love she'd had for Michael and the unforgiveness she held toward him now. It was also his responsibility to keep her mind from thinking clearly, thus being able to dwell on the truth of God's word that still resided within her spirit.

Dekar addressed the group huddled, unseen by natural eyes, in the dark corners of Zoe's new apartment. "Let's make sure we keep our stronghold secure. Keep her separated from those who would be a godly influence in her life. To turn her heart further away from her blubbering husband, I've brought in Adultery. He'll see to it that she's led down the path of infidelity. He's crafty at his trade and has trapped many unsuspecting victims into his snare. He is responsible for the destruction of so many homes and churches by sweeping unsuspecting prey off their feet and into his lair. This wretched young woman will be a piece of cake for him." Dekar let out a wicked laugh as he disappeared. He had to report to Beelzebub. He'd be proud of Dekar and his team. Dekar loved the accolades he received from his prince.

Michael tossed and turned, unable to sleep in the half-empty king-size bed he'd shared with Zoe. He was disappointed that she hadn't answered his call. He figured she was busy in her new apartment, but he knew she always kept her phone close by.

The house was so lonely without Emma and Zoe. The darkness seemed to magnify the despair and loss he was feeling, bringing on a barrage of negative thoughts. *Maybe I should sell the house. I can't afford it anyway. What if she never comes back to me? Or, even worse, what if she finds someone else? Maybe I should just give up.* Michael spoke into the darkness, knowing in his heart that he could never give up. "God never gives up on me, and I can't give up on my marriage or Zoe."

He whispered a prayer as he lay on his bed, tears rolling down either side of his face. "Father, please protect her. Show her the way back into Your arms as well as mine. Help her to forgive and heal her as she grieves the loss of Emma. Bring people into her life that will be a strong godly influence on her. Lord, give me grace and strength to wait upon You and Your timing. Help me to surrender Zoe into Your care and trust You to work in her heart as well as mine. Show me any doors I've opened to the enemy so I can quickly close them as I stand in faith for our marriage. In Jesus's name."

A popular worship song came into his mind. He began to sing it softly into the darkness of his room.

"Our God is greater, our God is stronger
God, You are higher than any other.

Our God is healer, awesome in power
Our God, our God."

The song rolled around over and over in his mind. A peace came over him as he drifted off to sleep.

Deuel stood over Michael as he spoke into his charges spirit. "*God never gives up on you, so you can't give up on Zoe.*" He was thankful that Michael wasn't giving into the spirit of Depression trying desperately to worm his way into his charges thoughts. As soon as Michael uttered the first word to the Almighty, he fought off the spirit with a well-executed jab of his sword. It pleased him to listen to Michael's bass voice singing the song of worship the Holy Spirit imparted into his spirit.

A host of angels joined him in worship along with Michael. Tonight, there would be no demons of discouragement or depression allowed to assault his charge. Worship was a mighty weapon to defend against the onslaughts of the enemy.

The angels began to chant in unison as Deuel's charge drifted off to sleep: "And now my head shall be lifted up above my enemies all around me. Therefore, I will offer sacrifices of joy in His tabernacle. I will sing, yes. I will sing praises to the Lord." The glory of the Almighty filled the room.

Grandma Abby sat in her recliner watching the latest reality show featuring couples dancing, provocatively dressed and often very sensual in their choreographed routines. "What is the world coming to?" The seventy-three-year-old yelled at the television. Disgusted, she grabbed the remote and turned the flat screen television off.

"*Pray for Zoe and Michael.*" The Spirit of God lovingly, yet authoritatively, commanded her.

She was aware of the fact that Zoe's marriage was in trouble and that she was faltering in her faith walk. It grieved her to the core that her granddaughter had left her husband. Her thoughts turned to Amos. *If only Amos would leave that dear child alone and let the Father take care of her*. She had suggested the possibility to Amos. However, he wasn't listening and as usual, had told her he didn't want to hear anything about her God.

So as she'd done many times before, she sat in her favorite chair till the wee hours of the morning and interceded until she felt the peace of God fill her spirit. "Good night, Lord." She rose from the chair as soon as she ended her prayer and shuffled into her bedroom. "Now, will you please let this old woman sleep in tomorrow morning? I need my beauty rest, You know."

She made it her habit to talk to the Lord as if He were in the room sitting right beside her. Rarely did a day go by when she didn't feel His presence. He was her constant companion. Their relationship had grown over the years due to quick obedience on her part and faithfulness on His. She was familiar with His voice even when He spoke in the gentlest whisper. He'd seen her through the loss of her husband and daughter and had faithfully provided for her every need. She was never afraid of being alone because He had given His angels charge over her, and He'd promised never to leave or forsake her.

She didn't question the loss of Emma just as she hadn't questioned the loss of her husband Tommy or her daughter. That was God's business. She was quite confident that she'd be reunited with them one glorious day. As a young girl, she'd surrendered her life to Him, and so far, He'd been faithful to His promises. "You work it out for them, Lord." She pulled the covers over her tired body. Satisfied the Father was well able to move in Zoe and Michael's affairs, she fell asleep as soon as her head hit the pillow.

8

I believed and therefore I spoke
—2 Corinthians 4:13

Zoe woke up late the next morning feeling nauseated. *Ugh, I must have overdone it with the wine.* She made a mental note to stick with one or two glasses a night instead of drinking a whole bottle by herself. Her head was swimming as she made a mad dash to the toilet. She sat on the cold tile floor, her head halfway inside the porcelain throne and vomited until it felt like her insides would come out.

Exhausted and feeling sorry for herself, she recalled that the last time she'd been sick was while pregnant with Emma. The thought made her heartache as much as her head was pounding. *What if I never get to have another child?* The idea only compounded her sadness.

Having purged her pizza and wine from the night before, she brushed her teeth and went into the kitchen to make herself a cup of coffee. The aroma of fresh coffee brewing had her back in the bathroom once again.

She protested as she finished vomiting. "I can't be sick today. I have way too much to do." It was Saturday, and she'd planned to unpack the last few boxes before going shopping with her dad. On Monday, she would be starting her new job at her dad's law firm and she wanted new clothes. "You know I think I need some shopping therapy." Zoe had informed Amos on the phone the

91

previous morning. It had taken only a slight hint, and he'd readily offered to take her on a shopping spree at his expense, of course.

Michael's familiar ring began to sound on her phone lying beside her on the bathroom floor. She was still feeling pitiful and miserable when she answered after the third ring. "Hello."

"Baby, are you okay? You sound awful. Are you sick?" Michael's voice was oozing with compassion, and she hated the fact that it made her feel a bit guilty.

"No, I'm fine. I think I drank a little too much wine last night while I was working on my apartment. That or the pizza I ordered didn't agree with me. But I'm feeling better now since I upchucked my guts."

"I wish I were there to make you feel better. I'd be more than happy to come over and take care of you."

"The always faithful Michael." She rolled her eyes as she walked into the kitchen to get a drink of water. "Sometimes I wish you'd just be mean to me or at least not be so damn nice." Something about being miserable made her want him to be miserable too.

The curse word stunned Michael. "Zoe, you know that's never going to happen. I told you I'm not going to give up on us."

"Michael, why are you calling?" She knew the answer even before she asked.

"Just to tell you I love you and miss you."

"Michael, I think it would be better if you didn't call me for a while. I need space. If you want to do something for me, then give me space."

"Baby, if you need space, I'll give it to you. But promise me you won't give up on us. Promise me you'll at least think about me. Zoe..." Michael's voice choked as he spoke her name.

"I just need to be left alone. I can't promise anything to you, Michael. I'm taking life one horrible day at a time. I know you love me, but please let me have some air." She hung up the phone as a fresh wave of nausea drove her back into the bathroom.

Zoe was feeling better later that morning as she met her dad at their favorite coffee shop. The memory of the last time they'd spent the day shopping together invaded her mind. It was the Sunday before Emma had died. Amos had pushed the baby around in the stroller, often sitting outside of the stores, keeping the toddler occupied and leaving Zoe free to shop. Unwelcome tears stung her eyes as a lump formed at the back of her throat. *How long is it gonna take for me not to want to bawl every time I think of her?* She wiped away a tear trying to escape and make its way down her cheek. She hated crying. It was a sign of weakness. She wasn't willing to give God the pleasure of seeing her cry any more than she'd given Barbara the satisfaction of her tears when she'd mistreated her as a young girl.

"Hey, Daddy." Zoe bent down and kissed Amos's cheek. He was already seated and had ordered coffee for the two of them.

"I got you your favorite white chocolate mocha without the whip because I know you're watching your girlish figure, even though that drink has a million calories and a mountain of sugar in it." Amos tried to be lighthearted as he placed the hot cup of coffee in front of her. His heart broke for his daughter. A pair of skinny jeans and loose-fitting tee shirt accentuated the weight she'd already lost from her tiny frame. Her puffy eyes had dark circles underneath them. It was apparent she'd been crying. "Where is our shopping excursion taking us today?" They usually rode together while leaving one of their cars in the coffee shop parking lot.

"Thanks for the coffee, Daddy. Well, I was thinking about Neiman Marcus, so why don't we just head to the Galleria. I want to find some clothes for my new job and shoes to match of course." She winked at her dad. It was an inside joke they shared. He always teased that she could open a shoe store with all of the shoes she owned. "A girl can never have too many shoes."

"How's the apartment coming? Have you got it whipped into shape yet?" He and Barbara had selected the apartment and paid six months rent in advance. She had so much on her mind that he didn't want her to have to worry about rent and certainly didn't want her in some dingy cheap apartment complex.

"It's nice, Daddy. Thanks. I unpacked all day yesterday, but I still have a few boxes to unpack. I'm gonna try to finish up this evening if I still have the energy." She let out a slight chuckle. "I think I had a little too much wine to help motivate me last night. I was sicker than a dog this morning. I won't do that again anytime soon. My stomach is still a little queasy."

"Zoe, you have to be careful mixing your medicine with the wine." Amos had a look of concern on his face.

"I know. I'll be more careful. Don't look so worried, Daddy. It's not like I'm becoming an alcoholic or anything."

Amos changed the subject. "Hey, I ran into an old friend of yours last week. Well, actually he ran into me. He had some legal business he needed to have taken care of, so he came to our office. Remember Zach, your first high school crush? I hope you don't mind, but I told him about Emma as well as the fact that you and Michael are splitting up. He was sorry to hear about it. He's a super nice guy and apparently doing well for himself."

"So you're our mutual friend." Zoe proceeded to tell him about Zach's message on her Facebook page. "He seemed to be genuinely concerned about me. I thought it was sweet."

"Well, what would it hurt if you went out to lunch or dinner with him? It'd give you someone to talk with besides your dear old dad. I think he'll be by the office on Monday so you may be seeing him anyway."

"We'll see. Daddy, I don't need you to play Mr. Matchmaker right now." Zoe took a sip of her coffee and glanced around the coffee shop. She couldn't help but notice a couple sitting at the table next to theirs, holding hands while lost in conversation.

"Daddy, I haven't written Michael off just yet. I was kind of hoping that time away from him would help me to get my mind clear and…I don't know, put things into perspective. I think so much has happened in such a short time. I feel like I've lost everything." She clenched her jaw to hold back the tears threatening to pour out of her bloodshot eyes and expose her vulnerability to everyone within view.

Amos reached out to pat her hand. "Honey, you know I only want what's best for you. I certainly don't want to be a negative influence on you. I just want to see my baby girl happy again. I miss your sweet smile and bouncy personality. If getting back with Michael is what would make you happy, I'm all for it."

"Do you think that will ever happen again, Daddy? When you lost Mom, how long did it take you to get to where you weren't drowning in sorrow all the time? I mean, I know it's only been a little over two months, but I feel like I'm on this emotional roller coaster and I just want to get off."

"Well, I can't remember to be honest with you. That was so long ago. But I do remember that having you helped me to get through it and then Bar…" He stopped short before completing his wife's name, not wanting to upset his daughter.

"I know. Miss Sexpot came along and made you feel all better." Zoe's voice was thick with sarcasm. "I'll never forget finding you two in bed together. It scarred me for life." She made a face and stuck out her tongue. "Eeeww."

"Zoe, I'm…" She held up her hand to silence him and interrupted before he could finish.

"Let's get on the road and get this party started, Daddy. I'm gonna wear you out today. I hope you wore your shoppin' shoes." She kissed him on the cheek as she rose from her chair. "My car or yours?" They made their way out of the shop.

Amos volunteered. "If I'm going to be spending all of my money, we might as well use all of my gas too."

Michael inched slowly along in the torrential rain with his windshield wipers swishing at full speed as he drove to church. Low, dark, ominous clouds filled the Houston skyline promising continued rain throughout the day. The weather suited his melancholy mood. *I'm not sure why I'm going to church when all I want to do is stay home, pull the covers over my head, and mope in bed.*

"God, can't I just have one day to feel sorry for myself? I've lost my family and…" Michael grumbled as he made his way into the church building.

Bob Cline, the ever-faithful door greeter, gave him a warm smile as he entered the church and folded his umbrella. "Michael, I'm so glad to see you. I've been praying for you and Zoe. I hope she's doing okay."

Give him a break. Michael knew he needed to control his sour attitude. *The sweet old man has no clue that your wife has left you.* He prayed silently. *Lord, help me to walk in love even though I'm going through this storm.*

"Hey, Bob. It's good to see you. I'll let Zoe know you've been praying. We'll take every prayer we can get." He half-hugged Bob before moving toward the sanctuary.

Several well-meaning friends flocked toward him questioning him on Zoe's whereabouts, how he was coping, and if there was anything they could do to help. He assumed word had already spread that she'd moved out. He was aware that several of her church friends, including Kira, had tried to talk her out of it when she'd confided her plans to them.

"Michael, can I see you a minute." Marcie caught him by the arm to pull him away from the small crowd.

"Hey, Ms. Marcie. Is there something I can do for you?"

"No, I could see that you might need some rescuing from all of their questions. Steve informed me that Zoe moved out this week. People mean well, but I could tell you were having a difficult time." Marcie smiled up at him sweetly. "If you'd like, you can go sit in Pastor's office while you wait for the service to start. It's quiet in there, and no one will bother you."

"Thanks, but I'm going to go on in and get my seat. Sooner or later, I'm going to have to face people anyway. I appreciate it though. I wasn't prepared for all the questions. I know news travels fast, and people are going to hear. What do I tell them?"

"Only what you want them to know, Michael. You might just tell people the best thing they can do for you and Zoe right now is pray. Steve and I are praying for you. I hope you are aware of that." She reached up and touched his shoulder. "We love you guys, and we're here for both of you. I've tried to call Zoe, but as you know, she won't answer my calls."

"Don't feel bad, Ms. Marcie. She doesn't want to answer mine either. She's asked me not to contact her for a while. It's driving me crazy. I love her so much."

"Oh, I'm so sorry to hear that. We'll just keep praying. Prayer is a mighty force, Michael. I don't understand why all of this has happened, but I believe God is going to work it all for your good. I'm sure of that. I know that sounds so cliché, but I really do believe it."

"Thanks. I do too, although I wish I could see God's goodness right now. You know what I mean? The last few months of my life have been pure hell. Excuse me for saying that. I'm gonna go on in. I'll talk to you later. Thanks for rescuing me." He turned and walked into the sanctuary.

"Lord, help that poor sweet guy." Marcie prayed as she watched him walk away.

"I'm not talking about a name-it-and-claim-it or a blab-it-and-grab-it Gospel." Pastor Steve spoke with intensity, pacing back and forth on the platform as he preached about speaking the word of God in faith. Michael, sensed the anointing on his pastor and took meticulous notes while following along intently.

"God didn't create this earth out of something that already existed. He simply said, 'Let there be.'" He had the congregation reading along with him in Genesis one. "Everything came into existence because God said."

"Turn with me to Romans four, verses seventeen through nineteen." He looked up at the congregation before reading the scripture aloud. "As it is written, 'I have made you a father of many nations' in the presence of Him Whom he believed—God, who gives life to the dead and calls those things which do not exist as though they did; who, contrary to hope, in hope believed, so that he became the father of many nations, according to what was spoken, 'So shall your descendants be.' And not being weak in faith, he did not consider his own body, already dead (since he was about a hundred years old), and the deadness of Sarah's womb."

"Abraham saw God do the impossible in his life because he called those things that did not exist as though they already did. He didn't have an heir to fulfill the promise that his descendants would be as numerous as the stars in the sky. But the word tells us Abraham spoke God's promise over his life."

"Abraham believed God, even when it looked impossible. He was one hundred years old, and Sarah's womb was as good as dead. Do you know what that means, folks?" He smiled broadly before continuing. "That means her womb didn't work anymore. In the natural, it was a hopeless situation. I'm sure Abraham's friends laughed hysterically at the thought of Sarah getting pregnant, but he didn't care if they thought he was crazy. God had spoken, and Abraham believed and repeated exactly what his God said."

"I don't know about you, but I've had some of those dead womb experiences. You know what I mean, we've all experienced times when we've had to believe God for something that appears to be overwhelmingly hopeless in the natural. In this scripture, we learn the key to seeing our desires come to pass. It's a key to seeing dead wombs and dead dreams filled with the promise of new life. It says right here that Abraham didn't even look at his own body. He didn't consider the fact that his wife was old and well past childbearing years. He didn't consider the impossibilities of his situation. He took God at His word and kept his eyes on the God of the impossible. The Bible tells us that with our God nothing is impossible." The crowd erupted in cheers and applause.

He continued exuberantly. "I'm almost ready to close, but first turn with me to second Corinthians four. Look at verses thirteen and fourteen.

He paused to allow the congregation a chance to locate the passage in their Bibles before reading it aloud. "And since we have the same spirit of faith, according to what is written, 'I believed, and therefore I spoke,' we also believe and therefore speak, knowing that He who raised up the Lord Jesus will also raise us up with Jesus, and will present us with you."

"If you want to measure your faith in any given situation, listen to the words coming out of your mouth. Are they words that line up with the promises of God, or are they negative words filled with doubt and unbelief? What is it that you desire God to do for you in your life? You need to speak God's word in faith over your situation. Get yourself in the Word, find a promise, and stand on it. If God has promised it in His word, it will come to pass if you'll stand in faith, confess with your mouth, and run doubt out the door." He closed his Bible and placed it on the pulpit before walking to the edge of the platform.

He closed out the service with an altar call for those who'd never accepted Christ as their Savior. Michael, encouraged by the message, approached Pastor Steve once the service had ended.

"Pastor, do you have a minute?" He reached out to shake Pastor Steve's hand.

"Michael, come here." He pulled Michael toward him and embraced him in a bear hug. "I'll always have time for you. Why don't you go to lunch with Marcie and me today? My treat."

"Thanks, but I told my parents I'd drive out and meet them after church. I just wanted to tell you how much I was encouraged by the word today. I know I need to keep my eyes on the Lord. Please be praying for us. Zoe's asked me not to contact her for now. I've been feeling pretty down about it."

"You can bet that Marcie and I will be praying. What about meeting one day this week for lunch?"

"Maybe so. I'll give you a call." Michael hugged his pastor again before leaving the church.

The rain was still pouring down, but his heart felt a little lighter as he drove off to meet his parents. The song he'd sung the night before was playing on the radio.

"Our God is greater, our God is stronger God,
You are higher than any other.
Our God is healer, awesome in power.

Our God, our God."

"I'm thinking about putting the house up for sale. What do you guys think about that?" Michael took a seat between his parents at the crowded restaurant.

Daniel spoke up after exchanging a confirming glance with his wife. "It's funny you should mention it because we just prayed about that last night. I know you and Zoe have been strapped financially ever since you bought that house. I think it might be a wise decision."

Michael smiled. "Yea, thanks for not saying 'I told you so,' Dad. I know we should've listened to you guys, but Zoe wanted that house, and she convinced me we needed it."

"Don't blame it all on her, son. You're the spiritual leader of your home. Zoe needs a leader, not someone who'll cater to her every whim. The Bible talks about counting the cost, and I don't think you two were wise in making that decision."

Michael looked sheepishly at his father. "I know, Dad. I guess I wanted it too even though I knew it was a bad decision."

Seeing Michael's obvious discomfort, Shara changed the subject. "We think maybe it would be easier for Zoe to consider reconciliation if you sold the house. It has to be a constant reminder of her baby's death as well as it is to you too; I'm sure."

"Well, since Zoe's moved out, there's no reason for me to continue living there. I can't stand looking at that pool every day, and the house is way too big for me. And really, Mom, I don't see Zoe moving back anytime soon. I talked to her yesterday, and she's asked me not to call her. She said she wants me to give her some space."

Shara put her hand on top of Michael's as she spoke soothingly to her son. "Oh, honey."

"I can't believe this has all happened. I feel like I'm living in a nightmare, and I just want to wake up. I can't see us ever getting back together. Zoe's never going to forgive me. I'm afraid she's walked so far away from the Lord that she'll never be able to find her way back. She can be so stubborn sometimes, and Amos isn't helping the situation. He's so overbearing and has made her think he's the only one who can make her feel better. He's never thought I was good enough…"

"*I believed, and therefore I spoke.*" The scripture popped into his head almost before he'd finished his sentence.

Reminded of Pastor Steve's sermon, he quickly corrected himself. "I take that back. I have to believe that God can restore what the enemy has stolen. I need to start speaking God's word over my marriage. That was the message in church today."

Daniel looked across the table at Michael. "That's right, son. We all do. It's easy to speak what we see in the natural. It takes a lot more diligence and determination to speak God's word in faith over our situations. You need to get together some scriptures that speak to you about restoration for your marriage. Pray them every day. When the enemy comes and lies to you and tells you Zoe will never come back, you quote the word back to him. That's exactly what Jesus did. He reminded Satan 'it is written.'"

"Do you have any idea where you will move to?" Shara glanced up from the menu she'd been reading.

"I don't know. I guess I need to find a realtor first and pray the house sells quickly. Zoe loved that house when we first bought it. But I'm gonna believe that when God restores our marriage, He'll help us to get a house we can afford that she'll love just as much."

"Amen." Shara smiled at him.

"I'll probably just move into an apartment for now. I don't want to buy another house until Zoe can help me pick it out."

Before leaving the restaurant, Michael and his parents held hands and prayed for God to lead Michael to an excellent realtor and for the house to sell quickly. They prayed for Zoe's heart to be restored to God and her husband and for God to comfort her as she grieved the loss of Emma. And they prayed for Michael to feel the constant guidance, comfort, and companionship of the Holy Spirit.

Michael noticed that the rain had stopped, and the sun was shining as he drove out of the restaurant parking lot. The most vivid double rainbow he'd ever seen blazed across the sky.

"Thanks, Lord. I needed that." Michael's heart felt lighter as he made his way home.

Deuel noticed Doubt and Negativity, demons that almost always worked side by side, lurking by the table Michael and his parents occupied. Their mission was to keep the seed of God's word from taking root in the heart of the believer. As Michael received the scripture spoken by the Holy Spirit and quickly changed his confession, the angel was empowered and sent the spirits scrambling as fast as they could away from his charge.

Deuel would do everything within his authority to ensure that the seed had time to bear fruit in Michael's life so that his charge would be able to enjoy a fruitful harvest of God's promises.

Barbara arose from the pew, edged her way past several people until she was standing in the middle of the aisle. The pastor continued to call people forward for prayer as the musicians played softly in the background. She started walking toward the front of the church as if an unseen force were pushing her along. God was dealing with her heart through her pastor's sermon on honesty and integrity. It was time to be open and honest with Amos about her relationship with Christ. *It's going to take a major dose of grace.* The thought, along with a twinge of fear came to her as she strolled toward the altar to one of the waiting prayer team members.

For several years, she'd wanted desperately to tell her husband that she was a believer in Christ but couldn't muster the courage. She despised herself for the deception but loved Amos and was afraid that if he knew the truth, he'd look at her differently. He'd think she was weak and using God as an excuse for escaping her problems.

"Satan is the father of all lies." The truth the pastor had spoken in his sermon reverberated in her spirit. He'd also stated that continuing in the sin of deception could allow for the enemy to bring destruction in your life. She certainly didn't want to give the enemy a foothold. And she didn't want there to be any hindrances to God answering her prayers for Amos to become a Christian.

The woman on the prayer team listened as Barbara confessed her sin with tears in her eyes. She prayed for Barbara and promised to continue praying for her throughout the week. "Let me know how it goes. I know God will go before you and give you the words to say."

Before leaving the altar, Barbara prayed a prayer of repentance. "Oh, God, please forgive me for lying to Amos all this time. I've been a coward and a liar. I know I need to be honest with him about my love for You. You have changed me so much and made my life more joyful than I could have ever imagined, and I love You with all of my heart. Lord, help me to be a woman of integrity and courage. I realize that no matter what my excuse is, You view lying as a sin."

She left with a resolve to talk with Amos that night.

Zoe spent Sunday morning working in her apartment. Her possessions found their place in her new home as box after box was emptied until only one remained. *Emma* scrawled across the top, warned her of its cherished contents: pictures, a baby album, and some of Emma's clothes and mementos she'd kept. Opening the box with shaky hands, she took out a picture of her baby at nine months old.

"My Emma. My sweet Emma." A dam had been breached. She sat on the floor and wailed. "God, why? Why?" She held the picture tightly to her chest as she railed at God. "How can I live without her?"

She pulled out the baby album. A pen still rested within its pages, ready to record each of Emma's milestones as soon as they occurred. The pen served as a bookmark of her last entry.

> Your first words…dada! Really, Emma Noel? Why couldn't you say mama first? Your daddy will never let me live this one down. You are our joy. We love watching you waddle around the house. You are a messy little goose, and I find myself constantly picking up after you. My living room will never be the same. But I wouldn't trade you for anything in the world.

After what seemed like hours spent pouring over every picture and reading each entry, she took several of the framed photographs and placed them around the apartment. "I'll never forget you." She kissed the picture of Emma taken on her first birthday as she spoke the words and placed it beside her bed.

She put the box, and what remained in it, into the spare room closet. Though it was still early in the day, she poured herself a generous glass of wine. Sitting on the couch, she watched the rain pelting against the glass doors that led to her patio. Suddenly reminded of an old nursery rhyme, she spoke into the empty room. "I feel like Humpty Dumpty. And all the king's horses and all the king's men could never put me back together again."

9

A bruised reed He will not break,
and smoking flax He will not quench,
till He sends forth justice to victory.

—*Matthew 12:20*

Zoe strolled nervously into the prestigious law offices of Pointer, Richards and Brighten located on the fifteenth floor of a downtown office building and was immediately impressed with the opulent reception area. Two expensive brown Italian leather couches and four matching wingback chairs were perfectly placed around several ornately carved wooden tables. A beautiful water sculpture took up the entire wall to the right of the reception desk, ushering in an atmosphere of tranquility, and above the sculpture was the name of the law firm in gold lettering. There was an archway on the opposite side of the desk leading back to the offices of the attorneys and their staff. An antique tapestry hung on one wall, and several pieces of expensive art adorned the remaining walls. Soft music played in the background. Zoe assumed the two people seated on one of the couches were awaiting their scheduled appointments.

"Hi, Ms. Davis. We've been expecting you. If you'll have a seat please, our office manager will be right out." The pleasant black girl at the reception desk smiled as she peered over the counter, pointed Zoe to one of the leather chairs, picked up the phone, and began whispering into it.

As Zoe obediently took her seat, the thought occurred to her that maybe she should have returned to her job at Dream Makers Employment Agency. Fear of having to defend her decision to leave Michael had kept her from returning to the Christian-based company. *Maybe this is a big mistake. Am I making too many changes all at once? I might be out of my league here.* But before she had time to dwell on the answers, an attractive young girl walked through the archway and came to where she was seated.

"Hello, I'm Tonya Mendez, the office manager. You must be Zoe Davis." The young woman shook Zoe's hand firmly. Though she appeared to be warm and welcoming, her professional manner made Zoe feel insecure.

"Hi, it's nice to meet you." Zoe stood as she responded.

"Come on back, and I'll show you around." Tonya turned and walked through the archway that led to the busy law offices. Zoe followed.

Tonya took her on a tour of the offices, introducing fellow employees as she led her around. They stopped in front of her father's office. His secretary, a woman she'd spoken to many times when calling Amos, gave them permission to enter. His spacious corner office overlooked the downtown Houston skyline. He motioned them with his finger to wait as he finished a phone call.

"Is Tonya taking good care of you?" Amos asked as he hung up the phone.

"Yea, but I don't know how I'm going to remember everyone's names or where everything is. This place is huge."

"Oh, don't worry." Tonya leaned against the doorway of Amos' office. "Before the week is out, you'll feel like you've been here forever. It just seems overwhelming at first."

"I sure hope so. We'd better be going, Daddy. Tonya says there's a lot for me to learn today." She hugged Amos before walking toward Tonya.

"You'll pick it all up quick. Be gentle with her Tonya." He winked at the young office manager.

"Of course, Amos. You know I'm nice to everyone." Tonya flashed Amos a flirtatious smile before turning to leave.

Zoe couldn't help but notice Tonya's flirtatiousness with many of the men, including her father nor the fact that most of them seemed to perk up when she entered their offices.

As they walked down the hall, Zoe was struck by the sudden thought that demons were lurking at every corner. Of course, she couldn't see them, but she could feel the hair stand up on the back of her neck. The thought left as quickly as it had come.

Tonya took her full circle around the office before returning to the front desk where she introduced her to LaDonna Starrett, the receptionist whom she'd spoken with upon her arrival.

Tonya stood to the side as LaDonna shook Zoe's hand. "LaDonna has been promoted to be my assistant. She'll be responsible for training you. So I'm going to leave you two ladies for now. Zoe, why don't you plan on joining us for lunch today? Unless you already have plans to have lunch with your father."

"No, that would be great." Zoe smiled at Tonya. "Thanks for showing me around."

She turned her attention back toward LaDonna, who'd already pulled up an extra chair. She gestured to Zoe to sit in the chair she'd previously occupied. LaDonna noticed the wide-eyed look of fear in Zoe's eyes. "Hey, there's no better way to learn this job than to jump right in."

She proceeded to explain the demands of the front desk, how to answer the phones, and what would be expected of her as the receptionist for Pointer, Richards and Brighten Law Associates.

Zoe wasn't the only one who had noticed the demons cowering in the corners of the law office. Ramiah had seen them too. He'd seen other angels as well. Most stood, basically powerless watching over their charges, their authority stripped from them due to prayerlessness on the part of those they guarded so faithfully.

Adultery, Lust, Greed, Jealousy, Competition as well as many other demonic spirits lurked throughout the offices and cubicles. It would be a challenge guarding Zoe in this place. There had been demons at her previous job, but this place was infested with them. The light of Christ was scarce to be seen except in one office they'd passed during the tour. There were a few dim lights emanating here and there, but these were not from fully surrendered, sold-out believers in Christ. These were Christians in word but not deed.

Carol Tatum, a young legal assistant, was a devout follower of the Almighty and His Son. The light of Christ flooded her office. Ozias, her angel, mounted guard beside her. She was a strong prayer warrior and spoke the word of God boldly. Ozias didn't allow demons access near her, and they scampered in fear when he accompanied her down the hallway or into other offices. She kept her witness among her peers, never entering into their office gossip or politics. Most of them referred to her as the holy roller or Jesus freak.

Ramiah greeted Ozias briefly. The Almighty expected them to work together to arrange a meeting between their charges. Ramiah smiled with approval. Carol Tatum would be a good influence in his charge's life.

He would pray to the Almighty for wisdom in the matter and His perfect timing.

Michael was stunned when he retrieved the postcard of a local realtor out of his mailbox Monday morning. Amanda Townsend's advertisement touted her knowledge of the area and her success at selling homes. Her picture was displayed prominently beside a sold sign in front of a magnificent home. Feeling like this was the confirmation he needed, he decided to give her a call.

He called her number and set up an appointment for later that evening. He spent the rest of the day making sure the house would be presentable when she arrived.

Zoe was reviewing her extensive notes and didn't notice the cocky young man walking casually up to the receptionist desk.

"Excuse me, pretty lady, can you help me? I'm here to see Amos Richards."

Startled, she peered over the counter of the desk to see Zachary Thomas standing in front of her looking like he'd stepped out of a GQ magazine. *He's even better looking in person than he was in his pictures.* Her face blushed at the thought. Feeling flustered and suddenly insecure about how she looked, she hoped her pale pink lipstick hadn't worn off from the coffee she'd been drinking.

"Well, how are you doing, Mr. Thomas?" Zoe tried to appear cool and calm. "Wow, it's been so long since I've seen you."

"Too long, if you ask me." He stared at her as if he wanted to devour her. "You haven't changed a bit. You're as gorgeous as ever." He cleared his throat, and his voice softened and became suddenly serious. "I just want to say again how sorry I am for your loss, Zoe."

"Thanks, Zach. I'm just taking one day at a time. My life will never be the same."

"Do you have lunch plans? Can I take you to lunch?"

"I'm sorry, but our office manager has asked me to lunch today." The thought of being alone with him made her nervous.

"Well, how about dinner? I know the perfect place to take you, and a night out might do you some good. I promise not to keep you out late."

His charm and the sweetness in his voice made it difficult to resist his invitation. "Okay. But I can't be out late. I have to be up bright and early in the morning for work." She lowered her voice just to be sure others waiting in the reception area could not hear her. "Let's make this clear; this is just dinner between two old friends. Nothing more. Okay?"

"Well, you may be old, but I'm not." He winked at her before continuing. "Of course. I know you're going through a difficult time. I just want to be a friend and cheer you up, if I can." He spoke a partial truth.

"Okay! Then have a seat, and I'll let Mr. Richards know you are here to see him, sir." She smiled playfully as she pointed in the direction of the waiting area.

She rang Patricia Knesek, her father's secretary, to notify her that Zach was waiting for his appointment with Amos. She found herself staring at him as he took a seat in the waiting area. *Oh, my lord, he is so good-looking.*

Amos greeted Zach with a handshake as he offered him something to drink. After discussing Zach's legal business, the conversation turned to Zoe. Amos liked Zach. He found himself wishing Zoe would be attracted to him. He was aggressive, had a great job, yet was trying to further himself by starting his own investment business. Amos couldn't imagine this young man having any problems getting the ladies with his charismatic, confident personality.

"So I suppose you saw my daughter at the reception desk?"

"I certainly did." Zach nodded in agreement.

"She doesn't need this job. I'd support her completely if she'd let me. But she said she wants to stay busy. I guess it helps her to keep her mind off things."

"I can understand that. She's going through a very difficult time." Zach tried to sound sympathetic.

"I think she could use a friend. You know, someone to lean on and confide in besides me. I know you two used to be friends." Amos hoped the young man would take the bait he was laying out.

"Well, Mr. Richards…"

"Amos. Son, you can call me Amos."

"Amos, I've made it known to her that if she needs a friend, I'm certainly available. I asked her out for dinner tonight, and she said she'd go."

"Great!" Amos beamed as he rose up out of the chair. He reached out to shake Zach's hand, indicating that their discussion had come to an end. "I hope you two have a nice time."

Zach was puzzled as he left Amos's office. It didn't seem to matter to Amos that Zoe was still married and, though it was only a friendly dinner date, going out with someone other than her husband.

He stopped at the reception desk to get Zoe's phone number and arrange a time to pick her up before leaving the office.

There was a definite spring in his step for the rest of the day.

"OMG! First day on the job and you've already got men asking you out." LaDonna stared after Zach as he disappeared into the elevator. "Girl, it took two months of me workin' here before anyone asked me out, and I guarantee you, he wasn't as fine lookin' as that guy."

"We're just old friends. It's not a big deal." Zoe protested, though inside she felt as giddy as a schoolgirl. She withheld from LaDonna that she and Zach had dated in high school.

"Well, honey, I wish all my old friends looked like that." The girl laughed heartily. "Umm-hmm. I could do some damage to that boy!"

Zoe instantly took to LaDonna. A beautiful girl in her mid-twenties, she was slightly overweight, though she joked about it as if it didn't bother her. "I'm my boyfriend's shade in the summer and warmth in the winter."

Zoe couldn't help but notice how beautiful her dark, silky smooth skin was or the fact that the young woman certainly knew how to dress to accentuate her robust figure. Her keen sense of humor kept Zoe in stitches as they worked together. The two bantered back and forth as if they'd been friends for a long time.

"Girl, you better tell me all about that date tomorrow. I'm gonna want me some details. You hear me?"

"I could spare you the wait. We are going out to eat, and that's all." Zoe enjoyed the banter. It felt good to smile and laugh with LaDonna. *Lord only knows how long it's been since I've had a good laugh.*

"Girl! What are you talkin' 'bout? One look in his eyes and your knees are gonna go all weak and wobbly. You're gonna be like putty in his hands. And if you ain't, you is crazy. You gotta promise me you'll tell me everything tomorrow."

Zoe laughed. "I promise, but I think you're going to be disappointed. There won't be much to tell. Dinner, that's all that's on the agenda."

Zoe had to admit that the thought of sitting across a table from Zachary Thomas already made her stomach turn summersaults. She caught herself thinking way too much about what she'd wear and was surprised at how often her thoughts turned to him throughout the remainder of the day.

Michael was outside watering the yard when Amanda Townsend pulled into the driveway.

"Your home is beautiful." She waved as she got out of her car, briefcase in hand. "Amanda Townsend." She introduced herself as she extended her hand out to Michael.

"Glad to meet you." Michael shook her hand. "Come on in, and I'll show you around. My wife and I have recently separated. I'm hoping that it's okay that she's not here."

"Oh, certainly. I'm sorry to hear that. Is the house in both of your names?"

"Yes." Michael nodded.

"Well, you can sign the contract, and either we can fax a copy to her for her signature, or you can take it to her if you'd like."

He took Amanda on a tour of the house. "Of course, we'll have to disclose that there was a drowning in the pool, but I don't think it will be a problem." She pulled paperwork from her briefcase and handed it to Michael.

"I've done a market analysis, and I think we can list your home for $400,000. It's a seller's market right now. I'm pretty sure I already have clients who'd be interested. This is a hot area, and the house is beautiful and in immaculate condition."

After signing his portion of the contract, he promised to get Zoe's signature and return it to her as soon as possible.

"Great. I'd like to get a sign in the yard by the end of the week."

"It'd be great if it sells quick. It's been hard living here since our baby…"

She cut him off. "Oh, Mr. Davis, don't worry. We'll get it sold. It's a gorgeous home with a great floor plan, and it's in a good area. There's no reason it shouldn't sell fairly quickly."

Michael felt optimistic as she pulled out of the driveway, both at the prospect of the house selling quickly and the opportunity to see Zoe. Since he had a good excuse, he didn't waste any time shooting off a text to her.

> Need to talk to you about the house. I'm putting it on the market & have papers for you to sign. Can I come by tonight so we can talk about it & you can sign the contract? How about dinner? I can bring something over if you don't feel like going out?

Racing to get home quickly, Zoe whipped in and out of traffic while she mentally perused her closet, still unsettled as to what she was going to wear to her dinner with Zach. A slight twinge of guilt made her uncomfortable as she read the text from Michael. *What in the world am I going to say to him? How should I answer? It's not a date. I'm just going out with a friend for dinner.* She replied while stopped at a traffic light.

> Sorry, I'm not feeling well. Had a long day. 1st day at work. I'm exhausted! Can we meet tomorrow?

She knew that her response would likely provoke a call from Michael and steeled herself for his familiar ringtone. It was easier lying to him by text. However, she knew she'd have no excuse not to answer if he called. *I don't want to deal with you tonight Michael.*

Michael felt rejected as he stared at his phone. He desperately wanted to hear Zoe's voice. However, being afraid of upsetting her he typed a quick reply.

> Ok, baby. I'll plan on coming by tomorrow around 7:00 if that's ok. I love you & I'm praying for you & for us.

A wave of sadness washed over him. The thought of spending another dismal night alone in the house made him want to cry. He couldn't believe that his life had taken such a 180-degree turn.

"Lo, I am with you always, even to the end of the age."

He recognized God's voice. "Thank You, Lord. I needed that." His responded audibly to the familiar voice. "God, this is so hard. I don't know what I'd do without You." A scripture popped into his mind, so quickly, he knew it had to be the Lord.

"A bruised reed He will not break, and smoking flax He will not quench, till He sends forth justice to victory."

Though he was unfamiliar with the passage, he was encouraged. He got out his Bible and meditated on the scripture, allowing it to soothe his spirit like a healing balm.

Barbara had worked all afternoon to prepare a romantic dinner for Amos. She'd sent the housekeeper home early so they could have the house to themselves. She was putting the finishing touches on his favorite chocolate cake when she heard him pull into the garage.

"Wow, what have I done to deserve this?" Amos leaned in and kissed her on the cheek.

"I wanted to surprise you and show you that I can still cook."

"Wow…it smells great. Pot roast? That's my favorite. I'll pour us a glass of wine. How's that sound?"

Barbara smiled up at him. "I already have some chilled. Go ahead and pour it, and I'll meet you in the dining room with our plates."

Amos was surprised to find candles lit, the dining room table beautifully set, and soft music playing in the background. "This is more than just a reminder that you can cook." He grinned as he shouted toward the kitchen. "Do I need to put on something more comfortable?"

She laughed as she entered the room with plates full of pot roast, potatoes, and green beans. "You'll really think I'm special when you taste the cake I made for dessert."

They shared the details of each other's day while enjoying a leisurely meal together. After serving dessert, Barbara knew it was time to confess the truth to Amos.

"Honey, I have something I need to talk to you about." Her voice became soft and serious.

"Oh heck, I thought you did all of this because you wanted my body." Amos could sense the tension in her voice.

"Well, we can talk about that later. But I have a confession to make. Amos, I have been keeping something from you. I've been afraid to tell you because I don't know how you'll take it, and I don't want you to be disappointed with me." Tears began to fill her eyes.

Amos was surprised by the emotion in her voice. "Honey, there's not much you could do to disappoint me." He put his hand on top of hers.

"Amos, I've become a Christian. I've been going to church with Sondra Beckman for over two years. I've often lied to you, telling you I was going to one of my charities or something so that you wouldn't find out. I was afraid of what you'd think of me. You've always been so down on Christians. I didn't want you to be down on me too. I'm so sorry I haven't been honest with you."

He stared at her in disbelief. "Honey, I feel rotten that you'd think you needed to hide that from me. I must be a real heathen for you to think you couldn't even tell me you were going to church." He tried to make light of the news. "I don't mind if you go to church. I just don't want you to be all radical like that crazy Jesus freak at my office or Michael and his family."

"I don't know if you'd call me a Jesus freak, but I know that Christ has been slowly but surely changing my life. It's not just about me going to church. Amos, I have a relationship with Jesus. I would love for you to have one too, but I'd never try to change you."

His voice began to rise in defense. "Why would you need to change me? I'm a good person. I don't cheat on my wife like the other partners at my office. I might have a few drinks now and then, but I'm not a drunk, and I've always allowed you to give to your charities. I've headed up a few of them myself. I can promise you this; I'll never be like Daniel or Michael Davis. That's just not me."

"Oh, Amos, this is really about me. I'm not expecting you to change. I've just felt so guilty for deceiving you, and I wanted you to know the truth. I don't want to have to hide my faith. It's become very important to me. It's who I am now."

"You've always been a wonderful, beautiful woman to me. I've never felt like you needed to change. I'm not upset with you. I just don't want you to be a holy roller, and I certainly don't want you to expect me to go strolling down any church aisles with you."

Barbara was relieved that Satan could no longer hound her with guilt for lying to Amos. His stronghold over that part of her life was broken. She knew she'd have to pray harder for Amos. He was going to be a tough nut to crack. She'd continue lifting him up to God and walking in faith that God would one day have Amos Richards's heart for good.

10

For I know the thoughts that I think toward you, says the Lord,
thoughts of peace and not of evil, to give you a future and a hope.
—*Jeremiah 29:11*

Zoe felt fuzzy-headed and couldn't recall where she was when she was star-tled awake. Puzzled by her surroundings, she sat up in the strange bed. Her cheeks flushed red hot as the realization hit her that she was completely naked in Zach's bed. The clock on the nightstand told her it was a little past three in the morning. After giving herself a moment to adjust to her surroundings, she inched her way out of bed, located her clothes lying scattered about the floor, and began to dress as quickly and quietly as possible. After a moment of searching, she found her purse on the bar in Zach's kitchen. She crept out of his apartment, being careful not to awaken him. She called for a taxi as she made her way down the elevator and into the lobby of his luxury apartments.

Memories of their evening came flooding into her mind. Zach had taken her to a ridiculously expensive restaurant where they'd been seated in a quiet, dimly lit corner away from most of the other patrons. She was pretty sure he'd arranged that beforehand. Their conversation had been a little awkward at first until she'd downed several glasses of wine. They'd gone from there to a downtown piano bar where they'd had a few more cocktails, which led to some rather provocative dancing. He'd kissed her passionately on the dance floor, telling her how good she felt and how he'd longed to hold her in his arms all night long. She knew she was drinking way too much, but it had helped her to relax and calmed her feelings of inadequacy around Zach. From there they'd ended up at his apartment where they'd had another glass of wine before things got heated, and she found herself unable to resist the passion burning inside of her. He carried her into his bedroom, making love to her before they fell asleep in each other's arms.

She berated herself in the backseat of the taxi. *For goodness' sakes, Zoe, you've only been out with him once, and you're still married.* Her head was still tipsy, and her stomach churned from the alcohol she'd consumed. She smiled as she reflected once again on the events of the evening. Zach had poured on the charm, and his irresistible good looks had melted all of her resolve to keep the night from developing into anything more than two friends out for dinner. Being with him had helped her, at least for one night, to anesthetize the pain of losing Emma. However, her life was a mess, and she knew she didn't need any additional entanglements at this point. She'd have to tell Zach they couldn't see each other again though the thought of his touch sent a chill of delight up and down her spine.

Michael's face suddenly dropped into her mind like a bad memory trying to resurface. It would break Michael's heart if he ever found out that she'd slept with another man. Though she couldn't forgive him for killing her baby, she didn't want to hurt him.

It was four-thirty in the morning before she was able to fall asleep in her own bed.

Adultery and Lust, like a proud peacock, paraded himself in front of the demons assembled before Dekar, their fierce ruler. His prowess at successfully arranging the seduction of his assignment into bed with a man who was not her husband was being touted by the group of demons.

Lust was the first one to gloat, wanting to be sure he received credit for his actions. "You should have seen him at work. She was so drunk that all she could think about was how bad she wanted him. I made sure that she was irresistibly attracted to the guy. Our plans worked better than we could have hoped for."

"Well done, my faithful servants. Beelzebub will be pleased with your efforts." Dekar's voice oozed with false pleasure as he commended the group before him. "However, this is not the time to be boasting and celebrating, you bunch of idiots. Your time would be much better spent calculating your next move very carefully. Do you not know this woman has several people praying for her? You certainly can't afford to slack off now. Tighten the noose around her neck. Beelzebub is never content with anything but complete victory."

Catching the underling off guard, Dekar violently grabbed him by the neck in one swift movement. Lust's eyes bulged out of their sockets as Dekar breathed his foul breath into the shriveling demon's face. "You'd better not screw this up, you cocky little runt, or else." He left the threat up to their imaginations as he loosened his hold on Lust's neck. The whimpering spirit scampered as far away from his grasp as he could.

Adultery spoke up, though he tried to steer clear of Dekar and his unpredictable temper. "Oh, master, don't worry. We've left no stone unturned. Her unwillingness to forgive has paved the way for us to slide in and out of her life with ease. And we've also recruited the strong spirits that dominate this young man's life. They've assured us their full cooperation as they also want to please our great prince. He opened himself up to our world through transcendental meditation and his new age beliefs a long time ago. He willingly gives his demons free entrance and does whatever they suggest to him." His face was contorted by his hideous smile as he wrung his hands together. "We couldn't possibly have chosen anyone more suited for the task of seducing her."

"We'll see. I know her guardian angel. Ramiah will look for every opportunity to fight for her. He'll enlist others. I've done battle with him before, and he's a formidable opponent. Remember, you must never underestimate the power of prayer. Go after those praying for her." Dekar barked back before disappearing into thin air.

Zoe was startled awake by the alarm clock on her iPhone. It was seven in the morning, but she could have used several more hours of sleep. Her queasy stomach and throbbing head served as a grim reminder that she'd had too much to drink the night before. She blushed at the thought of herself sneaking out of Zach's apartment in the middle of the night. *I wonder what he thought when he woke up and found that I'd just left?*

While showering, she recalled a frightening dream she'd had right before the alarm went off. She wasn't one to remember her dreams, but this one had been so vivid. In the dream, she'd been at Grandma Abby's house though her Grandma wasn't there. She was walking through the house, searching for someone, but she couldn't remember who she was looking for. She was in the living room when the house suddenly began to tilt. Rushing over to the window, she realized that the house was being swallowed by a giant sinkhole. She tried to run toward the back door and escape before it was too late, but the door was jammed. She remembered screaming before waking up to the sound of her alarm. She surmised that the dream must have resulted from having too much alcohol in her system. But it nagged at her. She remembered that God often spoke to Michael in dreams.

However, instead of seeking God for its meaning, she allowed her thoughts to roam back to her night of illicit romance in Zach's arms. She smiled at the memory of his hands gently caressing her body. She thought about how the two of them had become united in a moment of ecstasy, unlike anything she'd ever felt with Michael.

Ramiah stood positioned just a few feet from Zoe, as always, battle ready and waiting for her to speak the word so that he could take down her enemies. The Almighty had given her a dream to warn her that her life was taking a dramatic downward turn, far away from the shelter of the Most High. She was spiraling down into a pit that only promised despair and destruction. The Almighty desired to love and comfort her as He had when she was a child facing the loss of her mother and the rejection of her stepmom. Instead of embracing pain as a means of drawing closer to Him, she was, like so many in the world, taking the path of least resistance. A road that only ends in more misery.

He also saw the spirit of Lust whispering into her ear, reminding her of the night of passion in the arms of another man and the lustful feelings it had aroused within her. He wanted to run the intruder off, but Zoe seemed to hang onto every word as if it were a delicacy to be relished with each tempting bite.

Michael woke up feeling uneasy. He'd awakened twice in the night with an overwhelming need to pray for Zoe and an undeniable sense of foreboding. His thoughts returned to her during his morning devotions. *I'll surprise her at her office and see if she'll go to lunch with me.*

He knew he was supposed to have dinner with her that night but, after such a restless night, felt like he had to see her right away. God, I've just got to know that she's okay. He also prayed he would see a glimmer of hope for the restoration of their marriage when he looked her into her eyes.

LaDonna, itching to hear all about Zoe's date with Zach, bombarded her with questions as soon as she walked into the office. Though she was practically a stranger, her prodding didn't bother Zoe.

"Okay, let's have it. Where did he take you?" LaDonna was hungry for all the details of which Zoe wasn't ready to share. She leaned back in a chair next to Zoe, arms folded across her ample bosom. "Come on…you can tell me the truth. Your secrets are safe with me." Her childish curiosity brought a smile to Zoe's face.

"I told you it wasn't going to be a big deal. We went out and had a nice quiet dinner." Zoe tried to lie, but a slight curve in her lips confirmed LaDonna's suspicions that there was more to the story.

"Girl, who you be trying to kid? I wasn't born yesterday. So what else happened?" She smiled like a Cheshire cat.

"Nothing! We just ate and talked." The phone on Zoe's desk rang giving her the opportunity to ignore LaDonna's probing questions.

"You're not off the hook." LaDonna leaned in and whispered playfully so those in the waiting area couldn't hear her. "Just wait until lunchtime. Girl, I know you couldn't possibly go out with a man that's built like that and just eat and talk."

"You're crazy!" Zoe swatted her playfully. Normally, she would have been offended by someone as forward and pushy as LaDonna. She'd never been one to like people getting into her business. However, Zoe found her to be a comedic distraction from the familiar presence of grief that was always nearby and ready to infiltrate her thoughts. She welcomed any relief, no matter what form it took, to help her cope with the shattered pieces of her life.

As the morning progressed, she fought the urge to call Zach and apologize for the evening. *I must have been a drunken mess to just hop into bed with him like that. How can I ever face him again?* Though embarrassed by her behavior, she tingled with excitement at the thought of his touch. It was unnerving the way he'd captured her thoughts from just one night out.

With a candle burning and his favorite Zen music playing softly in the background, Zach sat on the bedroom floor in the lotus position. Bringing his mind into a focused level of consciousness, he tried to silence the worry that was threatening to steal his peace. His mother, a yoga instructor and well-known psychic reader, had taught him at an early age, how to meditate and access a power that went well beyond his natural ability. What had started out as a means to help a shy, lonely young boy come out of his shell had opened up a portal into the spirit realm for which he could communicate freely with spirit guides who promised him success in every area of his life. The adoration and obedience they demanded of him seemed small in comparison to the financial success and self-confidence they'd helped him achieve. He considered himself to be a spiritual young man, devoted to the spirits who were always ready and willing to come to his aid.

Today, he sought direction from his spirit friends, as he liked to call them. He was concerned that maybe he'd moved a little too quickly with Zoe and scared her off. It bothered him that she'd left sometime in the night without telling him good-bye. The evening had been intoxicating. He was enamored with her and wanted her more than anything. He'd make a deal with the devil himself if he had too.

His spirit friends had been faithful to him thus far. He'd solicited their help in getting Zoe to go out with him, and they had delivered. To his pleasant surprise, they'd even made sure he had favor with her father. The restaurant he'd taken her to, at their recommendation, had blown her away. She'd been impressed when he'd had a bottle of her favorite wine delivered to the table. When asked how he knew, he said it was just a wild guess. He was grateful for their faithful assistance and couldn't imagine his life without them.

Sometimes he heard their voices when he was deep in a trance, most of the time, however, they would merely impress a thought into his subconscious. Often, he might just see a picture in his mind and know that they were communicating something important to him. That's how he'd known the type of wine to order for Zoe. He'd seen a picture of the bottle while meditating that morning.

He fell into a trance as he repeated his familiar mantra, inviting the demons that disguised themselves as familiar friends. He was instructed to move slowly and use her vulnerability to his advantage. They suggested sending her roses and even told him her favorite kind, though he wondered how they knew these things.

Zach wasn't aware that he was dealing with devils of darkness. These seemingly friendly guides would turn on him the moment he wasn't obedient to their every whim. Though he thought they were doing him a favor, he was nothing more than a pawn in their deadly game, and they were using him to help destroy what remained of Zoe's faith.

Rising from his position on the floor, he grabbed his cell phone off the nightstand and called the florist. He was very particular about the type of roses he ordered and how he worded the card. He then hopped into the shower.

Zoe was startled when she looked up to see her husband standing in front of the reception desk. "Michael, what are you doing here?" Crazy thoughts flashed through her mind. *Does he know about last night? Did he follow us? Can he tell by looking at me that I've been with another man?* She hoped she didn't appear or sound as flustered as she felt.

Michael smiled down at her. "Well, I was hoping to receive a better welcome than that. I need you to sign this contract so we can get the house on the market." He waved a large envelope containing the contract as if to prove the legitimacy of his visit. "I thought that maybe we could have lunch together and discuss it."

"I thought you were coming by…tonight at…seven?" At that moment she was suddenly distracted by a man walking through the double glass doors carrying a bouquet of two-dozen long stem pink roses in a beautiful vase.

Ignoring Michael, the man approached the desk. "Excuse me; I have a delivery here for Zoe Davis."

"Ugh…um…I'm Zoe Davis." Her hands shook as she signed for the delivery.

Michael stared at her in bewilderment. "Who's sending my wife roses?" His face was crimson red.

"I…don't know." Zoe busied herself with the roses hoping that Michael could not read the lie written on her face.

LaDonna sat beside her; amused and thoroughly enjoying the drama being played out in front of her. "Girl, why don't you let me answer the phones for you while you take a break for a minute and talk to your visitor?"

"I'm not just a visitor. I'm her husband!" Michael glared at LaDonna.

"Why don't you open the card?" He pressed as he turned his attention back to Zoe. "I'd like to know who sent them."

Zoe, looking like a deer caught in the headlights, motioned for LaDonna to take her seat by the phones. "I'll be right back. I'm gonna take a quick break."

"Umm-hmm…" LaDonna shook her head in agreement.

Desiring to keep their conversation private and fearful of what LaDonna might say, given the opportunity, Zoe led Michael out of the law office and into the hallway.

"Zoe, what's going on? Are you seeing someone? Who would be sending you your favorite pink roses? I thought those were special between you and me?" Michael was unable to quell the fear and anxiety rising within him.

"I don't know, Michael. Probably Daddy sent them to me. But you weren't supposed to be here today. You were supposed to come tonight."

"Yea, God forbid I come to your workplace and find out that someone is sending my wife roses. I miss you, Zoe. I wanted to have lunch with my wife."

"I told you I needed some time to be alone."

"Time for what? Zoe, get the card and open it. I need to know who those flowers came from." Michael was insistent. Deep down inside he knew that Amos hadn't sent the flowers.

"No! It's not a big deal. I don't know of anyone other than you or my dad who'd send them. And since you didn't, they must have come from him." It didn't bother her at all to lie to her husband.

"Can we go talk over lunch?" Michael nervously ran his hands through his dark brown curls. "I need to spend some time with you, baby. I miss you so much." He reached out to grab her hand, but she backed away.

She loathed the desperation she heard in his voice and saw in his eyes. "Michael, this is not the time or the place for that. Can't you just come over tonight like we planned?" Her body language spoke volumes.

"Fine, but I'd like to see Amos before I leave."

This time, it was Zoe's face that turned beet red. "Why do you need to speak with Daddy?"

"It's personal!"

"Well, he's not in the office. He's out of town on business until Thursday." It was the truth.

"Okay, Zoe." Michael felt heartsick. "I'll be by tonight at seven." His voice softened. "Can I bring dinner over? Chinese?"

"Sure. That's fine. I'll see you then." He could hear the detachment in her voice as she turned abruptly to go back into the office. He was left standing alone in the hallway following her with his eyes, feeling helpless and defeated.

LaDonna's eyes rolled as Zoe came around the desk. "That was your husband? Honey, if that man were my husband, I'd be keepin' him warm and happy."

"Oh my gosh, I thought I was going to faint when that guy brought in those roses. Of all things, Zach would have to send pink long-stemmed roses. Michael is the only one who knows they are my favorite. How in the world could he have known?" Zoe didn't have to look at the card to know that Zachary had sent the beautiful flowers.

"Good guess? All I know is that he's hot after you. It must have been some heavy talking. Umm-hmm…some heavy talkin'!"

Zoe peeked over the counter to make sure Michael had disappeared into the elevator before opening the card.

Zoe,

Last night was incredible. I loved every minute of it. I want to see you again soon.

Zach

"Well, what's it say?" LaDonna peered eagerly up at Zoe as she placed the card back into its envelope.

Zoe smiled, unable to hide the excitement she felt. "I am not sharing this card with you on the grounds it might incriminate me."

LaDonna gave her a knowing look. "Girl, you are in deep trouble. Looks like you got two men ready to fight for you. And, one is your husband. That's shotgun stuff. What are you gonna do?"

"For now, cover my tracks." She picked up her cell phone to call her father. She wanted to warn Amos that Michael might call inquiring about the roses. She needed to tell him what to say, just in case.

Michael, hurt and confused, sat in his car in the parking garage of Zoe's office building. *What just happened? Could Zoe be seeing someone else? Who? Had she already met someone in her office? This quick? Could she have been seeing someone before Emma died?* The questions bombarded his mind in rapid succession like shots fired from a gun, strategically aimed at destroying his peace.

By Zoe's flustered reaction, he was sure Amos hadn't sent her the roses. And to add to his suspicion, she'd refused to open the card in front of him. He had a sinking feeling in the pit of his stomach.

"Okay, Father God. I'm trying to stay positive, but it's not looking good down here. Can't You give me a glimmer of hope? I sure could use it. What do I do?"

Frustrated, he pounded the steering wheel with his fist.

Michael called Brad Parker as he maneuvered his car onto the freeway. He was thankful when Brad answered after the second ring.

"Hey, Michael, how ya doin'?"

"Hey, Brad. Are you doing anything for lunch today? I could sure use someone to talk to."

"Just tell me where you want to meet, and I'll be there." Brad could hear the desperation in his friend's voice.

They discussed the time and place to meet before hanging up. Brad proceeded to pray for God's wisdom as he made his way to the restaurant.

Though it took everything within him, Zach refrained from calling Zoe before he boarded his private plane bound for New York. Heeding the advice of his spirit guides, he would take it nice and slow with her. In the meantime, he had other matters that required his immediate attention and concentration.

Brad and Michael sat opposite each other in a booth at their favorite Mexican restaurant. Brad thought back on happier times they'd shared in the restaurant, together with their wives, before his friend's life had been ripped apart by tragedy. Michael and Zoe had announced her pregnancy with Emma to Kira and him in this very booth. He was overwhelmed with sadness for Michael. *Who would have ever dreamed their life would take such a tragic turn?*

"Brad, I know that it sounds crazy, but I think she's seeing someone else. Or at least someone is interested in her. I think it's over. She's never coming back. You should have seen her. It's like she's an entirely different person. She had on this low cut blouse, and her skirt was so tight you could see every curve of her body. I've never seen her dress like that. And she was so distant with me like she couldn't stand the fact that I was there. I mean... she wouldn't even let me touch her. I don't know what to do."

Brad listened with compassion as Michael shared his heart. It was apparent that his friend was visibly shaken and in need of encouragement. He wasn't even touching his food and looking at his shrinking frame; Brad knew he needed the nourishment.

"Someone sent her roses today. You should've seen her face when they were delivered. She looked like someone who got caught with the hand in the cookie jar. I'm the only person who ever sends her pink roses. She shared with me when we first met that they were special to her. Zoe had a picture of her mom holding a bouquet of pink roses that Amos had given to her at the hospital when Zoe was born. Somehow, they made her feel close to her mom. Who could have known that? God, I'm so frustrated. I'm angry. Why is God allowing this to happen to me? What have I done? I've served Him all of my life."

"Michael, I wish I had all the answers. I know God's plan for our life is always perfect, even when it doesn't appear to be just or fair. I know He is working out His plan for you and Zoe. Sometimes we have to go through the storm before we can see the rainbow. Like Joseph in the Bible, you might have to go to the pit before you get to dwell in the palace. God's promise to you is that He knows the plans He has for you. You have to have faith that His plan is for your ultimate good. You only see a part of what's going on, but God sees the big picture from start to finish. And though it may take all that is in you right now, you're going to have to trust Him."

"You make it sound so easy. Man, I'm trying to walk by faith, but what would you do if you were in my shoes? I've lost my child, and that's a pain that is beyond belief. I think about her constantly. I know Zoe's hurting over losing Emma, but I have to look at that pool every day. Every day I'm reminded that I'm responsible for Emma's death!"

Michael fought back the tears. "I'm losing my wife who seems to have turned away from her faith. I'm putting our house up for sale, and I don't have a clue where I'll live when or if it sells. I can barely pay the bills, and I no longer have Zoe's income to help out with the house payment for a house that she just had to have. I can't stand one more lonely night of sleeping by myself in that huge empty house. I don't know how much more pit I can take." He used his napkin to wipe away the tears that slid down his cheeks. "I'm sorry, man. I know I probably sound like a whiner."

"Bro, I know I haven't walked in your shoes, and I don't mean to sound glib, but Jesus has. He's suffered loss. Everyone He loved rejected Him. His own Father turned away from Him as He hung on the cross. His disciples scattered when He was arrested in the garden. Peter even denied knowing Him. The Father understands. He lost His Son. He watched as the very ones He sent His Son to save, mocked and tortured Him."

"I know all that up here." Michael pointed to his forehead before placing his hand on his heart. "But here, it doesn't help the hurt I'm feeling. I read the word every day. I pray. But I just don't feel like I have enough faith to walk this out. I can't see Zoe ever coming back to me, and now I think she could be seeing someone else. I don't have the strength to fight anymore. I feel hopeless."

"Michael, as long as you have Christ, there is hope. And hope, the word tells us, is an anchor for our soul. It keeps us secure in Him. I know that Christ dwells in you, so no matter how hopeless you may feel, you have the hope of Christ. I can't promise you that things are going to turn out the way you want them too. I don't have a word from God on that, although I wish I did. But I can tell you that no matter what happens between you and Zoe, God is faithful. He'll see you through. He'll be with you every step of the way if you'll continue to trust Him."

"I know the Lord has people praying for you. Kira and I have been. I'm sure Pastor and Marcie are, as well as your parents. And, you know I'm here for you anytime you need to talk. Trust in the Lord with all of your heart, Michael. That scripture has powerful potential if you'll hang onto it."

Brad could see that his words were encouraging Michael. "Remember Pastor's message this past Sunday on speaking in faith. You need to speak what God says about Zoe and not what you see in the natural. Satan's more than happy to show you the negative side of her. For instance, Jesus said in John 10:28 that no one can snatch his sheep from His hand. So thank God that the enemy cannot have her because she belongs to the Good Shepherd. You are in a battle, and though you may be weak and tired, you are going to have to fight. But remember, you never fight alone because the Greater One lives in you and fights for you."

"Thanks, Brad. I know I can always count on you. Please keep Zoe in your prayers too. I think she's so angry at God that she's lost her way."

"She may feel lost, my friend, but God knows exactly where she is, and He knows how to keep her. Of course, I'll be praying for her."

Brad placed his hands on Michael's shoulders and prayed for him in the parking lot before they parted ways. He made Michael promise that he'd call, no matter the time of day or night if he needed someone to talk to.

He wished he could shake some sense into Zoe. It angered him as he thought about the pain she was putting his best friend through. *I always had my doubts about her faith. I wonder if she was ever even saved? Poor Michael, he deserves better than her.*

The Holy Spirit was quick to speak to his spirit. *Judge not unless you want others to judge you. I love Zoe just as much as I love Michael. She is my beloved, and she's desperately hurting. She's filling up her life with whatever she thinks will help mask the pain. She lost her child. I know what that feels like. My heart breaks for her and yours should too.*

Convicted by the words of the Holy Spirit, he bowed his head and asked for forgiveness for being so quick to judge. He prayed that God would give him a heart of compassion for Zoe and for the healing of her wounded soul.

"Michael, as long as you have Christ,

there is hope.

And hope, the word tells us,

is an anchor for our soul.

It keeps us secure in Him."

11

These things I have spoken to you, that in Me you may have peace.
In the world you will have tribulation; but be of good cheer,
I have overcome the world."

—*John 16:33*

Zoe felt emotionally drained by the time she opened her apartment door. Tired from a lack of sleep the previous night and mentally exhausted from training for her new job, as well as her encounter with Michael, she poured herself a glass a wine as she kicked off her heels. *What I need is a good hot bubble bath. But unfortunately, Michael will be over in an hour, so there's no time for that.* The thought of Michael showing up unannounced at her office infuriated her. *How dare he demand me to open that card in front of him. He needs to get on with his life and let me pick up the pieces of mine in peace.*

Her thoughts turned to Zach as she grabbed her iPad. She checked Facebook to see if he had sent a message or wrote on her wall. She'd been so busy training with LaDonna at work that she hadn't had time to check her phone, though she'd listened intently for a call or text to come through. She saw no new messages on Facebook. *Why hasn't he contacted me?* She found herself becoming anxious though she'd already determined not to see him again. Her resolve was waning as time ticked by.

Calm down, Zoe. The boy sent you roses. She'd left the roses at the office hoping Michael wouldn't bring them up again.

Suddenly her thoughts shifted as the dream she'd had earlier that morning came to her remembrance. She meditated on it as she sat on the couch sipping her Chardonnay. *Why was I at Grandma Abby's house in the dream? And why was the house falling into a sinkhole? That couldn't be good…*

A knock at the door brought her back to reality. Glancing at her watch, she knew it was Michael.

Ramiah looked on as Zoe sat on the couch, completely unaware of the demonic presence surrounding her. The enemy's attack was escalating as strongholds were fortified against his charge's life. A proverbial Pandora's box was opened. Anger, Anxiety, Lust, and a host of demons hung around waiting for opportunities to pounce on their unsuspecting prey.

He wanted desperately to slice these scoundrels to pieces, sending them trembling and shrieking in fear as he threw them into the pit. However, he was still held back by her lack of prayer and refusal to call on the Father for deliverance. His beloved charge was ignorant of the enemy's devices. She couldn't feel the invisible chains of bitterness and unforgiveness wrapped around her soul, nor could she see the incredibly intricate web of deceit he was spinning around her. She'd swallowed his lies hook, line, and sinker. Her feet were no longer equipped with the Gospel of peace but bound by shackles of rebellion. Her eyes were blinded to God's infinite love, and her ears could no longer distinguish her Shepherd's voice apart from other voices that clamored for her attention. Worst of all, she couldn't see that His arms were wide open, ready to receive her the moment she turned her life back over to Him.

It was difficult for him to witness the enemy brutalizing her. But he stood stalwart in the corner of the room praying to the Almighty even as demons mocked him. The Almighty had a plan. After all, it is written in the Scriptures that no one can snatch His beloved from His hands.

Yes, let the enemy mock him. He would wait patiently for the Almighty to turn it all around and set the captive free. The Great and Glorious One would have His vengeance on His enemy.

Michael stood at the door with a bag of Moo Goo Gai Pan and fried rice in one hand, a bottle of soda in the other, and the sales contract tucked under his arm. The smell of Chinese food filled the hallway as he waited for Zoe to come to the door. He felt so nervous he didn't think he'd be able to eat a thing. The scale showed a thirteen-pound weight loss since Emma had died. A telltale sign that this trial was taking a toll on his physical body as much as it was his soul.

"Hey, come on in." Zoe stood aside as she opened the door for him to enter, her lack of enthusiasm apparent in her voice. "That smells good, and I'm actually hungry for a change."

"Great. I got your favorite." Michael tried to sound upbeat as he pulled cartons of food out of the bag and onto the kitchen counter. "Where are your plates?"

Zoe pulled plates, knives, and forks out of cabinets and drawers. "Can I get you a glass of wine?" She regretted the question as soon as it escaped her mouth. She knew Michael had never drunk a drop of alcohol in his life.

"Seriously?" He looked stunned as he twisted the lid off of the soda bottle. *Maybe the other guy drinks.* The thought made him angry. "No, I brought a bottle of diet coke. It used to be your drink of choice."

"Sorry, I know you don't drink. But I don't see anything wrong with a glass of wine now and then. Jesus drank wine, ya know. Besides, since Emma's been gone it helps me to relax and sleep better at night."

"I'm sorry, baby. I know how hard it is. I hurt too. It's hard being in that big house all alone. I have to walk by the patio doors and see that pool every day. That's why I want to put the house up for sale."

"Well, it's fine with me, Michael. I could never, ever go back there again! Too many memories." Zoe choked back tears.

"Honey, you know we could start over somewhere else. As soon as I sell the house, we could look for something together." Disappointment filled him as he saw the empty look in her eyes.

"Zoe, do you ever see us getting back together again? I need to know. I'm trying to stand and believe God to restore our marriage, but I need you to give me some hope."

"Michael, I don't know. I'm just trying to take life one day at a time."

She took her drink and plate into the living room and sat down on the couch. Michael followed. It had always been their habit to eat in the living room in front of the television.

Michael sat down beside Zoe. "Can I pray for our food?"

Embarrassed that she'd already begun eating, she dropped her fork. They'd always prayed together before meals. "Sure."

Michael grabbed both of her hands before she could protest and began to pray. "Father God, I pray for Your presence here with us tonight as we discuss plans for our future. I pray for Your peace and that You would bless this food to the nourishment of our bodies. In Jesus's name. Amen!"

Before letting go of her hands, Michael looked into her eyes and pleaded. "I just don't want you to give up on the idea of us. We have so much history together and I know God wants to give us a future together."

With the excuse of reaching for her drink, Zoe pulled away and quickly changed the subject. "So, let me see the contract. I hope the house sells fast."

He took the contract out of the envelope and pulled a pen out of his shirt pocket. "Amanda, our realtor, marked the places where you need to sign or initial." He set the contract beside her phone on the coffee table.

He inquired about her job and tried to make small talk as she signed the papers. Her phone began to ring. Michael strained to see who was calling. His heart sank as he saw the name, Zach. Before she'd met him, she'd been crazy over a guy named Zach in high school until she'd found him cheating on her. *Surely it's not the same guy.*

She picked up her phone and silenced the ringer before turning it over so he could no longer see the screen. The phone buzzed indicating that the caller had left a message.

"Zach?" Michael's face flushed in anger as he bombarded Zoe with accusations. "Is he the one who sent you the roses? Zach, the guy you dated in high school before we met? Good grief Zoe, we've only been separated a few days. Is that why you want to live alone? Were you seeing him before Emma drowned?" By the look on her face, he knew his last question had hit a nerve.

"Really, Michael? How could you even suggest that?"

"I'm sorry, Zoe. But just the thought of you with another guy drives me crazy." Michael rubbed the back of his neck in frustration.

"Michael, let's just eat and be civil. I don't want to discuss my private life with you tonight."

"Your private life? You're my wife! Your private life has everything to do with me. It affects me. Don't you get that, Zoe?" Enraged, he stood and began to pace in front of the coffee table.

"Michael, don't force me to do anything that I'm not ready to do."

"Yea, what's that supposed to mean?" He turned to face her.

"I mean if you keep throwing in my face that I'm your wife and bugging me about what I'm doing or who's sending me roses…I might have to…file for…" She left the sentence unfinished, satisfied with the effect it was having. She knew by the clench of his jaw that her words had hit their mark.

"What, file for divorce? Zoe, what in the world has happened to you? Where is the godly woman I fell in love with? How could you have changed so drastically in such a short period of time?" He tried to calm down and lower his voice.

"Life happened, Michael. I lost my baby!" Zoe's voice grew louder and louder as she stood and wagged an accusatory finger at Michael. "Due to your stupid negligence, I might add. I don't see life the way I used to. I don't see God the way I used to. I'm certainly not hanging on to some pie-in-the-sky outlook like you. You can believe everything's just gonna turn out hunky-dory if you want to, but I don't think I have faith to believe that way anymore. If God were real and cared anything about me, He'd have saved my baby. That's the way I see life. That's what's changed me. Maybe Daddy was right all along. Christians are simply weak people who need a crutch to lean on." She knew her words had wounded him deeply, but she didn't care.

"Zoe, you can't mean that." Stunned, Michael shook his head in disbelief.

She handed him the papers. "I think you just need to go before this conversation gets out of hand."

"Zoe,—he grabbed the papers and shook his head—I don't understand what has gotten into you. Enjoy your dinner!" He slammed the door as he left her apartment.

Zoe reflected on the words that had almost come out of her mouth. *Would I consider divorcing Michael? I was in love with him such a short time ago. I always believed in 'till death do us part.' Why don't I feel anything for him now? He's such an awesome man of God. I guess life changes.* She turned on the television to silence the questions swimming around in her head and then picked up her phone to listen to Zach's message. At least he had called.

Michael drove around for about an hour before pulling into his parents' driveway. The thought of going home to an empty house was more than he could bear. He felt alone.

"Michael!" Shara looked surprised when she opened the door. Her smile quickly faded into a worried expression. "Honey, come in. You look terrible."

Falling into her arms, he broke down in the comfort of her embrace as he'd done when he was a small boy. He wept, long and hard.

After he'd gained his composure, she pointed towards the couch. "Sit down, honey. Can I get you anything? Are you hungry? Your father will be home shortly. He had a hospital visit to make."

"No, I just couldn't go home tonight." He looked miserable as he sat on the sofa. "Mom, I think Zoe's seeing someone."

He told Shara about the roses and how Zoe refused to disclose who'd sent them. He relayed their conversation over dinner and how it hadn't ended well.

"Mom, I feel like God has abandoned me or like He's punishing me. Maybe I've done something awful that I'm not aware of, and I'm being punished."

"God doesn't work that way. Michael, it's the goodness of God that leads us to repentance. He's not punishing you. You're His son. Would your dad kill your child and separate you from your wife because you did something wrong?" She continued without giving him an opportunity to respond. "No! Satan hates you. He's always seeking opportunities to steal, kill, and destroy. He's gotten a foothold in Zoe's life and is causing destruction. Unfortunately, you are in the path of that destruction."

"What about Emma? Zoe didn't have anything to do with her death. I caused it."

"Emma's death was an unfortunate, horrible accident. We live in a sin-filled world. Sometimes doors are opened just enough for the enemy to get his foot in the door and cause destruction in our lives and the lives of those we love. Remember, he seeks those whom he can devour. There are things we don't know and may never know this side of heaven. But I know God loves you, and He wouldn't take Emma away to punish you."

"What about David? He took his son away when he committed adultery with Bathsheba and then murdered her husband."

"Honey, I don't have all the answers. I wish I did. However, that was under the Old Covenant. Your sins were paid for by the death of Jesus on the cross. I don't think God took Emma because you sinned. But her death could have resulted from negligence in your or Zoe's spiritual walk. God doesn't call us to walk in obedience to the word for His benefit. The Bible tells us the wages of sin is death. It's for our benefit so that we might have life and have it in abundance. When we know the word and choose not to obey it, we are opening doors to Satan, giving him leeway, so to speak, in our life. I personally believe that one of the reasons God calls us to be a fasting and praying people, in constant communion with Him is so that He can reveal those open doors or opportunities we give to the enemy."

She sat beside him on the couch. "I recently heard a teaching about Hebrews 12:1. It says, 'Let us lay aside every weight, and the sin, which so easily ensnares us.' To ensnare means to skillfully surround. When we habitually and knowingly sin, the enemy has authority to skillfully surround us. It's our sin that leads us into his traps. First John 5:18 tells us that if we keep ourselves from sin, the enemy can't touch us."

"Mom, don't you think that's a little legalistic? I mean if my sins are paid for, why do I have to worry about opening doors to the enemy? When I pray for forgiveness, doesn't God forgive me and shut those doors?"

"Of course, He forgives you. However, you can be a forgiven child of God and still be walking in bondage to the enemy in areas of your life. Fear, doubt, and unbelief, anger, being unwilling to forgive…any of these can be opportunities for the enemy to get a foothold in your life, even though in other areas you may be walking in obedience. Our words, the Bible says, can bring forth life or death. By speaking negatively, or what the world has to say instead of what the word of God has to say, we can give Satan occasion to bring death into our life. Spiritual as well as physical death."

Michael pondered his mother's words. "The word says God has given us authority over the enemy. Maybe, when we fail to speak and act in faith, we forfeit that authority. I know I've always allowed fear to minister to me. I don't know why I give into it so easily. Even when I try to fight against it, sometimes it's too hard to be constantly guarding my mind and my mouth, and I give up and let fear and worry overtake me." A thought suddenly came to him. "You know, Mom, I was always so afraid of losing Zoe. I knew Amos didn't think I was good enough for her. She was used to living at a higher financial status than I could provide for her, and she's so beautiful. I felt like I lucked out when she agreed to marry me, but I always feared the day she'd realize she'd made a huge mistake in doing so."

Shara was overwhelmed with love and compassion for her son. He was a grown man yet, here before her, seemed like a small boy again searching for answers to life's questions. "Well, you could probably get better answers from your father. He certainly knows more than I do. Why don't you let me fix you something to eat?"

"Always the mom!" Michael offered a faint smile. "There's nothing in life a good home-cooked meal can't fix. Especially when it's your home cooking."

Shara rose from the sofa. "Well, it always helped when you were a little boy. Back then, it was a kiss and ice cream that did the trick. I have some Blue Bell if it will help."

"Yeah, I'll have some. A man still has to eat. I could use that kiss too." He winked at his mom.

She bent over and kissed his forehead and ruffled his hair. "One large bowl of cookies and cream coming up."

Zoe was startled awake by the ring of her phone. Though still groggy, she was pleasantly surprised to see Zach's name on the screen.

"Hey."

"Hey, beautiful. Did I wake you?"

"Well, I was watching TV, and I guess I fell asleep on the couch."

"Hmm…well, you didn't get much sleep last night did you?" He, of course, knew the answer.

"Zach, I have to apologize for last night. I've never done that before. I think I just had too much to drink. I mean…I don't want you to think I go around sleeping with guys like that. Maybe we shouldn't see each other again. I'm still married."

"Zoe, I don't want you to think I just want to hop in the sack with you. I genuinely care about you, and I know you are going through a difficult time. I should have been the one to stop what happened last night. I'm sorry. I'll behave better next time. I promise. But I have to see you again."

She couldn't help but smile. "Zach, I don't know. I want to see you too, but it just complicates everything."

"Okay, here's my offer, dinner and a movie Saturday? I'll pick you up around five o'clock, and I'll have you home by midnight. Scouts honor! How's that sound?"

"You were never a scout Zachary Thomas. Okay! But we're just going out as friends. Agreed?"

She couldn't see that he'd crossed his fingers before answering. "Agreed. So I'll see you Saturday at five?"

"All right. That sounds like fun."

"Great. Sweet dreams, beautiful lady." Smiling mischievously, he hung up the phone.

Shara's eyes filled with tears as she dished the bowl of ice cream for her son. The events of the past couple of months were too overwhelming to comprehend. She'd lost her only grandchild. She'd adored Emma from the moment she was born. Having never had a daughter of her own, she'd been thrilled to have a granddaughter. Her daughter-in-law, whom she'd loved like a daughter, was not only separated from Michael and the family but also seemed to have lost her faith in Christ. Shara couldn't even fathom the thought of Zoe going out with another man. And her beloved son was hurting beyond words. Her heart broke for him. He had always been such a sensitive young man and had set his life on a course to follow hard after God. It just didn't seem fair or just. A familiar scripture came to mind.

"These things I have spoken to you, that in Me you may have peace. In the world, you will have tribulation, but be of good cheer, I have overcome the world."

Grateful for the encouragement, she bowed her head and whispered a prayer. "Thank You, Father, that You have overcome the world. I know that somehow You will help us walk through this trial and that You will turn what Satan meant for harm into our good. Please help my son, Lord. His heart is broken. He's grieving the loss of his daughter and his wife, and he's looking for answers. Minister to him and give Daniel and me wisdom to know how to help him. Thank You, Father, for Your love and care. In Jesus' name."

12

Blessed be the God and Father of our Lord Jesus Christ,
the Father of mercies and God of all comfort,
who comforts us in all our tribulation,
that we may be able to comfort those who are in any trouble,
with the comfort with which we ourselves are comforted by God.
—2 Corinthians 1:3–4

Beelzebub wrapped up his address to the large gathering of rulers and principalities before him. "Let me remind you, your job is that of a seeker. And what are you to be seeking? You are to seek those who can be easily devoured, just like a hungry lion stalking his prey. You must move with stealth and act with superior hunting skills. If you are given an inch into the life of one of those worthless Christians, be quick to take a mile. Ferret out those who've separated themselves from the rest of their pack. Find ways to get your foot in the door of their lives. Pursue the weak and the vulnerable. Make it your quest to find those who are not praying and employing their angels to fight against you. You must constantly be watching and listening to discover their Achilles' heel. Manipulate their thinking so that they accept the thoughts you speak into their souls. The more you bombard them with evil thoughts, the less likely they are to resist. Most of them don't know how to keep their wretched traps shut. They'll begin to speak out of their mouths the seeds of doubt, unbelief, and the lies you plant within their hearts. They'll give you opportunities to bring destruction upon their lives by their very own words. Give them what they say."

Beelzebub had once been one of the most beautiful creatures in all of creation; however, centuries of rebellion toward the Creator had eroded any vestige of his former glory. He could appear as an angel of light, but he was indeed a hideous being to gaze upon. However, the demons before him praised their counterfeit king, bowing low in obeisance to him. Extremely fearful of his wrath, they would do anything to gain his approval. He transformed himself into a venomous serpent, hissed, and slithered out of their midst.

Ramiah placed the thought into Zoe's mind that she needed a cup of coffee. The order from On High was to get her into the breakroom at precisely ten forty-two in the morning. It was his assignment to make sure she was in the right place at the right time. For centuries, angels were responsible for making sure their charges made their divine appointments and well-timed encounters. It often took several guardians working together to be sure that their charges hooked up, as they liked to call it, for God's purposes. Though humans often believed it to be a coincidence when their paths crossed with someone who helped mold and shape their future; unseen beings were behind these well-planned moments in time.

Zoe was busy answering phones and greeting guests as they arrived for their morning appointments. She loved the hectic pace of her new job, which afforded little opportunity to dwell on her sorrows or contemplate her future.

The only challenge with working the reception desk was that it kept Zoe tied down to her desk. She called LaDonna, who was quickly becoming a friend, to relieve her so that she could go to the restroom and get a cup of coffee.

LaDonna plopped into the receptionist chair. "All right, girl, you'd better be quick 'cuz I got lots of work to do today, and I ain't got time for you to be runnin' to pee every ten minutes."

"Whatever! You just need to sit down here and answer the phones. Don't make me tell my daddy you are being mean to me." Zoe enjoyed bantering with her friend.

"Girl, don't you be pullin' that daddy card with me. You know I ain't afraid of ole' Amos. He don't scare me."

Zoe laughed. LaDonna was good for her soul. Her jovial personality was like a fresh breeze in Zoe's life. "Okay, Miss Priss. I'll be right back. Don't be flirtin' out here with the clients."

"Who me?" LaDonna chuckled before turning her attention to an approaching client.

After a trip to the restroom, Zoe headed to the breakroom. She saw the back of a female standing at the coffee pot and instantly recognized it to be Carol Tatum. She considered turning and walking out before Carol spotted her, but it was too late.

"Hi! Zoe Davis, right? You're Amos Richards's daughter." Carol's smile was warm and friendly. Oddly enough, when Zoe looked into her dark brown eyes, she sensed an overwhelming love and compassion pouring forth from her soul.

"Hi. Yes, I am." Zoe tried not to encourage any conversation with the girl. To be seen talking to or associating with her in the office was political suicide. Everyone knew she was a religious nut, and though they were cordial enough to her, most of the staff looked upon her as if she was a plague that might infect them if they came into contact with her. The girl would often bring her Bible into the breakroom at lunchtime and read it on the sofa while eating her lunch. Carol was known for playing Christian music in her office and had sticky notes with scriptures plastered all over her desk. Though she wasn't outspoken about her faith, her very presence made people feel uncomfortable. Everyone mocked her behind her back while she, unbeknownst to them, lovingly and compassionately prayed for the salvation of their souls. She was the last person with whom Zoe wanted to be seen carrying on a conversation.

"I've seen you around, but I haven't had the chance to introduce myself to you. I know you've been through a very difficult time lately, and I just want you to know that I've been praying for you. If you ever need anyone to talk to, I'm always available."

Zoe wondered if Carol was oblivious to the office gossip surrounding her. *It's her own fault. You can't go around wearing your faith like a banner in the office. It's unprofessional. Of course, it's okay to be a Christian, but she should keep it to herself, for goodness' sake, so she doesn't offend people.*

"Thank you. I appreciate your prayers. But I try very hard to keep my personal life separate from the office." Zoe concentrated on fixing herself a cup of coffee before exiting the break room, leaving Carol staring after her.

Carol watched as Zoe practically ran out of the breakroom. She'd felt empathy for her from the moment she'd heard about the loss of her child. She could relate to what Zoe was going through, having lost her son Jacob five years earlier. He'd drown in the bathtub at one and a half years old when she'd left him alone in order to grab clothes from his bedroom. She'd taken a few minutes to pick up the toys scattered about his room after stepping on one that had been left on the floor. Upon returning to the bathroom, she'd found him face down in the water. It had been a horrifying, life-changing experience from which she hadn't thought she would survive. However, she was grateful that through it all, she and her husband had come to know the Lord. They now had a beautiful three-year-old named Olivia, and though no one knew it yet, a set of twins on the way.

After hearing of Zoe's loss, Carol had been interceding for her and hoped to befriend her. She'd prayed and petitioned God for the opportunity to meet and let the grieving mother know that she was praying for her. She believed in the power of prayer. Prayer was what had gotten her through her season of walking through the valley of the shadow of death. Now, she knew it was her calling to comfort those in need with the same comfort she'd received from Christ.

She was aware that people in the office made fun of her because she didn't hide the fact that she was a Christian. She wasn't purposely trying to offend people with her faith. However, she couldn't separate herself from her faith either. She loved reading the word of God, and since she didn't have anyone to go to lunch with and didn't want to stay in her office all day, she enjoyed spending her lunch hour in the breakroom. The room was quiet at lunchtime, and the corner couch was comfortable.

Though it would be easy to be offended, she knew she was called to be a light to the lost, hurting, and broken. It was apparent that the Spirit of God residing in her made those walking in darkness feel uncomfortable around her. The word of God said that the world would hate her, and she expected nothing less. Like the Apostle Paul, she counted it a blessing that others mocked her because of her deep love and devotion to God. She couldn't judge her coworkers because she'd looked down on Christians too before she'd given her heart to the Lord. She desired to be the one her coworkers would turn to if or when they faced a life-altering crisis—just as her neighbor had been the one she'd turned to when she'd lost her sweet little Jacob.

She silently gave thanks to God as she made her way back to her office. *Oh Father, thank You so much for allowing me to be in the breakroom when Zoe came in today. I pray for future opportunities to show her the love of Christ and to be a friend to her. Thank You that You heal her brokenness. Turn her ashes to beauty and her mourning to joy. In Jesus's name.*

Shelesh gave Ramiah a high five before the two angelic beings parted ways. Since his charge had accepted Christ, warfare had increased, and he stayed on constant guard against her enemy. She'd fallen head-over-heels in love with the Son and desired to live a life of complete surrender to Him, which made her an increased target of the enemy. She was ceaseless in her praying, often lifting up her family and friends, coworkers, and even complete strangers she saw on the television newscast that were going through difficult situations. All of which kept Shelesh busy connecting with other guardians to see that her prayers were answered. Her prayers were a sweet smelling fragrance to the Almighty, and she always had His attention when she whispered her desires to Him.

Like Ramiah, he too had received instructions from the Almighty. Today, he'd made sure Carol's prayers were answered and that she was in the breakroom at just the right time to meet Zoe, the subject of her prayers.

Though she'd assumed the desire to befriend Ramiah's charge was solely her idea, the Almighty had seeded the thought into her spirit as she'd spent precious time in communion with Him.

It was always a joy for the angels to watch their humans giving God glory for what was, in actuality, His divine plan. Shelesh broke out in praise to the Almighty as Carol gave thanks to God.

"Girl, what took you so long? Did you stop to eat breakfast or something?" LaDonna pretended to glance at her watch.

"Oh my gosh, you'll never guess who I ran into in the breakroom."

"Who? The Pope?" LaDonna stood to make way for Zoe to take her seat at the reception desk.

"Almost. Carol Tatum. OMG, she dresses like a nun. No man's ever gonna see any of her skin. No, siree, Bob. She's all buttoned up from her toes to her neck." She knew that it was probably wrong to make fun of Carol, but everyone else did it, and she had a desire to fit in. "She was sweet though. She offered to pray for me."

"She needs to pray that your boyfriend would pick up his dang phone and give you a call. I haven't had anything juicy to talk about since you got those roses on Tuesday morning."

Zoe had been complaining to LaDonna that she hadn't heard from Zach since late Tuesday evening. Even though he'd asked to take her out on Saturday, she'd still felt slighted when he hadn't bothered giving her a call during the rest of the week.

"Thanks for relieving me."

"Yea, yea. I'm sure you'll be callin' me again in ten minutes. Later! Let me know if anything exciting happens." LaDonna waved her hand over her shoulder as she turned, hips swinging heavily from side to side, and walked away.

Grandma Abby prayed as she puttered around the house doing her normal Friday cleaning. She couldn't get Zoe and Michael off her mind. Barbara had confided in her that the young couple had separated. She'd been heartbroken at the loss of her great grandchild, but the thought of Zoe and Michael breaking off their covenant was unthinkable. She couldn't seem to help her granddaughter see the truth. She recalled the phone conversation they'd had earlier in the week.

"Grandma, I needed a break. I just couldn't live in that house anymore."

"Oh, honey, I understand that you're hurting, but you two should have moved out together. For goodness' sakes, let that house go back to the mortgage company if you have to. But your husband needs you right now as much as you need him. My dear girl, it's not God's will for you to separate or get a divorce especially when you have such a wonderful husband as Michael. I understand that you're grieving, and I know it can cause us to do crazy things, but you don't run to the world to see what it has to offer. You run into the arms of Christ. He's the only one who can heal your pain. Trust me; I know what I'm talking about. When I lost your mom, I thought I'd go crazy with grief. There were times I felt like my life wasn't worth living, but I never thought about giving up on God. I found that He was the only one worth hanging onto. Look how He has blessed me."

"Grandma, can we talk about something other than Michael or God. I just need time alone. Okay! Please, drop it!" Zoe had adamantly refused to broach the subject again.

Abby knew that her granddaughter could be stubborn and had agreed, reluctantly, to drop the conversation. Zoe had been more than happy to change the subject and talk about her new job and the friends she was making.

As she reflected on their conversation, Abby was afraid her granddaughter would live to regret the decisions she was making. She knew Zoe wasn't walking in the will of God for her life.

"Oh, Lord, Michael has such a pure heart for You. Zoe is blessed to have a man like that for her husband. Soften her heart. Lord, I think she's completely lost her way. Help her find the path that leads back to You. And please comfort poor, sweet Michael. He must be going through some kind of torment, Lord. He's lost his baby and his wife has left him. Oh, my heart breaks for that dear sweet boy. Give him grace to walk through this. Amen." She wiped the tears from her eyes. "Wake up, Zoe, before it's too late. It'd be a cryin' shame if you lost that boy for good."

Michael pulled up in front of the youth building at church. It was Friday night, and they were having a youth conference with a guest speaker, a popular praise band, and all the pizza you could eat. Donovan had made it clear that he needed to be at the conference if he wanted to remain on the youth staff. Though he'd been shocked by Donovan's lack of sympathy for his situation, he knew he needed to get back into the routine of serving as the assistant youth pastor.

The outpouring of support from the youth had genuinely touched Michael. Many came up to hug him and tell him how much they'd missed him. It blessed him when several of the kids informed him they'd been praying for him.

Michael got lost in worship as the worship leader led them into the presence of God. He was young, probably about nineteen or twenty Michael surmised, but he carried a strong anointing. The lyrics of each song ministered to Michael's battered soul. With arms raised in the air, he worshipped the Lord freely. It felt good to be in the presence of God.

The speaker, a dynamic, charismatic young man from Dallas named John Marc, took the platform after the worship service ended. Michael had heard him once before and knew the message would be excellent.

His message was a word of warning to the youth about doors they open to Satan, the enemy of their souls. He had a huge, bright red, six-foot cardboard heart in the center of the platform on which he'd painted the words *your heart* in white letters. Several cardboard doors surrounded the heart, each having something painted on it: lack of prayer, sin, rebellion, lack of knowledge, and unforgiveness. As he ministered, he went through different scenarios where the enemy would come to a door and find it opened a crack, if not wide open, because of sin that hadn't been dealt with, a lack of spending time in prayer or a lack of knowledge of the word, therefore giving the enemy entrance into a person's heart. He then went through other scenarios where the devil would find the door shut tight and locked because the person was not giving the enemy an opportunity to get a foothold into the door of their heart. Donovan helped him in the demonstration and played the devil. He brought the house down laughing with his animated imitation of the devil pulling on the door, straining with all of his might to get in. Most of the crowd went up for prayer during the altar call.

Afterward, Michael went over to talk with John Marc while the youth dived into the free pizza and soda. He gave him the short version of what he'd been walking through. He told him that the message had been a confirmation of the conversation he'd had with his mom earlier in the week.

John Marc ministered a word from the Lord to him. "Michael, I believe God wants you to know that He has wept with you in your hour of darkness. He's placed your tears in a bottle and holds them close to His heart. He's never left you for even a moment. He wants to remind you that He is for you and never against you. He also says that He will turn your mourning into dancing. Weeping may endure for a night, but be of good cheer because there will come a day when joy will return. God says you will be so surprised at how He can turn what Satan meant for harm into a precious pearl for you." He promised to keep Michael in his prayers.

He left the event feeling uplifted and encouraged. God had spoken to him. He knew that God saw him and had not abandoned him. God had heard his cries and understood the deep sorrow of his heart. The God, who'd created the universe and held the world in His hands, had wept with him. Though Michael knew that God hadn't specifically spoken to him about Zoe, it gave him hope that Zoe would return to him again to spend the rest of their lives together.

He texted his mom before leaving the parking lot to tell her about the word he'd received.

Zoe squeezed into the booth at the popular Houston nightclub surrounded by several men and women from her office. LaDonna, Tonya and several others had convinced her to join them for Friday night happy hour. They had ordered a round of drinks before several got up to dance.

Trace, a young intern from her office, pulled her out of her seat. "Come on, Zoe, let's dance."

"Oh my gosh, I haven't danced in a long time. I'll make a fool of myself." Zoe tried pulling away from him. At that moment the waitress came to the table with a tray of shot glasses filled with tequila.

"Here, drink this, and you'll be fine." He held up a shot of tequila, which she took and willingly chugged it down.

She felt liquid warmth flowing down her body as the alcohol hit her bloodstream. Amused, Trace watched as she took two more shots, giggled, and then grabbed his hand. "Okay, let's go."

"Wow, what was in that drink?" They made their way to the crowded dance floor. "I usually don't drink anything stronger than a glass of wine."

Smiling, Trace leaned into her ear and spoke loud enough so she could hear over the blaring music. "It was a shot of tequila. Haven't you ever drank shots before?"

She smiled and shook her head to indicate that she hadn't.

"It warms the soul." The DJ began to play a slow song, and he grabbed her hand and drew her to himself. They danced to several songs before rejoining the group back at the table.

The dancing, loud music and the warm liquor eased the constant ache in Zoe's soul. She was content, even if it was only temporary, to forget her pain and live in the moment.

After two more rounds of drinks and several trips to the dance floor, most of the group decided to head home or paired off into couples to continue the night together elsewhere. Zoe decided to head home though Trace tried desperately to get her to stay out with him.

"I can't, Trace. I'm sorry. I need to be going home."

She smiled at him. He was boyishly good-looking and had a promising legal career ahead of him. She was well aware that a guy like him was after one thing and one thing only. Though tempted, she wanted to be rested for her date with Zach the next day. *Besides, I don't know if I could trust myself to be alone with him.*

He held her hand as he walked her to her car. "I've had a great time tonight. I'd like to take you out sometime."

Zoe leaned against her car door. "Ummm…I'm not so sure that I'd feel comfortable dating someone I work with. But thanks for dancing with me tonight. I had fun!"

She left the club feeling woozy and a little queasy in her stomach. The room was spinning by the time she got up to her apartment. She could barely remember the drive home. After undressing and slipping into her nightclothes, she threw up in the toilet. *I'll never drink again.*

"*The wages of sin is death.*" The Lord whispered the scripture to her as she fell into a fitful sleep.

13

Delight yourself also in the Lord,
and He shall give you the desires of your heart.
—Psalm 37:4

It was ten in the morning before Zoe woke up. Her head hurt, her eyes were puffy and dark, and her stomach still felt a little uneasy.

She frowned as she gazed at her reflection in the bathroom mirror. "Great! Girl, you look a hot mess."

She showered and dressed before heading to the kitchen to make herself a cup of coffee. Her phone rang as she was pulling out a box of cereal from the pantry.

"How's my girl?" Her father's voice boomed into her ear.

"Hey, Daddy." Expecting the caller to be Zach, she was unable to disguise her disappointment

"Well, thanks for the warm reception. Were you expecting someone else?"

"Sorry! I just woke up. I went out with some friends from the office for drinks last night. I learned something new."

"Yea, and what's that?"

"Tequila is not my friend."

He laughed heartily. "Oh, those hangovers are no fun. You probably need to stick to your wine my girl. How about meeting your old man for lunch?"

"I can't today. I have plans tonight, and I don't want to be worn out, so I'm gonna hang out here and take it easy."

"Oh…anyone I know?"

"Maybe. But I'm not gonna tell you. I know it'll drive you crazy if I keep you guessing. And that's what you get for laughing at me for having a hangover." Her phone beeped indicating another call trying to ring through. "Oh, I gotta go, Daddy. I've got another call. I'll call you later." She connected to the incoming call.

"Hello." A tingle traveled up and down her spine.

"Hey, beautiful." She couldn't help but smile at the sound of Zach's deep voice.

"Hey. I thought maybe you forgot about me."

"Never. How could I forget someone as beautiful and sexy as you? Oh, sorry. I remember we're just friends. Probably inappropriate to say I think you're sexy."

Zoe giggled.

"I've been looking forward to today. How early can you be ready to go?" Zach was pleased that he'd apparently been on her mind during the week. *This is going to be a piece of cake.*

"Today? I thought we were going out tonight?" Her smile broadened.

"Well, if you don't mind, I'd like to pick you up around one. I was thinking we could drive to Kemah and eat on the boardwalk. How's that sound? I thought it was a little more creative than just dinner and a movie."

She was ecstatic. She had worried needlessly during the week that she hadn't crossed his mind, but she could tell he was as eager to see her, as she was to see him. "Awesome. I'll be ready at one."

Zach was once again thankful for the wise counsel of his spirit guides. He'd wanted to call Zoe every day during the past week to make sure he kept her interested, but they'd insisted he wait. "You have to play the game." They had wisely warned him. *Ah, the game.* He loved the game! It brought the added excitement to his life that he so craved.

They had also reminded him of how good she'd felt in his arms, the intoxicating smell of her perfume and the sweet sound of her voice. It wasn't that he needed Zoe. He just wanted her, and they made sure to feed his insatiable hunger.

Before hopping into the shower and getting dressed for the day, he lit a candle, put on his music, and then sat in his usual position on the bedroom floor, eyes closed and chanted himself into a deep trance. He didn't dare start out his day without first spending time in meditation.

Zoe rummaged through her overstuffed closet looking for the perfect outfit to wear. She was standing half-dressed before her full-length mirror when her phone rang again. She knew by the ring-tone that it was Michael.

"Crap!" Frustrated, she grabbed her phone from off the bed.

"Hey, Michael." She hoped that he could discern the agitation and impatience she felt.

"Hi, baby. Am I interrupting anything?" Michael was dismayed at Zoe's lack of enthusiasm.

"Not really. What's up?" As she listened to Michael, she stood before her mirror holding a sleeveless multicolored maxi dress up against her body and quickly decided it wouldn't do for her date with Zach.

"I wanted you to know they are showing the house today. Our realtor said this is the second time this couple has looked at it and thinks they might make an offer." The information was only an excuse to call.

"Oh, that sounds great. I hope it sells. Michael, have you given thought to what we'll do when it sells? I mean, we are going to split the proceeds, right?"

Her question was met with silence.

She grabbed another sundress from the closet as she continued the conversation. "I just think we need to talk about it so that it's not a problem at closing. I think fifty-fifty would be fair. Don't you?"

"You know as well as I do that I'm believing God to restore our marriage. You can have all of the money as far as I'm concerned."

"No, that wouldn't be fair. Michael, how can God restore what has been stolen away? How can you still believe that He will do that? Our baby is gone forever. I'm trying to forget the past and move on. It's just easier for me."

"Easier for you? That's great! What about what's easy for me? I have all the confidence in the world that I will see Emma again one day. Baby, we were a family before we ever had Emma. She was conceived out of our love for each other. I think the enemy has blinded you to that fact. God can certainly restore what the enemy has stolen from us. I also struggle every day with grief, but I miss you so bad it's killing me. I don't want to move on. I want us back."

Zoe rolled her eyes. She wanted the conversation to end so that she could get on with her day. "Well, Michael, honestly that's probably not going to happen. And the more time goes by, the more I just don't see myself getting back together with you. I'm enjoying my freedom. It's helping me to get through the pain of losing Emma."

"Zoe, have you spent any time praying about your decision because I don't think it's God's will for us to be apart?"

"No. I'm not praying about anything. I'm living my life, and I just want to forget the past and move on."

Michael was shocked when he realized she'd hung up the phone. He paced angrily back and forth across his living room. He could feel discouragement threatening to take hold of his soul and render him hopeless and defeated.

"Okay, Lord. What do I do now?" Michael sat down on the couch in his living room to quiet his mind so that he could hear from the Lord. A short scripture he'd once memorized as a young boy in Vacation Bible School came to his mind.

"Trust in the Lord, and do good."

He got out his Bible and opened to the scripture, reading the entire Psalm out loud before focusing on several verses: Trust in the Lord, and do good; dwell in the land, and feed on His faithfulness. Delight yourself also in the Lord, and He shall give you the desires of your heart. Commit your way to the Lord, trust also in Him, and He shall bring it to pass. He shall bring forth your righteousness as the light, and your justice as the noonday. Rest in the Lord, and wait patiently for Him.

He read the passage several times while meditating on its meaning. *I need to feed on the Lord's faithfulness while I wait patiently for Him to give me the desires of my heart. How can I feed on the Lord's faithfulness?* He got out a pen and paper and began to make some notes.

1. I will purposely praise God as I go through this trial. I will find something to praise Him for every day.
2. I will feed on His word. Besides my normal Bible reading, I will memorize a scripture a week that will encourage me. I'll start with this one.
3. I will speak His word in faith over the restoration of my marriage and my wife. I will not be moved by what I see or hear.

4. I will commit Zoe to Him and trust Him to work in her life as I pray for her every day.

5. I refuse to be anxious. I will trust in God's timing.

Glancing over his list, he felt satisfied. He dated and folded the paper and placed it in his Bible. He then took out another piece of paper and wrote down Psalm 37:3–7. He decided he'd carry it with him throughout the week and glance at it every chance he got until he'd memorized it. And then, because he knew God to be faithful, loving and true to His word, he prayed.

"Lord, I take authority over my emotions in the name of Jesus. I plead the blood of Christ over my mind, will, and emotions, and I command the spirit of discouragement to leave me now in Jesus's name. I put my hope and my trust in You, knowing that You are faithful, even when I am faithless. I may not have great faith, but I know I have mustard seed faith. I ask You to help me grow in faith to see my marriage restored. Today, I choose to think of You and Your loving kindness and goodness instead of dwelling on this situation. I forgive Zoe for hurting me, and I lift her up to You, Lord, and ask You to deal with her heart in Your mercy and love. In Jesus's name. Amen!"

Deuel rebuked the devil of discouragement just as soon as he heard his charge boldly going before the throne of grace. "The Lord rebuke you, Satan." His authority was heightened as Michael used the Name that was above every other name and pleaded the blood of Christ. Deuel smiled as he watched the trembling demon bow to the name of Jesus. The foul imp had no alternative but to flee.

Michael was spending more time in prayer, drawing closer to the Almighty for strength as he walked through this season of trial. Each new assault made him determined to seek after the Almighty that much more. Though he couldn't perceive it, his relationship with the Almighty was growing by leaps and bounds. He was developing unshakable faith and his spiritual muscles were growing stronger. The Almighty was taking him to new levels of glory though Michael often saw himself as weak and failing in his faith. Deuel knew that the Almighty was pleased with his charge as he hung onto the word in faith and trusted in his heavenly Father's love.

Even faith the size of a mustard seed is enough to move mountains and bring the Almighty great pleasure. Michael's spirit received the encouragement spoken by his angelic watcher.

The Almighty had a good plan for Michael's life. And he was right on course to see God's incredible plan unfold.

Zoe was filled with nervous excitement when Zach rang her doorbell. She looked stunning in a very short strapless yellow sundress and white sandals. With her long blond hair in a French braid, she looked like the teenager he'd dated in school.

"Wow!" Zach desperately wanted to sweep her up in his arms as he entered her apartment. "You look amazing."

"Thanks." Zoe was quite pleased with the effect she was having on him. It had taken an hour to decide on the perfect outfit and almost as long to get her hair and makeup just right.

He teased her about how youthful she looked as they made their way down the elevator and into the parking garage. "Man, I feel like I'm going out with a teenager. You look just like you did in high school."

He held her hand gently as they made the drive to Kemah. She felt comfortable with him. He was so easy to talk to and easy on the eyes. His quick wit kept her laughing during the ride. The sun shining brightly, the cloudless sky, and the smell of the ocean breeze as they neared Kemah added to the charm of the afternoon. She could feel the heaviness in her soul being lightened by the sheer enjoyment of being in his presence.

After a late leisurely lunch, they drove to Galveston where they parked and strolled hand in hand along the beach, lost in conversation. With his arm around her, they sat on the warm sand watching the sun disappear below the horizon. It was the perfect ending to an incredible day.

Their date had gone by too fast, and she wasn't ready to say good-bye as he pulled into the parking garage of her apartments.

"Michael, I've had such…" She stopped short, realizing what she'd said. "I mean…Zach…I'm so sorry. I don't know why his name popped out like that. I wasn't even thinking about him. I promise!" She could feel the heat rising in her flushed face.

"It's okay. You can call me anything you want. As long as you are here with me, I don't care." Zach leaned over to kiss her. "Can I walk you upstairs?"

She was afraid he could hear her heart beating wildly in her chest. "Umm… yea. I could pour us a glass of wine." She knew it might be dangerous to have him up to her apartment, but she didn't care.

Zoe was disappointed when he told her he wouldn't be staying. "We're going to keep this friendly, remember? I don't want to confuse you, and by your slip in the car, it's obvious your husband is still on your mind, at least a little."

"Zach, I didn't mean to call you Michael. It's just…I mean…I don't think it'll hurt anything if we have a glass of wine together."

"I've had a great time with you today." He kissed her one last time. A long, lingering kiss. "I'll call you soon." He left before her protest could convince him to change his mind. *You've got to play the game if you want the prize.* He smiled slyly.

Barbara was awakened in the middle of the night. She sensed the presence of the Lord in her bedroom and felt an overwhelming need to pray. She got out of bed so as not to wake Amos and went into her prayer room. She'd converted an area of her massive walk-in closet to be her prayer sanctuary. She'd bought a comfortable chair, ottoman, and an end table that fit nicely in one of the corners of the closet. The lamp on the table made the space feel warm and inviting. As a general rule, Amos had learned that if she was in her closet with the door closed, he wasn't to disturb her. But tonight, with Amos fast asleep, she didn't bother closing the door.

As she sat in her chair, the Spirit of intercession came over her. She began to weep and moan for her stepdaughter and son-in-law. The Holy Spirit was so strong upon her that she could feel the breaking of His heart for the couple. She lost track of time while praying fervently in the Spirit, often quoting scripture after scripture as the Spirit would bring them to her remembrance.

The Lord had placed such a love in her heart for Zoe. It was as if she'd birthed her from her own womb. She consistently prayed for the day the Lord would heal Zoe's old wounds and help her to forgive so the two of them could enjoy a close relationship.

When the burden to pray for Zoe and Michael lifted, she prayed earnestly for Amos's salvation before returning to bed. Glancing at the clock on the nightstand, she was surprised to see that she'd been praying for over two hours. She fell fast asleep, unaware that Amos lay awake beside her with tears streaming down his face.

Amos, unbeknownst to Barbara, had gotten up in the night. Hearing a noise and realizing that his wife was not in bed, he went searching to make sure she was all right. He paused by her closet door when he heard her crying. He realized that she was praying and, not wanting to eavesdrop, turned to go back to bed. Suddenly, it was as though his feet would not move. He was virtually frozen in place, mesmerized by the sound of the cries coming from his wife. It didn't sound like English, but the sound was beautiful, often changing from a melodic sound to a very authoritative tone. He was witnessing his wife having a supernatural experience with her God, and the two of them were one. It made him a little jealous of her obvious devotion to Him, and yet there was something so intriguing about it all.

He noticed a pause in her prayers as if she had finished, and then she began to pray for him. She prayed for his soul to be saved and for him to fall in love with God the way she had. She prayed for God's protection over him, for wisdom and favor in his business. She thanked God for giving her such a wonderful husband and the love of her life. Never before had he felt such an overwhelming love for her and profound gratefulness that she was his wife.

Just as quickly as he'd felt stuck in place, he sensed a release to return to bed. He was still awake a half-hour later when Barbara returned to bed. Unable to comprehend what had occurred, he was profoundly and unexplainably moved to tears.

Not wanting to startle her as she got back into bed, he pretended to be asleep. At least an hour had passed before he was able to drift off to sleep again.

Jasiel held Amos in place just before the entrance to his wife's prayer closet. Barbara had been praying fervently for Amos since she'd come to know the Lord. Because of her deep love for God and appreciation of all He'd done for her, she'd grown quickly in her faith and desperately wanted her husband to become a Christian too. She longed for the day when she could share her faith and love for Christ with him.

God had heard her cries and seen her tears and was intervening on her behalf. He'd also heard the prayers of Abby, Zoe's grandma. She loved him like her very own son and also never failed, night and day, to bring his name up to the Lord for salvation.

The Almighty had instructed Jasiel to wake Amos and direct him to the entrance of the closet. Jasiel was told to make sure that Amos heard his wife's petitions for his soul as his time for salvation was drawing near. When Amos had been sufficiently touched by the Spirit moving through his wife, Jasiel freed him to go back to bed.

The angel praised God that his charge's heart was softening, as evidenced by the tears flowing down his cheeks. Jasiel longed for the day when Amos would understand the plan of salvation, receive the love and acceptance of the Almighty, and surrender his heart to the Son.

He'd been held back from working in Amos's life for so many years. Though Amos appeared to be blessed financially, he'd suffered needlessly on many occasions. If he'd been a man of prayer and faith, Jasiel would have been able to intervene in some of the losses he'd incurred in his life, both physical and financial.

Neither he nor his first wife had even thought to pray during her long battle with cancer, though with her mother's help; she'd received Christ on her deathbed and was now enjoying her heavenly home to the fullest.

Amos could have spared his daughter and Barbara years of turmoil and strife if only he had engaged his angel into battle through prayer.

Jasiel was pleased. The tide was turning.

14

But those who wait on the Lord shall renew their strength;
they shall mount up with wings like eagles,
they shall run and not be weary,
they shall walk and not faint.

—*Isaiah 40:31*

Zoe was busy at work on Wednesday when Zach strolled into the office. Other than a few short texts, she hadn't heard much from him since their date the previous Saturday. He'd made no attempt to see her again, and she'd wondered if perhaps he'd been offended when she had accidentally called him by her husband's name on their last date. LaDonna and Tonya had encouraged her to turn the table on him and play hard to get.

"Hey, beautiful." He leaned over the reception desk to hand her a gorgeous bouquet of summer flowers.

Though she felt as though her heart had dropped down to her toes, she tried hard not to let him see the effect he was having on her. "Oh, hey, Zach. Are you here to see my dad? I'll let him know you're here." She picked up the phone as if to call Patricia, her father's secretary.

"Whoa, no I'm here to see you. I was in the neighborhood and was hoping you would have lunch with me. I brought you these flowers. I hope you like them."

"That's sweet." Her voice sounded as cool as a cucumber as she took the flowers from him. "But I've already made plans for lunch with a few of the girls here at my office."

"Uh, did I miss something? Have I done something wrong? You seem upset with me?" For a moment, he'd begun to doubt the advice of his trusted spiritual friends.

Zoe's eyes darted around to make sure that no one in the waiting room was listening or paying attention to their conversation before explaining herself. "Well, you haven't called me since Saturday, and I was beginning to think you weren't interested. Zach, I've been through a difficult enough time as it is, either you want to go out, or you don't, but please don't play games with me."

He pretended to be shocked before calmly offering his excuse. "Well, Zoe, for one thing, you are the one who told me you wanted me to take it slow. You said you wanted to keep it friendly. So I've been trying to go as slow as I can, but hey, I'd be happy to speed things up. Besides, my job keeps me in the air, and I don't always get an opportunity to make phone calls. I'll be leaving tomorrow to go back out of town, so what are you doing tonight?"

Blushing with embarrassment, she looked at him apologetically. "You're right. I did say that I wanted to be friends, didn't I? I feel silly now for being upset. How about dinner at my place tonight at seven?"

"Sounds great. I'll bring the wine." Zach gave her a look that made her feel like he was undressing her with his eyes. "I can't wait." He winked at her before turning to leave the office.

Zoe smelled the flowers and stomped her feet under her desk like a giddy little schoolgirl being asked out for the first time. She called LaDonna, unable to contain the excitement as she relayed her conversation and the news of her impending date.

"Oh, girl! I just knew that boy wanted you. Uh-huh, he's been playing you, and you called him on it."

"Well, it was really my fault. I was the one who told him to take it slow." Zoe felt the need to defend Zach. "Now, I've just got to figure out what in the world I'm gonna fix him for dinner. It needs to be something that will knock his socks off."

"Yeah, you know what they say, whoever *they* is, 'the way to a man's heart is through his stomach.' Girl, you may be knocking more than his socks off tonight."

"You're so crazy!" They both giggled before hanging up.

Amanda Townsend called Michael, relaying the news that she had a contract and earnest money for the house. She told him the couple was not only very interested in the house but also wanted to pay cash to speed up the sale. They were hoping to get the papers signed and to the title company before the end of the week.

Michael was thrilled as he hung up the phone with the realtor. He could hardly wait to tell Zoe the news. He called her cell phone, but she didn't answer, so he dialed her office number.

"Pointer, Richards and Brighten Law Associates, this is Zoe how can I help you?"

God, I miss her. He desperately wanted to see her. "Hey, baby! I've got good news."

"Michael?" Though she recognized his voice, she wanted to make sure it wasn't Zach.

"How many other men call you, baby?" His excitement was waning.

"Michael, I'm sorry I was distracted. What's your good news?" *He always picks the worse times to call.* Zoe rolled her eyes.

"We've sold the house. The people are going to pay cash, and they want to close as soon as possible. I'll be so glad to get out from under this note and away from this house. It's an answer to prayer. But I'm going to need to bring the contract by for you to sign tonight so that we can get it to the title company."

"Oh, Michael, I'm sorry, but I have plans tonight. Can you either bring it by here this afternoon or else maybe bring it by tomorrow night?" She hoped he wouldn't press for details.

Michael could feel the blood draining from his face as fear tried to inch its way into his thoughts. "What are you doing tonight? Are you going on a date?"

"As a matter of fact, I'm having someone over for dinner." She decided he might as well know that she was moving on.

"That's great, Zoe! I guess we'll just sell the house, and that'll be the end of our life together. We'll forget we ever had a beautiful child together. We'll pretend that we never made a vow before God, 'till death do us part.' I can't believe you. I'm beginning to wonder if you ever loved me or had a real relationship with God."

"Michael, I can't argue with you while I'm at work. Do you want to bring the contract by so I can sign it or not?" She was growing impatient and wanted the chapter of her life with Michael to be over and done. Her heart was as hard as a stone.

"Fine! I'll be there in an hour." This time, it was he who hung up the phone on Zoe. He remembered the list he'd made and the promise to surrender Zoe to Christ. He fell to his knees and raised both arms into the air in a stance of surrender.

"I will walk by faith and not by sight! I don't care what she says or what she does…nothing is too difficult for God! I will trust You, Lord. In faith, I worship You, Almighty God. I worship You. I choose to trust You."

Peace, like a warm blanket of love wrapped around his wounded soul, enveloped him, melting away the anger.

"You are my peace that surpasses my understanding."

Deuel bowed in adoration as the Presence entered the room. Kneeling down beside Michael, the Son cradled him in His arms while tears of mercy fell from His adoring eyes. His love was like a consuming fire that filled the room, and His voice resembled the sound of a thousand waterfalls. "*I Am your Jehovah Shalom.*"

An angelic host filled the atmosphere with boisterous songs of praise and worship to their beloved King.

Determined to sever all ties with Michael, Zoe called her dad's cell phone.

"Hey, my girl. I'm in a meeting across town. Can I call you back, or do you need to talk to me right now?" Amos, rose from his chair to exit the conference room.

"Daddy…" Zoe tried to hold back the tears, though Amos could hear the emotion in her voice. She heard him excuse himself from the meeting, saying that he needed to step out into the hallway for an urgent phone call.

"Zoe, what's wrong?"

"Daddy, I need a lawyer. I think I want to go ahead with a divorce from Michael. Can you refer someone to me?" Though family law wasn't his specialty, she knew he had contacts all over Houston.

"Honey, are you sure you want to do that right now? I mean, it's only been a short time since you lost Emma, and I'm afraid you might be acting a bit rashly." The sound of his sweet wife calling out to the Lord to save his daughter's marriage came flooding into his mind.

"Hello? Who are you, and what have you done with my daddy?" The change in his attitude took her by surprise. *What's gotten into him? Just a few weeks ago, he sounded excited at the prospect of me going out with Zach and starting over.*

"Zoe, you know I'll help you any way I can, but..." Amos searched his mind for the right words. "I just think we need to talk about it. Can we have lunch tomorrow? We'll talk about it then."

"Okay. But I've made up my mind Daddy. And you know me, once I've made up my mind, that's it. I don't see Michael and me getting back together, and I want to move on with my life."

"Zoe, I worry that a lot of what you're going through is a result of your grief. That's all. You know I want what's best for you. Please, let's just have lunch tomorrow, and we'll talk about it then. All right?"

"Okay, Daddy. I'll ask Patricia to put me on your schedule for lunch tomorrow so you can't back out. Love you."

"I love you too, sweetie."

Amos didn't understand the change in his heart, but something inside of him told him that he needed to buy some time for this marriage. He'd even thought about calling Zach and asking him to back off from pursuing his daughter but knew Zoe would resent him meddling in her affairs.

Michael was all business as he handed the contract to Zoe and directed her as to where she needed to sign. He told her he'd let her know when the closing was to take place and agreed that they could split the proceeds of the sale in half.

He couldn't help but notice that the pink low-cut top she wore revealed far too much cleavage when she bent over to sign the papers. He knew that other men coming into the law office would notice it too. He also saw the fresh flowers on her desk but didn't bother to comment on them or ask who'd sent them.

He was fuming as he walked out the door and onto the waiting elevator. He tried to turn his thoughts to the scripture he'd been putting to memory all that week.

"But those who wait on the Lord shall renew their strength. They shall mount up with wings like eagles, they shall run and not be weary, they shall walk and not faint. Isaiah 40:31."

By the time he reached his car, he could feel his anger subsiding as he determined, once more, to trust in the Lord and continue to pray for Zoe and speak God's word over her. It was tearing him up inside to think of her in someone else's arms, but he knew he'd have to trust God to work on her heart and remove this guy from her life. Nothing is too difficult for God; he reminded himself as he drove out of the parking garage. He prayed for strength and grace as he drove to his realtor's office.

Barbara could tell that something was bothering Amos when he came into the kitchen.

"Hey, sweetheart!" She wrapped her arms around his waist and kissed him on the cheek. "How's my guy today? You look like something is bothering you. Did you have a hard day at the office?"

Amos held her tightly. If at all possible, his love for her had deepened since the night he'd heard her praying for his soul. She was not only an attractive woman who could easily get a man much younger than himself, but she also had a beautiful heart. She was more radiant and tender since she'd become a Christian, and though he didn't understand it all, her relationship with God made her even more captivating to him.

"Nothing that can't be made better by spending time with my incredible wife."

"Just for that, I'm going to pour you a glass of wine." She kissed him tenderly before she released him from his embrace. "Tell me about your day." Barbara busied herself with opening the bottle of wine.

"Zoe called me today. She wants me to help her find a divorce lawyer."

She was surprised to hear the sadness in his voice. "I didn't think you cared if they got a divorce. I thought you blamed Michael for Emma's death and wanted them to divorce. Why do you sound like you're upset about it?" She handed him a glass of red wine.

Amos looked intently at her as he took a sip of wine, unsure how much he should tell her. He took another sip to boost his courage. He had a strange sense that the confession he was about to make was going to change his life forever.

"The other night, you got out of bed, and you were praying in your closet. I got up to check on you when I heard a noise and found that you weren't in bed. You'd left your closet door open. And I promise, honey, I didn't mean to spy or eavesdrop, but I heard you praying, and I was…I don't know…it touched me deeply. I know it sounds strange, but I even cried. I don't know why. I heard you praying for Zoe and Michael, and I realized how important their marriage vows were to you and, apparently, to your God. I started thinking about it, and I…don't want to get in the way of your prayers by helping her get a divorce, but I don't know what to do."

Barbara started to speak, but Amos held up his hand to indicate that he wasn't finished. It was obvious that he was trying to keep his emotions in check. Her eyes filled with tears. She knew that God was working in her husband's life and answering the prayers she'd been praying for over two years.

"I also heard you praying for me. I realized how important my becoming a Christian is to you. And though I know I'm not ready to change my life just yet, I want you to know I've been thinking about it, and I would be willing to go to church with you sometime."

"Oh, Amos! You don't even begin to know how happy that would make me." She wrapped her arms around him and kissed him. He embraced her affectionately.

"I see such a difference in you that somehow makes me want to be better. I don't want to be left out of any part of your life. But I don't know that I'm ready to be a holy roller either. Heck, I still like my glass of wine and my occasional cocktail." He smiled down at her.

"Amos, God takes us just as we are. You don't ever have to worry about changing for God to accept you. He loves you just as you are. He's changed me because the more I've fallen in love with Him, the more I want to change for Him so that I'm pleasing to Him."

"Well, I sure like the changes in you. You are more beautiful to me now than the day I first fell in love with my hot babysitter." He chuckled before turning serious once more. "Now, what do I do about Zoe? How can I put her off or convince her to wait?"

"I'm not sure, but I'll be praying for God to direct you and to somehow keep her from making that mistake. I truly believe God wants Zoe and Michael to get back together."

"Even after the way she's treated you, you love her, don't you?" Amos was amazed at his wife's compassion and concern for his daughter.

"As if I birthed her from my own belly! I pray for the day that she would allow me to be a part of her life."

"I know." He held her head against his chest. "I am a lucky man to have you. You know that?"

"You're blessed. But yea, I know. I know." They both smiled as he kissed the tip of her nose.

Though Michael didn't feel like going to church, he knew if he sat at home he'd drive himself crazy thinking about Zoe on a date with another man. However, instead of helping with the youth as he usually did on Wednesday nights, he felt led to go into the main sanctuary to listen to his pastor's message.

Michael soaked up every word as Pastor Steve taught on surrendering one's life completely over to Christ.

"God has called each one of us to live a life of complete surrender. What does it mean to surrender? It means you lay down your life, your dreams, and your desires before the throne of God and take up your cross, just as Jesus took up His cross. Surrender means that you say to God, 'Not my will but Thine be done.' It's an act of submission to the plan and purpose of God for your life." The pastor read from Proverbs 3:5–6, the scripture Michael had recently put to memory. He took it to be a confirmation that God was speaking directly to him through the message.

"What is it that you are holding on to so tightly that you are afraid to give over to God because you can't trust Him with it? Is it a child, your spouse, a dream for your future, or is it the need for an increase in your life? Or maybe it's a sin that you think no one else knows about, and you don't want to let it go?"

Zoe came to Michael's mind as Pastor Steve questioned the attentive congregation. Is it possible, he wondered, that he hadn't surrendered her over to God? What if God didn't choose to restore her to him? Could he surrender to God's will for his life, whatever it might be?

"You can't live a surrendered life if you are not willing to trust God with that person, sin, or desire you hold so tightly in your grasp. You have to give it all to Him. He promises that He will direct your path if you trust Him. He's promised you that He will meet your needs. He knows the plans He has for you that began even when you were still in your mother's womb. If you understood how very much God loves you, you wouldn't have any trouble surrendering to Him."

"Even Jesus had to surrender to the will of His Father." He read the passage in Luke twenty-two about Jesus agonizing in the garden while in prayer to His Father.

"Yet, in the end, Jesus surrendered His will and went to the cross for all of mankind because He knew it was God's perfect will for His life. And now He is seated victoriously at the right hand of the Father. When we give to God, His law of reciprocity is always at work, and He gives back to us in greater measure. So I encourage you to let go of that which you are holding onto and surrender your life completely over to God."

Pastor Steve called for the praise team to come up to the platform. They sang quietly in the background as he made an impassioned plea for those lost in their sin to accept Christ as their Savior. He then asked for those to come to the altar who were not living a completely surrendered life. Half the congregation went forward, including Michael. Brad and Kira, who'd been sitting beside him, went up with him.

As his pastor said a prayer, Michael envisioned himself placing Zoe in the palms of the nail-scared hands of Christ. With tears streaming down his face, he prayed in agreement with Pastor Steve. He felt as though a burden had lifted as he made his way back to his seat.

After the service, people continued to pray and fellowship together. Brad and Kira, along with Pastor Steve, asked Michael if they could pray with him. As they stood in a circle holding hands, he thought someone else had joined them when he sensed a warm hand on his shoulder. However, there was no one there when he turned to look. He felt bathed in love and the mercy of God as they prayed fervently for him. They prayed for grace as he walked through the fire of testing and for the peace of God to engulf him. He hadn't told any of them that he suspected Zoe was with another man because he didn't want to uncover her sin. But the Lord knew just how to lead them in a prayer that brought comfort.

Afterward, he went home and, to his amazement, went to bed and fell into a deep, peaceful sleep.

Deuel placed his hand upon Michael's shoulder as the small group gathered to pray for him. He wanted to support his charge and hoped he would feel the presence and strength of God through his touch. He, with a company of angels sent at the Father's command, encircled Michael as he slept that night making sure his sleep was peaceful and refreshing. They worshiped over him and could hear the booming voice of the Almighty singing along with them. The Almighty rejoiced over Michael with singing as He'd promised His saints in Zephaniah 3:17.

Zoe was busy in the kitchen preparing dinner when Zach arrived. She'd rushed home after a quick stop at the grocery store to purchase steaks for the grill. She strategically put on a pair of short shorts paired with a low-cut loose-fitting top and pulled her hair back in a ponytail.

"Wow, it smells amazing in here." Zach kissed her lightly on the cheek as he entered her apartment. "What's for dinner?"

"I hope you know how to grill steaks because that's what's for dinner. I'm making potatoes au gratin and some bacon wrapped asparagus. How's that sound?"

"Great!" He rubbed his hands together. "I can grill a mean steak. Do you want me to pour you a glass of wine first?" He busied himself with opening the bottle.

"Yea, that sounds good. I've been running around like a chicken with my head cut off since I got off work. I could use a glass to help me relax."

"Well, you certainly don't look like a chicken without a head. You look fantastic."

"Why, thank you." She smiled coyly as he handed her a glass of wine. She'd put more thought into what she was going to wear than the dinner menu. She knew that the way to get and keep a man like Zachary Thomas was to make sure that he was completely satisfied when he left her house.

He went out on the patio to start the grill while she put on some soft music. She'd already set plates on the coffee table and placed pillows on the floor. She wanted this night to be a night he wouldn't soon forget. She dimmed the living room lights and busied herself lighting candles around the apartment.

"You're so incredibly beautiful!" Zach was staring at her from the patio door as she bent over a candle. Before she could reply, he scooped her up in his arms and kissed her passionately. "Can we skip dinner and get to dessert?" He had a mischievous twinkle in his eyes.

Without waiting for an answer, he picked her up and carried her into her bedroom. They were deeply engrossed in making love to each other when the smoke detectors went off.

"Oh my gosh!" Zoe giggled as they both flew off the bed. She'd forgotten that she'd left the asparagus cooking in the oven. The bacon grease had smoked up the kitchen causing the smoke alarm to go off.

Zach burned himself while pulling the asparagus out of the oven. Dropping the pan, he let out a curse, causing both of them to laugh hysterically as they stood naked in the kitchen, surrounded by smoke with the alarm still buzzing loudly in their ears.

"We're going to have my neighbors calling the fire department." She opened the sliding patio door and fanned the smoke with a dishtowel.

Zach stood on a kitchen chair yanking the battery out of the smoke detector before placing his hand under the kitchen faucet to alleviate the pain from his burn.

While bending over to check on his hand, Zach again pulled her body to him and began to kiss her. She melted into his arms, and before long, they were back in her bedroom. The food remained on the counter, untouched all night long.

The two fell fast asleep after hours of spent passion, their bodies entangled together.

Zoe was already dressed for work, had coffee brewing and breakfast cooking as Zach entered the kitchen.

"I figured I'd feed you breakfast since we never got around to dinner last night. You must be starving." She was taken aback at how devilishly handsome he looked. She couldn't help but smile as she plated the last piece of bacon she'd been frying.

He picked up a piece of bacon and took a bite. "So, she can cook." He smiled broadly as he gently patted her on the behind.

She swatted him back playfully with the dishtowel. "Hey, I'd have fed you last night, but you never let me get around to it. Breakfast is almost ready. We're going to eat out on the patio if that's okay with you? I love the view when it's pretty like today." She'd already set the table on her patio and was carrying a carafe of coffee out the door, expecting him to follow.

"Zoe…I can't stay for breakfast. I have to fly my boss out to New York, and I can't be late." He stood with his arms crossed while leaning against the kitchen counter.

She turned and pleaded with him through the open patio door. "Well, surely you can stay for a quick breakfast. It's almost ready. I just have to get the biscuits out of the oven."

"No, I can't. I have to get back to my apartment and pack. I was going to do that when I got home last night, but… you kept me detained." He walked out onto the patio to kiss her good-bye.

"So you're just going to love me and leave me?" She looked at him with sad eyes as she set the carafe on the table. "You can't even have a cup of coffee?"

"Well, I don't want to leave you, but I have to. I have to make this flight. I'll call you later. Maybe we can get together next week." He drew her into an embrace, repeatedly kissing her neck though he displayed no real concern for her feelings.

"Next week?" Zoe backed away, her voice unable to hide her frustration. "Where are you going and how long are you going to be gone?"

"Don't worry, baby. I'll be back. I'll try to call you more often; I promise. Please don't be angry." He grabbed her again and kissed her in a lingering embrace, momentarily melting away the anger and apprehension rising within her. Afterward, he turned and walked out of her apartment, leaving her feeling empty and alone.

She brooded as she sat on the patio surveying the beautiful table she'd set and the food that was now getting cold. *I can't believe he couldn't even take time to enjoy the breakfast I cooked for him.*

She thought about the night they'd spent together. There had been a passion in their lovemaking that she could not deny. However, something was missing though she couldn't quite put her finger on it. Unlike Michael, who was so in-tuned to her every physical need and cared more about pleasing her than himself, Zach had been a demanding lover, almost selfish in his desire.

A melancholy feeling settled over her, and no matter how hard she tried, she couldn't shake it off. She decided to call in sick and spent most of the day in bed nursing her wounded feelings.

Dekar pompously stood before the gaggle of demons. Beelzebub had once again sent him to congratulate them and keep them focused on their attack against Zoe.

"She's in so deep; she'll never get out." Lust made lewd gestures toward the others.

"Yea, she's putty in my hands." Depression never showed any emotion other than sadness, but he was excellent at what he did and a tremendous asset at furthering the kingdom of darkness. Too many children of God had fallen headlong into his clutches, being so deceived by him that many had even taken their own lives.

"Good!" Dekar clapped his hands in approval. "The prince of darkness is pleased with each of you and how well you've united in your efforts. But you must remember that he will not be completely satisfied until her life has been destroyed with no vestige of her faith left intact. You must make sure that she never turns back to Jehovah. It sounds easy, I know, but she has so many of the saints praying for her. Continue to work together, and keep your eyes out for Ramiah. He'll wield his sword with every given opportunity. I don't have to remind you that his sword is empowered by the word of Jehovah. It is quick and powerful and able to divide between soul and spirit and joint and marrow. With just one swipe, he can tear down a stronghold that's taken us years to construct."

He slinked away into the darkness, off to encourage, instruct or rebuke similar groups as they worked to trap other unsuspecting Christians.

15

For I am persuaded that neither death nor life, nor angels
nor principalities nor powers, nor things present nor things to come,
nor height nor depth, nor any other created thing,
shall be able to separate us from the love of God which is in Christ Jesus our Lord.
—Romans 8:38–39

Michael worked diligently packing box after box of his, and what remained of Zoe's, possessions while his mom and dad tackled the daunting task of packing up Emma's room. As if time had stood still, her room looked exactly the way it had on the fatal day of her drowning. It had been his mother's idea to give most of her belongings to a crisis pregnancy center.

Brad and Kira were working in the kitchen while Pastor Steve and Marcie were busy pulling pictures off walls and carefully wrapping some of the decorations Zoe had left behind when she'd moved out. Several other church members had brought over food and offered help.

It had blessed him when three high school seniors, members of the youth group, had shown up bright and early to help. They'd given up their Saturday and were packing up the garage while intermittently jumping into the pool for relief from the sweltering heat. From the view out of his upstairs bedroom window, he smiled as he watched Victor Ramirez doing a cannonball jump

177

into the pool.

Michael was grateful for the love of his parents, the support of the body of Christ and the fact that he didn't have to face this day alone. Though he was glad to be moving, he'd dreaded having to handle all of their belongings and making decisions as to what he should keep, give away, or sell.

Praise music filled the house both upstairs and down. His dad had prayed before they'd begun that morning. He'd prayed for everyone's safety and that this change was just a step in the pathway of God's plan for Michael. It had lifted Michael's spirits. He'd awakened that morning with a sense of dread at the thought of packing away all of the memories this house had held in happier times.

He sat on the edge of his bed, thumbing through Zoe's Bible. He'd found it while cleaning out her nightstand. It grieved him that she'd left it behind. Michael opened the Bible to the page marked by an embroidered bookmark; a gift from Grandma Abby. A scripture caught his attention. Apparently, the highlighted scripture had been special to Zoe. He read it out loud several times.

"For I am persuaded that neither death nor life, nor angels nor principalities nor powers, nor things present nor things to come, nor height nor depth, nor any other created thing, shall be able to separate us from the love of God which is in Christ Jesus our Lord."

For a brief moment, Michael allowed himself the luxury to reminisce on the day he and Zoe had met. Her beauty, both on the inside as well as the outside, had captured his attention. She lit up every room she entered, but her love for the Lord had endeared her to him. He smiled as he recalled how she would witness to anyone on two legs when he'd first met her, often to his embarrassment. He remembered the young girl who loved to read her Bible and spend time in prayer. He thought back to their wedding day and how it'd been so important to her that those attending the ceremony felt the presence of the Lord as they made their vows together.

It saddened him to think of how the cares of life had slowly eroded her walk with the Lord. Her lust for things had somehow replaced her desire to seek God with her whole heart. An incessant desire to have the biggest and the best without patiently waiting on God to gradually increase them had put a tremendous strain on their finances, which had been a constant source of stress in their marriage. Though she had loved the big house, pool, and fancy car, having to leave Emma in daycare so she could work had made her question God's provision for them and the need to tithe. In her eyes, God was supposed to be like her natural father, Amos, giving her what she wanted when she wanted it.

In hindsight, he could see how he'd messed up too in that he'd allowed her to dictate most of the decisions because of her strong will and his inability to deny her what she wanted. If given a second chance, he knew he'd do things differently. He certainly wouldn't let the fear of losing her rule his life.

"Father, I thank You for this wonderful promise from Your word. No matter what it looks like to me, I thank You that You continue to hold my wife in the palm of Your hand. I thank You that she cannot be separated from You. I bind Satan and all of his forces from trying to keep her bound in sin, and thank You that You will send out warring angels to fight for her freedom. I thank You that Your mercies are new every morning and ask You to extend mercy to her today. I pray for Your will to be done in her life. Holy Spirit, I ask You to woo her back to her first love. Heal her brokenness. In Jesus's name. Amen!"

After his brief prayer, he put the Bible in the box with his own Bible and devotional books. Something told him not to put it away into storage. He hoped there would soon be a day when Zoe would hunger for the word of God once again.

Amos noticed his daughter was barely touching her food as he sat across the table from her at his prestigious country club restaurant on a beautiful Saturday morning. He'd wanted to take her to lunch earlier in the week, but she'd called in sick both Thursday and Friday.

"What's the matter? Are you still feeling ill? You look like you've lost a little more weight."

"Daddy, I have a confession to make. I wasn't sick. I'm just in a funk, and I didn't feel like going to work." Zoe didn't disclose the reason for her sour mood.

Amos assumed his daughter was still grieving the loss of her child and sudden changes in her life. "Do you want to talk about it? Are you having second thoughts about the divorce?"

She gave Amos a puzzled look. "Divorce? Oh no, Daddy. I'm still very determined to go ahead with that. That's not what has me down. It's probably just my hormones. You know how us women can be."

"Zoe, I've been thinking about this divorce business. Of course, I know several divorce attorneys, but I think it'd be better for you to give it a little more time just to be sure it's what you want to do. There's no reason for you to rush into a divorce. Michael's agreed to give you half of the equity from the house, and you've already gotten all the furniture and things you wanted."

"I just want to move on, and I don't feel like I can do that while I'm still tied to Michael. What's gotten into you, Daddy? All of the sudden you seem to be against divorce. Is Barbara putting thoughts into your head?"

He ignored her question. "I just want you to be sure of what you're doing, honey. You've been through so much emotional trauma. You're still grieving over Emma, and I worry about you making the wrong decision. You were crazy in love with Michael. I don't understand how you could just turn off your emotions toward him like someone turning off a kitchen faucet."

"You weren't too worried when I moved out of the house. You helped me get into my apartment. Something's changed, and I want to know what's up with you, Amos Richards." She felt betrayed by her father's sudden change in support for her decision.

"Well, I haven't changed yet, but I'm thinking about going to church with Barbara this Sunday." His eyes searched Zoe's face. He expected her to be happy. Amos knew she'd prayed for him to become a Christian ever since she was a teenager.

"What? I knew she had to have something to do with this. Since when is she going to church? Maybe it'll help soothe her conscience. She certainly needs to repent of her sins and the hatred that's in her heart." She pushed back her plate of food. "Now I've completely lost my appetite!"

"Zoe, I'm going to say this once, and I won't say it again." By the tone of his voice, Zoe could tell she'd pushed her father too far. His face turned crimson as he pointed his index finger angrily at her. "I will not have you disrespect my wife in my presence ever again. Do you understand me? If you only knew how much she loves you. She prays for you day and night! She's changed Zoe! She's not the woman that she was when you were a child, and it's time you forgive her and get over it. You're stuck in your past, and I'm afraid you're going to allow it to ruin your future."

"What's that supposed to mean?" Zoe eyes stung from the tears that threatened to make their way down her flushed cheeks. "How is my past going to affect my future? Are you not going to be a part of my life if I refuse to forgive her? Have you forgotten how horrible she was? She was cruel. She made sure that I knew Johnny was her only child. She hurt me and…" She jumped out of her chair, throwing her napkin on the table before finishing her sentence. "I'm leaving before one of us says something we might regret. Thanks for lunch, Dad. I'll find my own lawyer!" She turned and walked away. Several onlookers, their quiet lunches interrupted by her sudden outburst, stared in bewilderment.

"Zoe!" Amos called after her but she didn't turn around.

Zoe clasped the steering wheel so hard her hands hurt as she drove back to her apartment. Her father had never spoken to her in that tone. He'd always comforted her, and though he'd often made excuses for Barbara, he'd never defended her with such passion and conviction. She felt as though she'd almost been given an ultimatum: a choice between forgiving Barbara or giving up the closeness she'd always shared with her father. Once again, she felt like Barbara had the upper hand in her life, and, at that moment, she hated her more than ever. *How dare she come between my dad and me by pretending to be someone she's not.*

To add fuel to her fire, Zach still wasn't back in town. She had hoped they'd be able to spend the weekend together. However, she hadn't heard from him. Several of the girls from the office had asked her to go clubbing with them Saturday evening, but she'd held off from giving them a reply, hoping she'd hear from Zach.

Once home, she angrily threw her keys and purse onto the kitchen counter, slipped into a pair of sweats, and poured herself a glass of wine even though it was only two in the afternoon.

The bedroom door creaked open as two pairs of tiny feet bounded toward the bed. "Daddy, Daddy!" Two high-pitched voices shrieked in excitement. "Mommy says it's time to get out of bed. We want to go to the park."

Zach opened one eye as if to tease the two little faces hovering over him. He then, in one quick swoop, whisked up the twin girls and pulled them into the bed. Amidst giggles and squeals, he began to tickle his young daughters.

Their reinforcement entered the room. "Hey, sleepyhead. It's eleven in the morning. Are you going to sleep all day? We're bored, and you promised Lauryn and Lisha you'd take them to the park. It's a beautiful day outside." She pulled open the drapes before sitting beside him on the bed.

"Wow, I have been overtaken by women today." He sat up in bed. "Okay, girls, give me time to get a shower and get dressed, and we'll go have a picnic in the park. How's that sound?"

"Yippee!" The four-year-old twins jumped up and down on the bed with excitement.

"But first, your beautiful mommy has to come and give me a kiss."

Adele Thomas came and sat on the edge of the bed beside her husband. Zach embraced her tenderly as he kissed her, eliciting even more giggles from the girls.

"Good morning, my darling." Adel lovingly tousled his hair.

"Good morning, beautiful."

"There's nothing better than being woken up in my own bed by my two favorite munchkins. This out of town stuff is getting old. I hate being away from my girls." It was partially true.

"Well, get up, lazybones, and we'll spend the whole day together. You've been working so hard that we've felt ignored." She bent down to whisper in his ear in her thick French accent. "And, tonight…I'll remind you why you married a French girl."

"Ah ha!" Zach pretended a French accent as he bounded out of bed. "I will be ready in thirty minutes my loves." The girls squealed with laughter.

He grabbed his phone as he went into the bathroom to shower, leaving his wife and daughters to prepare for the picnic.

Before shaving, he sent out a quick text message to Zoe. It was the first time he'd felt like he could do so without getting caught.

Hey, beautiful. I can't get u out of my mind. Sitting here on the runway waiting to take off & I can't seem to think of anything but u. Sorry my job has kept me out of town so much lately. I'll be in the air again today so I won't get to call but hopefully,

I can call u tomorrow. Planning to be home early next week.

He then deleted all evidence of the text before getting into the shower.

His guides had promised him that he could have his cake and eat it too. He had an adoring wife. She'd been an up and coming model when they'd met on a chance encounter at a Starbucks in New York. Adele was drop-dead gorgeous. He'd been instantly smitten when he'd heard her place her coffee order in her French accent. From the moment he'd laid eyes on her, he knew she was someone he wanted. They'd dated only a few months before she had become pregnant. Though he'd panicked at the prospect of settling down into a completely monogamous relationship and becoming a father, his spirit guides had assured him that he could be happily married and have an occasional tryst without hurting anyone. So far, they'd been right. His girls brought joy to him and gave him a sense of being settled. Whereas, someone like Zoe excited him. She gave him something to look forward to, like a child anticipating that special gift on Christmas morning.

He whistled as the hot water rained down on him. *It's going to be a great day.*

Zoe called LaDonna as soon as she read the text from Zach. "Hey, girl. What time are ya'll going out tonight?"

"Oh, are you gonna go? I'm so excited! I'll come by and pick you up around eight tonight. You doing okay?" LaDonna could hear the despondency in Zoe's voice.

"Yea. I'm just kinda bummed. I got a text from Zach saying he's still out of town and has another flight today. He won't be back until sometime next week."

"Hmm. Well, don't you worry. You're gonna have guys falling all over you tonight. We're gonna have us a great time." She laughed mischievously. "I'll see you at eight. And hey, remember there are other fish in the sea."

"I know. I'll be ready at eight."

LaDonna had her suspicions about Zach Thomas, but she wasn't about to share them with Zoe. She'd give him the benefit of the doubt for now, but he'd better shape up, or she'd have to let Zoe know what she suspected. She didn't want to see her friend hurt. *Poor Zoe, she's already been through enough hurt to last a lifetime.*

The group of helpers laid hands on Michael as they surrounded him to pray for his move as well as his marriage to be restored. Pastor Steve led them in prayer and then, as the Spirit led, others prayed too.

Afterward, Michael addressed the group telling them how much he appreciated all of their support and help.

"Your prayers are so important to me. I know that it's your prayers that are helping me get through this season of my life and still be able to remain thankful to God and walk in peace. I truly believe in the importance of prayer and that it can change situations and move mountains. I'm standing for my marriage and believing in faith for restoration. God said in His word that He hates divorce, so I believe that I'm in His perfect will when I pray for my wife to be restored to me as well as to Him. Losing Emma has just been more than she can bear, but I know that one day, soon I hope, she'll be back with me and completely restored to God."

One by one, the group said good-bye and promised to continue to pray. His dad and mom were the last to leave.

"Are you sure you don't want to come stay with us, honey?" Michael could see the concern etched on his mom's face.

"No, I'll only be at Brad and Kira's for two nights. Don't worry, Mom. I'm going to be fine." He hugged her and his dad before watching them disappear down the brick walkway.

The movers would be coming on Monday morning, bright and early. Brad and Kira had invited him to spend the next couple of nights with them until his move into the new apartment not far from their neighborhood. He told them he'd join them shortly but wanted to spend a little time alone before going to their house for the night.

With the house now silent, he went out to the pool and stood by the spot where he'd retrieved Emma from the water on the day she'd drowned. It seemed like so long ago. Yet as if it were yesterday, he could still recall the sound of her giggles as she'd toddled through the house while he'd pretend to chase after her.

Sitting down on the pool steps, he allowed himself a moment to cry and grieve over his child. He knew she was in heaven and that he'd see her again one day, but his heart ached. Monday he'd be moving out of this house, leaving behind the memories, both good and bad.

"Daddy's so sorry, Emma. I should have taken better care of you. I wish I could turn back the hands of time and relive that day. I wouldn't be so stupid as to leave the door open so you could get out. You were probably searching for me. Please know Mommy and Daddy love you and miss you. We'll be with you again someday when God says it's time. Until then, my angel girl, rest in peace."

Tears streamed down his cheeks. Though he couldn't see into the spirit realm, Jesus sat next to him on the step, cradling him in His arms. Deuel stood behind him, sword drawn high in his right hand while his left hand rested on Michael's shoulder. Another angel carefully caught every tear and placed it in a bottle.

16

Behold, the former things have come to pass,
and new things I declare; before they spring forth I tell you of them.
—Isaiah 42:9

The music was deafeningly loud; the dance floor packed with bodies, and the atmosphere sparked with lust and anticipation as the girls entered the popular Houston nightclub. Three other girls from the office, Molly, Hanna, and Kim, had joined Zoe, LaDonna, and Tonya for their night on the town. They sauntered through the crowd and found a table in the back corner away from the dance floor. A waitress came and took their drink orders.

Zoe watched as her friends, well versed in the art of flirting, caught the attention of several hungry men, out on the prowl and hunting for their next meal. Tonya, Hanna, and Kim left to dance or mingle with the crowd after leaving their purses to mark their seats at the table.

The waitress bent down at the table, balancing a tray of drinks in her hand. "A gentleman at the bar bought this round for you ladies." She nodded her head toward an attractive man seated at the bar. "He likes you." She handed Zoe a drink. "He said he'd like to meet you, and he tipped me real big, so will you at least wave at him? Thanks, ladies."

"Well, why ain't he man enough to come over and introduce himself?" LaDonna took a drink of her margarita, tipping the glass in his direction as if to thank him. "Umm…I love a free drink…and the night's just beginning. We need to bring you more often, Zoe. You might just be our lucky charm."

"That was sweet of him." Zoe waved in his direction. "I can't believe he bought all of our drinks." She was naive and unfamiliar with how the game worked.

Molly Barnes leaned across the table to address Zoe. "Girl, that means he wants one thing and one thing only. Don't be fooled by his generosity. His pockets come at a price." The three of them giggled.

Zoe noticed the man walking towards her. "Oh, my gosh. He's coming this way." Before the girls could reply, he bent down and asked Zoe if she'd like to dance.

"Sure." She stood and offered him her hand. Turning back toward the girls, she shrugged her shoulders and made a funny face as she followed him out onto the dance floor.

They danced to several fast songs before returning to the table. Tonya was back at the table deep in conversation with a young man seated beside her and the rest of the girls were nowhere to be seen.

"So what's your name?" The guy leaned in towards her. The loud music had kept them from getting acquainted on the dance floor.

"Zoe." She took a sip of wine as she looked him over. *He's cute, though not as attractive as Zach or even Michael for that matter. He's built nice and obviously works out a lot.*

"Nice to meet you, Zoe. I'm Kyle. I'm kind of new to the whole club scene. I recently divorced, and I've only been clubbing once or twice. Can I get you another drink?" He waved at a waitress passing by.

"I'll have a scotch on the rocks, and the lady will have a…" He looked at Zoe.

"A glass of red wine please."

"So are you single?"

Zoe leaned closer to hear the question. "Huh? Sorry, I didn't hear you."

"Are you single?" He smiled as he leaned toward her to repeat the question into her ear.

"Oh, yea. I'm separated right now, but I'm working toward a divorce." It wasn't a lie. She just needed to find a good lawyer.

They sat and talked intermittently between dances. The more drinks they had, the friendlier they became. Tonya surprised her when she told her she was leaving with a guy she'd just met. LaDonna was still missing from the table, though Zoe assumed she was either on the dance floor or seated at another table with someone with whom she'd hooked up.

"Would you like to go get a bite to eat?" By this time, it was close to midnight.

"I'll have to find my friend and tell her I'm leaving. Can you wait while I look for her?"

"Sure." He motioned for the waitress to settle the bill.

Zoe walked around until she spotted LaDonna making out with a guy in a booth. She told her she was going to get a bite to eat with Kyle and that he'd take her home.

"Okay! I may have found someone myself. Ain't he pretty?" She nodded toward the guy as she winked at Zoe. "You sure you're gonna be okay?"

"Yea, he seems nice. He's recently divorced. I'll be fine."

Zoe went back to the table and retrieved her purse before she left, hand in hand with Kyle.

The Club Rendezvous was a popular Houston nightspot for those looking to hook up with a partner for the night, ease their loneliness, fulfill their lustful cravings, peddle or purchase drugs, as well as many other unsavory and unspeakable behaviors. It was dark and murky and infested with demonic activity, unbeknownst to the humans who came to have a good time and an innocent night of fun. These unsuspecting guests were blinded to the fact that nothing good happens in dark places. The spirits that claimed Rendezvous as their territory were well within their spiritual rights to latch onto and influence those who entered their habitat. They reveled in the darkness, lurking in every corner and crevice of the club, exciting passions, desires, and totally unethical and unlawful behavior in those who dared penetrate their lair.

Any angelic beings who were daring enough to enter were restricted to stand in the shadows and watch helplessly as demons strategically hooked their charges like hungry fish lured by tasty bait. Those they were called to guard were giving themselves over to darkness by their very entrance into the devil's playground. The poor, ignorant mortals who came in rarely left the nightspot untainted by the unseen chains wrapped tightly around their sin-stained souls.

Zoe and Kyle sat next to each other at a Denny's restaurant. She drank a cup of coffee and chewed on one of his pieces of bacon while he ate a sizable breakfast.

He shared about his divorce, and how hard it had been for him financially having to pay child support for his two children, but Zoe was reluctant to share any details about her private life. After an hour and a half of friendly conversation with him doing most of the talking, he drove her home.

Zoe, not wanting to be alone with her constant nightmares and depressing dreams, asked him up to her apartment for a drink. Much to his delight, he ended up spending the night.

The alarm he'd set on his cell phone woke her up early on Sunday morning.

"Oh my gosh, why is your alarm going off?" Her mind was still foggy with sleep as she drew close to him, hoping to enjoy another round of sexual pleasure. He'd been more than an adequate lover and she was hoping he wasn't in any hurry to leave her bed.

"I've got to go. I'm supposed to go to church. I'm being baptized this morning." He showed no remorse for the time they'd spent meeting each other's sexual needs the night before. He threw back the covers and bounded out of bed without so much as touching her.

"You've got to be kidding me!" Zoe bolted up in the bed; the white bed sheet pulled up to her neck as if now embarrassed for him to see her naked body. "What was I, your last supper?"

"No, I thoroughly enjoyed last night, and I wouldn't mind seeing you again. But I've made this commitment, and I have to follow through." Kyle busied himself with retrieving his clothes sprawled around her bedroom.

Zoe couldn't believe her ears. She'd have laughed hysterically if she hadn't been so shocked. *Does he have a clue as to what baptism means? Wait till the girls hear this one.*

"Where do you go to church?" She watched him put on his clothes.

He named a well-known and very popular interdenominational church. One Michael had always frowned upon, calling it a "feel-good" church. "I started going there to meet singles."

"Don't they teach you that you are not supposed to sleep around...especially the night before you are going to get baptized?" Zoe was unable to hide her outrage at the irony of the situation.

"Not really. The pastor preaches an encouraging message. That's what I like about the church. You leave feeling uplifted. He doesn't believe in all that talk about sin, hell, or the blood. He talks more about prosperity, blessings, God's love, and stuff like that. The music is upbeat too. You could go too if you'd like."

The thought seemed ludicrous to Zoe. "Ugh...no, I just slept with you, and to be totally honest, I can't even remember your name. I'm not going to be a hypocrite and go to church with you."

"Okay!" He shrugged as if unaffected by her attitude. "Can I get your number and call you some time. I'd like to see you again."

She held her hand palm side out in front of her face as he bent to kiss her. "No, I don't think so." She got out of bed wrapping herself in her robe while following him to the door of her apartment.

She slammed the door behind him. Angry, frustrated, and even a little ashamed, she lay down on her sofa where she cried herself back to sleep.

Kira busied herself in the kitchen before her family and their houseguest began to stir. It was her Sunday morning ritual to have her quiet time, get her shower and dress, and prepare breakfast before waking Brad and the kids. She was particularly excited this morning because God had awakened her in the wee hours of the morning and given her a word for Michael. Though she wanted to run upstairs and bang on his bedroom door at five in the morning, she'd asked God to show her His perfect timing for Michael to receive the word, which she knew, would bring encouragement.

She'd been interceding for Michael and Zoe ever since they'd lost their only child, and, for Zoe, even long before that. At least a year before Emma's death, Kira had suspected Zoe was going through a dry spell or a faith crisis of some sort. The fire that had once burned so brightly had become little more than a sizzle. Her once positive and uplifting friend had begun to murmur and complain about their church, being critical of the leadership, especially Donovan Scott, the youth pastor. She'd grumbled that she felt forced to work in the nursery when Emma was born.

If given a choice, she'd have chosen shopping or sleeping in over a Sunday worship service, and often did. With an unforgiving heart, she'd often confided in Kira the hatred she had toward her stepmom, retelling events from the past over and over again. She resented the fact that she and Michael lived from paycheck to paycheck and that he wasn't driven to success like her father. She'd begun to look at everyone through a pair of dark, bitter glasses. Kira had long suspected that the enemy had found a foothold and staked a claim on her friend's soul.

She too had felt the pain of loss when Zoe had turned away from their special friendship after Emma's death. They'd shared deep secrets, desires, and dreams together, shopped, and had play dates with their children. She and Brad would often double date with Michael and Zoe. They had even been at the hospital the night Emma was born to rejoice with their friends. Though she still loved Zoe dearly, her heart now broke for Michael as he struggled through his losses.

Kira, though she sought diligently after God, read the word daily and considered herself to be a woman of faith, rarely got a "word from God" for herself, much less anyone else. So she was very surprised when God had entrusted her with this precious gift for Michael. She'd carefully written it out just as God had given it to her.

For Michael August 15, 2012:

O you afflicted one, tossed with tempest, and not comforted, behold, I will lay your stones with colorful gems, and lay your foundations with sapphires. I will make your pinnacles of rubies, your gates of crystal, and all your walls of precious stones. All your children shall be taught by the Lord, and great shall be the peace of your children. (Isaiah 54:11–13)

God says you will not only be a father of natural children once again, but I will make you a father of many spiritual sons and daughters. Because you have held onto Me and My word through the furnace of affliction, I will give you the desires of your heart.

The sound of children will fill your home once again. As my word says in Psalms 127:4–5, Like arrows in the hand of a warrior, so are the children of one's youth. Happy is the man who has his quiver full of them. Joy will fill the walls of your home.

There will be many who look to you as a spiritual father. There are even those watching you now going through this fire of testing. I have made you a sign and a wonder to them as David was to those who witnessed his strong faith and trust in Me (Ps. 71:7). They speak of your faith and trust. They see your steadfastness in this hour of trial and are amazed at your spiritual fortitude.

I, the Lord, have called You in righteousness, and will hold Your hand; I will keep You and give You as a covenant to the people, as a light to the Gentiles, to open blind eyes, to bring out prisoners from the prison, those who sit in darkness from the prison house. I am the Lord, that is My name; and My glory I will not give to another, nor My praise to carved images. Behold, the former things have come to pass, and new things I declare; before they spring forth I tell you of them (Isaiah 42:6–9).

From your youth, I have called you. You have desired with all of your heart to please and serve Me. You've said, 'Here am I, Lord. Use me.' I have heard your cries. And even in this your darkest hour, I am preparing to use you for My glory. You will be a voice to the lost. You and your wife will be used to set spiritual captives free. My Word that is hidden in your heart will come forth with great boldness. Doors that have seemed shut will suddenly open for you because you have a humble and gentle spirit. I will do a new thing in your life. I declare it now.

She'd thought carefully before writing the words 'your wife.' She didn't want to give Michael false hope of restoration with Zoe, and she wasn't sure that God was speaking about Zoe either. *Possibly, God will give Michael another wife who'll bear him children.* Nevertheless, she felt like it was a word that would encourage her friend.

After writing it all down just as God had dictated it to her, she folded the paper and stuck it in her Bible. She would wait until the time was right to give the paper to Michael.

Michael was up early on Monday morning. The closing on his house was scheduled for nine in the morning and movers were coming at noon to move him into his new apartment. Though excited about the sale, he wasn't looking forward to living alone in an apartment. He'd enjoyed his short stay with Brad and Kira. They had made him feel welcomed and at home.

"I smell coffee." He walked into their spacious kitchen smiling. Kira was busy making pancakes and frying bacon. Brad was in the shower and the kids were still sleeping.

"Hope you're hungry this morning. I have a boatload of pancakes here. I think I got carried away." She placed two more steaming pancakes on top of the already mountainous stack. "I wanted to make sure I had enough to feed two grown men. Brad can put down some pancakes."

She eyed Michael as he poured himself a mug of coffee. "How are you this morning?"

"I'm good. Ready to get this sale over with, I guess. It's kinda bittersweet. That's the last place I ever held my baby girl, ya know? But, then again, I don't have to be continually reminded of my own stupid negligence and loss by looking out at that pool every day." Michael sat on a bar stool watching her cook breakfast while sipping on his coffee.

Kira heard the voice of God in her spirit. "*Now!*"

"Michael, I have something for you." She went on to explain how God had given her the word and how she'd written it down verbatim, just as He'd spoken it to her. "I've never received anything like this from God before, but I know it came from Him. It was like hearing a voice recorder in my spirit. I knew I wasn't making it up. If you'll watch these pancakes for me, I'll run and get it. It's in my Bible. I was waiting for the right time to give it to you."

Michael walked from around the bar to take her place at the griddle while she ran off into her bedroom. She reentered the kitchen holding out the folded piece of paper toward him.

"I'm going to take my coffee out by the pool and read it there, if that's okay?"

"Of course it's okay." She handed him a plate of pancakes. "You might as well take these with you too. The syrup and butter are on the counter. You can fix them however you like."

After smothering his pancakes with butter and syrup and adding a little coffee to his mug, Michael went outside to sit at the table beside Brad and Kira's pool. A large turquoise umbrella shaded the patio table from the already searing Texas sun. It took only seconds for beads of sweat to build on his forehead and neck though he barely noticed.

Hope rose up within him as he read and then reread the page. He received the words written by Kira's hand as if his Creator had stood before him and spoken them Himself. God's promise to him was that not only would he have children again but also for open doors for ministry.

He whispered into the unseen realm. "Will my children come from Zoe? Father, I desire her to be the mother of my children. I want to spend my life with her. I can't imagine a future without her in it."

"*Surrender.*"

The word popped into his spirit so quickly; he knew it was not his own thought.

"Okay. I hear you, Lord. I know I need to work on that. I'm trying. I know I lay her down on Your altar only to pick her back up again. I'm sorry. I surrender Zoe to You. I pray Your will be done, and for Your kingdom to come in my life. Whatever You have planned for me is for my good, and I will trust You."

Michael laid the paper on the table just as Brad walked out to join him.

"Mind if I join you?" Brad didn't wait for an answer.

"Well, it's your house, and since you're already pulling out your chair…I guess I have no choice." He smiled at his friend.

Michael read the paper to Brad as the two ate their breakfast.

"Pretty cool word, huh?"

"It sounds to me like God has an awesome plan for your life. Do you think He means that you'll have children from Zoe?"

"I hope so. I prayed about that. God's still been dealing with me about surrendering Zoe to Him. I find that I lay her in His hands only to pick her back up again. Man, it's hard! I want to stand for my marriage, but I'm still supposed to trust in God's ultimate plan for me."

Brad leaned back in his chair and tossed his napkin on the now empty plate. "First Peter 5:6–7 says, 'Therefore humble yourselves under the mighty hand of God, that He may exalt you in due time, casting all your care upon Him, for He cares for you.' To surrender is an act of humility and demonstrates to God that we trust in His ability to meet our need. We know we truly trust in

His love and care for us when we are willing to cast all of our care on Him."

He tilted his head to glance at Michael. "I certainly believe the word Kira gave you comes from the heart of God, but I would still put it on a shelf and ask God to confirm it and bring it to pass in His timing. One of the biggest mistakes we make when we receive a promise like that from God is to expect that it's going to happen right away. When our expectations go unfulfilled, we tend to lose faith and give up. But if our heart is surrendered, we can put the ball back in God's court, so to speak, and trust the One who spoke it to bring it to pass in His timing."

"Yea, you're right. I wish God, and I wore the same watch."

They spent the rest of their time making plans for Brad to be at the new apartment to meet the movers at noon in case his closing went longer than expected.

"I can't tell you how much I appreciate yours and Kira's help and hospitality. It's meant a lot to me." Michael took his last bite of pancake.

"No problem, bro! You know I'd do anything for you. I'm so glad we could help out. That's what friends are for. I know you'd have done the same for me." Brad stood and gathered their breakfast dishes.

"Well, I hope one day I can be half the blessing to someone else that you guys have been to me."

"Do you have to leave so soon, darling? You just got back, and the girls have been missing you terribly." Adele held onto Zach tightly as they waited on the curb for a taxi. He had a suitcase by his side that would never be unpacked. The closet in his Houston apartment was full of all the clothes he needed when in town. It was a merely prop to make his ruse seem believable to his wife of nearly five years. He could not risk her seeing lipstick stains or smelling another woman's perfume on his clothes.

"Sweetheart, you know I do this for you and the girls. I hate being away too, but I've got to fly out when they call me. I don't get to dictate my own schedule. I'm just thankful that I've had a few days off with my girls. I'll call you every chance I get. I'll miss you. You make this so difficult on me every time I fly out. How do you think that makes me feel?"

"I'm sorry, darling. It's just that I feel like a single mom sometimes, and I miss you so much when you are gone. You know I hate sleeping by myself."

A cab pulled up to the curb, and he opened the door and tossed in his suitcase before turning to kiss his wife tenderly on the lips. "So do I. I love you. I'll call you as soon as I can. Take care of my girls for me."

"Bye, darling." She blew him a kiss as the cab pulled away from the curb.

After giving the taxi driver his destination, he waved good-bye, promptly picked up his cell phone, and dialed the number he'd been waiting anxiously to call.

"Pointer, Richards and Brighten Law Associates, this is Zoe how can I help you?"

"Hey, beautiful. I've missed your voice. I've been thinking about you a lot." Zach relaxed in the seat as the cab headed toward the airport.

Her heart skipped a beat even though she did little to hide the anger in her voice. "Zach, you've been gone for almost a week, and I've hardly heard from you! Where are you?"

"Well, I'm on my way to the airport right now. I'm flying home and hoping to have dinner tonight with the sexiest, most beautiful woman I know. I thought I'd better take you out so that we don't set your place on fire again. How about I pick you up at seven?" He disregarded the anger he detected in her voice.

She tried to play hard to get. "I don't know. What if I told you I had plans tonight with someone else since you've been ignoring me?"

"I would never ignore you, Zoe. I've texted you every chance I could. Besides, you are way too beautiful to ignore. I can't wait to hold you in my arms. Seven?" He was cocky, and she fell for it.

"Okay. I'm gonna cut you some slack, but you'd better have a good reason for not calling me. And you'd better not be going out of town tomorrow." She was giddy with anticipation of being in his arms again. "Do you hear me, Zachary Thomas?"

"Oh, yes, ma'am! I think I'm scheduled to be in town most of this week. Um…I just checked my schedule. I'm not scheduled to fly out again until Thursday or Friday. I'll be working from my apartment. So we can spend some time together. How's that sound?"

"Great! I'll see you tonight at seven."

A smug smile enveloped his face as he hung up the phone. The thought of seeing Zoe made the difficulty of juggling two lives worth the trouble and risk.

"One of the biggest mistakes we make when we receive a promise like that from God is to expect that it's going to happen right away. When our expectations go unfulfilled, we tend to lose faith and give up."

17

And forgive us our debts, as we forgive our debtors.
—Matthew 6:12

Grandma Abby dialed her granddaughter's cell number from the old rotary dial phone hanging like a testament of times gone by on her kitchen wall. She was not one to worry, but concern filled her heart for Zoe since she'd not heard from her in almost two weeks. She missed the days when her only granddaughter, young, energetic, and desperately needing a mother's love had often begged to hang out at her house. They'd spent many hours picking fresh berries along the back fence behind her house and transforming them into the best jam in Austin County. She remembered how a young Zoe loved to work in the vegetable garden with her during the long, hot Texas summers, never complaining as she weeded or picked the ripened vegetables. And even though she often complained that her church was old and boring, she loved the Sunday school and Vacation Bible School, even opting to be a helper once she'd outgrown the program.

Before Emma's death, Zoe would bring the baby out at least twice a month so she could bond with her great grandma. Oh, how she missed those days. Though Amos and Barbara tried to visit as often as possible, she was lonesome for her granddaughter.

"Little Emma's death changed everything, Lord. I don't mean to complain, and I know You see the big picture, but it's hard to rejoice in this trial. I miss my Zoe." She often spoke to the Lord as if He were standing beside her.

"Hi, Grandma!" Zoe was embarrassed that her grandma had not even crossed her mind in days. "How are you? I'm sorry I haven't called or been out to see you lately, but my new job has been keeping me very busy." It was a lie, but she didn't want her Grandma to think she didn't care for her. Grandma Abby was one of her favorite people and her connection to her mom's past.

"Hello, my dear. I haven't heard from you, and I've been thinking about and praying for you and Michael. I wanted to see how you're doing."

Zoe cringed at the mention of prayer and Michael in the same sentence. "I'm doing okay, Grandma. I still have those nightmares I told you about. You know, I dream that I'm looking for Emma and can't find her. Or I dream that she's crying out for me, and I can't get to her in time. I always wake up in tears and stressed out. But other than that…I guess I'm okay. I like my new job. Remember I told you I went to work for Daddy's company?"

"Zoe, I may be in my seventies, but there's nothing wrong with my memory. How's Michael?"

"Sorry, Grandma. I couldn't remember how much I've told you. It's probably me with the memory problem. Umm…Michael sold the house. That's great news. We have agreed to split the proceeds. I think he's moved into an apartment. We haven't talked much beyond that."

"Oh, dear, I'm so sorry to hear that. Zoe, Michael is a good, godly man and those are hard to come by. This old lady doesn't know much, but I do know most men these days don't know how to love and respect a woman like he does. Why are you running from him when the two of you desperately need each other right now?"

"Grandma, I've told you before I just don't want to talk about it. No offense, but it's my life. I just can't get over the fact that he let Emma drown. He should have been paying better attention to her. He was supposed to be watching her. I can't forgive him for that."

"You can't or you won't? Zoe, you're still holding onto grudges!" Though she knew she was pressing an issue that might cause a breach between them, she boldly continued. "You've nurtured your hatred toward Barbara all these years, and now you're going to turn on the one man who truly loves you, because of your unwillingness to forgive. It breaks my heart. Your father told me you're mad at him right now too. Honey, you're going to have to learn to forgive and forget. Christ forgave you when He hung on that cross for your sins. Or are you mad at Him too? You know the Lord's Prayer says we are to forgive as Christ has so graciously forgiven us."

Zoe rolled her eyes and tried to change the subject. "When are you going to come see my new apartment? You'd love the view of downtown. I could come get you and bring you here on a Sunday afternoon. We could have lunch. How's that sound?" She loved her Grandma, but she wasn't about to let her preach to her or judge her actions. It was her life, and she'd live it the way she darn well pleased.

"My dear girl, I go to church on Sundays. Have you forgotten? You used to love to go to church, remember?"

"Grandma, please drop it." Zoe could no longer hold in her frustration. "I love you dearly, but I'm not going to discuss my private life with you, Daddy, or anyone else. I'm old enough to make my own decisions. Listen, I have to go. But I'll call you, and we can get together for lunch. Okay?"

"Zoe, I'll just say this before I hang up. You may not have taken it seriously when you asked Jesus into your heart as a young girl. But God did. He marked you as His. One way or another, I have no doubt that He'll woo you back. You can run from Him, but you cannot run far or forever. Please, dear, remember that He loves you and has a good plan for your life."

"Okay, Grandma. Listen, I've got to go. Love you." She was shaking with anger as she hung up the phone. She couldn't put her finger on exactly what had fueled the fire raging inside of her. Maybe deep down inside she knew her Grandma was right. She was running from God.

Well, God, You had your chance with me, and You blew it. She wiped away the fresh tears that stung her eyes.

"Hey, ya wanna go to lunch?" LaDonna asked as she leaned against Zoe's desk.

"No, I can't. I'm going out with Zach tonight. Besides, girl, I have gained weight. My waist is expanding from going out so often. If I don't slow down, I'm gonna have to buy new clothes."

LaDonna leaned over the desk to get a good look at Zoe. "Girl, where do you think you gained weight? In your big toe?"

"I'm serious. My scale says I've gained two pounds. I can't afford to gain weight. I think I'm gonna grab a salad from the café downstairs and eat in the breakroom today. You care to join me?"

"Honey, you know I don't do salads, and I certainly don't do skinny. I have to have me some meat and potatoes to keep this body lookin' good." She moved her hands in an exaggerated motion down her body in mock accentuation of her curvaceous figure. They both giggled. "So where are you and Zach going tonight? Did you find out why he hasn't called?"

"No, he said he's just been busy. I believe him. He says when he's in the air he can't just pick up his phone and call me. I'm not sure where he's taking me. What should I wear?"

LaDonna raised her eyelids as if to question Zoe's judgment. "Well, I don't know that I'd trust a guy who slept with me and then didn't call for almost a week. Girl, he better be callin' and courtin' if he wants some more of this!"

"He texted me several times." Zoe felt the need to defend Zach.

"Hmm…" LaDonna turned and walked away, her hips swinging behind her.

I guess I have to defend myself to everyone today. She was still stinging from her conversation with her Grandma.

Ramiah stood by Zoe's side. Working in conjunction with Ozias, he was hoping to get her into the break room at lunchtime to have another encounter with Carol Tatum. The Almighty deemed her instrumental in making sure Zoe fulfilled her destiny. Though her grandma had planted seeds during their phone call that morning, the Holy Spirit wanted to be sure they were watered and made fertile so they could grow and bear fruit in her life. It was becoming increasingly difficult to get his charge to follow his leading at all since gross darkness was blinding her eyes and deafening her ears.

He was glad when he realized she'd taken the thought he'd spoken into her spirit and claimed it as her own.

Zoe sat at a large round table in the break room, munching on a salad while glancing through the Facebook news feed on her iPad.

"Hi, mind if I join you?" Carol Tatum, all smiles, entered the room. "I usually have the room all to myself. It's nice to have some company."

Zoe noticed she had a Bible under her left arm while she carried a brown bag in one hand and a diet soda in the other. She placed them on the table before Zoe could protest.

"Umm…sure." Zoe pulled her iPad, salad, and water closer as if the girl might contaminate her things by looking at them. She pretended to be deeply engrossed in her iPad, hoping to avoid any conversation with Carol.

Carol opened her well-worn Bible to a bookmarked page and began to read silently. Zoe searched her mind thinking of excuses she could make to leave. The open Bible made her uncomfortable.

Carol sensed her discomfort. "I hope you don't mind if I sit here and read?"

"Ugh, no. Actually, I…I'm a Christian too."

"Really?" Carol acted genuinely surprised. "That's awesome. What church do you go to?"

Looking stunned, Zoe immediately regretted her former statement. *I'm an idiot for engaging this girl in conversation.* "Well, I don't go to church right now…I used to go all the time though." She knew she'd already said too much and could tell that Carol, who'd temporarily shut her Bible, was ready to talk.

"Oh." Carol felt a strong prompting by the Holy Spirit to share how she'd come to faith in Christ. "I used to be lost as a goose. No one around here would believe it, but I was a pothead, and my husband and I were major partiers. We met in a bar of all places. Neither one of us came from a church background. I didn't even know what it meant to be saved." She talked with ease as she relayed her testimony. "We had an adorable son named Jacob. He was the love of my life. One night I got distracted cleaning up his room while he was in the bathtub, and he drowned. I have to admit; I was probably high as a kite. As I know you can probably relate, I was devastated. I had horrible nightmares every night. I'd dream that I was going to check on him because I could hear him crying, but when I'd go to look, he wasn't in the tub, and I couldn't find him. The dreams haunted me for months. I'd wake up sweating, and my pillow would be wet with tears."

Zoe looked as if she'd seen a ghost. She wanted to escape this girl's story but was somehow drawn into it. She was shocked to learn that this strange girl had experienced the loss of her child by drowning, followed by the similarly horrific nightmares she herself had been enduring. She listened quietly without showing any emotion.

Carol interpreted Zoe's silence as permission to continue her story. "My neighbor, who was at the scene to help when the ambulance arrived, was what some refer to as a holy roller. She'd tried several times to witness to me before the accident, and, I hate to say it, but I wasn't very nice to her."

Zoe's eyebrows rose as a slight smile flashed across her face.

"Oh, I know, that's what people call me." She waved her hand in the air as if the thought didn't bother her. "Anyway, after the accident, my neighbor became my rock and a constant source of encouragement to me. She invited my husband and me to her church more times than I can count. She wouldn't give up on us. Finally, we were so desperate for peace and healing from our constant grief that we decided to accompany her a couple of months after Jacob's death. That was five and a half years ago. It's all history from there. I fell in love with Christ, and He radically changed my life. He forgave me of my sins and didn't condemn me for the death of my son. He totally washed away my guilt. He's done so much for me that I can't help but want to serve Him and be a witness for Him."

Zoe stared in disbelief. This woman's story was so eerily similar to hers except her loss had led her to Christ while Zoe's had driven her away from Him.

"Did you and your husband stay together?"

"Yea, we have a beautiful little three-year-old named Olivia, and I recently found out I'm pregnant with twins."

"Oh, wow!" Zoe couldn't help but like this girl. She found her to be warm and friendly. "I'm very happy for you. My daughter drowned too. My husband was supposed to be watching her, but he left our back door open. He thought she was asleep while he was on the phone in his office. She wandered outside, probably looking for him, and drowned in our backyard pool." Zoe was caught off guard by the tears that flowed effortlessly down her cheeks. "I'm sorry." She apologized as she wiped them away with a swipe of her hand.

"Oh, don't be sorry. You're still grieving the loss of your baby. It has taken me years to get to the place where I can talk about Jacob without bawling. So are you and your husband still together?"

"No! I still blame him, and...well, I can't forgive him. I find it impossible to even be in the same room with him. I'm filing for divorce."

Zoe scanned Carol's face expecting to see judgment in her eyes, however, she exuded nothing but heartfelt compassion and sympathy for Zoe.

"Do you mind if I pray for you?" She stretched her hand across the table to grab Zoe's.

As if waking from a dream, Zoe snatched her hand away from Carol's, gathered up her things, and stood to leave.

"Thanks for sharing with me, but I really need to go. I…I'm sorry."

Carol watched Zoe leave the breakroom before bowing her head to pray.

Zach showed up at Zoe's door promptly at seven with two dozen of her favorite pink roses in hand. He pulled her toward him as soon as she opened the door, kissing her passionately before holding her at arm's length. "I've missed you. You look beautiful. If I weren't starving, I'd be tempted to stay here, take your clothes off, and make mad passionate love to you."

"Well, since it took me an hour to figure out what I was going to wear, you're definitely taking me to dinner, Zachary Thomas. Besides, I'm starving too."

He took her to The Americana, an expensive restaurant in the downtown district where they were led to a secluded booth. She was sure he'd tipped the maitre d' generously to secure their privacy.

Seated almost on top of each other, Zach talked about how busy his week had been with constant travel. He suddenly realized he didn't have her full attention. "Earth to Zoe, are you paying attention to me? You look like you are a thousand miles away."

"Oh, sorry. Yea, I'm listening. I heard everything you said." However, in truth, she'd been thinking about the conversation she'd had with Carol earlier that day. She couldn't get the girl's story out of her mind. It was uncanny that it was so similar to hers. Yet, Carol seemed to be so happy.

"You've hardly touched your food. I thought you were starving? Is something or someone else on your mind?"

"Nope, just you." She kissed him. "I'd like another glass of wine if that's okay." *Maybe another glass of wine will get Carol's story off my mind.*

"I have a better idea. I'm going to order a bottle to go. We'll take it to your place. I can get you drunk and take advantage of you. How's that sound?" His eyes twinkled mischievously.

She grabbed the collar of his polo shirt and pulled his face close to hers. "First off, you don't have to get me drunk to take advantage of me. Second." She kissed him as she pressed her body provocatively close to his.

Afterward, he raised his hand to gesture for the waiter. "Check please, right away." They both laughed with expectation of the night ahead.

A night of wild passionate love with this man will help me forget all of my cares. She clung to him as they walked arm in arm to his waiting car.

There was a hush throughout the congregation as Pastor Steve made the announcement that Sunday morning. You could have heard a pin drop in the packed sanctuary as he told the church of the indiscretion of one of their staff members.

"It is with great sorrow that I have to inform you we've had to ask Donovan Scott to resign as our youth pastor effective immediately. As many of you may have already heard, Donovan has been accused and arrested for child molestation of one of the precious young girls in our youth. To say I'm grieved over this matter would be an understatement. I'm not at liberty to give out details because there is an ongoing investigation by the police. Nor do we want to bring further damage to this young lady by exposing her name, but I would ask that you keep her and her family in your prayers. God knows who she is. I'm sure it will probably come out through the media and rumor mill, but for now, I think it would be best to allow her and her family privacy as they deal with this horrific incident. I'd also ask you to keep Donovan and his family in your prayers. He is still our brother in Christ, and I don't believe this is the time to throw stones, gossip, or alienate him. I've told him and Theresa that they are still welcome in this church though he is not allowed to work or serve in any capacity. We are all subject to temptations of the enemy, and, therefore, we need to extend grace and love instead of shooting our wounded. I believe this is a test to see how we as a church body respond toward those who fall in our midst. Are we going to help them back up and pray for their restoration, or are we going to throw stones? I trust you will commit yourselves to prayer in this matter, walk in love, and forgive even as Christ has forgiven you of your sins."

Michael was as stunned as the rest of the church. He had wondered why Donovan hadn't been at the meeting on Wednesday and why it had been Pastor Steve who had called to ask him to lead the youth group that night. *How could this happen to someone who seemed so on fire for God?* His thoughts turned to Donovan's wife and how devastated she must be. His heart suddenly broke for the couple. He prayed silently for both of them as well as the young girl involved. He prayed for the church and that they would recover from this devastating news. He also prayed for those visiting the church for the first time that day and asked God to allow them to hear the love in Pastor Steve's heart for his body. And, despite this news, that somehow they'd still hear the good news of the Gospel as the sermon was preached. He thanked God for Pastor Steve and that he was not a man who would try and hide or cover up this ugly stain or revel in exposing the sin of one of his members. He knew his pastor would be grieving and praying for Donovan's complete restoration just as much as he would be praying for the soul wounds of this young girl to be healed.

After the service, Pastor Steve grabbed him by the arm just as he was heading down the aisle to leave. "I have some things to finish up here, but I need to talk with you. Would you be available to go to lunch with Marcie and me today? It'll be my treat."

"Sure, I'd love to. You know I can't resist a free meal." Michael tried to be lighthearted, hoping to ease the tension he knew his pastor was experiencing.

They agreed to meet at a nearby restaurant and that he'd go on ahead and reserve a table while Pastor Steve finished closing up the church.

The angelic host assigned to guard and protect New Zion Fellowship filled the sanctuary. Gleaming swords darted left and right to ward off vicious attacks of devious spirits desperately wanting to plant seeds of distrust and accusation into the hearts of the worshippers.

Beelzebub had assumed that victory was undisputedly secure when he'd successfully enticed the youth pastor to fall headlong into the clutches of Lust. He'd hoped to not only destroy the young man, his marriage, and ministry but also his victim, sending her into depths of shame and depression that would follow her for years to come. But his greatest desire was to see the church fall.

He hadn't planned, however, on the pastor being so forthcoming with his congregation and loving toward one of his black sheep. No, knowing mankind the way he did, he'd assumed he would try to cover up the matter and quietly kick the villain out on his heels.

He had sent one of his most trusted servants, Bithron, well known for living up to his name, which means divisions, to head up the attack. He'd given him specific orders: use Gossip, Backbiting, Murmuring and Complaining to wear down the saints of New Zion Fellowship when this sin is exposed and sow mistrust of the pastor into the hearts of his parishioners.

What he hadn't counted on was the pastor being a man of great integrity and faith, given to mercy and compassion, leading the church into a time of intercession for the perpetrator and his victim. He cringed as they cried out for the complete restoration of the young man and healing for the young girl he'd molested. And to make matters worse, after they'd spent time in prayer that morning, they penetrated his kingdom of darkness giving angels even more power to defend against his forces as they wholeheartedly dived into triumphant worship of Jehovah singing songs of deliverance and victory.

Bithron called his troops to retreat before leaving the battle with his tail tucked between his legs, his pride severely damaged, and licking his wounds like a dog beaten by a sly cat.

Michael could see the pain etched on his pastor's face as he and his wife approached the table. Being the good shepherd that he was, Michael knew Steve would be hurting immensely for his flock, especially for the one that had gone astray and those deeply wounded by his transgressions.

"That was pretty heavy today, huh?" Pastor Steve sat down across from Michael.

"Well, I certainly didn't see it coming. It's pretty unbelievable. I've had a few problems with Donovan in the past, and Zoe didn't like him at all, but I would have never in a million years imagined that he would sexually abuse one of our youth. I feel for Theresa. She must be devastated."

"Yes, it's all pretty devastating. We've been so grieved over this." Marcie wiped tears from her eyes. "All I can think about is that poor young girl. I pray this incident doesn't turn her heart away from Christ. Donovan claims the girl came onto him and that the affair was mutual, but he should have known better. She's only fifteen. The parents are, understandably, wanting to see him imprisoned and labeled a child molester for the rest of his life. It's unbelievable how so many lives can be affected by the sin of one individual."

Pastor Steve tenderly patted his wife's hand. "God will turn this around for good. I believe the enemy gave it his best shot, but God will see that we grow stronger as a body, and as long as we walk in faith and love, we'll see restoration. But the key is to walk in love. We have to love these hurting parents who are angry with Donovan, as well as the church. We need to reach out to them and offer whatever help we can. But we must also reach out to Donovan and Theresa and make sure they know we still love them."

Their conversation was interrupted as their waiter came to take their orders. Pastor Steve resumed the conversation once the young man had left the table.

"Michael, I've been spending a lot of time in fasting and prayer since this matter was brought to my attention. God has shown me that you are to take over as our youth pastor. I'm asking you to come on staff full-time. I know I can't possibly pay you what you've been making as a programmer, but I know you've been called into ministry, and it's been the desire of your heart for a long time."

Michael looked at his pastor in disbelief. "I don't know what to say. I…"

"I know you think it's the wrong time because of your separation from Zoe and you're still dealing with the loss of Emma. However, I think it will be a great opportunity for you to move forward into your call, and it might help you to keep your focus on Christ as you walk through this difficult season."

Pastor Steve took a drink of iced tea before continuing. "Now more than ever, we need someone we can trust to nurture this youth group back to health. I'm sure we're going to lose quite a few of our kids because of this ordeal with Donovan. We need someone our parents can trust."

"Everyone adores you. We believe they'll trust you too." Marcie smiled convincingly at Michael.

"I'll need to pray about it. I know God has called me to ministry, but I just don't know if I'm ready. I mean…my life is a mess. I'm not sure that I feel equipped right now."

"You'll never do anything for God if you wait until you feel ready. It's when we feel incapable that we are in the best position for God to use us. You've heard the saying, 'God doesn't call the equipped. He equips the called.' There's a lot of truth to that. God isn't looking at your ability. He's looking at your heart and your desire to serve Him with your life. He simply needs a willing vessel, not one whose life is in perfect order."

"I'm honored that you would ask me. Can I pray about it and get back to you later this week? I'd like to talk to my dad about it too if that's okay."

Pastor Steve assured him that there was no one better suited for the position. "We'll be praying too." He chuckled. "But while you're praying, can you lead the group again Wednesday night?"

Michael nodded. "Sure, that'll be fine."

18

"Dad, I've been praying for ministry doors to open for so long, but it doesn't make sense to me that God would open the door when my life is so messed up. Do you think I'm ready for this?" Michael sat across from his father in his parent's kitchen.

"Son, remember the story of Moses. He murdered a man, was fearful, and had a stutter, but God saw a leader in him and chose to use him to deliver the Israelites out of Egypt. There are many examples of people in the Bible that God called into service whose lives were less than what we'd deem to be perfect. Look at the Apostle Paul. He was a murderer of Christians when God called him to bring the Gospel to the Gentiles. Peter denied Christ, yet God used him mightily to build His church. Man looks at the outward appearance, but God looks on the heart. You are looking at your external circumstances, but you don't see the whole picture. God knows you right down to every hair on your head. If He says you're ready, then I believe you are ready."

Daniel paused to take a bite before continuing. "It's because you feel inadequate that I believe it's most definitely God opening the door. In

Second Corinthians 12:9, God says, 'My grace is sufficient for you, for My strength is made perfect in weakness.' It's when we are weak that God's grace is manifested in our lives, making us able to do what He has called us to do despite our ability or circumstances. Son, you need to accept this position with the full assurance that God has opened the door for you and will equip you."

"Okay, I think I will. I'm going to call Pastor Steve in the morning and accept the job." A smile stretched across his face as he looked from his dad to his mom. "You guys have been such a blessing to me. I don't know what I would have done without you in my life. I want you to know how much I love and appreciate you."

"We are proud of you. You've been through so much, and yet you're still seeking after God with all of your heart." Shara stood, walked around the table and wrapped her arms around her son's neck.

"Okay, okay, enough with the mushy stuff." Pride and joy filled Daniel's heart though he pretended to be put out by his wife's display of emotion. "Let's have some pie and ice cream. My son's going into the ministry, and we need to celebrate."

Michael laughed as he squeezed his mom tightly. "Well, at least he didn't tell you to kill the fatted calf."

That night sleep evaded Michael. A long, arduous battle for Michael's destiny was mounted. The enemy bombarded his mind with thoughts of inadequacy, fear of failure, and doubt. Knowing that his best work is done under the cloak of darkness, the enemy sought to use the nighttime, when Michael should have been resting and being refreshed, to wear him down. It wasn't that he was afraid of Michael taking a ministry position. The previous youth minister had allowed pride and the illusion of power to take control and had, in the process, destroyed his witness. No, he didn't fear position. But what he did fear was Michael walking in obedience, full of faith and discovering the complete truth of who he is in Christ, and turning the battle toward his kingdom of darkness. So he sent his best liars to deceive him.

"Your life is a failure. How can you possibly think you have anything to offer those kids?"

"Why would God call you into ministry? You weren't even responsible enough to

take care of your own baby, much less a group of over seventy teenagers."

"Just because your father is a preacher doesn't mean you'll be any good at it."

"What if Pastor Steve and your father were wrong and you're not ready?"

"You'll never make enough money in the ministry. How will you win Zoe back on a minister's salary? You know how important money is to her. She'll never come back when she realizes that you've changed professions."

"How will you come up with a sermon every week for those kids? Do you know how difficult that will be?"

"It doesn't matter what you do. Zoe will never come back anyway."

"What if you fail? Donovan was funny, and the kids loved his sermons. What if you're boring? What if…what if…what if?"

One by one the negative thoughts assaulted his mind all night long. Michael tossed and turned and wrestled with the enemy praying for sleep that persistently eluded him. As soon as he would cast down one negative thought, two more would ambush his mind. By midmorning, he was mentally and physically exhausted.

He sat up in bed and turned on the bedside lamp. "God, help me!" By now it was nearly four in the morning.

Deuel heard the Holy Spirit speak into the spirit realm where truth speaks louder than the lies of the enemy.

"My grace is sufficient for you, for My strength is made perfect in weakness."

Michael suddenly remembered the scripture his dad had spoken the night before. As he began to recite it over and over to himself, he felt strength flooding into his spirit.

Deuel called on several angelic warriors, and they began to do fierce battle in the heavenlies. They violently assaulted the enemy attacking his charge.

Once again, the Spirit encouraged Michael. *"So do not fear, for I am with you; do not be dismayed, for I am your God. I will strengthen you and help you; I will uphold you with my righteous right hand."*

Michael grabbed his Bible, searched his concordance, and found the passage in Isaiah 41:10. He read the scripture out loud and boldly began to pray against the spirit of fear.

If he could have seen into the spirit realm, he would have witnessed the disappointment on Satan's face at the realization of another failed attempt against God's anointed. He would have seen demons being put to flight as valiant warriors battled on his behalf.

The Holy Spirit, directed by the Father, continued to empower Michael's spirit. *"You did not choose Me, but I chose you and appointed you so that you might go and bear fruit—fruit that will last—and so that whatever you ask in My name the Father will give you."*

Michael didn't have to look the scripture up. He knew it was located in John 15:16. God had spoken the scripture to him as a young teenager when he'd first heard the call into ministry. It was a scripture he'd quoted back to God many times when praying for a future ministry position. After nearly an hour of waiting before the Lord, listening for His voice and receiving His truth, a peace and reassurance came over him. He gave thanks to the Lord before turning out the light and falling into a deep, restful sleep.

The next morning, Michael knelt beside the desk in his apartment with his head bowed. "Father, I believe it's Your will for me to step into this ministry position. You know my heart is more than willing to serve You. I only ask that You would give me a pastor's heart for these kids like that of my father and Pastor Steve. Help me to encourage them and use me to bring healing to our youth group. Give me wisdom and anoint me to be the leader they need. I surrender my life to You. If You desire to use it in spite of my faults and failures, here I am. My greatest desire is to serve You and Your body. In Jesus's name."

After his prayer, he called Pastor Steve to tell him that he would accept the position. Excitement filled his spirit at the thought of stepping into the destiny God had for him. *True, I've always wanted to pastor a church, but you've got to start somewhere.* He knew better than to despise the day of small beginnings.

"Excellent!" Pastor Steve, seated at his office desk, raised his hands in thanks to the Lord. He was convinced that Michael was exactly who the youth needed and a man the congregation could trust with their children.

"I'm excited! I have a few programming jobs I'll need to finish up here, but I think I can do it within a week or so." He felt hope flooding his spirit for the first time in a long time.

"Well, feel free to go ahead and get situated in your office here. I want you to know how proud I am of you, Michael. I know you'll be an excellent youth pastor. I've seen how the youth look up to you and how they've surrounded you during this season of trial. They love you, and they'll listen to you."

After their conversation, Michael began to pour himself into studying for the message he'd deliver that night to his youth group.

Michael found his way to the table where Brad was seated munching on chips and salsa. "Hey, thanks for meeting me."

Brad stood to greet him, and they exchanged a half-hug handshake. "You know me. I'll use any excuse I can to eat me some good Mexican food."

"I want to go over my first message with you. I need you to be honest and tell me what you think."

"No worries, bro, I'll be brutally honest. You're not nervous about teaching a bunch of teenagers are you?" Brad teased as he studied the menu.

"Yea, of course, I am! My message is going to touch on Donovan and what he did, and I want to be sure I'm handling it just right. I think it's important to address it with the kids instead of just sweeping it under the rug."

"That was pretty ugly, huh? I mean, dude, the guy messed around with a kid that was half his age. I can't believe he would risk his marriage, his ministry, and most of all, his witness like that. If I were that girl's father, I'd probably beat the you-know-what out of him."

Michael could hear the disgust in Brad's voice and chose his words carefully so as not to offend his friend. "I know Donovan could be obnoxious and prideful, and he took advantage of me on more than one occasion, but he's still a child of God, and as difficult as it is, I don't think we should be judging him. I'm not taking up for what he did. Trust me. I think the guy must be sick to molest a young girl. But I also know that God still loves him and extends grace to him as hard as that is for us to conceive. What I needed when I felt so guilty about Emma's drowning was grace. Someone to tell me…it's gonna be okay. God can turn it around. I think we need to pray for God's mercy and grace to completely restore Donovan."

"Oh, man, you already sound like Pastor Steve, and you're making me feel like I'm the one who's lost. I guess I'll have to start calling you Pastor Michael." Though he tried to make light of the conversation, Brad knew the Holy Spirit was speaking to him through his friend. "Or I could call you Saint Michael.

That sounds better."

"Whatever! Are you gonna listen to my message, or do I have to find someone else to preach to? Preferably someone who's a little more spiritual?"

"Okay, okay, I'm listening. I just figure if I act up like the youth, it will help you be better prepared. Preach on!"

Michael took out his notes and began sharing the heart of his message with Brad. "I'm going to be talking about the choices we make, both good and bad, and how they can affect everyone around us. My main scripture is Deuteronomy 30:19. 'I call heaven and earth as witnesses today against you, that I have set before you life and death, blessing and cursing; therefore choose life, that both you and your descendants may live.' I plan on using the example of Donovan's mistake and bringing out the fact that he had a choice, and unfortunately, his choice led to death instead of life. This young girl lost her innocence and possibly the trust of men in authority. He'll probably lose his freedom by having to spend time in prison and maybe even his marriage, and the church has suffered through his sin as well. On the other hand, I'm going to bring in the story of Joseph in Genesis 39 where it talks about how his master's wife tried to tempt him into having an affair with her, but he refused. His choice eventually brought life for his family when they were able to come to Egypt for food during the years of famine."

He paused and looked up at Brad. "How does that sound so far?"

"So far, so good." Brad motioned for Michael to continue.

"I'm also going to use the story of Joseph and how he extended grace and mercy to his brothers even though they were the ones who sold him into slavery. I plan on sharing with them that we will all sin and make mistakes in our walk with the Lord, and at some point in time, we may be the one in desperate need of mercy and grace. I thought I'd end it with a time of worship where anyone who wants can come up to the front and pray for Donovan, his family, the young girl or the church. What do you think?"

"I think it sounds awesome. I especially like the fact that you want to give the kids a chance to pray for Donovan. I think it will help usher in forgiveness and healing to our youth. I'll be praying for you tonight, but I know it's going to be great."

"Thanks. I appreciate you listening."

They ended their time together praying for the youth meeting, Donovan and his family and, as always, for Zoe.

Zoe's cell phone rang as she walked briskly through a department store. None of her friends had been available for lunch, and she didn't want to risk running into Carol in the breakroom, so she was out shopping on her lunch hour. She couldn't help but smile as she immediately recognized the familiar ring. Having recently put Zach on her favorites list, she'd set his ringtone to be the summer's most popular hit, "Call Me Maybe" by Carly Rae Jepsen.

"Hey! I didn't expect a call from you. Didn't we say good-bye this morning?" She blushed as she thought back to the time they'd spent making love that morning before departing each other's company.

"Umm, we sure did, and it was very nice." Though she believed he was taking a group of business executives to a trade show in New Orleans, he had failed to mention that he would be flying home afterward to spend time with his wife and daughters. True, the CEO of his company lived in New York, and he flew him to and from New York on a regular basis, but it was also the place of his permanent residence. Of course, Zoe was unaware of that fact. He told her as little as possible about his schedule so as not to get caught in a lie.

"I'm waiting on my passengers to get settled, and my copilot left the cabin for just a second, so I wanted to take a minute to call you and tell you that it's been a wonderful couple of days. I'll miss you. I'll call when I can, but I can't promise anything."

"Okay. I'm so glad you called me. I want you to know, Zach, that you have made the last couple of weeks bearable for me. I mean, you've just helped take my mind off of my grief and the loss of my baby. I don't know what I'd have done if you hadn't shown up at just the right time. You've helped me to move on with my life."

"Oh, so I'm just a distraction?" A twinge of guilt made him uncomfortable when she mentioned her recent loss. He knew at some point that he'd have to give her up since he wasn't willing to leave his wife or his twin daughters. *Just enjoy it while you can. It's not your fault she lost her child.* He soothed his conscience with the knowledge that he was helping her get past her grief.

"No, you're not just a distraction, but you certainly make a good one."

"So, it's Friday night. What are you going to do tonight? I hate the thought of you going out and meeting someone else."

"You don't have to worry about that. I'm going to take it easy and get some sleep tonight. I'm dragging today. Thanks to you."

His copilot walked backed into the cockpit, giving him the signal that it was time to get going. "Hey, I've got to go. I think we're ready to get moving here. I'll call you when I can." Without giving her time to say good-bye, he hung up.

Though it had ended abruptly, the call had uplifted her spirits. She'd been so down knowing he would be gone over the weekend, leaving her all alone once again. A lingering grin lit up her face as she made her way back to the office.

Zach phoned his wife upon his arrival in New York. It was Monday morning, and he'd spent the whole weekend in New Orleans.

"Hey, baby, how's my girl? Guess who's in New York?"

"Zach, you're home?" Adele beamed from ear to ear.

"Yes, I'm only home for a few days though. My boss wanted to fly home to New York, but he plans on flying back to Houston in a couple of days. So how about you and I go out tonight for a romantic dinner? Can you get a sitter for the girls?"

"I'll see what I can do. I'm so excited you're home. We've missed you so much. The girls can't wait to see you." Adele had no idea that her husband had not only been cheating on her with Zoe, but also, during his brief stay in New Orleans, he'd met another woman at a bar and spent the weekend with her.

"Okay. Give me about an hour and a half, and I'll be home. I love you. I've missed you too."

Zoe sat opposite Dane Smith, a popular Houston divorce attorney her father had recommended, though he'd tried once again to talk her out of seeking the divorce. The mere thought of their conversation still conjured up feelings of anger and betrayal. His concern over her getting a divorce had caused a rift in their relationship. She was positive her stepmom was behind his change of heart.

"Zoe, I don't think it's a good idea to go through with this right now. You never know, your feelings for Michael can change. Give it some time. It's only

been three months. For goodness' sake, honey, I just think you are rushing this."
Amos argued when she'd pressed him for an attorney's name and number.

"Daddy, I have feelings for someone else already. Michael and I are over. I've told you, I don't think there's even a remote chance we'll get back together." She was bound and determined to get the divorce out of the way so she could be free to pursue a deeper relationship with Zach. Thoughts of him now occupied her mind night and day. Zach filled such a void in her life left empty by the loss of Emma.

Though he spent quite a bit of time out of town and barely communicated with her when he was gone, she was sure he was crazy about her too. It was as if fireworks went off whenever they were together. Though she had to admit, their relationship was fueled by their undeniable sexual attraction to each other more than anything else; they still shared some common interest.

After giving the attorney a retainer and answering all of his questions, she was promised a relatively quick and straightforward divorce as long as Michael agreed to it. *That might be a problem.* She was sure Michael would put up a fight.

Though he was dismayed that his charge was walking further and further away from the Almighty and down a path of certain destruction and despair, Ramiah wasn't about to give up on her. The Lord of hosts had many humans interceding for her, and though it looked like darkness was prevailing, the Lord always had a way of winning over the darkness.

He wasn't sure what it would take to turn her heart around, but as he'd seen in times past, sometimes the darkest hour came just before the dawn. He was certain of one thing: the Almighty would not let go of her.

A chill went through Zoe's body as she stared at the calendar on the desk. It was a warm Wednesday morning at the beginning of September. Zoe knew the chill that penetrated her bones had nothing to do with the weather, and everything to do with the fear that engulfed her. It had occurred to her that morning while getting dressed for work that she'd not only skipped her monthly cycle; she couldn't remember when she'd last had a period. She'd also been suffering from bouts of nausea, and there was no denying the sudden weight gain in her midsection. That morning she hadn't been able to fit into an outfit she'd worn just two weeks prior.

She could easily think of an excuse for each one of these symptoms. Her body might still be off cycle due to the stress of losing Emma. She wasn't positive, but she didn't think she'd had a period since her death. Her upset stomach, which she'd been experiencing for some time now, was probably the result of mixing wine with the drugs she'd been taking for the last several months. She ate lunch out often with her friends and had been cooking for Zach or going out with him quite a bit when he was in town, which she surmised, could have resulted in the few extra pounds.

Sweat beads broke out on her forehead; panic enveloped her. "Oh, God, please, I can't be pregnant. Not now." It was not so much a whispered prayer as a desperate plea. She made up her mind to go to the drug store after work and purchase a pregnancy test. Zach was coming over for dinner, but she could take it in the morning. Her stomach felt knotted with nerves as she contemplated the possibility of it being positive.

Zach had been in town for a few days, and they were enjoying a happy rhythm of seeing each other whenever possible. She hated it when he was out of town, but she used the time to go out with friends, though she never dated anyone else. And though she was keeping it a secret from Zach, she was diligently working on getting her divorce from Michael so that she could be free for whatever the future might hold.

Ugh, this is not a good time to come up pregnant.

19

Eye has not seen, nor ear heard,
nor have entered into the heart of man
the things which God has prepared for those who love Him.
—*1 Corinthian 2:9*

"I'm flying out of town tomorrow. I'm not sure when I'll be back." Zach and Zoe lingered in Zoe's bed, wrapped in each other's arms. He feared she would be angry but knew he needed to get home to his wife and the girls. He'd promised Adele he wouldn't miss the twin's dance recital that Friday evening.

Surprisingly, Zoe felt a sense of relief at the thought of him leaving. She didn't want him to know she suspected she might be pregnant with his child. And, if the test proved to be positive, she'd have time to figure out exactly what to do about it.

"What, are you ready for me to leave?" Zach was surprised by her lack of protest. He kissed her gently all over her face. "You don't seem to be too upset. Are you as crazy about me as I am about you?"

"Absolutely!" She ran her hand up and down his bare back. "I have a lot going on at work, and I'm going to be busy for the next couple of days. But you'd better not be gone too long. I get lonely when you're not here."

They made love one last time before he got out of her bed to take a shower. She hoped he'd leave in time for her to take the pregnancy test before having to leave for work. She couldn't bear the thought of going through the entire day without knowing for sure.

They enjoyed a cup of coffee together on her balcony before he held her tenderly and kissed her good-bye in the doorway.

The ringing of the phone interrupted Amos's breakfast. It was unusual for the house phone to ring, especially early in the morning. Except for the occasional annoying solicitors, most people contacted him and Barbara on their private cell phones.

"Hello!" He didn't have the patience for solicitor calls this early in the morning.

"Is this Mr. Amos Richards?" The female voice on the other end of the line inquired.

Amos didn't try to hide his annoyance. "Yes, who wants to know?"

"Sir, this is Officer Debra Simpson with the Sealy Police Department. Do you know a Miss Abigail Ruznick? She had your number written above her phone as a number to call in case of an emergency."

Amos suddenly became concerned. "Yes, she's my mother-in-law. Is she all right?"

"No, sir. I'm sorry to inform you that we found her deceased in her house early this morning. A member of her church had asked us to check up on her. She wasn't in church on Sunday morning or Wednesday night, and apparently, she never missed. An officer spotted her body on the floor in the kitchen through her window. We had to break a window in order to gain entrance into the house. We believe she'd been deceased for several days. We have released her body to the local mortuary since we saw no signs of foul play. It looks like she might have had a heart attack or a stroke."

Amos choked back a sob. He dearly loved Abby. She'd been like a mother to him ever since he'd met his first wife. They'd helped each other through the grieving process when Claire had died, and she'd helped him take care of Zoe until he'd met and married Barbara. It was no secret that she'd prayed for him and Barbara when they were going through a difficult season in their marriage. He and Barbara tried to visit her at least two or three times a month. *When was the last time I talked to her?*

"Sir, would you like to write down the name and number of the funeral home?"

"Yes, just one moment. Let me get something to write on." He put the phone down on the kitchen counter while he rummaged through a drawer in search of writing material.

Barbara walked into the kitchen. "Amos, who's on the phone? What are you looking for, honey?"

He snapped his fingers impatiently at her. "Quick, I need some paper and a pen. It's the police on the phone. They found Abby dead in her kitchen this morning."

"No!" Barbara put her hand over her mouth. "Oh, no." She helped him find paper and a pen, and he returned to the phone to take down the needed information before thanking the officer and hanging up the receiver.

"Oh, Amos, I'm so sorry. I know how much you loved her, and she loved you. She has taught me so much about the Bible and God's love. I'll miss her."

"Yea, she could get on my nerves with all her God stuff, but she was a sweet old lady, and I know she loved me like a son. I guess she's in heaven now since she was such a good soul."

"No, she's in heaven because she had an intimate relationship with Christ. That's one of the things she drilled into me. She told me over and over that I couldn't work my way into heaven by making up for my past mistakes. 'There's only one way to heaven,' she'd say, 'through an intimate relationship with Jesus.'"

"Well, I'm sure if He's there, then she's there with Him, and that must make her very happy." Amos had recently started going to church with Barbara, but he hadn't made up his mind as to whether or not he believed in what the preacher had to offer. As an attorney, he could make an argument for both sides of the coin: for belief and unbelief.

A frown came on his face. "I'm going to have to call Zoe. She's going to be crushed. She adored her grandma."

"I'll pray for God to give you the words to say and that He will comfort Zoe." She reached up to hug her husband. "I'm so sorry."

He kissed her on the lips before grabbing his cell phone off the table. Barbara went into her prayer closet to pray for her husband as he delivered the awful news to his daughter.

Zoe was devastated by the news of her grandma's passing. She recalled, with feelings of shame and remorse, the last conversation she'd had with her grandma. She'd promised to have lunch with her but hadn't kept her promise. *As a matter of fact, I never even bothered calling her back. I've been so wrapped up in my own affairs that I forgot all about her.*

"Daddy, what are we going to do without her? I feel terrible because I haven't seen her in several months. I've been so busy trying to get my life in order and dealing with my own grief that I didn't make time for her, and now she's gone. I loved her."

"I loved her too, baby. Would you like to go with me to make funeral arrangements for her? You can help pick out a dress for her to wear and… umm…a casket." Amos feared that the word would conjure up recent memories of Emma's funeral.

"Yes, I'd love to. I'll call the office and let them know I won't be coming in today." She felt it was the least she could do for her grandma. Guilt flooded her soul. *She must have been so lonely. Why is it that we realize how much we love and need our family and how important they are to us when they're gone? If only I'd told her how much I loved her and how precious she was to me.* Tears of remorse spilled down her cheeks.

"I'll pick you up at ten. Will that give you plenty of time to get ready?"

"Yea, I'll be ready." She hung up the phone, sat on the edge of her bed, and bawled. Tears of pain and grief came pouring forth like a breached dam.

She cried out in anger and frustration. "Why, God? Why now? Haven't I been through enough? What have I done to make You want to punish me like this?"

She forgot about the pregnancy test she'd placed on the back of the toilet as she hurriedly dressed to meet her dad.

Zoe ran her fingers caressingly over several of the dresses neatly hanging in her grandma's closet. Finding the one she was looking for, she held it to her face and breathed in the lingering fragrance of her grandma's favorite perfume.

Her voice was muffled by sobs as she whispered into the dress. "Oh, Grandma, I'm so sorry I didn't get to tell you good-bye or how much you've meant to me. I wasn't very nice to you the last time we spoke. I'm going to miss you so much. I'm sorry you were all alone."

She pulled the dress from its hanger and laid it on the bed to get a good look at it. It was a lilac dress that had small white daisies embroidered on it and a feminine lace collar. She had given it to Abby on Mother's Day several years earlier.

Amos walked into the room. "Is that the one?"

"Yes, I think she'd like wearing this one. It was her favorite. Michael and I took her shopping and bought it for her for Mother's Day several years ago." She turned back to the closet and pulled out a pair of cream-colored low-heeled pumps. "I think she always wore these with it. She complained that they hurt her feet, but she wanted to look good." The thought brought a slight smile to her face. "You know how she just loved to look good."

Amos chuckled. "Yep, that was your grandma. The society queen. Well, she'll look great in that. We need to get going. We have a one-thirty appointment at the funeral home."

"Okay, Dad. Let me grab a necklace for her to wear, and I'll be right out." Zoe went to the dresser beside her grandma's bed. The Bible sitting open on top of the dresser caught her attention. Picking it up, she held it gingerly in her hands as the cover had almost separated from the pages. Though the page was well highlighted, and copious notes were written in the margins, one scripture caught Zoe's eye.

> Eye has not seen, nor ear heard, nor have entered into the heart of man the things which God has prepared for those who love Him. 1 Corinthian 2:9

For a moment, Zoe thought about what her grandma might be experiencing in heaven. *She's with Emma. She's holding her and loving her. And she's united with Momma.* She felt a burst of excitement, and tears of joy filled her eyes.

"Zoe, are you ready?" Amos's voice brought her back to reality.

"Just one minute." She grabbed a strand of faux pearls from her grandma's jewelry box and dropped them into her purse. She tucked the Bible under her arm and carried the dress and shoes into the living room of the small wood-frame house where Amos waited.

"Okay, let's go do this." Zoe wiped tears from her already swollen eyes.

Amos stroked her hair as he had so many times when she was a little girl. "Are you going to be all right, baby girl?"

"Yea, I'm just going to miss her. But I know where she is, and I know she's with Momma and Emma, and as strange as it sounds that makes me happy." She smiled up at her dad as he opened the door and stepped aside for her to exit the house.

Ramiah stood praising the Almighty as his charge picked up the Bible. He was pleased as he witnessed her glancing at the scripture. The word lit up the entire room, filling every crook and corner with its eternal light. By the smile on her face, he knew she'd received its message and the peace and comfort it afforded.

After making final arrangements at the funeral home, Zoe and Amos met with the pastor of the First United Methodist Church in Sealy. Pastor Rick Brown shook Amos's hand and hugged Zoe enthusiastically.

"Zoe Davis, how are you? Why I remember you coming to church with Ms. Abigail and attending our Vacation Bible School every summer when you were just knee-high to a grasshopper. It's so good to see you. You're all grown up. I'm sorry for the loss of your little girl. Ms. Abigail told us about it, and we've been praying for you and your husband. We sent flowers to the funeral. I hope you got them."

Zoe was surprised that the mention of Emma didn't sting as much as she would have expected and embarrassed that she'd never sent out thank you notes for the flowers received at Emma's funeral. "Thank you, Pastor Brown. It's good to see you too. Yes, we got the flowers. It was very thoughtful of you. The church looks the same as it always has."

"Your grandma was thought of highly. She had many friends, and so many of the young women looked up to her as a spiritual mother of sorts. She had a lot of wisdom and such a servant's heart. If anyone needed a meal or a ride, she was the first one to offer assistance. Our congregation will miss her." The pastor sat at his desk with his chin perched on his hands. Amos and Zoe sat on the couch in his small but comfortable office.

Amos offered thanks to Pastor Brown for his willingness to hold the funeral at his church. "Of course we'd like you to officiate her funeral. I know she would have wanted that. I'm not sure how many people will attend since Zoe and I are her only living relatives, but…"

The Pastor interrupted him midsentence. "Oh, you can bet the place will be packed. As I said before, she's one of the oldest members of our church, and she was very well loved. She was here long before I took this pastorate, and I've been here for over forty years.".

Zoe's phone buzzed loudly indicating an incoming text. "Excuse me. I should have silenced my phone." She reached into her purse to silence the phone and spotted a text from Zach.

> Hey baby, I'll b home in about an hour. Can't wait 2 see u &
> the girls. I love u and I've missed u like crazy.

She was stunned as she read the text several times. Her face turned bright red as she stared in disbelief.

Amos noticed that she was visibly shaken. "Honey, is everything okay? You look upset."

"Ugh…I'm…umm…no, I'll be right back." She quickly rose from the couch and headed toward the office door. "You guys go ahead without me. I'll be back in a minute." Zoe felt dizzy as she exited the pastor's office.

Oh no. Her head was swimming. *This can't be. I must have read the text wrong. There's got to be an explanation.*

She walked into the dimly lit women's restroom, trembling as she pulled out her phone and read the text once again. She put her hand over her mouth to stifle a scream. Questions swarmed around in her mind like bees buzzing around a hive. *Is Zach married? Is that where he goes when he leaves me? Is that why he doesn't call? Why would he search me out to have a relationship with me if he were married? And the girls…does he have kids? How could I have been so blind?*

Suddenly nauseated, she entered a stall and heaved violently into the toilet; her stomach quickly relieved of its contents from lunch. Afterward, she sat on the floor sobbing uncontrollably.

Amos, wondering what was keeping Zoe, kept glancing at his watch as the two men discussed the order of Abby's service. He informed Pastor Brown that he had no clue as to what songs should be played or scriptures read.

"I'm not a religious man. But I will talk with my wife and daughter. They may be able to come up with some appropriate songs and scriptures."

"Mr. Richards, I must make it clear to you that I will have to preach the Gospel message if I am to do this funeral. It's what your mother-in-law would have wanted. Ms. Abigail was a strong believer. I believe that when we die in Christ, we have the hope of eternal life. And those who die in Christ will be reunited with Ms. Abigail again in heaven when they go home to be with Jesus. It's the only comfort I can offer to those who are grieving. And, of course, I'll want to give people an opportunity to accept Christ as their Savior. Is this all right with you?"

Embarrassed, Amos shifted on the couch. "Sure."

Once again, he looked at his watch, realizing over half an hour had passed since Zoe had left the room. "If you'll excuse me, Pastor. I believe we have settled all we need to settle for now. I'll get back with you on the songs and scriptures as soon as I confer with my wife and daughter. Do I need to write you a check now?"

"Oh no. Ms. Abigail was a dear member. We don't charge for the use of our building or even for my services when officiating a member's funeral. You are welcome to give a love offering if you so choose, but it is not required. I'm sure our congregation will also want to have a lunch in the fellowship hall immediately following the funeral if that is all right with the family. It won't be anything fancy, probably just sandwiches, chips, and salads. Oh, and hopefully dessert." He smiled at Amos as he rose from his chair.

"Yes, that would be nice. Now, if you'll excuse me, I need to check on Zoe. I'm concerned since she never came back." Amos shook hands with the pastor and walked down the hall toward the foyer of the church. Seeing no sign of Zoe, he proceeded out to the car. She was leaning against it; her arms crossed tightly against her chest, her head bent down staring at the ground. He assumed she was grieving the loss of her grandma when he noticed her eyes were puffy from crying.

He hugged her tightly before opening the car door. "Sweetie, I'm sorry. I know you've already been through so much. I'll do anything I can to help you. You know that, don't you?"

Zoe realized he thought she was upset over Grandma Abby's passing. She supposed she was grieving, but it was the loss of so much more than just Grandma or even Emma for that matter. It felt as if an invisible hand was squeezing the life out of her heart. The pain was almost more than she could bear.

Neither spoke a word as they made the forty-minute drive back toward Houston.

It grieved Ramiah to see the tremendous pain, grief, and disappointment engraved on his charge's face. All the pain Zoe was experiencing, he knew, was purposed to draw her closer to the Almighty. And though the Almighty hadn't caused the pain and would have preferred she not go through it, He would most certainly, like a master artist, used it to mold and shape her life into a beautiful creation.

Ramiah looked on as Jesus sat beside Zoe during the car ride home, sometimes stroking her hair, patting her arm or holding her tightly against His chest all the while making intercession to the Almighty for His beloved child.

If she only knew how much the King of kings treasured her. She would turn to Him and respond to His overwhelming, unconditional love.

Ramiah bowed his head and joined the King in intercession to the Almighty on his charge's behalf. He could hear the great cloud of witnesses, those who knew and loved her and had been a part of her life and lineage, gathered around the throne mixing their prayers with his and the Kings. It was like a majestic symphony. The fragrance of the prayers mingling together always made Ramiah stand in awe of the power of such an Almighty, All Powerful Creator, Whose power no foe could withstand.

Zoe entered her luxury apartment, took off her jewelry and clothes, put on her pajamas, threw herself on her bed, and welcomed the sobs that came in torrential waves. She beat her fists on the bed like a child throwing a temper tantrum. Anger oozed out of every pore of her body. She hated Zach for betraying and making such a fool of her. She hated Michael for causing her baby's death. She hated herself for not being there for her grandma and being so blinded by Zach's charm. But most of all, she was angry at God. How could He allow so much pain in her life? How could He just stand by while her heart was being shattered in two? After she'd wallowed in self-pity and self-loathing for what seemed to be hours, she got up to wash her face.

The nausea that had been plaguing her reared its ugly head as she stood at the bathroom sink. She sat down on the cold tile floor, her head held in her hands as her elbows straddled the toilet. After the vomiting spell had passed, she noticed the box with the pregnancy test staring at her from the top of the toilet. Rising up, she went to the sink to rinse out her mouth. She was stunned by her appearance in the mirror. Her makeup was running down her face, her eyes nearly swollen shut from crying, and her nose was beet red. She leaned against the granite countertop, held her head in her hands, and sobbed once again.

She felt alone, she felt betrayed, but most of all, she felt utterly hopeless. She'd hit rock bottom, the very end of herself. It seemed as if she had no one in whom she could trust or turn to.

Michael received a call from Barbara late that evening informing him of Grandma Abby's passing. He wondered what he should do. Barbara told him how upset Zoe had been at the funeral home.

"Amos says the poor girl was beside herself with grief. She didn't utter a word the whole ride home, and she looked terrible when he dropped her off at her apartment. I don't know what I can do except to pray for her, but frankly, Michael, we are very concerned about her state of mind. This is just so much loss for her to deal with."

"I agree with you, but I don't know what to do. She refuses to answer my calls and has told me that she doesn't want to see me. What do you suggest I do?"

"Just go over and check on her. Maybe she'll open up to you. She knows how much you loved Abby too. If nothing else, maybe she'd let you pray for her."

Michael felt fear for his wife's well-being trying to creep into his soul. He knew she had medications in her apartment that, if abused, could end her life. *What if she was to overdose on something?* The thought of her running into Zach's arms for comfort brought on further anxiety.

He felt a strong pull on his spirit to pray for wisdom and guidance. Though he was concerned for Zoe, and his heart ached for her loss, peace settled over him while he prayed. He sensed the Father speaking to his spirit. *"I've got this, and she's going to be all right."*

Michael questioned as to whether or not he'd heard from God. He felt led to pray in the Spirit, allowing his spirit man to be still so that he could hear God's voice. After several minutes had passed, a scripture bubbled up from within him like water suddenly bursting forth out of a freshly dug well.

"I also count all things loss for the excellence of the knowledge of Christ Jesus my Lord…"

Michael got out his Bible and looked up the familiar passage of scripture. He turned to Philippians 3:8 and read the scripture in context with the entire passage. Philippians 3:7–11 stood out to him, and he believed God was revealing to him what He planned to do in Zoe's life. Praising God, he took out his journal and wrote *A Prayer for Zoe* at the top of the page, and underneath, he wrote a prayer, personalizing the scripture passage so that he could begin to pray it over her daily.

A Prayer for Zoe

But what things were gain to Zoe, these she has counted loss for Christ. Yet indeed she also counts all things loss for the excellence of the knowledge of Christ Jesus her Lord, for Whom she has suffered the loss of all things. And counts them as rubbish, that she may gain Christ and be found in Him, not having her own righteousness, which is from the law, but that which is through faith in Christ, the righteousness which is from God by faith; that she may know Him and the power of His resurrection, and the fellowship of His sufferings, being conformed to His death, if, by any means, she may attain to the resurrection from the dead. Hallelujah!

He then prayed the prayer out loud and followed up with his own words to the Father. "Thank You, Father, that You are giving me a faith vision for my wife. Thank You that You can and will take all of this devastating loss in her life to draw her into a deep, abiding relationship with You. Thank You that her faith will be deepened by this tremendous trial she is walking through. I will stand in faith with You and pray for her eyes to be opened and her ears to hear Your voice saying to her, 'This is the way, walk in it.' I thank You for the day that she will be able to look back on her life and count all the things that she has lost as nothing in comparison to the future she has with You. I know the day is coming when You will restore to her the joy of her salvation. I praise You for speaking to me today and giving me a fresh hope for Zoe. In Jesus's name."

After he had spent time in prayer, he picked up his cell phone to text Barbara.

> I didn't talk to Zoe but I did talk to God & He specifically told me that she's going to b ok. He's going to use these trials to draw her back to Him. I know Amos won't understand all of this but please tell him not to worry. God's words to me were, 'I've got this & she's going to b all right.'

She quickly responded to his text.

> Thanks. I believe & will b standing n faith with u. Nothing is impossible with our God. He was able 2 change me & He's working on Amos slowly but surely. I know He can turn this around 4 His good.:)

Michael smiled at her response, put his phone on the charger, and went to bed.

Worry and anxiety had stealthily tried to creep into the room as Michael listened to the report about Zoe. Deuel heard the Holy Spirit speak the word *"pray"* into his charge's spirit. Thankfully, when Michael hung up the phone, he obediently went into intercession. Deuel, fueled by Michael's prayers, took his sword and assaulted the foul spirits before they even knew what had overtaken them. A smile of satisfaction came over him as he listened to his faithful charge in earnest, heartfelt prayer for his wife. It brought great pleasure to see Michael obeying the voice of the Spirit and walking in faith toward the Almighty. He bowed his head and prayed for Michael to hear a distinct word from heaven.

20

"Well, today is the day of reckoning. You might as well get this thing over with." Zoe was overwhelmed with dread as she dragged herself out of bed. She hoped with all of her heart that she was wrong though she had a gut feeling the pregnancy test would be positive.

After eating a few saltines to help settle her already queasy stomach, she proceeded into the bathroom and took the test. The results stared back at her, an ugly reminder of the adulterous affair in which she'd participated. Her time with Zach had filled more than a void in her soul caused by the loss of her child. He'd impregnated her with his illegitimate seed.

How could I have been so careless about my birth control? She thought she noticed a slight bulge in her stomach though she figured she couldn't possibly be more than six or seven weeks along. Unlike the joy and excitement, she'd experienced upon discovering her pregnancy with Emma, dread, fear and shame consumed her.

She tried to weigh her alternatives while soaking under a hot shower. Seething with anger, she nixed any notion of informing Zach of her pregnancy with his child. The hatred and bitterness she felt toward him were like bile eating away at her soul. She'd completely ignored his text the night before and had even been awakened at two o'clock in the morning by an incoming call from him. He'd left a message asking why she hadn't responded to his text.

Since bringing this child into the world wasn't an option, she settled on the only reasonable choice available to her. She'd call her gynecologist and get a reference for an abortion provider. Even as she made her decision, she imagined a slight movement deep within her body as if the child was protesting his or her determined fate.

Michael stared in stunned disbelief at the divorce papers he held in his hands. Though he desperately tried to recall scriptures that could speak faith into the confusion now threatening his peace, his mind drew a blank. His entire body shook as he sat on the edge of the couch reviewing the papers along with a letter requesting his signature of consent.

Though God had given him a reassuring word the night before, he was battling with doubt and unbelief. *God, what are you trying to tell me? If I sign these papers, I'm agreeing to a divorce that I don't want. But if I get an attorney and fight, it'll only drive Zoe further away. What do I do? Is my marriage really over with? Am I supposed to just move on?*

A barrage of thoughts bombarded his mind. He questioned words that had been spoken into his life. Grabbing his Bible off the coffee table, he took out the folded piece of paper that contained the word Kira had received from God and written down for him. He read the word carefully, as he'd done on numerous other occasions when in need of encouragement. He'd assumed God was going to restore his and Zoe's marriage, but maybe God planned on bringing someone else into his life. He couldn't fathom loving anyone like he loved Zoe.

Uncontrollable anger rose up within him. *How can Zoe just throw our lives away? How can she be so hard-hearted?* He paced back and forth in his apartment trying to get his anger under control. He thought about his wife in the arms of Zachary Thomas, and a rage aimed at the young man filled his heart. At that moment, though it was so contrary to his nature, he felt hatred toward another human being.

"For we do not wrestle against flesh and blood, but against principalities, against powers, against the rulers of the darkness of this age, against spiritual hosts of wickedness in the heavenly places."

Michael knew instantly it was the still small voice of God trying to get his attention. He also knew that he could be obedient and heed the voice that reverberated in his spirit, or he could continue allowing his emotions to rule over him.

In an act of surrender, he fell to his knees. "Father, forgive me for my anger. Help me to work through these emotions. I realize Zoe and Zachary are not my enemies. I bind Satan, in the mighty name of Jesus, from operating in Zoe's life. I bind the spirit of adultery that is trying to tempt her away from our covenant vows. I bless Zoe right now and pray that You would keep Your hand upon her. And, Father, I bless Zachary. I pray that if he doesn't know Christ as his Savior, the Holy Spirit will draw him into receiving Jesus as his Lord. I pray not my will but Yours be done. I know that nothing is impossible for You. Even if I sign these papers and the divorce goes through, You are a big enough God to put our marriage back together again. However, if it's never going to happen, help me to move on and trust You for my future."

Knowing that it was out of his hands, he signed the papers, put them in the return envelope, and placed them in the mailbox before heading to his new office at New Zion Fellowship.

Zoe's workday had just begun when her cell phone, which was tucked in the top drawer of her desk, began to buzz repeatedly indicating an incoming text. She opened the drawer and peered at the screen on her iPhone. The text was from Zach. She rolled her eyes as she snatched the phone up quickly to read the message.

Hey beautiful, y haven't u answered my text? I miss u & I'm worried about u. R u all right? I will try 2 call u around 1 p.m. today. I accidentally sent u a text that was meant for my sister. She was house sitting 4 me while I was gone. Hope u didn't misconstrue that text. I'm sorry if it upset u. U know I'm crazy 4 u. Please answer the phone when I call today. I want 2 hear ur voice.

What a big, fat liar. She fumed as her fingers typed a response.

Really Zach? Do u always call ur sister "Baby" & tell her u
miss her like crazy? Do I appear 2 b that stupid? And what
'girls' were you referring to? Game over. Ur married. Admit it.
Don't bother calling or texting me again. Ever!

Just as quick, a reply from Zach flashed across her screen.

Please Zoe! I can xplain. Can we talk about this when I get
back in town? Can I call u 2night?

Outraged, she sent one last message to him before stuffing her phone back
into the drawer.

No! Don't bother!

She made no mention in the text that she was pregnant with his child and
that later in the day she was going to set up an appointment to abort the fetus
in her womb. She didn't plan on sharing that information with anyone.

Michael stood; arms crossed over his chest, carefully perusing the youth
room. The clamor of video games filled the room, mingled with the sounds
of chatting and laughing youth hanging out on cushions strung about the
floor, eating or drinking whatever they'd purchased from the youth snack
shack. Some of the girls chattered in the foyer of the youth building while
the guys played basketball in the parking lot under the careful supervision of
adult leaders. Christian rap music blasted through the speakers, adding to the
orderly chaos of the Friday night back to school youth rally.

He'd preached a strong message that night, encouraging the kids to be
leaders in their school and examples to those who were lost and hurting.

"You might be the only Jesus your classmates ever see. You are called to be a light in this dark world. You can't let the world around you mold and shape who you're going to be. You're called to be leaders, not followers. Your classmates might make fun of you and ridicule you for your beliefs, but you'll be the person they run to when they're in trouble and need prayer."

He'd felt a strong anointing and God's presence during the service. Even some of the kids who regularly misbehaved and distracted others during the meetings were unusually attentive. Afterward, the room had been filled with joyful exuberance during game time. The youth seemed to have bounced back from the shock of losing their previous youth pastor under such appalling circumstances.

Though he'd been served divorce papers that morning, he was determined the enemy would not get the victory. He'd made up his mind that he would praise God even in the midst of the storm. He wanted to be sure his life was a witness to the youth God had entrusted him to lead.

As he surveyed the room, he felt nothing but joy and satisfaction at seeing so many young kids present and enjoying themselves on a Friday night. *God, You are truly faithful, and I'm so grateful to You.*

A triumphant Deuel praised the Almighty as his charge gave thanks to God. Though the enemy had tried earlier in the day to get Michael to harbor anger and hatred in his heart toward those who'd hurt him, he'd instead chosen to do battle against the powers of darkness.

Of his own accord, Michael had chosen to bless and not curse. He was focusing on the blessings God had recently brought into his life instead of setting his mind on the adverse circumstances surrounding him.

Deuel beamed with joy knowing his charge was persevering under pressure and enduring hardship like a valiant soldier.

Kira was in the church parking lot with Debi Feldman and Cheryl Perkins. All three worked as adult leaders for the youth. Kira had volunteered when Michael took the youth pastor position. The leaders usually hung outside after the meetings, making sure the hormone-flaring pubescent youth were keeping their hands and lips to themselves. Though public displays of affection were strictly prohibited, it wasn't uncommon to find a young couple kissing between the youth building and the main sanctuary or in some dark corner of the parking lot. The church had installed floodlights between the two buildings, but the kids still managed to find a secluded place if the adults weren't cautiously watching their every move.

Cheryl Perkins spoke in a low voice so as not to be overheard as the three huddled together. "How do you think Michael is doing as the new youth leader?"

Kira spoke while keeping her eyes fixed on a young couple walking in the parking lot. "I think he's doing a fabulous job. The kids were so attentive. You could have heard a pin drop when he was speaking tonight."

Debi Feldman shook her head in agreement. "I think he's doing a great job. The kids seem to love and respect him. I've noticed how attentive they are when he speaks?"

"Yea." Cheryl glanced at the group playing basketball. "I just think it's a shame Zoe couldn't be here to witness what an awesome job her husband is doing. I heard they're getting a divorce. I've also heard that Zoe has changed. My cousin Gail works in the same law office as she does. You know how news travels around an office. She says Zoe's become somewhat of a party girl. I'm only telling ya'll because I think we should be praying for her."

Kira could feel her blood beginning to boil in anger as the conversation turned toward her friend. Though she didn't agree with Zoe's actions, she didn't feel like it was appropriate for them to be discussing her private life.

Debi added to the conversation before Kira could say a word. "I wasn't going to say anything, but I saw her about two weeks ago at a Starbucks. I couldn't believe how she was dressed. She had on a low-cut top and a pair of skin-tight jeans. And she was with some guy I've never seen before. He was good looking, and she was hanging all over him. I couldn't believe it. It hasn't been that long since her baby drowned. If you ask me, she didn't appear to be grieving at all. I was shocked. I hope Michael doesn't know about it. I think we need to be praying for him."

Kira, incensed, remained silent. Being mild-mannered and one who avoided confrontation at all cost, she wasn't sure how to respond.

Cheryl had a sour look of disapproval on her face. "My cousin says that her daddy is a very wealthy attorney and that Zoe was brought up living a life of luxury. Michael probably couldn't keep her in the lifestyle she was accustomed to. Poor guy. It makes you wonder if maybe God didn't let her baby die so He could get a hold of her heart. She obviously wasn't saved, or else she's walked away from the Lord. You'd have hoped it would have had the opposite effect on her and that she'd be broken. I know I would be. I can't believe Michael could have been so blinded by her."

Kira had finally had enough. It was apparent the two women didn't know that she'd been best friends with Zoe and still cared deeply for her. She and Brad often fasted and prayed for her and Michael to reconcile. *They're acting more like two sharks chomping on bait the enemy has fed them than godly women trying to be mentors for the youth.*

"Ladies, I can't believe that you would, under the guise of prayer, discuss Zoe as if you personally know what's going on in her life or her heart. I'll have you know that she is a Christian. And unless either of you have ever walked in her shoes, you have no right to judge or talk about her behind her back. I would suggest that you both keep your gossip to yourselves and pray for her. I know for a fact that she's grieving and hurting. God loves her, and I'm sure His heart breaks for her. Frankly, I'm ashamed that I even stood here to listen to this garbage and allowed it to pollute my spirit. And I'll remind both of you that gossip is listed in the Bible as a sin. So maybe I need to pray for the two of you." She was shaking when she turned and walked away, leaving them with their mouths gaping open, hoping she'd silenced their vicious rumors for the time being.

Oh, God, I know I wasn't very nice or gentle, and I'll probably have to apologize to them, but I couldn't bear to hear them gossiping about Zoe like that. Forgive me for my anger.

It was in the wee hours of Saturday morning that Zach crept downstairs in the darkness of his New York apartment. Adele and the girls were sound asleep, but he'd been awake all night fretting over the loss of his relationship with Zoe. *How could I have been so careless to send her the wrong text?* She'd brought him such pleasure, and he wasn't ready for it to end.

Sitting in his meditation pose, he tried desperately to quiet his mind so that he could hear from his trusted guides. They were silent. No matter how hard he tried, he couldn't seem to connect with them. Confused and feeling rejected; Zach felt abandoned in his hour of need.

Demons crowded around him though he couldn't see nor sense their vile presence. They shrieked with glee at his obvious confusion and displeasure. They tormented him with fear of his wife finding out about his indiscretions and the threat of losing his two daughters. Lust burned within him for Zoe as they hurled reminders of their sexual encounters. He was despondent at the mere thought that he would never have her again.

"What an idiot!" A demon danced wildly around Zach. "To think we would be your friends. Oh, yea, we'll guide you, right into hell."

Fear wrapped himself around Zach, engulfing the young man. "You're just a pawn you fool. How does it feel to be used?"

Michael sat opposite his dad, a pile of pancakes in front of each of them as his mom continued cooking breakfast. The smell of bacon frying, hot syrup, and pancakes filled the Davis kitchen.

"Zoe's filed for divorce." The words took Daniel and Shara by surprise.

"Oh, Michael!" Shara turned from her position at the stove to face her son. "I'm so sorry to hear that."

Daniel swallowed a mouthful of the hot pancakes. "It's not over till the fat lady sings. God always has the last say."

"I know. At first, I was angry. But I decided I needed to trust God and, once again, surrender Zoe over to Him. I'm still believing for Him to restore our marriage, but I'm open to whatever His will is for my life."

"He will lead you, son. Stay connected to Him, and He'll show you His will. You have no control over Zoe's decisions. But God will turn this situation around for you as long as you're seeking Him. I can't promise that Zoe is going to have a change of heart, but I know He has His hand on your life, and He'll bless you. We'll just continue to pray for her."

"Her Grandma's funeral is on Monday in Sealy. Do you guys want to go?" Michael looked from his mom to his dad. "I'm not sure how she'll receive it, but I plan on going, and I know Pastor Steve and Marcie, as well as Brad and Kira, are going too. We want to show her that she is still loved and in our thoughts."

"Of course we are going." Shara patted Michael's back as she placed a plate of bacon on the table. "Grandma Abby was such a precious lady. She'll be missed. We want Zoe to know we still love her too. I think it'll be great for her to see so many of us supporting her. We sent flowers from the church yesterday. Did you think to send flowers, Michael?"

"Yea. I sent a plant to Zoe's apartment. Do you think that's okay? I wanted to be sure she'd know I sent it. I was afraid it might get overlooked at the funeral home."

"Yes, that's fine." Shara, having finished cooking, sat down at the table between the two men she loved. "Michael, eat up. You're looking way too thin. You could certainly stand to gain a few pounds."

Michael laughed as he put another pancake on his plate. "Maybe I should come over here more often for breakfast. Mom, it looks like you were expecting an army."

"How's the youth group?" Daniel, satisfied with his breakfast, leaned back in his chair.

"It's going great. We had a back to school rally last night. I'm enjoying my job. We have a great group of kids and adult leaders."

"I'm proud of you, Michael." Daniel flashed a smile at his son. "I see you growing in your faith, and even though I know you've been through such a difficult time, you just keep standing and trusting God. I don't know if I could have withstood the trials you've been through, and are still going through, and held so strong."

"Dad, I don't feel strong. I know the Holy Spirit is helping me. I just try to lean on Him each day. But I have to tell you, sometimes I get down and don't think I can press through one more day. I get so frustrated when I falter in my faith. God speaks to me, and I'm encouraged, but then something happens, and I'm struggling again. I often feel like a failure."

"Michael, that's why we are told to walk out our faith. It's a walk. All of us stumble from time to time. Even when we hear a clear word from God, we're still not immune to struggles, especially when the enemy makes the path look so impassable and the mountain so immovable. But the important thing is that you keep putting one foot in front of the other, you keep getting back up when you fall, and you run to the One Who holds onto you and will never let you go. That's what's important."

Michael confided in his parents the anger and hatred he'd felt toward Zoe and Zachary. "You know in Ephesians 4:26 and 27 where the word says that anger gives place to the devil? I could feel the presence of the enemy coming into my living room when I was harboring hatred toward Zach. And then I heard God's voice telling me that my battle wasn't with flesh and blood. So I started coming against Satan and his attack. And, believe it or not, I even asked God to bless Zachary. I can tell you this—holding onto the hatred made me feel horrible. My flesh wanted to go beat the guy's face in. I didn't feel God's peace until I turned everything over to Him and prayed for him and Zoe."

"Umm, that's my boy." Daniel beamed from ear to ear. "That's my boy!"

Kira sat in bed next to Brad; her pillow propped up against the headboard, with a hot mug of coffee resting on her lap. Their children, Simon and Rebekah, were in the living room watching cartoons while eating their cereal at the coffee table, a Saturday morning tradition in the Parker house.

She relayed the events of the previous night at the youth rally to her husband. "Brad, I was so angry at those girls. I feel terrible about what I said to them, but they were judging Zoe. I certainly didn't want to hear the things they were saying about her."

"Honey, I have to admit, sometimes I get mad at her too when I see Michael struggling. It makes me angry to think of how she's blamed him for Emma's death and put such a guilt trip on him."

"I know, but I can't help but think of how she must be hurting. Imagine if something happened to Simon or Rebekah. I'd be devastated. We each have our own way of dealing with grief. I think Zoe's dealing with it the only way she knows how. Unfortunately, she wasn't strong enough in her faith to handle it the way Michael has. But I can't say how well I'd handle it either if you or one of my babies died. My best friend since childhood lost her dad when she was a teenager. She told me her mom, who'd been a stud Christian all her life, started going out to bars to meet men. You hear all the time about older men remarrying, sometimes just weeks or months after their spouse dies because they don't want to be alone."

"If you remarried that quick, I'd come back and haunt you." Brad nudged her.

She laughed as she nudged him back. "Are you kiddin' me? I wouldn't want to have to train another man. It took me too long to get you in shape." Her face became serious once again. "Brad, we can't give up on praying for her. I sense in my spirit that Zoe is still hurting. Sometimes when I pray for her, I weep, and I believe that it's the Holy Spirit weeping through me for her."

"Yea, I still pray for her. It'll be interesting to see how she responds to us at the funeral Monday."

"I worry about how she'll respond to Michael. I pray she doesn't make a scene. I certainly hope her new boyfriend isn't there. That would crush Michael."

"Then I might have to make a scene. I'd hate to see the guy die at a funeral." Though he spoke in jest, concern filled Brad's heart for his best friend.

"Brad, you have to trust God to take care of Michael. Don't you go acting like a redneck and getting into trouble." She kissed him on the lips before getting out of bed to check on the children.

Skandalon

21

There is a way that seems right to a man, but its end is the way of death.
—Proverbs 14:12

A mos held Zoe's hand as they walked the aisle to their seats on the front pew of the little Methodist church. A small choir sang, "In the Garden" as an elderly woman pounded the keys of an old upright, and slightly out of tune, piano. Zoe kept her head down so she wouldn't have to make eye contact with the other mourners. She couldn't help but notice how faded and worn the red carpet had become over the years. The sanctuary wasn't at all how she'd remembered it from her childhood. It seemed tired and worn out as if it needed a revival as much as some of its attendees. The musty smell reminded her of Grandma Abby's old house and, for some reason, made her think of the frailty of life and how, even when we refuse to embrace it, time changes things.

Barbara followed behind the two of them. Though Zoe had argued vehemently, Amos had insisted his wife would be attending the funeral, and he'd asserted; she would sit beside him in the front row where she belonged.

Once they had taken their seats, and the last note of the hymn was sung, Pastor Brown came in through a door off the right side of the small platform. He asked everyone to stand as he opened the service in prayer and then asked everyone to be seated as the choir sang another hymn.

Afterward, Amos made his way up to the platform. Zoe was touched as he spoke affectionately about Grandma Abby and how she'd been like a mother to him over the past thirty years. She could hear laughter coming from behind her as she relayed stories about what a spitfire she'd been and how the two of them had butted heads on more than one occasion. He had people roaring as he relayed the story of a time when he'd been dating Claire, and Abby had run him out of the house by hitting him repeatedly with a broom handle for bringing her daughter home past curfew. "I never did it again." Amos chuckled, folded the notes he'd used and then walked back to his seat.

Several of Abby's friends from the church also gave very touching eulogies before the pastor began his sermon.

"I'd like to begin by reading a scripture found in Proverbs 14:12. 'There is a way that seems right to a man, but its end is the way of death.' I know that might not sound like a scripture you'd normally hear at the funeral service of a godly woman like our dearly loved Ms. Abigail as we affectionately called her around here." He pointed at the closed casket housing Grandma Abby's body. "You see, though Ms. Abigail's body is in that casket, her spirit never tasted or experienced death for one millisecond. How do I know that you might ask? Because I know Ms. Abigail loved Jesus with all of her heart. She lived her life seeking to please Him from the moment her feet touched the floor in the morning until she laid down to sleep at night. She was a faithful servant, and I happen to know she spent hours in prayer interceding for many of you seated in this congregation today."

He turned his gaze toward Zoe and her father. "Zoe and Amos, I'm sure you both know she spent countless hours praying for the two of you and your families. It wasn't uncommon to find her sleeping in her old recliner during the day because she'd been up all night praying."

"Ms. Abigail believed that Jesus Christ was her Savior and had no fear of death. We'd discussed it on several occasions. She told me to make sure that when this day arrived, everyone at her funeral would know she was rejoicing in the arms of her beloved Savior and that this was a day to celebrate her life, not mourn her death."

You could hear the sound of the crinkled pages of the pastor's Bible as he turned to another scripture passage. "In John 14:1–6, we hear of a conversation between Jesus and His disciples. 'Let not your heart be troubled; you believe in God, believe also in Me. In My Father's house are many mansions; if it were not so, I would have told you. I go to prepare a place for you. And if I go and prepare a place for you, I will come again and receive you to Myself; that where I am, there you may be also. And where I go you know, and the way you know.' Thomas said to Him, 'Lord, we do not know where You are going, and how can we know the way?' Jesus said to him, 'I am the way, the truth, and the life. No one comes to the Father except through Me.'"

He placed his Bible on the podium and walked to the edge of the platform to address his audience. "Notice that Jesus said He's prepared a place in His Father's house for those who put their faith in Him. He also makes it clear in this passage that the only way to get to that place is through Him. He said, 'I am the way, the truth, and the life. No one comes to the Father except through Me.' The place Jesus is talking about is the eternal destination for those who die in Christ or, another way to put it, in a personal relationship with Him. Though our bodies die, if we are born again, our spirit and soul go on to live for all eternity with Christ in that place He has prepared for us. It's the place Ms. Abigail is at right now even as we celebrate her life."

He walked back around the podium and looked down at his notes before continuing. "John 11:25–26 says, 'I am the resurrection and the life. He who believes in Me, though he may die, he shall live. And whoever lives and believes in Me shall never die.' Ms. Abigail never felt death. Oh, her body stopped working and is no longer housing her spirit and soul, but as far as she was concerned, she just moved on. I like to call death for the Christian 'moving day.' Her spirit and soul packed up and moved out of her old body and into the new house Christ prepared for her. Isn't that glorious news, folks?"

He paused as several shouts of "Amen" and "Hallelujah" could be heard throughout the sanctuary.

"Now, I want to turn your attention back to my opening scripture passage." He reread the passage. "'There is a way that seems right to a man, but its end is the way of death'. Just like those who live eternally with Christ, there is a real place called hell where people who've chosen not to believe in Christ as their Savior live eternally separated from Him. Now, many in the world, maybe even some of you seated in this building today, believe that they are living their lives the right way." He emphasized the word, *right*.

"They might even believe they are good people. They don't smoke or chew or hang out with people who do..." Several people chuckled. "But they are still living a life that leads to death, eternal separation from God the Father and His Son, Jesus Christ. Unfortunately, many won't realize this awful truth until the day they are faced with the end of life as we know it here on earth."

Pastor Brown looked up. "Bear with me just one more minute. I'm almost done. Now can you imagine the horror to find out that you've lived your whole life the way you thought was right only to find when standing before the great throne of God, that your way was the wrong way? Friends, there is only one way! Jesus made that clear when He stated that He is the way. I would urge you today, as I know Ms. Abigail would urge you if she were standing here before you, if you've never asked Christ to be the Lord of your life…today is a great day to do it. I can't imagine a better way to honor the life of this godly woman than to surrender your life to Christ."

He sat down while the choir sang an old hymn that had been one of Grandma Abby's favorites, "Just As I Am."

When the song was over, he stood, making an impassioned plea for those who did not have a personal relationship with the Lord to accept Christ. "Folks, we are talking about life and death here. We are not guaranteed a tomorrow. This could be your very last day on earth. Where will you spend eternity? The choir is going to sing that song once more. While they are singing, if you'd like to make Jesus your Lord, make your way down this aisle. I'll be waiting here to meet you."

Zoe was shocked to see her father stand and walk boldly, without hesitation, toward Pastor Brown. The pastor smiled as he put his hand on Amos's shoulder and whispered into his ear. She could see Amos shaking his head in agreement to whatever the pastor was saying.

Pastor Brown turned his attention back toward those seated in the pews while still holding his hand on Amos's shoulder. Amos's head was bowed, but Zoe could see tears pouring down his cheek. "Is there anyone else?" Pastor Brown waited patiently, but no one else responded to the call.

The pastor then led Amos in a sinner's prayer, asking the congregation to repeat it along with Amos. The room erupted in applause afterward. Even Zoe smiled as she clapped her hands together in unison with the rest of the congregants. Amos, with moist eyes, was smiling as he walked back to his seat. Pastor Brown then invited everyone to pay his or her respects to the family before heading to the cemetery.

Jasiel walked alongside Amos as he made his way up to where the pastor was standing, beckoning the lost to accept the greatest invitation of their lives. He'd been waiting expectantly for this moment for quite some time. He burst into praise as his charge repeated the sinner's prayer. An innumerable company of angels also looked on with awe, and great joy as his charge experienced the incredible privilege of being born into the kingdom of God. Heaven exploded with praise.

One of the highest privileges of the angels was to gaze upon the salvation of man and witness the rebirth of a spirit. Jasiel couldn't fathom how any human could hear the truth of the word of God and turn down so great an invitation.

Michael filed in behind the long line of those waiting to pay their respects to the family. The line inched slowly along. He watched as people stopped to hug and speak words of comfort to Barbara, Amos, and Zoe. His heart broke for his wife as he noticed her frequently dabbing tears from her red, swollen eyes. She had no idea that he'd come and would probably be surprised that his parents, Pastor Steve and Marcie, as well as Brad and Kira, were right behind him in the procession line.

Finally, he was standing in front of Amos and Barbara. They both stood to embrace him. "Michael, you should have been seated up here with us. Grandma Abby loved you dearly." Barbara embraced him.

"I'll miss her. She was such a sweet lady and a great cook." Michael shook Amos's hand, smiled and moved toward Zoe.

"Michael…thanks for coming. How did you hear about it?" She looked up at Michael from her seated position in the pew. It was evident by the sheepish look on her face that she had not expected him to be there.

"Barbara called me and told me." He bent down to hug her. "Mom and Dad are here too as well as…"

She stood when she saw the others following close behind him. "Guys, thanks so much for coming. It blesses me to see ya'll here." Shame and embarrassment filled her heart as she gave each one a heartfelt embrace. It touched her deeply that they were there to comfort and support her. She'd done her best to write each one of them out of her life. Yet here they were, their eyes filled with nothing but love and compassion for her.

She glanced at Michael. "Are ya'll going to the cemetery and staying for the dinner?"

"No, we are going to go out to eat, and then we're heading back into Houston." They had all agreed beforehand to have lunch at a popular family diner in town since they had no idea how Zoe would respond to their presence at the funeral. He wondered if, just for an instant, he'd seen disappointment in her eyes.

He gently took hold of her hand and leaned in to whisper into her ear. "Baby, I'm here for you if you need me. You know you can call me anytime. I love you." He squeezed her hand and then walked away without giving her the opportunity to respond.

Michael, his parents, Pastor Steve and Marcie, as well as his best friends Brad and Kira sat around a large round table in the family style restaurant, having already retrieved their food from the buffet line. They held hands while Daniel Davis led them in a prayer.

"Father, as we join hands in fellowship around this table, we want to give You praise for this day and the salvation of Amos Richards. We are so thankful to You for saving his soul. We ask You to be with Zoe and Amos as they walk, once more, through the valley of the shadow of death. Comfort them and extend your grace to them during this season of their lives so that they see You in a greater measure. We continue to ask You to restore Zoe and Michael's marriage and stand upon Your word that says, what God has joined together let no man separate. Now, Father, we ask You to bless this food to the nourishment of our bodies. In Jesus's name, we pray and praise You. Amen!"

Everyone joined in unison. "Amen!"

Michael looked around the table. "I know I shouldn't be, but I'm still so amazed that Amos gave his life to the Lord. I've been praying for him for so long. He was always so opposed to Christianity."

Pastor Steve nodded. "It just goes to show you nothing is impossible with God. Never give up because it's all in His timing. It was Amos's time. That was a very nice funeral. The pastor did a great job. I could feel the presence of the Lord in that little church."

"Poor Zoe. She looked so broken. My heart aches for her. Sometimes you wonder what in the world is going on. I know God loves her and is working for her good but for goodness' sakes. She lost her grandma just a few short months after losing her baby. That seems like more than one should have to bear." Kira wiped tears of sympathy from her eyes.

"I agree." Shara shook her head in agreement. "But we have to believe God is faithful. He loves Zoe, and He'll use everything she's going through to take her from glory to glory. In His wisdom and sovereignty, He knows exactly what to use to bring about His perfect plan for her. Despite what it looks like now, one day we will all look back in awe at what He has done in her life. He makes all things beautiful in His time."

Later that evening, after a long, hot shower Zoe sat on the couch in her apartment relaxing with a glass of wine. She busied herself by searching her Facebook news feed on her iPad while the television blared in the background. An overwhelming sense of loneliness and depression enveloped her.

After tossing the iPad aside, her mind went back to the moment she'd seen Michael flashing his dimpled grin while standing over her at the funeral. It had surprised her that she'd been so moved by seeing him there. She'd forgotten how incredibly handsome he was. She felt guilty that she hadn't thought to tell him about Grandma Abby's passing, yet he hadn't appeared to be upset with her in the least. Just the opposite, he'd confessed his love to her. *If only he knew how I've slept with other men and that one of them was married while the other was a pathetic one-night stand.* Shame washed over her. *I'm pretty sure he wouldn't tell me he loved me if he knew I was pregnant with another man's child.*

"Oh, God, my life is a mess. What am I going to do?" It was a cry from deep inside of her battered, broken soul.

She caught a glimpse of Emma's picture on the fireplace mantle. *My sweet, precious Emma.* Thoughts began to swirl around in her head as she placed her hand on her abdomen. *This child might be my only chance of ever becoming a mommy again. How can I take its life? What choice do I have? What would people think if they knew I was pregnant with a married man's child? What would Michael think? What if, in some weird way, this baby was a gift from God? That's an incredibly stupid thought. How could this child possibly be a gift from God?*

Her heart swelled with pride as she thought about her father walking boldly up in front of everyone in attendance at the funeral to accept Christ as his Savior. As a teenager and young adult, she'd prayed diligently for her father's salvation. She'd given up hope of it ever happening and had ceased praying for it. It had embittered her toward God and drained her of faith to see her prayers unanswered for so long. Now, here he was accepting Christ, and she was the one who felt like the prodigal.

Suddenly, a scripture she'd heard at the funeral came to mind. *"There is a way that seems right to a man, but its end is the way of death."*

She could easily see how the path she'd chosen was leading to death. *Oh, I know I'm saved, but I've been living my life for myself. Even before Emma died, I was so spoiled and self-consumed. As long as I got what I wanted and needed, I didn't care too much about anything else.*

For the first time in a very long time, she bowed her head and uttered a short but heartfelt prayer. "God, I've made a mess of everything. I've done things I'm so ashamed of. I don't even begin to know what to do or what my future holds. Please help me to find my way back to You. Forgive me of my sins and lead me. Forgive me for the bitterness I've harbored in my heart. Lord, heal my brokenness." Tears poured down her cheeks. "This pain is unbearable. It hurts to think I'll never see my little girl again. I can't imagine that You could love me after all I've done. But if You could, I know I need You. Jesus. Please help me, Jesus."

As she sat quietly on her couch, tears streaming down her face, she thought she heard a faint voice in her spirit. *"I heal the brokenhearted, and I bind up their wounds."*

However, knowing how ugly her heart must look to God, she decided it must have been her imagination.

Ramiah knew a great battle was brewing. He looked on with triumphant joy as he watched the Son standing beside his beloved charge, cloaked in radiant light. He heard Him whisper into Zoe's spirit and then, in a rumbling voice, He proclaimed to the hosts in heaven and on earth. "I Am the Lord her God. I go before her. I will fight for her."

A host of angelic beings appeared. They, along with Ramiah, worshiped the Son. "Deserving is the Lamb, Who was sacrificed, to receive all the power and the riches and wisdom and might and honor and majesty and blessing!"

Great fear and trepidation pierced the core of even the boldest of demons at the presence of the Son. Ramiah, feeling a fresh surge of strength, started slinging his gleaming two-edged sword. The moment Zoe invoked the name of Jesus, Self-pity and Selfishness screamed in terror as they scrambled to escape the tip of his weapon. He knew he'd severely wounded Unforgiveness and Bitterness, though the wounds did not appear to be mortal. Several other angelic beings, dispatched at the sound of the Son's majestic voice, made great strides against defiant spirits of Rebellion and Promiscuity with whom Zoe had grown so attached and familiar. The angels fought with the word of God, speaking with determined authority as they struck the demons with their powerful swords.

Ramiah yelled triumphantly as he watched demon spirits running for cover. "You can run, but you cannot hide from the Almighty. The light of His glory expels darkness."

Why would the enemy ever think he has a chance of winning against the Almighty? One would think he'd learned his lesson. He reflected back to the glorious day when he'd witnessed the Son rising from the dead, carrying with Him the keys of death and Hades. The enemy had thought he'd been supremely victorious. Satan presumed he'd won the epic battle. He'd reveled in the horrific crucifixion of the beloved Son. But he hadn't counted on the resurrection. He hadn't even seen it coming. Yet, though history had repeated itself over and over again, he was still so foolish to believe he could win over the Lord's anointed.

Carol sat on her couch with her Bible opened on her lap. Her husband, a security guard working the night shift, had left several hours earlier, and her daughter had already been tucked snugly into bed. She'd felt a definite stirring in her spirit while having her quiet time with the Lord, to pray for Zoe. She'd prayed in the Spirit for quite some time when God quickened a scripture to her. It was a familiar passage, but she wasn't sure exactly where it was located. After searching through the concordance in the back of her Bible, she found the scripture and obediently wrote it down on a piece of stationery as she felt God had instructed her to do.

She had no doubt in her mind that God would, at some point in time, make a way for her to share the scripture with Zoe.

22

And from the days of John the Baptist until now
the kingdom of heaven suffers violence,
and the violent take it by force.

—*Matthew 11:12*

One week after the funeral, Michael found himself once again praying against the kingdom of darkness. The Lord had awakened him in the night after speaking to him in a dream.

In the dream, Michael had seen what appeared to be a prison cell shrouded in a dark cloud. As he approached the cell, he saw the shadow of a woman, her arms and feet shackled to either side of the small cell. Demonic spirits were poking and prodding her heart and mind. Others tormented her by hurling lying accusations against her. He could see that she was in pain and fearful for her life, but she didn't know how to break free of her tormentors. She noticed him standing outside of the cell looking in at her. "Michael, please pray for me. Help me. I can't get free, and they want to kill me. Please, Michael, please help me." In the dream, he quickly dropped to his knees and began to intercede for Zoe. He then heard what he believed to be the audible voice of God speaking into his spirit. "*The kingdom of heaven suffers violence, and the violent take it by force. Michael, get up and pray for Zoe.*"

Suddenly awake and alert, he shot out of bed, washed his face, and set his heart to pray, fueled by the picture in his mind of his wife being tormented by the enemy.

"The Lord rebuke you, Satan. I bind you and your cohorts from attacking my wife. I take the authority Jesus gave me, and I command you to get your hands off her. I plead the blood of Jesus over Zoe. No weapon formed against her shall prosper in the name of Jesus. Zoe is a child of God, and she rests under the shadow of His wings. Jesus said in His word that He has given her eternal life, and you cannot snatch her out of His hands. The love of God has been shed abroad in her heart, and therefore, she does not walk in fear but in the perfect love of God. Zoe has the mind of Christ and holds to the thoughts, feelings, purposes, and intents of His heart. She rejects you and your demon forces, choosing life over death…"

He continued to pray the word of God over Zoe with great authority, often going back and forth between praying in English and praying in his heavenly prayer language, allowing the Holy Spirit to pray through him with words and utterances he couldn't understand with his natural mind. He felt invigorated. He could sense the tremendous spiritual battle being waged in the heavenlies for his wife's soul.

After several hours of intense prayer, he showered and prepared for work. Though it was early Monday morning and he knew he had a long day ahead, Michael was surprised at how energetic he felt after so little sleep.

Zoe sat in the crowded waiting room of an abortion clinic listening for her name to be called. Her thoughts went back to a phone conversation she'd had with her obstetrician the day before. He'd made it clear that he was not in favor of abortion and didn't believe it was ever the answer to an unwanted pregnancy.

"Zoe, there are thousands of couples desperately waiting to adopt a baby. Why don't you pursue having the baby and giving it up for adoption?" He'd tried his best to convince her. Armed with thirty-five years of experience as a doctor, he'd seen the physical damage, emotional heartache, and lifelong devastation caused by abortion.

"Dr. Fields, I know this may sound selfish, but I don't think I could give up a child after carrying it in my body for nine months. Besides, it's not just that I don't think I can have this baby, but I've been on medication for anxiety and depression, and I've been drinking pretty heavily. I didn't know that I was pregnant. I'm afraid the baby could have serious health problems."

The doctor thought carefully before answering. "Yes, that's always a possibility, but I've seen women do everything right in their pregnancies and still have mentally or physically impaired babies. You have to trust God. He's the One Who gives life and has the authority to take it. Besides, there are many couples that have children with mental or physical development problems, and yet their families are thriving. Having a child with a physical or mental handicap is not the end of the world. We can run tests early to see if there are any problems, and maybe that would help to ease your mind. Why don't you come in and let me examine you? We can determine how far along you are and go from there."

"I'm sorry, Doctor, but I've already made up my mind. I don't have the same excitement with this baby as I did with Emma. It's different. I…I just don't think I could do it. I'm sorry, but I really would like the number of an abortion provider."

Reluctantly he'd given her the number of well-known abortion provider located in downtown Houston, though he'd asked her to please pray about her decision.

Molech, the chief power over the downtown clinic, and Murder, his fearsome accomplice wholeheartedly agreed to collaborate their efforts with Dekar and his demon forces as soon as they saw Zoe walk onto their property. This was their territory, and they were exceptionally skilled at getting young women to sacrifice the life of their unborn children all in the name of 'choice.'

"We'll need to be aggressive with this one." Dekar felt the need to warn Molech. "She has the potential to escape our clutches if we are not cunning and ambitious in our approach. There are many praying for her, and Ramiah, her guardian, has already done heavy-duty damage to my forces. Beelzebub has gotten involved with this case. He has laid claim to the life of her seed. I have Guilt and Shame ready to bombard her just as soon as it's accomplished. My ultimate goal is to call in the spirit of Suicide once those two have overtaken her."

"You don't have to worry. I can smell this child's blood even as we speak.

Rarely do those who come into my house leave without their minds made up to sacrifice their child. This isn't my first assignment, you know."

Molech appeared perturbed that Dekar would dare question his ability. "I have had centuries of experience. They always leave believing they've made the right decision. I'm so good at what I do, I can convince them that their baby's life will even be better off dead. Can you imagine how stupid you'd have to be to believe that lie?" He doubled over in laughter. "Your dead baby is better off…" By this time, he was rolling on the floor with laughter. "It's a lie that's worked for centuries. When the Israelites would sacrifice their children in the fire, I'd tell them that their lives would be blessed because of their supreme sacrifice, and their babies would go straight to Paradise. And they believed me hook, line and sinker."

Dekar did not appear to be impressed. "Well, as I said, she has many praying for her, and I've seen what the power of their prayers can do. Don't underestimate it!"

"The baby is as good as dead." Molech glared at Dekar. Murder nodded his head in agreement, a wicked smile covering his gruesome features.

"Ms. Davis, we can set up the procedure for Friday at ten in the morning. How does that sound?" Sally, a seemingly compassionate and cheerful assistant at the clinic, searched Zoe's face for agreement. The clinic doctor had already examined her, and though it had made her feel nauseated, Zoe had listened attentively while the procedure had been sufficiently explained to her. She'd stated before the exam that she didn't want to know how far along she was or anything about the life hidden inside of her womb.

"Well, I was hoping I could get it over with tomorrow." The prospect of going through with the abortion was beginning to unnerve her. Though the staff at the clinic had referred to the baby in her uterus as nothing but mere tissue, she knew better. Her friend Kira, a radical pro-life advocate, had been vehemently against abortion and had, on more than one occasion, shared with her how abortion providers refer to the pregnancy as "tissue" or "contents," rarely referring to it as "your baby."

"I'm so sorry, Ms. Davis, we don't like it or think that it's right, but the State requires, by law, we must wait for at least twenty-four hours after your initial consultation before we can perform the procedure. Of course, we believe, given it is your body, you should be able to have it done whenever you wish." Sally placed her hand gently on top of Zoe's. "I know you want to dispose of this problem as soon as possible so that you can get on with your life. I completely understand." She smiled sweetly at Zoe while patting her hand as if she were a little girl in need of reassurance. "Now, don't forget you'll need someone to accompany you and drive you home after the procedure."

Zoe left the clinic feeling discouraged and depressed. She recalled the excitement she and Michael had shared when they'd discovered she was pregnant with Emma. During the second month of that pregnancy, she'd thought she was going to miscarry and had been delighted when they'd finally passed the three-month mark. Every month, she'd posted on Facebook the different changes her body and baby were undergoing. *This pregnancy won't be celebrated.* The thought made her sad. *If I can help it, very few people will ever even know I was pregnant.*

She imagined she felt a slight flutter in her abdomen, though she knew she couldn't be far enough along to feel the baby move.

"LaDonna, I have a really, really big favor to ask you." Zoe leaned across the table and spoke in a low voice. She had told LaDonna she wanted to treat her to a nice lunch and had taken her to a fancy bistro close to the office. She'd even ordered wine for the two of them hoping to butter-up her friend. She waited until they were almost finished with their meal before springing her request on LaDonna.

"Sure, honey, whatever you need. What's up?"

"I need you to promise that you won't tell a soul. Nobody. I can't let this get out. Do you promise?"

LaDonna's eyes grew big and round with excitement. Intrigued, she swore herself to secrecy. "Absolutely." She made the sign of the cross over her chest.

"I don't know exactly how to say this. It's not something I'd normally ever consider doing…I…." Zoe sputtered, finding it difficult to say the word.

"Good grief, girl. Spit it out! Are you wantin' to rob a bank?" She leaned forward in her chair and laughed, a little tipsy from her second glass of chardonnay.

"No, I'm having an abortion." Zoe imagined every head in the restaurant turning in her direction though she knew the place was so loud no one could have possibly overheard. "I'm pregnant with Zach's baby, and he is no longer in the picture. There's no way I can have his child!"

LaDonna's eyes were as big as saucers, sparkling from the effects of the wine. "Oh my gosh!" She covered her mouth with her hand. "Girl, why didn't you tell me? What happened with Zach? I knew you hadn't mentioned him in a week or so, but I just thought…oh my gosh…" She stared at Zoe in stunned disbelief.

"I'm telling you now. I found out he is married. He accidentally sent me a text that was meant for his wife. That's why he was always going out of town. And they have children. I told him never to contact me again." Zoe watched LaDonna go from stunned to speechless. Her mouth fell open, but words would not come out.

"I was too ashamed and embarrassed to tell you. I know you and Tonya tried to warn me about him, but I just wouldn't listen."

"I knew it. I just knew it." LaDonna shook her head.

"And I found out that I was pregnant around the same time. I know I should have been using birth control, and I thought I was, but…well, that's how I got pregnant with Emma. I've never been good at keeping up with that stupid pill."

"Oh, girl." LaDonna was visibly shaken. "I can't believe it. After all you've been through. I'm so sorry. That dog. He's worse than a dog. If I could get my hands on him…"

"I know. I was beyond hurt. I fell for him, ya know? It's like I can't get a break in life."

"Oh, you poor baby."

"I need someone to go with me. Do you think you could somehow be off on Friday? I don't want anyone to know. Not even Tonya. Promise me you won't tell a soul?"

"Oh, I promise. I think I can take off Friday. I'll ask for a vacation day. But how are we gonna do this? I usually cover for you."

"Well, why don't you ask for Friday off when we get back to the office? I'll just call in sick Friday morning." Zoe offered a weak smile. "You know they won't fire the boss's daughter."

"Are you gonna tell your dad?"

"No!" Zoe was emphatic. "I don't want anyone to know. My dad is old-fashioned about this kinda thing. He was crazy about Emma, and he might try to talk me out of it."

"You have my word." LaDonna pretended to zip her lips. "You know I'll be there for you. I'll do whatever I can to help you."

"Thanks for being such a good friend, LaDonna. It feels like we've been friends forever." Zoe hugged her before the two of them got into her car to make the short drive back to the office.

Barbara turned as Amos walked into the kitchen. "Hey, sweetie, how was your day?" She smiled lovingly at him. "I'm making you a sandwich. I have Bible study tonight, so I need to leave in about fifteen minutes."

"What if I said I'd like to go with you? Would that be okay? I mean…if I'm going to be a Christian, I guess I'd better learn how to act like one." He winked at his wife before kissing her tenderly on the lips. "I'll just need a minute or two to get ready. I can eat the sandwich in the car if you'll drive."

"Oh, Amos, that would be wonderful." Tears filled her eyes. "Do you know how long I've been praying for this? It's such an answer to prayer." She patted him playfully on his behind. "Go get ready."

At that moment, she was grateful that she'd placed Amos in the Lord's hands and tried to live her life as a witness to her husband. Many times she'd thought about giving up when it didn't look like he would ever surrender his life to Christ, but she'd persisted in prayer and walked by faith and the reward was incredible. *Amos is going to Bible study with me tonight.* A smile danced across her lips at the thought.

She whispered a prayer as she finished making his sandwich. "Lord, You truly are an awesome God. I stand amazed at Your goodness to me. I pray that You will minister to Amos tonight. Draw him to You, Lord. Thank You so much for saving him. I love You more than words can say."

"Girl, you have to promise not to tell a soul. The reason I asked for Friday off is 'cause I'm gonna take Zoe to get an abortion. You know that cute guy she was seeing?"

Tonya responded on the other end of the line. "You're kidding? Yes, but I thought he was crazy about her."

"He was crazy about her, but he is also married." LaDonna proudly shared the tidbit of gossip as if it were a precious morsel of food to be savored by its recipient.

"What? Oh no he didn't! Poor Zoe! After all she's been through."

"She told me not to tell, so you can't tell anyone. You have to promise. Zoe'd hate me if she knew I told. But I didn't wanna lie to you. I just thought you should know the truth."

"Girl, you take the day off and don't you worry about it. Let me know how everything goes. You'll have to call me after you drop her back off at her apartment."

"Umm hmm, you know I will." LaDonna felt a tinge of guilt in sharing Zoe's secret, but it was certainly overshadowed by the smug satisfaction of being able to divulge such an important piece of information. Besides, she knew Tonya wouldn't tell a soul. She trusted her.

Carol was pouring herself a cup of coffee when Zoe walked into the breakroom on Thursday morning. It was barely after ten, but she'd already heard a terrible rumor that was going around the office. She prayed that it wasn't true and searched Zoe's face carefully to see if there were any signs as to its viability.

"Hey, Zoe. How are you doing?" She smiled at Zoe as if she had never heard the dreadful news.

"Hi, Carol. I'm fine, thank you." Zoe hid behind a fake smile and did not attempt to make further conversation. She acted as if she was engrossed in fixing herself a cup of coffee.

Carol suddenly remembered the paper in her purse. "Oh, I have something for you in my office. I'll go get it and bring it up to your desk."

"Uh, you have something for me?" Zoe raised her eyebrows in surprise.

"I was praying for you the other night and I believe God gave me a scripture for you. I wrote it down on a piece of paper. I just remembered that I had it in my purse. I'll go get it and bring it up to you."

Zoe was touched that this girl, who hardly knew her at all, had spent time praying for her. She had no time to respond, however, as two girls from accounting were walking into the break room, and she didn't want them to see her chatting with Carol and assume that they were friends.

She noticed that the girls seemed to be staring at her but quickly brushed it off as her imagination.

The spirit of Gossip was having a field day. He made sure the news of Zoe's affair with a married man as well as the fact that she was pregnant and contemplating having an abortion circulated around the office. He influenced those who were a little reluctant to spread the news, making sure someone came into their path or called on the phone at just the right time to incite them to share the juicy gossip.

The tongue is like a fire. He took pride in his craft. *If you spark a match in just the right place at just the right time, a flame is sure to burn. Man will never learn to tame his tongue.*

Zoe unfolded the pretty piece of stationary Carol had dropped on her desk. She was shocked beyond words to see the scripture that had carefully been written on the page.

> There is a way that seems right to a man, but its end is the way of death. Proverbs 14:12

Oh my gosh, that's the same scripture I thought I heard God speak to me. How could Carol have known that? She reread the scripture. A chill went down her spine, and she could feel the hair rising on the back of her neck. She didn't know what to make of it. Was it a specific word from God for her? She remembered the prayer she had prayed on the couch in her living room asking God for direction. Was He somehow speaking to her? Was He trying to lead her? She folded the piece of paper and shoved it into her purse.

23

Before I formed you in the womb I knew you;
before you were born I sanctified you.

—*Jeremiah 1:5*

Michael stood in front of the bathroom mirror shaving. An unexplainable and overwhelming urgency to text Zoe wouldn't leave him. She'd been on his mind ever since he'd awakened that morning, and he'd already spent a considerable amount of time praying for her. Giving in to the urge, he grabbed his phone and shot a quick text to her before dressing for work.

> Hey, I just wanted u to know I'm thinking bout u. I can't get u out of my mind. I know u have been thru a tough time lately. I'm here if u need anything. I'll always love u.

Still unable to shake the feeling of uneasiness, he sent out a group text to his mom, dad, Kira, Brad, and Barbara requesting prayer for Zoe. Though he couldn't put his finger on it, he had a sense that something major was going on in her life.

Zoe felt the warm tears stinging her eyes and a lump forming in the back of her throat as she read the text from Michael. *His timing is uncanny.* It warmed her heart to know that Michael was thinking about her.

She'd suffered a sleepless night and dreaded the day that loomed before her. After a quick shower, she dressed in a comfortable pair of baggy sweatpants and a tee shirt. The clinic had told her to dress comfortably. She berated herself for feeling so emotional and tried to convince herself that things would work out for the best. "Let's go get this over with, and everything will be okay."

However, as the minutes ticked slowly by, she found it more and more difficult to believe that anything would ever be okay again.

Though it didn't seem possible, she thought she could feel a flitting in her womb as if the baby was as apprehensive about the day as she was. She tried to ignore the feeling as she waited. To make matters worse, LaDonna, was running late to pick her up for the appointment.

Ramiah was not going to give up without a fight. He knew that his charge was having misgivings about aborting the life in her womb. The Almighty had sent the child's angel ahead, and Ramiah was working closely with him, as well as others to make sure Zoe didn't take the life of her unborn baby. This child was not a terrible mistake as Zoe assumed, but was formed and fashioned with a specific calling and destiny already established by the Creator.

Ramiah was aware that once she stepped onto the enemy's territory; it might be more difficult to convince her to have a change of heart. He was familiar with the power of Molech and his murderous minions. "Greater is He that is in Zoe than he that is in this world." Ramiah decreed into the heavenly realm.

He'd been working diligently over the last few days to ensure that Zoe would have a change of heart. Working with Ozias, he'd seen to it that Carol and Zoe ran into each other and that Carol gave her the scripture passage in a timely manner. He and Deuel were the instigators of the well-timed text Michael had sent to Zoe earlier that morning. Traffic delays, the work of several angelic beings, had ensured the tardiness of LaDonna's arrival, giving Zoe even more time to ponder the fate of her child. Things were certainly looking up, but he couldn't take anything for granted until his charge resolved to save the life in her womb.

Zoe arrived at the abortion facility thirty minutes late. Besides the usual early morning traffic, it had begun to pour as soon as they had pulled out of the parking garage of her apartment, making the drive even longer.

LaDonna gasped as she pointed to a protestor positioned directly across the street from the clinic. He was holding a sign that stated: "It's a child, not a choice." The rain didn't seem to deter him.

"What an idiot." She could tell that the sign unnerved Zoe. "I'll bet he's never been pregnant. He doesn't know what it's like to be in your position. Just ignore him."

Zoe looked down and asked LaDonna to drop her off at the door before going to park the car. She could hear the man shouting from across the street.

"Can I talk to you for a moment before you go in? I can offer you other options." His shouts could be heard above the noise of the pouring rain and cars that whizzed by the clinic. "Ma'am, I want you to know that God loves you and the child in your womb."

She turned and glanced in his direction before walking through the clinic doors. She was surprised to see that the young man, dressed in shorts and a red wife-beater tee shirt, had tattoos all over his body and long hair to his shoulders. *Funny, he doesn't seem like someone who'd care enough to stand outside of an abortion clinic fighting for the life of the unborn.*

"I'm Zoe Davis. I called. I have a ten o'clock appointment, but I'm running late." She spoke to a young girl seated at the reception desk.

"Yes, ma'am. If you could have a seat, someone will be with you shortly." The girl smiled politely.

Within minutes, she was called back up to the desk. "Ms. Davis, I'll need your payment for the procedure. Would you like to pay with cash or by credit card?"

Zoe had withdrawn the cash from her account so that there wouldn't be a paper trail or record of the procedure. "Cash."

She pulled the bank envelope from her purse containing the six crisp one-hundred-dollar bills. Without realizing it, she'd also grabbed the piece of stationary Carol had given her and handed it, along with the money to the receptionist.

"Oh, is this yours?" The receptionist held the paper out toward her.

Zoe's face turned crimson. "Yes." With trembling hands, she took the piece of paper from the girl before returning to her seat. She didn't need to open the paper. She knew what it said. She'd memorized the scripture.

"You okay, honey?" LaDonna motioned for Zoe to take the seat beside her. "You know everything is going to be just fine. It'll all be over before you know it."

"Sure. I just wanna get this over with." Zoe clutched the paper in her hand.

Molech smacked the underling demon hard across the back of his impish body. "You imbecile. You can't control her better than that? Why didn't you have her throw the stupid piece of paper in the trash along with the envelope?"

"I'm...sor...ry...so...sorry. It wo...wo...won't hap...happen again." Besai did his best to move out of striking range of Molech. He'd been attached to the receptionist all of her life by way of a curse that had been spoken over her since before she'd been born. Her father had repeatedly told her mother from the moment he'd learned of her conception that her life was a waste of breath on the earth. He'd never wanted a child and had tried to talk her mother into aborting her. Besai had impressed the desire upon the girl to work at the clinic. However, he often regretted placing himself under the direct authority of Molech. He was a harsh taskmaster who did not tolerate failure. If Besai made one mistake, which he often did, Molech was quick to punish with a beating.

"If that girl changes her mind because of your foolishness..." Molech didn't have to finish the sentence. Besai knew what the outcome for such a grievance would be. He'd surely suffer the consequences.

He marched toward Zoe, sat in the chair beside her, and began to whisper into her soul. "*Just get this over with, and you can continue on with life as if none of this ever happened. It'll be over before you know it. You can ask forgiveness later. It's all going to be just fine.*" He continued with his rambling until a nurse came to take her back to the pre-op area.

The King of kings stood next to a frightened Zoe as she entered the cold, sterile room. His light radiated every crevice of the murderous chamber. Every demon present trembled before Him, bowing down to His unequivocal lordship. An overwhelming and all-encompassing love for His beloved poured out of His being like a rushing spring.

The scars on the palms of His hands were visible as He placed them on Zoe's barely swollen abdomen. The heavens shook at the sound of His voice. The child in Zoe's womb kicked as the voice of the Lord reverberated in its newly fashioned ears.

Ramiah smiled as the Lord stood over his charge. He knew that the prayers of the saints had reached the Father's ears, and the Almighty was intervening in Zoe's life as well as the life of her unborn baby.

Zoe was alone after a nurse had taken her vital signs and reviewed all the paperwork as well as what to expect after the procedure was completed. Her hands shook as she undressed from the waist down and positioned herself, as she had been instructed, on the table. Looking around the sterile room she could feel the fear rising within her. She tried to breathe deeply to calm her nerves. Suddenly, a familiar scripture passage came to mind.

"Before I formed you in the womb I knew you; before you were born I sanctified you."

She gasped as she meditated on the scripture. *Where did that come from?* Suddenly, as if a veil was ripped from before her eyes, she understood what she was about to do. She was about to take the life of a child. Her child. Whether she loved the father or not, it didn't matter. She placed her hand on her abdomen. *God knows this child.*

"Oh, God, if you want me to have this baby, please give me a sign."

She'd barely whispered the prayer out loud before hearing a loud raucous coming from across the hall. A girl shrieked as if in mortal pain. "My baby, my baby! What have I done? Oh, God, what have I done? Get away from me." Zoe realized that the poor girl had come to herself too late.

She hopped off the bed just as a nurse opened the door. "Oh, goodness. What are you doing, Ms. Davis?" She entered the room, shutting the door behind her. "The doctor is ready to begin the procedure. I'm so sorry you had to hear that."

"I've changed my mind. I can't go through with this." Zoe scrambled for her clothes.

"Now calm down, Ms. Davis. It will be over in just a few minutes. Everything will be all right. It's quite normal to become frightened at the last minute." The nurse tried to sound calm while trying to convince Zoe to get back onto the table.

"I'm not frightened. I've changed my mind. I'm not going to have the abortion." Zoe's voice took on an angry and defensive tone.

"Ms. Davis, girls often think they have a change of heart only to come back several weeks later. By then the procedure is more complicated and much more expensive. It's best to get it over with now."

Zoe, indignant at the nurse's persistence, stood and looked her squarely in the eyes. "Listen to me. I'm not having this abortion today or ever. I have decided to have this baby. Now if you will excuse me, I'm going to get dressed and leave the clinic."

The nurse turned, walked out of the room and slammed the door behind her. Zoe could hear arguing in the hallway and assumed it was between the nurse and the doctor.

She cradled her hand on her womb. "Okay, God, I'm depending on You to help me get through this." She snatched up her purse, walked out the door and down the corridor all the while ignoring the stares that followed her.

"LaDonna, let's go." LaDonna was glancing through a magazine while talking on the phone and hadn't even noticed Zoe walking toward her.

"Is it over already?" LaDonna looked bewildered.

"No. I couldn't go through with it. Can we please get out of here?" Zoe didn't wait for her friend but walked straight toward the exit.

"I'm coming." LaDonna threw down the magazine, picked up her purse, and hustled after Zoe.

Zoe began to cry as they sat in the car. "I just couldn't do it. Did you hear that woman screaming in there?"

LaDonna dumbly shook her head. "I didn't hear a thing." She put the car in gear and began to make her way out of the parking lot.

"Slow down, please. Stop in front of that guy." Though puzzled, LaDonna stopped as Zoe had requested directly in front of the drenched young man boldly holding his sign of protest on the sidewalk.

Zoe rolled down her window. "Thank you for being out here today. I want you to know you were instrumental in me changing my mind. I didn't go through with it."

The young man reached into the car and hugged Zoe. "God bless you. Several years ago my girlfriend aborted my baby without telling me. I wasn't a Christian at the time, but I knew it wasn't right to take the life of an unborn child. After I became a Christian, I heard someone speaking at a pro-life rally, and since then, I've been coming out to this clinic every Friday. My girlfriend has regretted the abortion and has told me that if someone had been here to give her another option, she might have changed her mind. I want to make sure women know there is a God who offers hope. I'm happy you had a change of heart. I know God will be with you and help you through this. Do you need a number for a crisis pregnancy center?"

"No. Thanks again. I'll be fine." Zoe waved at him before the car pulled away and headed toward her apartment.

Molech raged as Ramiah lead Zoe out of his death chambers with the life inside of her womb still very much thriving. Seething, he summoned those working under his authority and beat each one until they whimpered for mercy. Even Murder, a demon that was as powerful and equal in rank, stood back out of the way to steer clear of Molech's violent, unrelenting rage.

Molech viciously attacked an underling. "I told you to watch out for that angel. I warned you that he'd be a problem. He came prancing in here as if the stench of death didn't bother him at all."

"You are not worthy to be called servants of the prince of demons you fools. Every last one of you will have to stand before him and give an account. I will not suffer for your incompetence."

One by one, the wounded demons scampered, desperately searching for a place to hide in the dark corners of the clinic, hoping to stay out of the way of Molech until he'd calmed down. They were used to his violent rampages and even expected it whenever they lost a patient over to the light. Time had trained them to lay low until his anger subsided.

Amos stood, arms folded against his chest, by the large window in his office staring pensively out over the downtown skyline. Since he'd given his heart to Christ, all hell was breaking loose in his life. His daughter, with whom he'd always been close, was hardly talking to him, and he was concerned because she'd called in sick but wasn't answering her phone. He'd tried calling her three times, and she hadn't picked up or returned his calls. He could tell something was bothering her, but she wasn't confiding in him as she'd always done before.

And to make matters worse, he and Barbara had gotten into one of the worst arguments of their marriage the night before. Down deep he knew it was his fault, but he wasn't ready to admit it to her. She believed that since he was now a Christian, they should start tithing ten percent of their monthly income. He thought back to the conversation they'd had the night before.

"Are you nuts? Do you know how much ten percent of my monthly income would be?" The thought of giving in to such an idea seemed absurd.

"Amos, it's the right thing to do. God prospered you even when you didn't desire to live your life for Him. I've been praying for a long time to be able to give God what is rightly His. It's important to me. You make enough money that you won't even miss ten percent."

Amos had defended his case, his voice rising in anger. "Are you kidding me? Honey, we are still putting John through college, and we need to think about our retirement too. Besides, that's one of the reasons I've always resisted going to church. All they ever want is your money. Your church looks like they are doing well. Why do they need my money? Have you seen the car your pastor drives? And if he lives anywhere close to the church, I'm sure he owns a very nice house."

"Honey, it's not about what kind of car pastor drives, how nice a house he lives in, or how well off our church is. You get paid well for what you do. Why shouldn't he get paid just as well for what he does? Tithing is about giving to God what is due Him. He's given us so many wonderful blessings in our life. We live in this incredible house in one of the most prestigious neighborhoods in Houston, we have a beach house, your firm is prospering, and we are both healthy. Is it too much to ask of you to give Him back only ten percent of what

He's blessed you with?"

Amos, feeling guilty, was furious at her for pressing the issue. "If giving away my hard-earned money is so important to you, then maybe you need to get a job and give away your income. Then you'd see how I feel about giving away what I work so hard for. I don't mind giving in the offering plate from time to time but not ten percent of my income. Now I don't want to hear another word about it." He'd stormed out of the room without giving her another opportunity to reply.

They'd sat opposite each other at the dinner table in total silence, and for the first time, she'd slept in the spare bedroom. He thought she was being ridiculous. He knew he shouldn't have allowed his temper to flare at her, but she'd kept pestering him about giving away his money. Surely God didn't need his money.

He continued to brood as he studied the rain now pelting against the window. His mood deteriorated as he thought about the news he'd just received. One of his largest and most lucrative clients had called to inform him they were going to go with another law firm. He'd held their account for years and won many important cases for them saving them millions of dollars. Now, just like that, they'd decided to go with another firm. The CEO's son-in-law had gotten a job working with the competition and had convinced his father-in-law to switch his business over. It was nothing personal, the CEO had assured him. *Ha, it's certainly personal to me.* He was going to have to break the news to the other partners, and he knew they'd be upset about it.

When it rains, it pours. He took a seat behind the massive oak desk. He picked up his cell phone and tried to call his daughter one more time.

24

Therefore, as the elect of God, holy and beloved,
put on tender mercies, kindness,
humility, meekness, longsuffering; bearing with one another,
and forgiving one another, if anyone has a complaint against another;
even as Christ forgave you,
so you also must do. But above all these things put on love,
which is the bond of perfection.
—Colossians 3:12–14

Before making her way up to her apartment, Zoe thanked LaDonna for taking her to the clinic and pleaded with her to keep her pregnancy a secret.

"I know it will become obvious soon enough, but I'd like to be the one to tell people, and I don't know exactly when or how I'm gonna want to do that."

She had no idea that over half the staff of Pointer, Richards and Brighten Law Associates, thanks to the fact that LaDonna found it difficult to keep such a delicious secret to herself, had already heard through the grapevine that she was pregnant and supposedly getting an abortion.

Zoe dialed the office number of her obstetrician as soon as she'd put her keys and purse down on the kitchen counter.

"Hi, this is Zoe Davis. I'd like to make an appointment to see Dr. Fields as soon as possible."

"Ms. Davis, can I ask what is the nature of your visit?"

"Yes, I'm pregnant." An unexpected burst of joy and excitement bubbled up within her.

The woman on the other end of the phone congratulated her before setting up an appointment. She informed Zoe that the earliest date she had available was three weeks away.

"That's fine. I don't think I'm that far along anyway, and I know all the right things to do." Zoe wrote the appointment date and time down on a piece of paper.

After hanging up the phone, she promptly marched into her bathroom. Though they'd served her well as a crutch for the last several months, and she wasn't sure how she was going to live without them, she gathered up the bottles of antianxiety medications and sleeping pills and dumped them ceremoniously down the toilet. She then proceeded to her kitchen and emptied an open bottle of wine as well a brand new bottle of vodka into the kitchen sink. *If I'm going to have this baby, I'll have to quit putting this junk into my body.*

Standing against the kitchen counter, she prayed as she cradled her abdomen with her hands. "God, I hope I haven't already caused damage to this child. I know I don't deserve it, but I pray this baby would be healthy. I believe You have a plan for my child and that You want this child to live. So please lead and guide me each step of the way."

Ramiah was joined by a host of angels as he praised the Almighty. He was witnessing the fruits of his labor as well as the prayers of so many persevering saints. He basked in the heavenly light that filled Zoe's apartment. She was taking a step in the right direction. And though it was only a slight move, she had prayed, which gave him the authority to act on her behalf.

He bowed down to the ground and proceeded to recite scriptures in the form of a prayer to strengthen his charge and help further align her to the will and purposes of God.

"Zoe honors You, Almighty God, and brings glory to You with her spirit, soul, and body. She is strong in You and in the power of Your might. She is well able to overcome every obstacle the enemy places in her path because You have declared that she is an overcomer. The Greater One lives in her, abides in her, and has His being in her. No weapon formed against her will be able to prosper. She hears the voice of her Shepherd and is obedient to His voice. You, Lord God will cause her thoughts to become agreeable to Your will, and so shall her plans be established and succeed. She is your workmanship recreated in Christ, and no foe can snatch her from Your all-powerful hands."

He felt strength begin to surge through his being as he prayed. He arose and winked at Zephon, the angel assigned to the child in Zoe's womb. He'd been lying prostrate beside Ramiah, lost in the worship of the Almighty. The two had been working in conjunction to save the life of the baby in Zoe's womb.

"Arise, my friend! There is much to be done and many more battles to be fought, but we will go in the strength of the Almighty."

Zoe's phone vibrated on the kitchen counter. She had placed it on silent mode before entering the clinic. It was Amos calling.

"Hey, Daddy."

"Where on earth have you been?" Amos couldn't hide the frustration in his voice. "I've been calling you for hours. Why haven't you been answering your phone?"

"Wow, slow down, Ole Man. I'm sorry, but I can't explain it over the phone. Would you like to meet me for dinner? I kind of need to talk to you."

Amos could feel his anger subsiding. "I suppose. But you need to answer your phone when I call you. I was worried sick about you."

"Daddy, I'm a big girl. You don't need to worry about me. I just wasn't in a place where I could answer. We'll talk about it later. Is five o'clock okay? Can we meet at the club?"

"Yea, that's fine. I'll see you there." Amos felt a little better after hearing her voice and knowing she was okay. *Now, I'm going to have to figure out a way to make up with Barbara.*

Pastor Steve tapped on the door of Michael's office. "You got a minute?"

"Sure, come on in, Pastor." Michael motioned to the chair in front of his desk. "What can I do for you?"

"Michael, I'm going to be going out of town next month for ten days." He sat down in a chair facing Michael. "I've been listening to some of your podcasts that you've put up on the youth website. They're anointed. I'm proud of you. You're doing a great job. I've also noticed our youth numbers have increased since you became our youth pastor."

"Thanks. That means a lot to me that you would take the time to listen." Michael blushed at the compliment. He smiled at his pastor, though he was uncomfortable receiving praise.

"I'd like you to preach for me while I'm out of town. Would you mind stepping into the pulpit for me?" He was pleased to see the surprise in Michael's eyes.

"Pastor, I would be honored. A couple of days ago I felt like the Lord gave me a message, but I thought it was a word for the body and not just the youth. I told Him that He would have to open the door for me to preach it."

"Yep, that's how God works. Michael, I know you are called to be more than just a youth pastor. Not that a youth pastor isn't a high calling. Lord knows our youth need someone like you who'll lead by example and teach them the word of God. But you have a pastor's heart, and I know God has anointed you for even greater things. I want to help you reach your full potential."

"That means the world to me. I truly appreciate you giving me this opportunity."

Pastor Steve stood to leave. "Do you have big plans for the weekend?"

"No, not really. Brad and Kira invited me to hang out with them tomorrow, but other than that, I have no plans."

"Have you heard anything from Zoe?"

Michael shrugged his shoulders. "Not since the funeral. I texted her, but she didn't respond. The Lord woke me up this morning to pray for her. I felt this intense spiritual warfare. I've never experienced anything like it."

Pastor Steve's eyebrows shot up in a look of surprise. "Really! What time was that?"

"Umm…"—Michael thought for a moment—"I think it was around three this morning. Why?"

"The same thing happened to Marcie. She told me the Lord woke her up about three-thirty this morning. She sensed an overwhelming urgency to pray for Zoe. She even used the same words as you just did. She said it was intense spiritual warfare."

"Wow, maybe God is doing something in her life."

"God is always doing something in all of our lives. We just need to pray that He is turning her heart back to Him and to you." Pastor Steve grinned at Michael. "Have a good weekend. I'll see you Sunday."

"You too, Pastor."

"Yes!" Michael excitedly pumped his fist up in the air and back down again once the pastor had left his office. "Thank You, Father."

"How come you're not having a glass of wine?" Amos waited for the waiter to walk away before questioning Zoe. "Don't you want something to drink besides tea?"

"Dad, I'm not drinking because I'm pregnant, and I think Zach is the father."

"Zoe, you two should have been more careful than that. What are you going to do? Does he know?"

"No, he doesn't know, and I don't plan on telling him. Remember the day at the funeral home when I got upset and left the office while you and the pastor were talking about the funeral arrangements?" She didn't give him time to respond. "Well, Zach accidentally sent me a text that had been meant for his wife."

"What? He's married?" Amos was stunned.

"Yes, and I don't think he lives in Houston. I think that's why he was always going out of town. He was going home to her. And to make matters worse, he has children."

"I'll kill that…Zoe, you've been through so much and now this. That no-good…" He sat back in his chair and clenched his fist.

"Now, Daddy. Just let it go. I'm way over him. He was a wolf in sheep's clothing. I'm not sure why he pursued me, but it's my fault too. I shouldn't have been so stupid and gotten involved with him so quickly. I wish I could say I was vulnerable because of Emma's death, but to be honest, it kinda started before she died. He'd contacted me on Facebook, and I was physically attracted to him or at least the pictures I saw of him. But I didn't do anything with him until I moved out from Michael."

"Well, what now? What are you going to do about the pregnancy?"

Zoe looked sheepishly at her father. "I'm ashamed to say it, but I was going to get an abortion today. That's why I was out of the office and why I didn't take your calls. But I couldn't go through with it. I know you'll think I'm crazy, but I felt like God spoke to me and told me He wants me to have this baby."

"Zoe, I'll support you in whatever you decide to do. You know that. But it's going to be difficult to raise a child on your own." His face softened. It was the first time he'd seen hope in his daughter's eyes in a very long time.

"I know, Daddy. But I don't see that I have a choice. I know I could never give this baby up for adoption. Not after carrying it in my body for nine months."

"How far along are you?"

"I think I'm only about nine or ten weeks, though I'd swear I've felt it move already. I'm guessing that happens when it's your second pregnancy. I've made an appointment to go see my doctor. I should find out then." Zoe squeezed Amos on the arm. "Relax, Dad! It's not the end of the world. Women have babies out of wedlock nowadays. It'll be okay. Besides, I have you."

"And Barbara. You know she could be a big help to you too." Amos waited for her usual outburst of anger at the mention of his wife, but to his astonishment, it didn't come.

Between bites of his dinner, Amos told her about the argument he'd had with Barbara the night before. "I just don't get this whole tithing thing. Why is it such a big deal with her?"

"Dad, I can honestly understand her point. Michael drilled into me the importance of the tithe even before we got married. The tithe is a demonstration to God of our obedience, and it helps protect our hearts from the love of money. There is absolutely nothing you have that you didn't receive from God. The Bible says that He gives you the ability to get wealth. He is the One who prospers the work of your hands. It all belongs to Him. You wouldn't be a big shot lawyer or have that mansion you guys live in if it weren't for Him. Is ten percent really too much to give Him in return?"

Amos chuckled as he pointed his finger at her. "You sound like a little preacher. I never thought I'd see the day you agreed with Barbara about anything." He nodded his head in agreement. "Alright, I'll give it some thought."

They finished their meal, and he kissed her on her forehead before helping her into her car. "Take care of my new grandbaby."

"I will." Her heart was content as she drove back to her apartment.

Amos carried a bouquet of three-dozen red roses and placed them gingerly on the coffee table in front of Barbara.

"Honey, I'm sorry. I shouldn't have…"

Quickly rising to her feet, she wrapped her arms around him. "Sweetie, it's me that needs to apologize to you. I shouldn't expect you to change just because you've asked Christ into your heart. I need to let the Holy Spirit work in you and teach you and trust God to direct your life. I'm so sorry that I made an issue out of tithing. I promise never to do that to you again." She picked up the roses and breathed in their fragrance. "The flowers are beautiful. Thank you, sweetie."

"Well, I shouldn't have lost my temper with you. I'm sorry too. But you'll never guess who took up for you today?" There was a twinkle in his eyes.

She cocked her head to the side as she looked up at him. "I've seen that look in your eyes before when you're arguing your case in court, and you know that you have information that's going to change the course of the trial. So what is it? Who took up for me today, counselor?"

"I had dinner with Zoe, which is a whole nother matter, and I told her about our disagreement. She said she understood how you felt about the tithe. She said Michael had drilled into her the importance of it and how, even when their finances were tight, he still tithed."

She motioned for Amos to sit beside her on the sofa. "Really!" Barbara looked surprised. "I'm shocked."

"I know. I was too. She didn't even have her normal hissy fit when I mentioned your name. I certainly didn't expect her to take your side." He laughed as he kissed her gently on the tip of her nose.

"She's pregnant! The father was a guy she dated a long time ago before she met Michael. Apparently, he's a real jerk. He chased after her even though he knew she was married, but she found out he's married and has kids."

"Oh no, Amos! What is she going to do?"

"She went to have an abortion today."

Barbara's hand flew to her mouth. "Oh, dear Lord."

"It's all right. She couldn't go through with it. I think it's going to be hard on her raising this child alone, but I told her we could help her. And you know what?"

"What?" She ran her fingers through his grey hair.

"She didn't even flinch when I suggested that we would be able to help her out."

She hugged him tightly around his waist as she buried her head against his chest. "Oh, Amos, nothing would make me happier than to have Zoe allow me into her life."

"Well, keep up your praying. It looks like there might be a crack in the dam."

Propped comfortably up in her bed, Zoe took her grandma's Bible out of the nightstand drawer where it had been kept since the day she'd retrieved it from her grandma's house. She recalled how precious the word had been to her as a teenager. It had been her comfort and refuge when she'd felt so utterly rejected during the turbulent times of living with Barbara. As she held the Bible on her lap, she thought about how the scriptures had been her compass, the light directing her path into a relationship with God that had led her eventually to Michael. She smiled as she recalled how Michael's zeal and love for the Lord had attracted her to him. She felt a sadness wash over her and an aching for the life they'd shared together. *How did it all get so messed up? God gave me such a sweet gift, a husband who loved me with an unselfish, unconditional love, and I somehow managed to screw it all up.* She wiped away a tear that fell from her eyes.

"Lord, what do I do now? Lead me as I begin to read your word. Speak to me. I need Your direction for my life as I carry this child."

She flipped the Bible open and looked down at the open pages, hoping something would catch her eye. A passage of scripture in Colossians chapter three was highlighted, and there were notes scribbled in the margin in her grandma's shaky handwriting. She read it out loud.

"Therefore, as the elect of God, holy and beloved, put on tender mercies, kindness, humility, meekness, longsuffering; bearing with one another, and forgiving one another, if anyone has a complaint against another; even as Christ forgave you, so you also must do. But above all these things put on love, which is the bond of perfection."

She glanced over at the note written in the margin beside the passage.

Love must be worn daily for all to see
My life a display of His tender mercy.
To walk in humility and patient with all
Showing kindness to those who stumble and fall.
And how would they know it's for Him I live,
If I choose to be angry and not to forgive?

The poem made her smile. She thought about her conversation with her dad earlier that evening. For whatever reason, she hadn't felt the surge of hatred and anger when he'd brought up Barbara's name. She certainly didn't feel the familiar loathing toward Michael she'd nursed in her heart since Emma's death. However, she still hadn't completely forgiven them either.

She allowed her mind to think back to the time when Barbara had raised her, mistreated, and rejected her, showing blatant favoritism to her brother John. She then prayed aloud.

"God, help me to forgive. I choose today to put on the garment of forgiveness. Help me to love Barbara the way you do and to see her through Your eyes. Please forgive me for holding onto bitterness and unforgiveness for so many years."

The dust that had clouded her vision for so long was instantly wiped away, and she was suddenly aware of the change in Barbara toward her and her father. She'd proven her devotion for Amos and that she wasn't a gold digger as Zoe had always accused her of being. She remembered how awful she'd been to her on the day Emma had died. For the first time, she felt a sense of remorse for her behavior. Her heart broke for Barbara.

"Oh, God, I'm so sorry. How could I have been so ugly to her in front of everyone? She must have been humiliated. Please forgive me."

Her thoughts then turned to Michael. She'd been unfair and cruel to him. How his heart must have broken to lose both his daughter and his wife at the same time. She sobbed as reality hit her square in the face. If the tables had been turned, Michael would have readily forgiven her, and though his heart would have been broken, he would have claimed Emma's death to be nothing more than an accident. She prayed through the sobs now racking her body.

"Father, I was so unfair to him, and I certainly don't deserve his love or forgiveness. Please forgive me for allowing myself to be filled with such hatred and animosity. Emma's death was a horrible accident, and I could very well have been the one to have left that door open. Oh, Lord, I have failed Michael, but most of all, I failed You. Please forgive me and change my heart. Renew in me a right spirit and restore to me the joy of my salvation. In the name of Jesus. Amen!"

A peace settled over her as she allowed the tears to continue their cleansing work. She knew there had been a breaking in her heart and that she'd opened the door for God to begin the healing process. Though she couldn't see into the future for herself and the child she carried, she knew God was with her, and He would help her. She sensed His presence as she turned out the lights. That night she slept deeply. There were no haunting dreams of Emma crying out to her, just a sweet, peaceful, refreshing sleep.

Dekar, breathing heavily and spurred on by fear of facing his prince, stomped back and forth in front of the underlings arrayed in military formation before him. Venom spewed forth from him as rage contorted every feature of his ugly being.

"You're incapable of following the simplest of orders. You had one measly assignment—to turn that girl completely away from her faith. You have the entire arsenal of the kingdom of darkness at your disposal. Yet you continue to fail. You had her securely entangled in your web, but you have allowed her to escape. To say that your lord, Beelzebub, is infuriated with the lot of you would be an understatement. You are a disappointment to your ranks…"

The demons cowered as his ranting continued. The more he ranted, the angrier he became, and so the more he ranted. They had nowhere to hide from the pummeling blows he randomly delivered on the one who happened to be within reach as his anger reached a crescendo. Most of them whimpered and cried out in fear as they cowered before him.

"If you want something done right, you have to do it yourself." Dekar smacked the head of Guilt. The demon howled in agony. "I suppose I'll have to show you morons how it's done."

25

And let us not grow weary while doing good,
for in due season we shall reap if we do not lose heart.
—*Galatians 6:9*

Zoe was seated on an examination table half-dressed and covered with a paper sheet, anxiously awaiting Dr. Fields, her obstetrician, to enter the room. There was a slight tap on the door before the elderly doctor poked his head into the room.

"You ready for me?" Dr. Fields had been her doctor for years, and she felt comfortable with him. He'd delivered Emma. He was slightly obese and had begun to lose most of the hair on his graying head, but he was a jovial man, a soft-spoken Christian with an excellent bedside manner. He was the type of doctor who never rushed his patients, allowing them ample time for asking questions, which often made him run late for his other appointments. Zoe had always considered that he was well worth the wait.

"As ready as I'll ever be." Zoe shifted on the bed nervously.

"Zoe, I can't tell you how thrilled I was when I heard you'd decided not to abort this baby."

"I just couldn't do it. I was in the room and ready to go, but I chickened out, I guess you could say. So, here I am."

"Well, let's listen to the heartbeat. I'll exam you, and then we'll do an ultrasound and see how far along you are."

With his nurse's assistance, he ran the fetal monitor over Zoe's belly. He glanced at Zoe. "That's a nice, strong heartbeat you've got there."

A tear rolled down the side of her face as she listened to her baby's heartbeat for the first time. It was as though with every beat of its heart her baby made a declaration. "I'm alive!" At that moment, she fell in love.

Dr. Fields patted her arm after the exam. "Well, everything looks fine. After you get dressed, the nurse will take you for the ultrasound. We'll talk in my office afterward." He exited the room.

As she dressed, she recalled how Michael had been with her at every appointment during her pregnancy with Emma. They had proudly posted on Facebook a picture of the two of them holding Emma's first ultrasound picture. Her emotions were off the chart. She went from being ecstatic at hearing the baby's heartbeat to a sense of being alone with no one to share the excitement of the moment.

A tap on the door interrupted her thoughts. "Are you ready?" The nurse peered around the open door. Zoe shook her head and grabbed her purse. "Well then, follow me."

Zoe was led to a small room with a sweet female technician. "Hi, my name is Rachel. I'll be doing your ultrasound today. Just hop up here on the table, and we'll get going."

Zoe was amazed as she viewed the monitor. The baby appeared to be sucking its thumb. The little feet pulled in toward its chest in opposition to the intrusion as the ultrasound wand passed over her abdomen.

"Do you want to know what you're having?" Rachel kept her eyes on the screen as she moved the wand slowly back and forth.

"You can tell this early? Sure!"

"See that?" Rachel paused the wand on Zoe's belly. "It looks to me like your having a boy."

"A boy!" Zoe stared at the image. "Oh my gosh, I'm having a little boy!" Tears of joy streamed down her cheeks. "Does he look all right? Ten fingers, ten toes, and all of that?"

"Well, I'm not allowed to go over the report with you. But Dr. Fields will review the results with you when you meet with him in his office. Okay, Ms. Davis. I'm finished."

The technician, finished with her portion of Zoe's appointment, led her into the doctor's office. "Just wait here, and he'll be with you shortly. Congratulations!"

Zoe seated herself on a leather wingback chair in front of the doctor's messy desk. It wasn't long before Dr. Fields entered the room and seated himself across from her.

"Well, everything looks good. I'm going to set your due date to be March fifteenth. It's hard to tell exactly because you can't remember when you had your last period, but the ultrasound seems to indicate that the baby is on target for that date. I'll see you back here in a month." He looked at the calendar on his desk. "That puts you back in here around November fourth. My nurse will help you set up a monthly appointment schedule. Do you have any questions?"

"Doctor you know I've been very concerned about the drugs I was taking, and I'm ashamed to say, much of the time I mixed them with alcohol. I was wondering if you could tell by the ultrasound…does the baby look okay? I mean…do you see any problems?"

"Everything appears to be fine." He came around the desk and patted her on the shoulder. "Let's just make sure that from here on out we take care of this baby."

Zoe left feeling as though a huge burden had been lifted. She was overjoyed that her baby boy appeared to be healthy with a strong heartbeat.

She sat in her car for a moment to allow the news to soak in. *A boy.* Michael had wanted a boy when she'd found out she was pregnant with Emma, but he'd cried, along with her, when they'd witnessed Emma's beautiful little image squirming on the ultrasound screen for the first time. He was smitten with his daughter from that moment on.

"Oh, God, I am so thankful that this baby boy is healthy, but I'm afraid, and I feel so alone. I never imagined it would be so lonely to go through this without someone by my side."

As soon as she'd uttered those words, she heard a voice, so real and so loud it sounded as if He was sitting in the seat beside her. "*I go before you. I Am your rear guard. I set the lonely in families.*"

At first, she was stunned to hear God's voice. She'd never heard the audible voice of God before, though Michael claimed he'd heard it several times. She looked around in the parking lot to make sure she hadn't heard someone else talking or a radio coming from a nearby car. There was no one in sight. Then she reflected on His last words. "*I set the lonely in families.*" She wasn't sure what they meant to her specific situation, but the fact that she'd heard God's audible voice excited her and filled her with hope as she drove back to her office.

Michael was in his office bright and early on a mid-October morning excitedly preparing his first sermon to be preached from the pulpit of his church the following Sunday. The dark sky outside his office window signaled the first cool front of the season was about to blow in. Even the threat of rain couldn't dampen his spirit.

He'd already spoken to his parents and invited them to attend the service, which, much to his surprise, they were both excited and had agreed to be present, front and center, to see their son preach his first sermon.

He felt blessed that his dad, who rarely missed a Sunday at his church, would leave his pulpit to his associate pastor to come and support him. However, the person he truly wished to be there to hear him preach for the first time, more than anyone else was Zoe. No one understood his vision of one day becoming a pastor more than her. He'd shared his heart with her from the time they'd met, and she'd always encouraged him and told him she had faith that God would bring it to pass. He wanted her to see the beginnings of the fulfillment of God's promise.

Though his expectations were not very high, he decided it wouldn't hurt to invite her. *All she can do is say no.* Before he could change his mind, he typed out the text.

> I'm going to b preaching this Sunday @ church. Thought I'd see if u could come. I would love to look out & see u smiling back @ me. I know it's a long shot but thought I'd ask anyway. I miss u.

"Okay, Lord, I did my part."

Monday mornings were usually busy for Zoe, and it was close to lunchtime before she had time to slow down and glance at her phone. She was pleasantly surprised when she read Michael's text. Pride filled her heart at the thought of him preaching his first sermon. She knew he'd do a sensational job. He had a gift of sharing the word. She'd heard him witness to people on numerous occasions and had always been mesmerized whenever she heard him share the Gospel.

For a split second, the thought of going crossed her mind until she looked down at the growing bulge in her abdomen. Though she was barely showing, she was finding it increasingly difficult to hide her little bump. She still hadn't told anyone except her father and LaDonna.

She could only imagine how people would speculate and gossip. But, even worse, what would Michael say once he found out that she was pregnant? No, she wasn't ready to face him and maybe never would be.

She didn't know if her mistakes could ever be fixed, but at least she was getting her life back on track with the Lord. She'd spent time in prayer that morning and had even read a passage in the Psalms. The thought had occurred to her while having a devotional time that she needed to find a church. She was too ashamed to face the members of her old church and wouldn't want to bring further reproach on Michael. Suddenly, she felt as though shame and disgrace would completely overwhelm her.

Her thoughts formed into a silent prayer. *Oh, God, I can see how I have made such a mess. I am so ashamed of how my life has turned out. I've disgraced Michael, and I don't know that I could ever see him face to face again. I know I've asked for Your forgiveness, but I don't know how to forgive myself.*

"Ready?" LaDonna interrupted her thoughts as she came around the corner of the hallway.

Zoe jumped in her seat. "Oh gosh, you startled me."

"Yeah, you looked like your mind was somewhere a thousand miles off. Sorry, I didn't mean to startle you. Let's go to lunch. I'm starvin'." LaDonna stood impatiently in front of Zoe's desk, purse and keys in hand. "Here comes Sandra. Let's go."

Zoe moved out of her chair so Sandra, the new relief receptionist, could take her place. "Okay, okay...let me get my purse."

As they headed toward the door, LaDonna leaned in close so that only Zoe could hear. "Now that you are eating for two, I'll bet you're starving too."

"Unfortunately, I've been eating for two for a while now, and it's showing. Do you think anyone knows?"

LaDonna turned away from her gaze so that her friend wouldn't be able to discern the deception in her reply. When several people in the office had approached her about Zoe, she'd realized that her secret hadn't been safe with the few people in whom she'd confided. "No, I doubt anyone knows. You don't look pregnant. Just pudgy."

Zoe looked dismayed as they entered the elevator. "Great, I think I'd rather look pregnant than pudgy."

Dekar watched as Shame and Disgrace viciously attacked Zoe. Since his last report to Beelzebub hadn't been favorable, he'd decided he would personally supervise this attack.

Utilizing the talents of Shame and Disgrace was a tactic he'd used for many millennia, and it almost always worked. He'd discovered, through experience, that when Christians fall into sin and then decide to turn back to Jehovah; they were the best weapons to discourage spiritual growth. Oh, his prey might enter back into worship, prayer, and even attending church, but her power would be hindered because she wouldn't be able to forgive herself.

The dynamic duo of Shame and Disgrace would make sure she felt like she couldn't measure up to other Christians by constantly reminding her of her past sins. They would make her feel unworthy of Jehovah's love, or anyone else's for that matter. They were brilliant in their methods and had an enormous success rate. He was confident that they'd be able to keep this weakling from being of any effect in the kingdom of Jehovah.

Though she'd finished her lunch and it was almost time for her to be back in her office, Carol felt led to hang around a few more minutes in the breakroom. When Zoe walked in carrying leftovers from her lunch, it was apparent to Carol why she'd felt inclined to wait.

"Hey, Zoe." She greeted Zoe cheerfully as she walked toward the refrigerator.

Zoe had been lost in thought as she entered the room and jumped as Carol's greeting took her by surprise.

"Oh, hi, Carol. I didn't see you sitting there."

Carol stared pensively at Zoe. She seemed to have changed though she couldn't quite put her finger on what it was that made her appear any different from any of the other times they'd spoken to each other. She was aware, as was most of the office thanks to the gossip that was circulating that Zoe had recently had an abortion. It had upset her at first, though she knew it wasn't her place to judge. No, it was something else, she thought pensively. Zoe looked softer. Her face didn't seem to be marked with the anger and bitterness that usually marred her countenance.

Carol stood from her seat, pushed her chair under the table, and walked toward Zoe. "How are you doing?"

Zoe sensed the compassion in Carol's voice and decided that she might be someone to confide in. "You know, I would like to get together and talk with you. Would you be able to have lunch with me tomorrow? It'll be my treat."

"Hey, I never turn down a free lunch. I'd love to go to lunch with you."

"Great. I'll talk to you tomorrow then."

Carol smiled knowing that God had just arranged another divine encounter between her and Zoe. "God, You are simply amazing!"

Zoe sat Indian style on the couch watching one of her favorite television sitcoms. Her cell phone, perched on the armrest of the sofa, began to buzz indicating she'd received a text. It was from Michael.

Hey baby, did u get my text earlier today?

She smiled as she read his text. She could almost hear his gentle voice calling her baby, the pet name he'd always called her and spoken in such a way that could melt her to the core. Until, of course, she'd went off the deep end, walked away from God, and ruined her life for good.

She typed out a brief reply.

I can't come. Sorry. I know u'll do great.

"Oh, God." Sobbing, she covered her face with her hands. "How could I have let him go? How could I have been so blind and foolish to leave him?"

She was overcome with sadness and a deep longing to see Michael.

She thought of the upcoming holidays spent alone without him or Emma. She'd been sharing her Thanksgiving and Christmas holidays with Michael ever since she was seventeen. The thought of being alone hit her like a ton of bricks, and a deep feeling of loneliness invaded her like an unwelcome guest, bringing fresh tears.

Rising from the couch to grab a tissue from a box on the coffee table, she felt a robust kick from the baby in her womb.

She placed her hands on her shifting abdomen. "I know little man. I need to get over myself and move on. You're the one who gives me purpose and something to look forward to."

Michael, though he felt like it was in vain, texted Zoe one more time before going to bed to be sure she'd received and read his first text. He sighed as Zoe's reply came through on his iPhone.

I figured she wouldn't come, and I was right. The rejection he felt was enough to make him want to give up on her altogether. *Maybe I just need to move on and forget about my life with Zoe. Maybe it's over. She apparently doesn't care or want me back, so why bother fighting?*

"God, I'm tired of this fight." Michael leaned his head back against the wooden headboard and sighed deeply.

A scripture passage came into his thoughts.

"Let us not grow weary while doing good, for in due season we shall reap if we do not lose heart."

Grabbing his Bible off the nightstand, he turned to the familiar passage. Because he spent so much time in the word, reading and studying it, he knew where to locate the scripture. He read it out loud.

"'Let us not grow weary while doing good, for in due season we shall reap if we do not lose heart.' God, are You saying to me that if I keep standing, she will return? Because that's the way, I view this scripture. Are You saying to me that our marriage will be restored if I continue to fight? Nothing in the natural makes me think Zoe will ever come back to me, so I could sure use some encouragement here."

He sat still in the silence of his bedroom, but all he could hear was the sound of the ceiling fan whirling softly above him. He spent several more minutes in prayer and worshiping God but didn't receive anything further from the Lord, though he sensed an incredible peace.

He returned the Bible back to his nightstand, turned out the light, and went to bed.

Deuel backed the spirit of Rejection into a corner and swiped him with his sword before the demon vanished from his presence. Out of the corner of his eyes, he noticed Discouragement slither quietly into the room, trying to avoid his detection.

"Oh no, you don't, you slimy snake." Michael's prayers mixed with worship gave Deuel authority and power to come against the ugly creature. "The Lord rebuke you! Now go in the name of Jesus."

"Okay, I'll leave. Just don't use that name. I hate that name." Discouragement slithered away as fast as he could—his mission foiled.

26

I can do all things through Christ who strengthens me.
—Philippians 4:13

"**O**rder whatever you like. It's my treat." Zoe glanced up from the menu she was perusing. She sat across the table from Carol in an Italian restaurant that was bustling with lunchtime customers.

They spent their time in superficial conversation until the waiter brought their food. Carol had spent most of her evening and much of the morning praying for God to guide her in her conversation with Zoe. She knew that the girl sitting opposite her was troubled, heartbroken, and had been through so much turmoil in such a short time. She waited to take her cues from Zoe and was relieved when Zoe finally opened up.

"I know you probably think it's strange that I asked you to lunch, but I feel like it just makes so much sense for me to confide in you. I can't tell you how shocked I was to find out that you'd been through a similar situation…I mean losing a child. And, well…" It was obvious that Zoe was searching for the right words, but Carol sat quietly and patiently waiting and listening. "I don't know any other way to say it, but…I'm pregnant." Zoe scanned Carol's face for any signs of disapproval. She was surprised to see compassion in her lunch companion's eyes.

"The father is a married man, but at the time I had no idea he was married. I would never have gotten involved with him if I had. Not that I'm trying to defend my integrity or anything because, honestly, I was still married at the time. I was going to have an abortion, but I just couldn't go through with it. I hope you won't judge me too severely for that."

"Zoe, first off, I'm not your judge. Thanks for confiding in me. I'm glad you decided to keep the baby."

"It's a boy." Zoe's was beaming from ear to ear. "I feel like God is giving me a second chance at being a mom."

"Oh, Zoe! That's so awesome. I'm so happy for you." Carol sensed Zoe had so much more to share with her. "How far along are you?"

"Well, the doctor says I'm due around the middle of March. But I can't remember the last time I had a period. I think the stress of Emma's death kept me from having one. Also, I was taking prescription drugs and drinking pretty heavily which could have prevented me from being regular. Anyways, I think he's off, but I didn't want to tell him that. I figure I'm probably not due until late in April based on the first time Zach and I slept together. Emma was early though so this one could come early too." Zoe took a bite before continuing.

"At first, I was in shock when I realized I was pregnant. I found out around the same time I discovered the guy I was seeing was married. But I'm excited about it now. My only regret is that I feel so alone. It was strange going to the doctor, experiencing the ultrasound and making plans without my husband. When Emma drowned I blamed Michael. I guess my walk with Christ wasn't as strong as I thought it was, and I walked away from the Lord as well as my husband. I let grief consume me and drive me to do things I never thought I could do. And now that I can see clearly, I'm pregnant with another man's child. I've really screwed up my life."

"Zoe, I know it sounds so cliché, but the word says that God can take everything that happens in our life and turn it for our good. Do you realize that before you were born, He knew that you'd be going through this and He already has a solution? His love for you has not changed one bit."

"I do believe He can turn it for good. I'm having a baby. I've missed my precious Emma so much, and I can't believe I get to be a mom again."

"Do you love Michael? Have you forgiven him?" Carol noticed the look of surprise on Zoe's face.

"You know, I think I do still love him. I hate myself for letting him go. He's such a great guy. He's preaching his first sermon Sunday. He invited me, but I can't face him, and I don't want him to know I'm pregnant. Do I forgive him? Hmm…I think I do, but forgiveness has always been so hard for me. It's so hard to let go of the hurt, ya know?"

"Have you ever hurt Jesus?" Carol could see Zoe was taken back by the question.

"Well…yea…I'm sure I have. Gosh, I think divorcing my husband, having an affair along with some other things I'm too ashamed to tell you. Yes! I've definitely hurt Jesus."

"Do you think He has to wait to get over the hurt before He can completely forgive you, or do you think He simply forgives?"

Zoe thought for a second before answering. "I'm sure He simply forgives, but I'm not Him."

"Do you believe that He lives in you? Because His word says that the Greater One lives in us, and we can do all things through Christ who gives us strength. It also says His grace is sufficient for us to help when we are weak. Please, don't think I'm preaching at you. I had to ask myself these same questions when Jacob drowned. I couldn't get past the pain I felt I'd caused my family and myself. And until I learned how to forgive completely, I wasn't able to move on in life and live in the victory that Christ paid the price for me to live in."

Carol felt pressed by the Holy Spirit to continue. "Zoe, forgiveness isn't an option with Jesus. We forgive because He forgave us. It's so important for our freedom. Jesus doesn't command us to forgive for His sake. It's for our own good. When we are unwilling to forgive, we give place to the enemy to bring destruction in our lives. It's not worth it. We don't wait until we feel like forgiving. We step out in faith and trust that the feelings will follow."

"I know you're right. I've heard all of that before, and I know it in my head, but I guess I've never put it into practice. But even if I forgive Michael, it's still too late." Zoe placed her hand on her abdomen.

"It's never too late with God. Just begin to work on your relationship with Him and put your future in His hands. Trust Him to work it all out for you as you love and follow Him to the best of your ability."

Finished with their meal, Zoe paid the check, and they rose to leave. "Thanks, Carol. You've given me a lot to think about. Would you mind if I bring my lunch from time to time and eat with you in the breakroom? I know you read your Bible at lunch, and I don't want to interrupt or impose on you."

"I'd love for you to join me whenever you like. But, you know, you might get a bad reputation for eating with me. Everyone thinks I'm a holy roller." Carol laughed heartily.

"Well, I've already made a mess of my reputation, don't cha think?" She was surprised at how easy it had been to talk to Carol and how much she'd enjoyed her company.

Later that night, as she sat in bed reading her Bible, Zoe pondered over her conversation with Carol. Using the concordance in the back of the Bible, she looked up and read as many scriptures on forgiveness that she could find. Taking out a sheet of paper, she wrote down the ones that ministered to her. The one that stood out to her the most was in the Lord's Prayer.

"And forgive us our debts, as we forgive our debtors." She read it over several times, allowing herself to meditate on the meaning of the words. She knew the Lord was telling her she needed to forgive Michael in the same way she wanted Him to forgive her. While she meditated on the scripture a picture of Barbara kept popping into her mind.

"Oh, Lord, I thought I'd forgiven her?"

"Have you asked her to forgive you?" The question quickly came to her mind followed by a passage of scripture she'd written down on her page. She glanced at the page and read the scripture out loud.

"Matthew 5:23–24, 'Therefore if you bring your gift to the altar, and there remember that your brother has something against you, leave your gift there before the altar, and go your way. First, be reconciled to your brother, and then come and offer your gift.'"

She desperately wanted to experience the freedom Carol had talked about, and if it meant she needed to go to Barbara and ask for her forgiveness; she was willing to be obedient. After several minutes of agonizing thought, she prayed.

"Lord, I know I've harbored hatred toward Barbara for so many years. I ask You to forgive me and cleanse me from hatred and unforgiveness. I don't want to give the enemy a place because of my unforgiveness. I want to ask her for forgiveness, but I know I'll need Your grace. I ask You to go before me. I ask for the grace to forgive Michael and Barbara completely so that the memories are no longer mingled with pain. Help me see Barbara and Michael through Your eyes and to love them the way You love them. In the name of Jesus. Amen!"

She didn't feel any different, but she felt content as she fell asleep thinking about the life in her womb.

Zoe may not have felt different when she prayed, but Ramiah, her faithful guardian angel knew a major turn of events had occurred in the spirit realm. Doors that had been opened to the enemy for years—small entrances into her life to cause heartache and pain, and to bring destruction—were suddenly slammed shut. He saw several demons scampering away with the realization that they no longer had authority to take up residence in Zoe's life.

He began to dance and praise the Almighty as other angelic beings joined in his celebration of the One they wholeheartedly served and adored.

Every time their praise reached a harmonious crescendo, being joined by the angels and elders around the throne, they were compelled to sing and praise Him that much more. Ramiah was filled with ecstasy as all of heaven joined in to celebrate in the joy of his charge breaking free from the stronghold of the enemy.

Barbara was busy preparing for her women's prayer group, which met every other Friday at her house, when the home phone rang. She assumed it was probably one of the ladies calling to let her know she wouldn't be able to make it.

"Hello."

"Hello, Barbara, it's Zoe." Zoe never called Barbara, and her shaky voice on the other end of the line conjured up disturbing thoughts of Amos being hurt.

"Hi, Zoe, is Amos all right?" She could feel fear rising up from the pit of her stomach.

"Oh, yes, I'm sorry, he's fine. He's in his office; I think. I was actually calling to see if I could maybe come over to talk with you tonight. Do you guys have any plans?"

Barbara breathed a sigh of relief. "No, we don't have anything planned for tonight. Would you like to come for dinner?"

"No, I'd like to spend some time alone with you, if that's all right. I need to talk with you."

"Well…sure. Anytime will be fine." Barbara hoped her stepdaughter didn't notice the hesitation in her voice.

"Okay, I know you guys eat around eight when Dad gets home, so I'll come right after work if that's okay with you."

"That sounds fine. I'll see you then."

"Okay, thanks." The line went dead. Shocked, Barbara stared at the receiver. *What in the world is going on with her? Was I mistaken, or did Zoe actually sound nice?* Before turning her attention back to preparing for her meeting, she lifted up a short prayer to the Lord.

"Lord, I ask that you prepare my heart for whatever Zoe has to share with me tonight. Help me to respond in love toward her at all times. I pray for Your presence to be here in the midst of us and that You would bathe both of us in Your peace and love. In Jesus's name. Amen!"

Zoe was so preoccupied that she didn't see him walk in. She was stunned when out of the corner of her eye she saw a huge bouquet of pink roses.

"Hey, beautiful!" Zach leaned over the desk.

A scowl crossed Zoe's face. "Zach, I can't believe you'd have the guts to show your face in this office. What in the world are you doing here?" Zoe tried to keep her voice down so the waiting clients wouldn't overhear her conversation.

Zach set the roses down on her desk and began to talk fast. "Zoe, just let me explain. I haven't been able to get you out of my mind. I think I'm really in love with you, and…"

She didn't allow him the opportunity to finish his sentence. "First off, I doubt you know what true love is. Second, you can take your roses off my desk and get out. I told you that I don't ever want to see you again, and I meant it. I can't believe you have the audacity to show your face. Does your wife know you are here?"

Zach appeared to be visibly shaken. "Zoe, please. I know I messed up. My wife found out about us and told me I had to make a choice." It was nothing more than another desperate lie, but he was prepared to say whatever it took to win her back. "I miss you and…"

"Out!" Her voice rose as she pointed her finger toward the lobby doors. He turned to leave. "Take your roses too." He grabbed the roses, turned, and walked out the glass doors. Several faces turned toward her as she sat at her desk trying to gain her composure.

Her whole body was shaking. The magnetic physical attraction, which had drawn her to him when she'd first seen his picture on Facebook, was gone. However, she had been terrified that he would discover she was carrying his child and want to be a part of his life. She'd been careful to keep her growing bump tucked safely underneath her desk.

Oh, God, thank You that he couldn't tell I was pregnant. Then the thought came.

Can you forgive him?

Gosh, God, can't a poor pregnant girl get a break here? She thought about the question for a moment before responding. *Yes, I guess I can forgive him, but I don't want him to be a part of our lives. Is that wrong?*

"*Forgive!*"

"Can I fix you a cup of coffee or get you a glass of tea?" Barbara tried to calm the anxiety looming inside of her.

Zoe took a seat on the luxurious leather loveseat in the living room. "No, I'm fine. The house looks great. I forgot how beautifully you decorate." Zoe, feeling anxious herself, wanted to set Barbara at ease as quickly as possible.

"Thank you." Barbara blushed as she sat on the edge of Amos's leather recliner opposite Zoe.

"I know you're wondering why I'm here, so I'll just spit it out. I came to apologize to you and ask for your forgiveness for the horrible way I've treated you. I want to say I'm sorry for how awful I was to you at my wedding, when Emma was born and when she…" She choked on the last words, but Barbara knew what she'd wanted to say.

"Oh, Zoe, it's me who needs to apologize to you. I was the stepmom from hell. I was immature and selfish when I met your dad, and I was such a horrible stepmom. I can't even begin to tell you how sorry I am. I know I hurt you terribly, and I didn't blame you for hating me. I deserved it. I wasn't even aware of how horrible I'd been until I became a Christian. I'd do anything I could to turn back the clock and do it all differently, but I can't. Please forgive me."

Zoe had tears in her eyes. The genuineness of Barbara's apology touched her deeply.

"The truth is, I need a mom right now. I'm pregnant, and I'm afraid of going through this pregnancy alone. I feel like I don't have anyone to share my excitement with. I was hoping you'd consider going with me to my doctor appointments and being my delivery room coach when the baby arrives."

Tears of joy streamed down Barbara's face. "I'd be honored. Your dad told me about the pregnancy. We'll do whatever we can to help you and stand with you. You could even move in here for now if you want…" She stopped short, not wanting to overstep her bounds in this budding relationship.

"Thanks, but I need to learn to live on my own since I'm going to have to raise this child for the rest of it's life. I'd love for you to help me get a nursery ready though. I haven't got anything prepared."

"Absolutely! I'm thrilled that you'd ask. Do you know what you're having yet?" Barbara was beside herself in awe of the goodness of God. The road to reconciliation had been so long, it was hard to believe that their battle had come to an end.

"Yes, you and Amos will be the proud grandparents of a baby boy." Zoe smiled, wanting to make sure Barbara understood what she was saying. "I'm so sorry I never let you be a part of Emma's life. But I want you to be this little guy's grandma so you'd better start thinking about what he's going to call you."

"Zoe, I don't know what to say. I think this is one of the happiest days of my life. It truly is. Thank you so much." She jumped out of the recliner and rushed over to hug Zoe. The two wept in each other's arms.

A door slammed in the kitchen. "Honey, I'm home. Is that Zoe's car out front?" Amos was still yelling as he made his way into the living room. "Well, I'll be…" He was stunned to see his wife and daughter embracing.

"We're having a boy!" Barbara turned toward Amos, beaming even as tears of joy fell down her cheeks.

Amos smiled at the two women. "Well, you two look a sight, and I don't smell any food cooking, so should we go out and celebrate my new grandson?"

He then went over and held them both, one in each arm. "I've waited a long time to see my two girls loving on each other. A long time."

27

*Surely He shall deliver you from the snare of the fowler
and from the perilous pestilence.*

—Psalm 91:3

Michael stood confidently behind the plexiglass pulpit. His stomach had been in knots, his throat parched and dry all throughout the praise and worship service, but now, standing before the congregation, he felt nothing but peace.

"I'd like you to turn with me in your Bibles to Matthew chapter sixteen. We are going to read verses twenty-one through twenty-three."

"From that time Jesus began to show to His disciples that He must go to Jerusalem, and suffer many things from the elders and chief priests and scribes, and be killed, and be raised the third day. Then Peter took Him aside and began to rebuke Him, saying, 'Far be it from You, Lord; this shall not happen to You!' But He turned and said to Peter, 'Get behind Me, Satan! You are an offense to Me, for you are not mindful of the things of God, but the things of men.'"

Michael looked out at the congregation. "Jesus is telling His disciples that He is going to suffer at the hands of the religious leaders and die for the sins of this world. He was trying to prepare them and yet, at the same time, encourage them that His death was not the end. In three days after His death, He would

309

rise from the dead. However, because they didn't quite understand the methods and motives of God, Peter rebuked Jesus and told Him that He was wrong in thinking this could happen to Him."

Michael felt the presence of God with him as he continued. If he could have seen in the spirit realm, he'd have witnessed thousands of angels in attendance, praying and praising as he ministered the word. His personal angel, Deuel, stood beside him, his legs spread apart, one hand by his side while the other rested on his mighty sword in a defensive stance.

"According to *Webster's Dictionary*, the word *offense* means an act of stumbling or a cause or occasion to sin. The Greek translation of the word *offense* is *skandalon*. It means a trap or a snare. Jesus recognized the enemy was using Peter, one of His own disciples, to bring an opportunity for Him to be trapped or ensnared, keeping Him from obeying the will of God and fulfilling His destiny and calling."

"The very nature of a trap is that it generally doesn't appear to be a trap at all. It appears as something tempting or appealing rather than something dangerous or threatening."

Michael turned the pages of his Bible. "Psalm 91:3 is a scripture we are all familiar with. 'Surely He shall deliver you from the snare of the fowler and from the perilous pestilence.' A fowler is one who catches birds in a trap or snare. The fowler represents the enemy of our souls. His goal is to set out the perfect bait that's going to entice us to enter into his trap. We are told in Second Corinthians 2:11 that we are not to be ignorant of Satan's devices, or he will be able to take advantage of us."

"I want to talk about one of the most common traps of the enemy and one he used in my life. Fear. Most of you know what has taken place in my life over the last six months. On May seventeenth, a day forever etched in my mind; I was watching my little girl while my wife was at work. She drowned in our pool. As a matter of fact, I was on the phone with Pastor Steve when she woke up from a nap and wandered outside through a door I'd carelessly left open. Then, as if that weren't enough, my wife became so distraught with grief that she was unable to forgive me for the accident and has since filed for divorce. I don't believe my baby girl drowned because I was being punished or because Zoe and I were in some way disappointing to God. However, a very wise woman, my mom who is sitting right here in the front row, reminded me that we can open doors of opportunity to the enemy. We can, by our lack of diligence, sin in our life, unforgiveness, fear, or lack of obedience…open the door, so to speak, to Satan, therefore becoming trapped. Hosea 4:6 tells us, 'My people are destroyed for lack of knowledge.'"

"I used to be fearful of losing my wife. When I first met her, I felt like she was the most beautiful woman I'd ever seen, and I couldn't believe she could possibly be interested in me. I was raised in a very godly home, and I'm proud to say I was a virgin when Zoe and I married. I loved God with all my heart and loved memorizing the Bible. All I ever wanted to be in life was a pastor just like my Dad. I knew most girls my age weren't going to fall for a shy, awkward, gospel geek." The congregation laughed.

"We met at summer camp, and I was astounded when she agreed to date me when we returned to the real world. Then several years later, when she agreed to be my wife, I was in awe to be marrying such an amazing woman. She came from a very affluent home, and I always worried that I wouldn't be able to support her and keep her in the lifestyle she'd been accustomed to. I always feared one day she'd wake up and realize I wasn't good enough or that I'd fail her in some way. And sure enough, I did. Exactly what I feared happened."

"Fear does not come from God. It comes from the enemy. The word tells us that God has not given us a spirit of fear, but of power, love and a sound mind. The more I allowed fear to permeate my thoughts, the more I gave it place in my life, and it became, I believe, an open door to the enemy. First John 4:18 says that perfect love cast out fear. I wasn't trusting in the perfect love of God to keep my marriage. I wasn't standing against fear. Instead, I gave it place in my life by focusing on it and agreeing with it. Therefore, it became a snare or trap I was caught in. I've since learned that when the enemy tempts us, we need to focus on the exact opposite of what he places before us. Instead of concentrating on fearful thoughts and the 'what ifs' the enemy brings to mind, I'm learning instead to turn my focus on God's love. I've written down scriptures that talk about God's love for me, and memorized them, reciting them to myself whenever fear rears its ugly head."

He continued his message talking about the traps of pride, offense, materialism, religion, worldly pursuits, busyness, and unforgiveness before winding down and giving those who were unsaved a chance to accept Christ as their Lord and Savior. He also gave an altar call, giving those who felt like they might be trapped by the enemy a chance to be set free.

Michael was surrounded by people after the service telling him how much the message had ministered to them and how blessed they were by the sermon.

Once the sanctuary had cleared out, he caught the eye of his father and mother. Daniel came over and hugged his son tightly. "I'm so proud of you, son. You did an excellent job. I felt the presence of God, and I can see that you are clearly called to minister the word. That was a great message."

Michael smiled as his mother also hugged him and told him how blessed she'd been by the message. He thanked them for their support. However, as grateful as he was, he felt disappointed that Zoe hadn't been there. He'd hoped he might see her face out in the congregation even though she'd told him she couldn't come. He assumed she was probably out having a good time with her boyfriend. *Why in the world would you think she'd come to listen to you preach?* Though he was excited that God had used him to help others gain freedom from the enemy, he still wanted Zoe to be free to serve God and another opportunity to be the man she loved.

"You're going to lunch with that weird girl again? That makes the fourth time this week. What's gotten into you?" LaDonna had come to ask Zoe out to lunch and didn't try to disguise her disapproval of her friend's growing relationship with the girl she deemed to be a religious nut.

"Yes, I am." Zoe felt the need to defend her new-found friend. "We have a lot in common. She's pregnant too. I know I never told you, but I met my husband at a church camp and used to consider myself a believer in Christ. She's helping me find my way back to Him, slowly, but surely. Besides, she's sweet, and I don't think people should judge her or make fun of her just because she loves the Lord."

LaDonna wanted to say more on the subject but bit her tongue, reminding herself that Zoe was one of the founding partner's daughters and could, if she chose, cause her to lose her job.

"Well, you go, but I'm not joining ya'll. I don't want to be a Bible thumper. I don't want some old book telling me what I can and cannot do. I believe in God but not the way she does."

LaDonna turned in a huff and walked away from Zoe's desk. Zoe knew it would probably be the end of their brief friendship. Suddenly she realized that she had not been a witness to LaDonna or any of her other coworkers, and it grieved her to the core. She asked God to forgive her.

A thought struck her as she watched LaDonna disappear around the corner. *Maybe LaDonna is one of those traps the enemy set for me.* Zoe had listened intently to Michael's message on Sunday morning as it streamed live on the Internet. She'd been proud of him and wished more than ever that she could have been there to support him in person. She had taken extensive notes and afterward looked up each scripture reference and studied it out carefully, allowing the meaning to penetrate her heart. She wanted the word to transform her life. She'd even prayed the prayer of deliverance along with others in the congregation desiring to be set free.

"Excuse me, Pastor Michael, do you have a minute?" Michael looked up to see an attractive young woman standing in the doorway of his office. He recognized her as someone relatively new to the church. He knew that her name was Sophie Patterson and that she was a single mother of two. She wore a pair of faded blue jeans and a pink camisole top. Her brunette hair was cut in a cute bob hairstyle that shaped her pretty round face perfectly. She had the most gorgeous blue-green eyes he'd ever seen.

"Umm…hello…what can I do for you?" Michael rose from his chair and motioned for her to come into his office. She took a seat in front of his desk.

"I hope I'm not disturbing you." She didn't wait for a response. "I was here signing my children up for the fall harvest party and wanted to stop by and personally thank you for the message last Sunday. It was awesome, and I felt like it was just for me. I'm a single mom. I've made so many mistakes in my life, but I'm trying to get my life back on track with the Lord."

Michael was touched by how sincere and sweet she sounded. "Thank you!" He grinned across the desk. "I appreciate you taking the time to come by and tell me that." He was surprised at how nervous he felt in her presence. Her perfume filled the room, and he found himself drawn to her mesmerizing eyes. They were not only beautiful but lit up whenever she smiled.

"We haven't met in person, and I wanted to introduce myself. I've wanted to get involved in the church, and I thought maybe you might need help in the youth. I'm not a mature Christian by any means, but I am a school teacher, so I do know how to watch kids."

Her smile warmed his heart, which he noticed, was beating rather rapidly. He couldn't remember being affected by a woman like this in a long time. "Sure, we can always use extra help in the youth." Generally, he would pray and seek the Lord in such matters.

"Great!" Sophie clapped her hands together. "When can I start?"

"Well, we meet an hour before the youth arrive, to pray. So, how about six o'clock next Wednesday? I'll introduce you to everyone and pair you with Kira. She'll show you the ropes and help you until you feel comfortable."

"I'll be there. Thank you so much for the opportunity. I'm looking forward to getting to know more people in the church." The room became awkwardly silent. "I guess I'll see you Wednesday." She stood and walked toward the door turning back toward him before leaving. "Pastor Michael…"

"Just call me Michael." He blushed.

She smiled. "Okay, Michael. Thanks again. I'm so excited."

He flashed a schoolboy grin at her. "I'm excited too. We can always use the help, and I think you'll be a great addition."

She turned and walked away, leaving him drooling on his desk. *What in the world just happened?* He knew he'd felt attracted to her although he was committed to praying and waiting for Zoe. He excused his behavior to being caught off guard by her beauty. He tried to get back to his studies, but his thoughts kept returning to Sophie.

Dekar could see that his plan of attack against Zoe was unraveling. Ramiah was able to contend against his forces because she was praying and studying the word more. To his dismay, she was even quoting scriptures as she prayed. One swipe of Ramiah's sword and his underlings were forced to retreat. So he'd come up with another plan, a subtler one. He would come through the back door so to speak. He knew he had to be cautious as he set his scheme into action. Deuel was a formidable foe, wise to Dekar's tactics. But Dekar was sure his plan had a chance. He'd use a weapon that had been beneficial to him for centuries…physical attraction or chemistry, as the world liked to call it.

Carol and Zoe talked nonstop during their lunch hour. As far as Zoe was concerned, the time had passed much too quickly. She'd shared with Carol about Michael's message and how God had revealed some of the traps in her own life. Carol promised to go online and listen to the podcast later that evening once her daughter was in bed.

They'd also compared notes on their pregnancies and talked about names for their respective children. Zoe loved having someone with whom she could share the joy and excitement of her pregnancy. She could feel her son kicking and moving more and more each day, reminding her that a new life, one she would be solely responsible for, would soon be coming into the world. She'd confided her fears to Carol.

"You'll be fine, Zoe. Remember, you're never alone. God promises to be a Father to the fatherless. He'll help you raise your son until you meet someone who can be a father to him."

"Oh my gosh, I could never imagine trusting anyone again after what happened with Zach. Besides, I don't know if I'll ever meet anyone who can measure up to Michael. I know he made a mistake, but he was a great daddy. He adored Emma."

"Have you given any thought to maybe going to Michael and telling him what happened? He knows about Zach anyway, right? If Michael loves you unconditionally, he will accept you as you are. Pregnant. After all, Joseph loved Mary when she was pregnant with God's Son."

"I couldn't possibly…I've thought about it, but…I don't know. If the tables were turned, and I found out Michael had a child by another woman, I don't think I could be a good, loving mother to that child or forgive Michael enough to take him back. Maybe I still have unforgiveness issues, but I also have to think about my son. I want him to feel loved and accepted. Even though I've forgiven my stepmom, I still remember what it feels like to be rejected by a parent. I don't want that for him. If I have to raise him by myself, so be it."

Carol shrugged. "Okay. I'll just keep praying for God's wisdom and direction in the matter for you. In the meantime, I have two coming, and I still haven't decided on a name for either one of them. You're going to have to help me."

They spent the rest of their time laughing hysterically over some of the ridiculous names they came up with for their babies.

Zoe returned to her desk thankful that God had sent Carol into her life at just the right time.

"Kira, have you met Sophie? She'll be helping us with the youth. I told her she could hang with you until she feels comfortable." Michael noticed the surprise on Kira's face. It was their practice to pray about all new adult leaders at their monthly leadership meeting before asking them to join the team.

"Hi, Sophie. Yea, we met a couple of Sunday's ago. I'll be happy to show you the ropes. Tonight's the harvest party so we might have our hands full."

"Great! Well then, you are in good hands." Michael smiled at Sophie before turning to Kira. "Can you finish introducing her around? I need to take care of a few things before the party starts." He then turned and walked away from the two women.

There was a nagging uneasiness in his spirit. He knew he should have sought God before asking Sophie to join the team. He realized the moment she showed up for the youth event that he'd made a mistake. However, she was so sweet and seemed very eager to help. Besides, he rationalized, what could it hurt? It might help her in her growth with the Lord.

"So how long have you been coming to church here?" Though Kira's tone was sweet, she wanted to find out as much as she could about this girl who'd apparently captured Michael's attention. *I wonder if she is trying to weasel in on Michael.* She knew the girl was a single mom and, therefore, might be looking for a husband to help raise her young children. *Michael might be easy prey.*

"Oh, I guess on and off for about four months. I've tried a few other churches as well, but I love Pastor Steve's preaching. I haven't made any friends here, so I wanted to get involved. What about you? How long have you been going here?" Her voice was soft and smooth like butter.

"Brad and I were here when Pastor Steve started the church in his home. Brad's on the board and is an elder. So what brought you to this church?"

"Honestly, I wanted better for my kids. My dad has been in and out of prison so many times I've lost count. My mom raised me. I wanted my children to be brought up in a more stable environment. I've already been married and divorced twice, so I thought maybe I might find a godly man in the church.

We live in an apartment just a couple of blocks from here."

Kira felt a tinge of guilt for judging the girl. *It seems like she's had a rough life. Maybe God brought her here for us to love on. Just as long as she doesn't think she's going to sink her teeth into our sweet Michael.*

"Come on; I'll introduce you to everyone."

Michael noticed Sophie bent over her left back tire as he walked toward his car. The parking lot was almost empty except for a few folks who'd hung around to help clean up the grounds after the harvest party. No one else had seen Sophie trying to change a flat tire on her own. Her two children were seated on the curb.

"Hey, do you need help with that?" Michael knelt down beside Sophie.

"Oh gosh, thanks, Michael. I came out after picking up the kids, and my tire was flat. I thought I might be able to master it on my own. It always looks so easy when someone else does it."

She laughed as she stood to her feet. "I'd be glad to let you help. I know the kids are worn out." She glanced toward her children.

"So, you have a boy and a girl?" Michael busied himself with changing the tire.

"Yes, Dakota is four and my baby girl, Saige, is just turning two this month. I have my hands full, but I love them with all my heart."

"I know what you mean." Thoughts of Emma came flooding into his mind.

"I heard your testimony Sunday. I'm so sorry for the loss of your little girl. I would be devastated if anything happened to one of my babies. It's hard being a single mom, but I wouldn't trade them for anything in the world."

The compassion in her voice touched Michael. "There you go, all done. Ya'll can be on your way now. Your children have been remarkably patient."

She laughed while picking up her daughter. "Oh, don't be fooled. They're just tired. Listen, I owe you. How about dinner this Saturday night? You can come hang out with us. Saturday is always movie night."

Michael hesitated. "I don't know. I…" He couldn't come up with a good reason as to why he shouldn't go. "Well, I guess I can. Give me your number and address." He took out his cell phone to put in her information.

"Come around six, if that's okay." She gave him her number and address before strapping the children into their car seats. "Thanks so much. I'd probably still be down there reading the manual."

"Anytime. I'm glad I could help." He watched her back out and drive away. He sensed that she was attracted to him and knew he shouldn't have accepted her invitation, but he felt an almost magnetic pull toward her. She was so sweet and easy on the eyes.

"I'm just saying I don't think we should be trying to do the Holy Spirit's job. He's quite capable of training this girl up in the way of the Lord. God was patient with us when we got saved. Remember?"

Brad and Kira were in a heated discussion as they prepared for bed. She'd complained about the new girl Sophie during the short drive home from church. Their argument had escalated when Brad hadn't agreed with her opinion of what should be done about the matter.

"Brad, you should have seen the way she was dressed. I'm just asking if you think I should talk to her about dressing a little more modestly?" Kira folded her arms over her chest.

"I think that's Michael's job as the youth pastor, don't you?"

"Well, normally yea. But I think this girl is in hot pursuit after Michael, and he may not be able to see clearly. She's drop-dead gorgeous, and he doesn't have a wife to help balance him out in this area." Kira, perturbed at Brad, threw the decorative pillows off of the bed and onto the floor.

"No, but he is a man of God, and he listens to the voice of the Lord. I'm sure he'll do what's right. Besides, we weren't perfect when we came into the church, and we can't expect others to be. We have to love the fish God brings to us. Not kill 'em and eat 'em." Brad pulled the covers back and got into bed. "I don't want to argue with you. I just think you have a problem with this girl because you want Michael and Zoe to get back together. I know she's seeing someone else, or at least that's what Michael told me. So it might be time for him to move on. We have to trust Michael to follow God. Let's just pray about it and see how God wants to handle the situation."

"I know you're right, but I think he should have waited to have her join the team. No one really knows her. I'm just sayin'…" Though her feelings were hurt, she couldn't stay mad at Brad. He always tried to follow after God's will.

"Wait, what did I hear? Could you say that a little louder? I'm what? Did you say that I'm right?" Brad grinned.

"Oh hush." She hit him playfully over the head with her pillow. She loved that he could always turn an argument around and make her laugh.

28

Beloved, if God so loved us, we also ought to love one another.
—1 John 4:11

Michael was startled awake by a dream early Friday morning. In the dream, he saw himself standing before a door. He sensed that someone was standing on the other side of the door. His excitement to open it and discover who was on the other side was tangible even within his dream state. He could hear laughter and someone humming a melody he'd never heard before. As he reached to put his hand on the beautiful crystal knob, a grotesque being grabbed him from behind. He'd come from out of nowhere. Michael struggled to get free and tried desperately to shout the name of Jesus, but before he could get it out of his mouth, the ugly being turned into the most beautiful angel he'd ever seen. Confusion and fear pulled him out of a deep sleep. He grabbed the pen and notepad, which he kept on his nightstand, to document the dream.

Though it was barely four in the morning, he threw back the covers, having decided to get out of bed and pray. Michael washed his face and fixed himself a cup of hot coffee before sitting on his bed to pray.

"Father, I know that was a warning dream, but what are you warning me about? Holy Spirit, You are the interpreter of dreams, so I ask you to show me the meaning of this dream." He sat quietly, giving the Holy Spirit opportunity to bring revelation while he pondered the dream.

Why did the demon turn into an angel? The scripture passage in Second Corinthians 11:14 came quickly to him. Satan transforms himself into an angel of light. It was a scripture he knew well. He wondered who was on the other side of the door. He remembered that he'd heard someone laughing and humming. *They sounded happy. Who was it, Lord? Who does the being represent in my life?* He had more questions than answers after spending over an hour and a half in prayer.

All throughout the day, his mind kept going back to the dream. He remembered the dream he'd had just before Emma drowned. He didn't want to miss God's warning ever again.

Zoe hummed softly as she made her way home from work. An old familiar tune kept bubbling up in her spirit. She sang aloud as the words came flooding back to her remembrance.

> Into my heart, into my heart,
> Come into my heart, Lord Jesus;
> Come in today, come in to stay;
> Come into my heart, Lord Jesus.

She wiped away tears falling on her cheeks as she sang the hymn over and over again. And then suddenly, she heard a voice rumble up out of her spirit. It was distinctive and authoritative yet filled with compassion.

"I'm already here! I never left your side."

The voice, which she knew to be her Lord's, took her completely by surprise. She pulled the car over into a fast-food restaurant parking lot and put it in park. She prayed through the sobs that poured out from deep within.

"Oh, God. I don't deserve Your love, but I thank You so much for loving me even when I was unlovable. I'm so grateful that You never gave up on me though I gave up on You. I love You so much and want to serve you and fulfill the destiny You've had for me from the foundation of the world. Thank You for giving me another chance. Thank You for this baby in my womb and keeping me from making the awful mistake of aborting him. Thank You for Carol's friendship. You are so good to me, and I'm so thankful."

Every tear had cleansing power to wash her heart and soul. She could feel shackles being broken, and the weights being removed. Her spirit soared as she sang another familiar hymn, "I Surrender All."

"Lord, please use me for Your glory. I want that more than anything. I desire to walk with You the way Michael and Carol walk with You. I surrender my life completely over to You. Have Your way in me."

She wasn't sure how long she'd sat basking in the presence of the Lord, but she sensed that somehow she was different. *Amazingly, here in the middle of a parking lot in Houston, I've had an encounter with the God of this universe. He has set me free and renewed me.* A broad smile framed her glowing face, the first genuine smile that had touched her lips since Emma's death.

Michael stood in front of Sophie's apartment. He'd almost called and canceled on her twice but felt it would be impolite. *It's just a thank you dinner* he kept reassuring himself.

His palms were sweaty as he rang the doorbell. He heard laughter and tiny feet racing toward the door, followed by Sophie's voice gently reprimanding her children.

"Hey, come on in." Sophie, looking beautiful in a flowered print maxi dress, was completely out of breath. "I'm sorry I'm so out of breath, but I had to race these two rug rats to the door." She laughed as she stepped aside for him to enter.

"What smells so good?" Michael followed Sophie into the kitchen. The children resumed their places on the couch watching a cartoon video.

"It's lasagna. My kids love it, so I thought you might like it too. Would you like a glass of wine?" She picked up a bottle of red wine and began to pour into one of two wine glasses sitting on the granite counter.

"Well, I…guess. Sure. I don't usually drink, but one glass won't hurt." He smiled weakly; he didn't want to embarrass her or make her feel judged by making an issue of her offer. *What is it about this woman that makes my knees turn to rubber?*

"Dinner's almost done. I hope you're hungry because I made enough to feed an army. My Dakota can put away some lasagna for such a small boy." Sophie handed him the glass. A chill went up his spine as their hands touched.

Michael felt his face flush as he took a sip of the wine. It helped calm his nervousness. He felt like a silly schoolboy unable to think of anything to say. Her calm voice broke the silence.

"I'm so glad you've given me the opportunity to help with the youth. I enjoyed the harvest party the other night. I can tell the youth love you."

"Thanks, I enjoy working with them. I'm glad you've joined us. You know I've only been the youth pastor now for a little over two months. So I'm kind of new at it although I was a volunteer leader for several years with the previous youth pastor."

"Well, I think you're good at it." She looked up and smiled at him as she busied herself with making a dinner salad.

He couldn't help but notice the curves in her body as she bent to check on the lasagna in the oven. She caught his glance out of the corner of her eye.

"I think it's ready. Let me get my kids washed up. I warn you though, dinner time can be loud in our house."

"That's okay. I miss loud. My apartment can be lonely and quiet."

The evening was fun. The children asked him every question their active little minds could conjure up. They wanted to know if he had a dog, if he had a house, and if he had a mommy and a daddy. They were also quick to inform him that their daddy didn't live with them. They wanted to show him their rooms and all of their favorite toys and even requested he read them a story before going to bed, which he did.

Sophie walked him to the door. "I think Dakota and Saige enjoyed your company as much as I did."

"Thanks. I enjoyed them too."

She stood barely an inch away from him looking up into his eyes. He could smell her hair and feel the heat of her body close to his. "I hope you enjoyed my company too."

He felt his face flush again. He wanted to draw her into his arms and kiss her. The physical attraction he felt toward her was overwhelming. However, his spirit was stronger than his flesh. *I'd better get out of here before I get into trouble.*

"I did. Thanks again for dinner. I enjoyed it." He could feel her disappointment as he turned and walked toward his car. By the time he reached it, she had gone back into her apartment and shut the door.

He took a moment to bridle the passion he felt burning within. He wanted to knock on Sophie's door and show her how very much he'd enjoyed her company, but he knew he might be opening a door that wasn't supposed to be opened just yet.

Michael couldn't see the spirits of Lust and Sensuality that Deuel fought hard to keep at bay. They were aggressively attacking his charge using his loneliness and physical attraction to try and entice him into a trap. Deuel had tried desperately to get Michael to cancel the dinner, but to his charge's credit, he didn't want to hurt the girl's feelings. It wasn't that she was a bad person. On the contrary, the Almightly loved her unconditionally and was looking out for her best interest too. However, she was still prey to these horrid spirits because of the promiscuous lifestyle she'd led in her past. She didn't have enough of the word of God within her to know it was wrong to dress provocatively to gain the attention of a man. She was still doing what the world had taught her: using the power of seduction to get what she wanted. She was lonely and desired, more than anything, a godly man to spend the rest of her life with and help raise her two children. However, Michael was not the right man for her. The Almighty had a different plan for Michael, and it was Deuel's responsibility to make sure God's plan came to pass in his charge's life.

Zoe's friendship with Carol was growing, and Carol had invited her over for dinner so she could meet her husband. As she made the twenty-minute drive to their house, she reflected on how they'd discovered, during lunches shared together and late-night phone conversations that they had a lot in common. God was using Carol as a positive influence, helping Zoe grow stronger in her faith walk.

Carol had invited her to go to church with them the following Sunday though Zoe turned her down. She'd relayed to Carol that, for the first time, she was going to attend church with Amos and Barbara. They were going to go as a family. Since it would be the Sunday after Thanksgiving, even her brother John was coming in from College Station, where he was still attending school, to join them. She was looking forward to it. It was her first Thanksgiving with Barbara, Amos, and John since she'd left their home following her graduation from high school. She and Michael had always spent the holidays with his family since she'd refused to be in Barbara's presence. She tried not to dwell on the fact that Michael and Emma wouldn't be there to share in the joy of their reconciliation.

God was restoring her family, and for once in her life, she felt free from the unforgiveness that had kept her bound for so many years. The difference in her countenance was astounding. Even Amos had remarked that she appeared to be happier and more content though he credited it to her pregnancy. She and Barbara spoke on the phone almost every day, making constant plans for the nursery and talking about every aspect of her pregnancy.

She'd decided to name her son Amos Michael Davis. Amos had strutted around like a proud peacock for days after she'd told him. It had tickled her and Barbara to see him so excited. The baby gave her something to look forward to. She felt like her life had meaning and purpose once again.

She was excited to meet John and Olivia whom she'd heard so much about. However, just as she was pulling into Carol's subdivision, her phone rang.

"Hello." She spoke into the car audio system.

She could hear the controlled panic in the voice on the other line. "Zoe, it's Carol. We're on our way to the hospital. My water just broke, and I'm having contractions. It's too early, and I'm so scared. Please be praying. Pray that my babies are okay."

"Oh, my gosh. I certainly will. I'm coming to the hospital. Tell John that I'm coming. I know I probably can't do anything, but I want to be there for you. I'll call my stepmom and ask her to pray too." Zoe was already turning the car around to head toward the hospital before they hung up from their conversation.

"Oh, Lord, please keep those babies safe. Carol has already gone through the loss of a child, and I know how devastating that can be. I know she's a lot stronger than I am in her relationship with You, but she's scared. Give her and John a peace that surpasses their understanding. I pray for wisdom for her doctors and Your guidance in this situation. In Jesus's name."

She could feel little Amos kicking and squirming in her womb as if in agreement with her prayer.

Zoe prayed silently as she paced in the crowded waiting room. It was well over two hours before John came out to give her an update on Carol and the babies. Zoe could see the strain all over his face.

"She's doing good. They are giving her meds to stop the contractions and help the babies' lungs grow stronger. She's going to have to stay in the hospital until she delivers. She's barely twenty-six weeks, and the doctor wants to hold her off as long as possible. She said she wants to see you, but the doctor told her that's not gonna happen tonight. They want to keep her as calm as possible. We appreciate you coming. Just knowing that you are here is a comfort to her. Oh, by the way, I'm John." It was the first time he smiled since he'd come out to meet with her.

"I feel like I know you already. Carol talks about you all the time. Is there anything I can do to help? Do you have someone taking care of Olivia?"

"Yes, my mom came over to the house and is spending the night with her. Right now, I think we just need lots of prayers. I've contacted our pastor, and he's assured me that he would put us on the prayer chain at church."

"Well, you know I'll be praying, and I've asked my stepmom to put ya'll on the prayer chain at her church as well. Please tell Carol I love her, and that I'll text her tomorrow to see how she's doing if that's okay." She picked up her purse in preparation to leave.

"Sure. That'd be great. Hopefully, she can have company tomorrow. You know her. It's not going to be easy to keep her in bed and away from Olivia."

"Tell her I said to rest because Amos wants his little buddies to be healthy." She smiled and gave John a quick hug before leaving the hospital.

She prayed the entire drive back to her apartment.

Zoe sat in the crowded sanctuary of Barbara and Amos's church sandwiched between her dad and brother John. Except for her grandma's funeral, it was the first time she'd set foot in a church since Emma's death. She listened intently as the young, highly animated and energetic pastor preached on the subject of love. She could feel the Holy Spirit's presence in the sanctuary and knew she was right where she needed to be, devouring every word.

"Jesus said if we love Him, then we are commanded, it's not just a sweet suggestion but a royal command, to love our neighbor as our self. How did

Jesus prove His love for us? He laid His life down and nailed it to the cross along with our sins. He tells us in First John 4:11, that if God so loved us, we also ought to love one another. God loved us by sacrificing His only Son. Parents, how many of you would sacrifice your only child to save the life of another? I have three children, and although sometimes I'm tempted…" He stopped and smiled while the congregation laughed. "I love them, and though I love every one of you dearly, I would not sacrifice one of my babies' lives for yours. But God loves us so much that He was willing to sacrifice His only Son so that we could live in a love relationship with Him."

"Romans 5:5 reminds us that God's love has been poured out in our hearts by the Holy Spirit. Therefore, I have the ability and capacity living within me to love just as He loves. I can love because Love, with a capital L, lives in me. First John 4:8 says that God is love. If He is love and He lives in me, then it stands to reason that I can love others just as I am loved by Him. Loving others is so very important to God because love is the essence of who He is. We need to be praying to have His love flowing through us more than we pray for great assignments or spiritual gifts because, without His love as the foundation, these are nothing."

Zoe got lost in the message. She thought about Grandma Abby and how she'd neglected her in the last few months of her life because she'd been engrossed in her self-centered lifestyle. She'd gotten so wrapped up in her loss that she hadn't reached out to her grandma. She thought about Michael and how he'd loved her unconditionally. He'd continued to love her even when she'd strayed from her marriage and her faith. He was an example to her of Christ's love. She found it unbearable to think that she'd squandered such a love. She glanced down at Barbara, who was beaming from ear to ear as she listened to her pastor. Today was a special day for Barbara, having her husband and children in church with her. Barbara had tried so many times to reach out to her in love, and Zoe had turned her down coldheartedly. She was thankful God's love had mended the gap between them.

Her mind then turned to her friend Carol. She had told Zoe how she'd often prayed for her even before they'd become friends. Carol was certainly a demonstration of God's love to her. She was a person who loved selflessly, even when love wasn't reciprocated in return. She silently thanked God for her friend. She was teaching her, by example, so much about love and forgiveness and dealing with tragedy.

The pastor, having come to the end of his message, gave an altar call for those who would desire to walk in the God-kind of love, who wanted to go deeper in their love walk and demonstrate God's love to the lost and hurting world around them. Zoe could feel the tug of the Spirit but felt timid about going up to the front of the church. She leaned over her dad and looked at Barbara.

"Will you go up front with me?" She mouthed the words to Barbara.

Barbara didn't say a word but grasped Zoe's hand, and the two walked the aisle, tears streaming down both of their faces, to the front of the church where several members of the prayer team were waiting to pray with those in need.

Zoe felt like God was continuing His cleansing work in her life as the woman prayed boldly for her, without even knowing exactly why Zoe'd come to the altar. She then prophesied over her.

"God says He is doing a new thing in your life. He wants you to know He is your God, and He is and has always been, in the midst of you. He says He's giving you a new heart today, and He's washing you and cleansing away the past. There is a call on your life, and everything you've been through has been to bring you into this place and prepare you for your destiny. He will use you to comfort others with the same comfort you have received from Him."

Zoe was amazed as she listened to this stranger speak over her. It was as if the woman had peered into her soul. She thanked her and was about to return to her seat when she suddenly turned back around.

"My friend is in the hospital expecting twins. It's way too early for her to be having the babies. Will you pray for her with me?" The three women joined hands as the prayer team member prayed for Carol, John, and the babies.

She felt a refreshing joy as she walked back to her seat arm in arm with Barbara.

29

Though the fig tree may not blossom, Nor fruit be on the vines;
Though the labor of the olive may fail, And the fields yield no food;
Though the flock may be cut off from the fold, And there be no herd in the stalls
— Yet I will rejoice in the Lord, I will joy in the God of my salvation.
—Habakkuk 3:17–18

"**A**re you doing all right?" The delivery room nurse stroked Carol's hand. Carol nodded affirmatively, though she was far from being all right. She was in a surgical room awaiting the birth of her twins who were insistent on making an early arrival. The medical staff had tried their best to hold off the labor, but apparently, God had another plan because her contractions kept coming. She'd barely begun preparing their nursery. To say she felt stressed and scared was an understatement. She was concerned for the life of her twins yet excited to see the gifts God was placing into their care.

John bent down, his face next to Carol's, encouraging her as the doctor performed the C-section. "Don't cry, baby. It's going to be okay. We have to trust God and His plan. We've prayed in faith. Now we have to put them into His hands."

"Almost there." The nurse informed the worried couple.

Carol heard the slight squeak of her first tiny premature twin as she made her entrance into the world.

"It's a girl!" The doctor held up their baby girl before quickly handing her off to a waiting nurse and busying himself with the next delivery.

Carol watched as the staff of nurses and pediatrician hovered over her new daughter. "Her name is Faith Alexandria."

She was so preoccupied with trying to get a glimpse of her new baby girl that she momentarily forgot she had another child ready to greet the world.

"Ahh…and you have a boy!" The doctor had a worried expression on his face as he handed the baby over to a nurse. He was aware of the loss of their first son and their hopes that one of the babies would be a boy.

The tiny boy didn't make a peep. "Is he okay?" Carol could sense the fear rising within her.

"His name is Christian Jacob." John smiled down at his wife. He and Carol had come up with two boy names and two girl names since they'd chosen not to know the sex of the babies until they were born. They'd wanted it to be a surprise from God. They'd also determined their top two favorite names in case they had one of each sex.

"How are they? Do they look okay?" Carol's joy and excitement was intermingled with a sudden worry and dread. "I didn't hear Christian make any noise." Though little Christian, weighing two pounds and one ounce, barely weighed more than his sister, Carol was concerned that she still hadn't heard a cry coming from the tiny infant. "Will someone please tell me how they are doing?"

A pediatric nurse came and bent over Carol. "We are still examining them, but your daughter appears to be doing fairly well. We are trying to stabilize your son. The doctor will come and speak to you as soon as we have them situated and stable in the NICU."

John kissed Carol tenderly. He had tears in his eyes. They got a brief glimpse of their babies as the nurses whisked them off in their incubators to the NICU. John clasped his wife's hand, and they prayed together for their children while the nurses prepared to take her back to her room.

Zoe tried to call Carol as soon as she got into her car. Though she was surprised when her friend didn't answer her cell phone, she assumed she was probably in the bathroom or taking a shower. She was excited to tell Carol she'd prayed for her and the babies at the altar, but she also wanted to share how great the message had been and how it had ministered to her. She felt it was important to let her know that she'd been a great example of God's love to her. She called the number once more, but when she didn't get an answer, she went on to meet her family for lunch.

Michael was about to open his car door when he caught a glimpse of Sophie walking toward him, Dakota and Saige following close behind her.

"Hey, I saw you walking out of church, so I thought I'd come say hi. That was a great service. I just love Pastor Steve. I always feel like he's talking directly to me." The children tugged on the hem of her jacket as Sophie chattered away.

Michael smiled and nodded toward the children. "I think they're ready to get going."

"Mommy it cold. Wet's go." Saige pulled on Sophie's hand while whining in her childish voice.

"I know it's cold baby. Just a minute." Sophie picked up her daughter and slung her on her hip before turning her attention back to Michael. "I think we're going to grab a burger. Do you want to join us?"

Michael was about to say no when Dakota piped up. "Yea, Mista Michael. Come eat with us. Pweese!"

"How can I turn down an invitation like that?" Michael laughed. "Where are you going?"

"We're going to the McDonald's over by my apartment. Is that okay with you?"

"Sure. I'll see you there."

After nearly four hours, Carol and John were finally told that they could go down to see their babies in the NICU. John wheeled her down through the maze of corridors and to the place that would become familiar to them in the weeks to come. The doctor had tried to prepare them for what they would see, but to Carol's absolute horror, nothing could have prepared her for the sight before her. Both babies were hooked up to ventilators, were on warming beds, and wore tiny blindfolds over their eyes to protect their paper-thin eyelids. Their little bodies were swallowed up by IV lines and wires that were attached to different areas of their miniature appendages. They appeared to be so frail and helpless. Carol buried her head in John's shoulder and cried.

"I know God is sovereign and that He loves us and these babies. I know He can turn this for good, but it's just so hard. I don't understand it."

John held her tightly. "I know, honey. I don't understand either. We're going to have to trust and lean on Him. We need to speak His word and keep our eyes on Him no matter what the doctors tell us. Okay? We are in a battle, and we are going to have to fight. It's not a time to crater to fear."

"Okay." Carol was barely able to squeak out the word. She knew her husband was right. This was one of those times when her faith was being tested, and she was going to have to stand, speak God's word over her children and believe even in the midst of this situation.

Still leaning on John's shoulder, she asked him to say a prayer. With his arms wrapped around her, he began to pray for their children. "Father, these are Your babies. You love them infinitely more than we could love them. You knew them in Carol's womb. You gave them life and called their little spirits into being. We choose right now to trust you for Faith and Christian. We ask You to continue the growth process that You began when You planted them in Carol's womb. We ask You to completely heal them and keep them healthy so we can take them home to train them up in the way You would desire us to. We speak life and health over their tiny bodies. We pray for wisdom for the doctors and nurses and that You would direct them as they care for them. We ask for grace and courage as we walk through this trial. Help us to be a witness of Your love to all we come in contact with in this hospital. We also pray for all of the other babies in this NICU and their families. We ask that You would heal them and bless them. Father, we love You and put our hope in You. Though the fig tree may not blossom, nor fruit be on the vines; though the labor of the olive may fail, and the fields yield no food; though the flock may be cut off from the fold, and there be no herd in the stalls, yet we will rejoice in the Lord. We will joy in the God of our salvation. In Jesus's mighty name, we pray. Amen."

He bent down and kissed Carol tenderly on the top of her head. "Remember when we were first taught that scripture after we'd come to Christ. We had to learn to praise God even after losing Jacob. Well, we have to praise Him now and trust that His plan for our lives is perfect. He's already brought us through so much. How can we not trust Him? I love you. We have each other, and God has us. No matter what happens, we have to praise Him."

Ozias and Azaliah, their guardian angels, as well as the angels that had been assigned to surround and protect the children, formed a circle around the little family. They prayed and worshiped the Almighty. Though human ears could not hear the incredibly beautiful harmonious sounds coming from them, the angelic choirs of heaven could and joined in with their songs of worship. The Almighty could hear it too, and though it couldn't be seen with natural eyes, a shaft of light brighter than the sun shone down from heaven and penetrated into the sterile NICU as John prayed. He and his family were completely enveloped in the light.

Michael sat across the table from Sophie in the McDonald's restaurant. Sounds of children joyfully screeching as they romped on the indoor playground, people laughing and talking at almost every table, babies crying mixed with the chorus of people ordering food at the overflowing counter made it difficult to have much of a private conversation. For that, Michael was grateful. He enjoyed watching the children play. He'd missed that since Emma had died. Being here in the midst of such a noisy, crowded place topped being alone in his apartment on a Sunday afternoon.

Sophie carefully kept her eyes on her children as they mixed and mingled at play with other boys and girls.

"I have to watch Dakota. He'd have all of them in single file marching to his drumbeat if he could. He can be pretty bossy."

Michael flashed her a dimpled grin. "You have great kids. After losing my baby girl, I can appreciate the simple joy of just watching children play. It's amazing how much personality such little people can have."

"Yea! I love my babies. They keep me busy and on my toes all the time, but my life would be empty without them."

Michael glanced at Sophie as she watched her children playing. She was a natural beauty. *She would be beautiful even without a lick of makeup.* It felt comfortable to be sitting with her even when they weren't sharing conversation. But something was nagging at him. He felt the discomfort of the Holy Spirit, though he didn't know why. The longer he sat there, the more uncomfortable he felt. *What is it, Lord?*

He leaned in toward Sophie to be sure she'd hear him. "I think I'm going to have to get going. I'm going to tell the kids good-bye. I enjoyed our lunch. Thanks for inviting me."

He could tell she was disappointed that he was leaving though they'd been there for at least forty-five minutes. He knew she was just as attracted to him as he was to her and that she was searching for something more than just a friendship. She wanted a husband, a lover, and someone to be a father for her children.

"You're leaving so soon?" She didn't try to hide the disappointment in her voice. "Well, I guess I'll see you Wednesday night at youth group then. Thanks for joining us. I know the kids enjoyed you being here. And thanks for buying our lunch. That's not why I invited you, ya know."

"I know."

She went to retrieve Dakota and Saige from the play yard. "Mr. Michael is going to have to leave, so you need to tell him thank you for coming and buying our lunch."

Both children came bounding over to the table. Dakota whined his disapproval that Michael was leaving so soon. But Michael was especially touched as tiny Saige pursed her cute little lips and kissed him while wrapping her arms around his neck. "Tank you, Miser Michael."

Sophie gave Michael an awkward hug. "Thanks again for buying our lunch. I enjoyed you coming with us even if it was so noisy in here that we couldn't hear ourselves much less each other."

"You're welcome. I enjoyed it too. I'll see you guys soon."

He left the McDonald's feeling somewhat out of joint. Though he knew he hadn't done anything wrong, he felt like something wasn't quite right. *Maybe God doesn't approve of me getting close to Sophie and her children.*

Zoe entered Carol's room with a bouquet of beautiful fragrant flowers in one hand and two huge balloons, one pink, the other blue. Her makeup was streaked from crying, and she was visibly shaken and out of breath.

"I got here as soon as I could." She set the flowers on the nightstand beside Carol before reaching over to give her friend a hug all the while still holding onto the balloons. "How are you feeling? Are you doing all right?"

"I've felt better. I haven't had much time to rest. We've been down in the NICU. They just gave me a pain pill, so I'm beginning to feel better." Tears formed in her eyes. "Oh, Zoe, they are so tiny, but they're so beautiful."

"I love the names Faith and Christian." Zoe straightened up and went over to greet John. "Congratulations, Daddy!" She offered a weak smile as she hugged him. "I'm so sorry! I was hoping ya'll would be able to hold off the delivery for at least another week or so."

John had been the one to call her after he and Carol had returned to their room from their first NICU visit. He'd given her a report on the condition of the babies and told her he thought his wife could use a visit from her.

"Is there anything I can do for you guys?" Zoe turned her attention back to Carol.

"No, John's mom is at home with Olivia, and our church is already lining up meals for us for the next several months. My parents are on the way from West Virginia. They'll stay at the house and take turns watching Olivia. I'm just glad you're here with me."

They made small talk for several minutes before it became apparent to Zoe that the pain medication was beginning to affect Carol. Her eyelids were getting heavy, and the trauma of delivering preemies by C-section had taken its toll on her.

"Listen, you look like you're fading fast. I'm not going to stay, but I promise to come back by tomorrow after work. Just keep in touch with me, and let me know how ya'll are doing. Call anytime, night or day. I promise I will be praying."

Carol barely protested the fact that Zoe was leaving. She was fast asleep before Zoe had even reached the elevator at the end of the hallway.

Michael sat on the bed, took the wrinkled piece of paper out of his Bible, and reread the word God had given him. God had promised that one day he'd have children again. He couldn't see it ever happening with Zoe and didn't understand why God was making it clear to him that he wasn't to pursue a relationship with Sophie. He knew she wasn't as strong in her walk as he was, but Zoe hadn't been either when he'd first met her.

He'd spent quite a bit of time in prayer the previous evening when he'd come home from his lunch with Sophie and her children. The nagging feeling he'd had just wouldn't go away, and during that time of prayer, he sensed God was speaking to his heart about his desire to have a relationship with her. Though she was beautiful, and he enjoyed being with her, God made it clear that it wasn't in His plan. He couldn't help but wonder why. He could easily see himself with her, and even being a father to her children. He realized he'd almost been trapped by his own emotions and a strong desire for a relationship. *How foolish I am to get myself into a trap right after I preached on it.*

"Not my will but Yours be done, Lord. I will continue to wait and praise You in the midst of my circumstances."

Loneliness filled his heart. He hated coming home day after day to an empty apartment. He tried to block out the silence with the television but only ended up watching shows he knew he shouldn't be watching.

The Lord had spoken to him one night when he was in the middle of watching a comedic sitcom that promoted homosexuality, sexual promiscuity, and foul humor, not to mention using offensive language which he knew was wrong.

"*What if demonic spirits are released into your home and given permission to affect your life because of some of the shows you are watching?*" It had come to him as a thought, but he knew God had been the one posing the question to him. It had startled him, and he'd immediately turned the television off. Since then, he'd tried to be more cautious as to what he allowed into his eye gate.

He knew he was going to have to tell Sophie he would not be able to see her again outside of the church. It wasn't as if anything had been said or even started between the two of them, except he knew she was interested in him and suspected she was aware that he was attracted to her.

He wished he'd prayed about her joining the youth leadership before inviting her onto the team. *It's going to be awkward seeing her on Wednesday nights.*

"Father, please prepare her heart. I don't want to hurt her. I'm very sorry I didn't seek you before striking up a friendship with her and asking her to join the leadership team. I ask for Your forgiveness. Please give me the words to speak to her. I know You love her and don't want to see her or her children hurt. In Jesus's name, I pray."

Dekar was disgusted as he looked on with rage at the demons cringing before him. He let out a slew of expletives as he ranted and raged at them.

"Are Jehovah's angels too strong for you?"

One demon was brave enough or, more likely, crazy enough to answer him. "But, my lord, greater is He that is in them than our most excellent Beelzebub. We have no power over them when they call on the name of Jesus and submit themselves under His authority. What more could we do?"

"What more could we do?" Dekar mimicked the whiny demon. "You could stay and fight instead of giving in every time someone utters that blasted name." His whole face distorted with rage.

"We desperately needed that young man to be trapped by his emotions for the girl. I gave you Promiscuity and Lust to make sure they were physically attracted to each other. I put Loneliness under your authority to help matters along, but you blundered the whole coup when you hightailed it too quickly."

"Sir, I beg your forgiveness, but I don't think this guy is going to break too easily. He's sold out. He stands against temptation by the power of the Holy Spirit. He understands and walks in his authority as a believer. He knows who he is in Christ and is obedient to Jehovah's word. He seeks Christ for direction on a daily basis. But our biggest problem is that he understands the power of love. We've tried everything we could think of, used every weapon imaginable, including the loss of his child and the divorce from his wife. We've even tried getting him hooked on television programs that would give us a foothold in his life, but the Holy Spirit revealed our strategy. How can we fight against such a strong follower of Jehovah?"

Dekar thought for a moment before he relented. "You may be right. We'll have to find another way to get him into our net." He kicked the demon hard before sending him back into the nest of demons standing before him.

30

Be still, and know that I am God.

—Psalm 46:10

Carol and John stared down at the frail, tiny body of their two-day-old baby boy. The doctor had informed them that Christian wasn't doing well and wasn't responding to treatment. He'd developed an infection in his underdeveloped lungs. The doctors and nurses had encouraged them to spend time with him because they weren't expecting him to make it through the night.

Carol cried and prayed intermittently as she stared down at the perfectly formed body of her little son. *How could anyone ever take the life of a child in the womb?* Gazing at Christian, she knew he was more than a blob, more than a fetus; he was her precious gift from God. She might have to entrust him back into the arms of Jesus until she could be reunited with him again one day. That was her hope. One day, she would be reunited with him should his life on this earth be cut short.

"How could anyone ever abort their child?" She leaned her head on John's shoulder. "Look how perfect he is. I want so much for him to live, but I don't want him to suffer."

"I know, baby. I feel the same way. Life is precious and so fragile. Though he's only two days old, I feel connected to him. I can't imagine my life without him." Tears streaked down John's face as he stroked Christian's little hand.

Glancing at the monitors hooked up to her baby, Carol could tell it was becoming increasingly difficult for him to hold onto life. A nurse came over to check on him and smiled sadly at them.

"Can I get either of you anything? Would you like for me to take him out so that you can hold him? I'm not God, and He can certainly turn this around, but it's not looking good for your son. I don't think it would hurt anything for you to hold him."

Both Carol and John looked at her and nodded. They had yet to hold Christian and wanted the opportunity while there was still life in his tiny body. The nurse gingerly handed him into the arms of Carol, who was now seated in a rocking chair beside the incubator. She held him close, and sang softly into his ear. John bent down and kissed him on the forehead before taking pictures with his smartphone as she held their son.

It felt like only minutes, but after an hour and a half, she gave him to John. Then, as quickly as he came into their world, he passed into eternity while in John's arms.

"We'll see you on the other side, little buddy." John cradled the lifeless little body in his arms.

They prayed over their son one last time and, before going out into the waiting room to inform their family of his passing, prayed for strength and grace for themselves as they walked through the valley of the shadow of death once again. Their only ray of sunshine was that little Faith seemed to be doing well, getting better, and gaining strength hour by hour.

Zoe knew immediately upon walking into Carol's room that something was terribly wrong. She'd not yet heard the tragic news of Christian's death and had brought a pink and blue stuffed animal for each of the children, as well as a larger pink bear for Olivia. Carol's eyes were red and swollen from crying. John sat in the window seat with his parents on either side of him. It was apparent that everyone was upset.

"Oh no, what's happened?" She rushed to Carol's bedside.

"Zoe, we lost Christian about an hour ago. He developed an infection in his lungs. But we got to hold him, and John took some pictures and a video. He's with Jesus now, and we know he's not suffering."

John walked over to the bed and took his wife's hand into his. "And, he's with Jacob."

Zoe's eyes betrayed the horror she felt. How could her friends seem so calm as they told her of the loss of their child?

"Oh my gosh, I'm so sorry. I...don't know what to say. I'm..." She tried to control the emotions rising within herself.

"I'm so glad you're here, Zoe. I wanted to tell you face-to-face. We are hurting, but it does not alter our faith in God or His promises."

Zoe felt confused. "Why would God allow this? I mean... you've already lost one child. I couldn't bear it if anything happened to Amos, not after losing Emma. If God would take Christian and you guys are so strong in your faith...I just don't know what hope I have for Amos Michael."

John put his hand on Zoe's shoulder to comfort her. "Zoe, we don't know why God allows these things to happen. We live in a fallen sin-stained world where bad things happen to good people who love and serve God. We have a very real enemy who comes to steal, kill, and destroy, and he hates us with a passion. We'll just have to continue asking God to reveal the why behind what happened, though we may never know this side of heaven. In the meantime, we have to trust that somehow God will turn this around for our good and use it for His glory."

"I don't know if I could look at it so spiritually if it were me. I'm trying to trust God that He can turn Emma's death into something good. So far, I haven't been able to think of one good thing that has come out of it." She suddenly realized how selfish she sounded in light of their loss. She turned her attention back to Carol. "I'm sorry. I don't mean to make this about me. Tell me what can I do for you?"

"Zoe, little Amos will be fine. Don't worry about him. We have a bit of good news too. Faith is doing well. She's a fighter."

"I'm so glad to hear that. I can't wait to meet her."

Carol showed Zoe the short video and pictures John had taken of her and Christian in the NICU.

"Are you going to have a service for him?" Zoe tried desperately to choke back sobs. She wiped away tears as she glanced at the photos.

"Yes! I can go home tomorrow. We'll plan it then. Our pastor is already working on a few of the details for us. I don't know what we'd do without him or our church body. Having faith on our side makes this so much more bearable than when we lost Jacob."

Zoe's mind was in turmoil, and her soul was filled with fear as she left the hospital. *How can they have so much peace? How would I respond if anything like that happened to Amos? Oh God, I feel like I'm just getting my faith back on the right track. Please don't let anything happen to this baby. I don't think I could bear it. I don't think...*

Suddenly, in her spirit, she heard a gentle whisper, and she knew it was the voice of God.

"*Be still and know that I am God.*" God's voice brought instant peace to her soul. Though it wasn't necessarily a promise that nothing bad would happen to Amos Michael, it was a promise that God was with her and in control. She knew that no matter what happened, she could lean on the everlasting arms of her Savior and trust in Him. Just as the Holy Spirit was helping her friends, He would undoubtedly be her Helper too.

Though Michael had contemplated all day long what he'd say to Sophie when he saw her, he had knots in his stomach as she walked up to him in the youth room. She was early, and except for a few kids playing video games in the game room, there was no one else present.

"Hi, Michael. I need to talk to you."

He could see by her countenance that something was bothering her. "Sure, I need to talk to you too. What's up?"

"I don't know how to say this, and I feel like maybe I tried to move too fast, but I had this weird dream last night, and I just know, for whatever reason, God doesn't want us to see each other. I know it sounds goofy. I mean nothing has actually happened between us, but I..."

Michael breathed a sigh of relief. "No, it doesn't sound goofy at all. God spoke the same thing to me. I was going to tell you tonight. I prayed last night that He would prepare your heart, and I guess He did. I think I'm still supposed to continue to stand and believe for my marriage. It's already been six months since she left, and it doesn't look like even a slight possibility that she'll be back, but I know there is nothing too difficult for God."

"I want God's best for you, and I want His best for my children and me. I know He has someone for me. I started coming to church because I was so sick and tired of guys wanting me for one thing and one thing only. You are such a gentleman, Michael, and you gave me hope that there are nice Christian guys out there. I would still like to help out in the youth if that's okay? If not, I understand."

"No, I'd love for you to continue working with us as long as you don't think you'll feel awkward around me. I'll be praying for God to bring someone into your life. I have to admit, for a little bit; I thought it might be me. You are very beautiful, inside and out, and you're a great mom to Saige and Dakota. I know God has awesome plans for you."

She smiled sweetly at him. "Thanks. I appreciate your friendship. I've got to go get the kids settled in their classes. Kira is watching them for me. I'll see you later."

As he watched her turn and walk away, Michael was in awe of how God had worked the situation out. "Thanks, Father. You're so faithful. Give her the desires of her heart."

Carol, still recovering from delivering twins, walked slowly down the aisle of her church with John by her side. It was hard to believe that a little less than two weeks ago she'd been pregnant with her babies and attending Sunday service. She determined that though she'd lost Christian, and Faith was still in the hospital, she was not going to give in to the depression or gloom that kept trying to drag her down. She hugged several people as she made her way to the front of the church and thanked them for their presence as well as their words of condolence. Her arms felt empty, but her heart was grateful that God had spared Faith and was uplifting her and her family.

Friends and family filled the sanctuary as well as members of her church that she'd never even met. It was as though God Himself was surrounding her. She stopped to hug Zoe, who was sitting with Amos and Barbara.

"Thank you so much for coming, ya'll. It means so much to John and me. We are so grateful for all the support. Mr. Richards, the flowers from the company are gorgeous. Please tell everyone thanks."

Amos stood and hugged her. "You take as much time off as you need. Don't worry about your job. It'll be waiting for you if you want to come back. You just concentrate on that baby girl that's still in the hospital."

Carol was touched by his concern. "Thank you so much, Mr. Richards. I can't tell you what that means to me."

"We are so very sorry for your loss." Barbara clasped Carol's extended hand. "If there is anything we can do for you, please let us know."

Zoe smiled up at her friend through tears in her eyes. "I can honestly say I know what you are going through, and I want you to know I'm here for you. Anytime, day or night, if you need someone to watch Olivia while you are up at the hospital to give your mom a break. Anything. Okay? We're praying for you."

"Thanks, Zoe. I know you are. I feel everyone's prayers carrying me." She hugged Zoe before continuing her journey to the front pew.

The service was a celebration of a little life barely lived. Colorful blue and yellow balloons were tied on every pew as well as throughout the front of the church. Beautiful arrangements, many with tiny blue teddy bears, filled the front of the sanctuary. The miniature blue casket was covered with a mixture of white and blue carnations and roses. Praise music played softly in the background.

The pastor's message was one of hope and expectation of the day they would all be able to behold this beautiful baby boy once again, as long as they were in a covenant relationship with Christ. He talked about how in this life, we often have more questions than answers. "One day, we, in Christ, will stand before the King, and we'll know Him face-to-face, and all of our questions will be answered, all of our pain will be erased, and there will be no more reason for tears."

The service ended by each person writing a message of love, condolence, or a prayer on a balloon. All together they released the balloons into the atmosphere in an act of unity.

Carol wrote on a large yellow balloon.

See you on the other side, little man. Kiss Jacob for Mommy.

Her smile was mingled with tears as she watched the balloon drift away into the clouds.

Gloom stared at the balloons in disbelief. How in the world could she be playing with balloons when he'd done his very best to speak despair and gloom into her soul? It infuriated him that she was even smiling as she released it. He was perplexed. Every time he shot a poisonous dart toward her, she refused to allow herself to dwell on the thought. She cast them down just as quickly as he spoke them into her soul. The thoughts fell by the wayside as she replaced them with scripture or a word of praise to Jehovah. She was the type of human he loathed. He knew he was rendered powerless as long as she refused his thoughts.

"Just wait until she gets home, and she's alone." Depression wrung his hands together. "She won't be as strong as she is here surrounded by the prayers of the saints."

Gloom starred at Carol in utter despair. "I don't know. She seems to be resolved to praise Jehovah through this trial. Besides, you and I both know; she is never really alone. Ozias never leaves her side. And she has the Holy Spirit with her at all times."

Upon hearing their conversation, Ozias raised his gleaming sword toward them. "The Lord rebuke you, Depression and Gloom. Be gone in the name of Jesus."

Fearful for their existence, they quickly fled.

Michael sat on the couch flipping through channels on the television. It was a Saturday night, and he was home, once again, alone. He hated the quiet that permeated his small apartment. He wasn't interested in anything on the television, but it provided noise as well as something to occupy his time.

He thought about Zoe and wondered what she was doing on this Saturday night. *I'll bet she's out having a great time.* The thought saddened him. *Or even worse, she's probably snuggled on her couch in her boyfriend's arms. She probably never gives me a second thought.*

A lying spirit saw an opportunity to pounce. *"You know she doesn't love you anymore. You might as well forget about her. The word Kira gave you probably wasn't from God. It was just a word to give you false hope. Zoe is enjoying her life without you. You might as well give up."*

He glanced at the picture of Zoe and Emma on the coffee table. "God, are you going to bring Zoe back to me? Are you going to restore our marriage? How long do I have to wait?" He could feel himself sinking into hopelessness.

Turning off the television, he put praise music on in his apartment. He began to pace back and forth as he praised. *The way to fight against hopelessness is to worship God.* He sang along with the songs as he lifted his hands toward heaven.

"I will wait upon the Lord. I will trust You as I wait. I place my life in Your hands. I will worship You alone, and I won't give into fear and depression."

He could feel the spiritual atmosphere changing from hopelessness to trust. Loneliness was replaced with the peace of Christ's presence, as he pressed deeper and deeper into worship and praise. He repented for questioning God's timing, doubting His plan, and listening, even for an instant, to the lies of the enemy.

The lying spirit hightailed it out of his presence as soon as he began to praise because spirits of darkness cannot remain in the presence of praise.

The Father smiled down upon him. The smile of a Father well pleased with His beloved son.

Zoe was over at Amos's and Barbara's, helping decorate for an office Christmas party that would be held at their house that weekend. She enjoyed spending time with them, especially Barbara. With their past dead and buried, they had forged a strong bond, became the best of friends, and when Barbara had asked her to help, she'd been quick to agree. Amos sat on the sofa watching the two busily turning the house into a winter wonderland.

"Zoe, with what happened to Carol, we'd just like you to consider moving in with us until Amos is born. We don't want you living alone. What if you went into labor or something happened, and you couldn't drive yourself to the hospital?" Driven by fear after hearing about the loss of Carol's premature baby, Amos tried to talk Zoe into temporarily moving in with him and Barbara.

"Daddy, I'm fine. I'll be okay. If anything happens to me, I'll call 911. Besides, I'm never alone. God is always with me, and He watches over me."

"That's great, but He also wants us to use wisdom. Please think about it. We're just concerned, and we want to make sure you and the baby are safe. If anything happened…"

Zoe shared the scripture God had spoken to her the night she'd left the hospital after learning of Christian's demise. "Dad, God specifically spoke to me. I heard His voice. Be still and know that I am God. At that moment, He took all of my fear and anxiety and gave me such a peace. I'm comfortable in my own apartment. Barbara and I are getting the nursery ready, and I don't want to leave it. Maybe during the last week or so I'll consider coming to stay with ya'll. How's that?"

Barbara patted Amos's hand. "She's made up her mind Amos, and we need to listen to her. She can hear from God, and I believe He'll protect her."

Amos shot her a whose-side-are-you-on glance. "Okay, I can see I'm outnumbered now. I never get my way. But you have to promise you'll call no matter what time of day or night if you feel even the slightest twinge."

Zoe laughed. "Okay, Daddy, I promise. And you have to promise me that you won't worry so much."

"That's probably not going to happen." Barbara winked at Zoe. "Your dad still needs to be delivered from worry."

31

Now to Him who is able to do exceedingly abundantly
above all that we ask or think, according to the power that works in us,
to Him be glory in the church by Christ Jesus to all generations,
forever and ever. Amen.
—Ephesians 3:20–21

"Oh my gosh, Carol, she's so tiny! She's like a little doll." Carol handed Zoe the small bundle wrapped in a fuzzy pink blanket. "I'm almost afraid to hold her."

"Don't worry she's fine. She has to contend with Olivia. Her little sister is always in her face and wanting to kiss her. Thank God for daycare." Carol laughed as she stroked the baby's face. "She's doing great. So far, we haven't seen any major side effects from her preemie birth. God's had His hand on her for sure. She's up to seven pounds two ounces."

"Oh, that's awesome. So how are you doing? I mean with…"

"You mean with the loss of Christian? I think I'm doing okay. Now that we have Faith home with us, I don't have a lot of time to dwell on the loss. It still hurts, but I try to give that hurt over to the Lord every time I find myself dwelling on it. I think of him in Christ's arms and with Jacob, and it gives me peace. I'm not saying it's easy, but I know I have to trust God."

"When I grow up I want to be as strong as you are."

"You're probably stronger than you think. I've seen you grow immensely since we've become friends."

Zoe stared down at the infant in her arms. "I'm trying so hard. I'm reading my Bible every morning and spending time in prayer. I've been going to church with Dad and Barbara. I want to have a strong faith like yours that can endure anything. I think that's where I failed before. I depended more on Michael's faith and his relationship with the Lord. I foolishly believed that was enough. But I've come to realize that I need to have my own walk with the Lord. If I have to go through a difficult time, I want to be able to handle it the way you do, completely trusting in Christ."

Carol smiled warmly at Zoe. "We're getting close to meeting little Amos. I can't wait. Faith will have a little playmate. And, who knows, maybe one day…"

They laughed. "You never know." Zoe placed her hand on Carol's arm. "Carol, I'm so thankful for your friendship. I was a real snob when we first met. Please forgive me for that. I can't imagine my life right now without you in it. You've been such an encourager to me."

"Stop! I'm still hormonal, and you'll get me crying. I'm thankful for your friendship too. I have to admit; I was getting lonely at work. I was beginning to dread going until God sent you."

"Isn't it amazing how God brings people into our lives at just the right time? I mean, if I wouldn't have started working at the law firm, we wouldn't have met. Who knows where I'd be?"

Carol thought for a moment before responding. "I believe God has a path for each of us to take. Even when we take detours, He's able to get us back on course. He loves us enough to give us the leeway to make mistakes so we can learn from them. But in due season, He places us where we need to be and sets up divine appointments to get us back on the right path. I don't know where I'd be in my life without Him. My greatest regret is that it took me so long to find Him."

Zoe looked thoughtfully at her friend. "I know what you mean. My greatest regret is that I let the world creep into my relationship with Him. I think I'd still be with Michael if I had been more serious about running after God. My lawyer called yesterday to tell me the divorce is final."

Carol could sense the regret in Zoe's voice. "Zoe, you never know what God might do. Is Michael in a relationship?"

"I don't know. I haven't heard from him in a while. I heard a rumor that there was a new girl at his church pursuing him. Heck, I don't blame her. When he smiles, those dimples of his can melt any heart." Zoe put her hands on her swollen abdomen. "At least, I have my little man on the way. It won't be long, and he'll be keeping me busy."

"Oh, that reminds me. I'll be right back." Carol left the room.

Zoe looked down at the sleeping baby in her arms. "God, I know this pregnancy probably isn't what You would have chosen for me, but I'm so grateful for this baby in my womb. I'm so thankful that he's healthy."

Carol came back into the room with a large plastic tub. "These are Jacob's baby clothes that I saved. I want you to have them. I don't plan on getting pregnant again, so I won't be needing them."

"Oh, Carol, are you sure?" Zoe handed Faith back to Carol and opened the tub as if it were a treasure chest of goodies. "Oh, look at these. They're adorable. I can't wait to show Barbara."

"I know your parents can afford to give you much nicer clothes, but I wanted Amos to have these. Consider it a late Christmas gift." Carol smiled as Zoe showed excitement over every outfit, squealing with glee as she held each item out in front of her.

"I love them. Thank you so much, Carol."

"You're welcome. Now let's put Faith down and eat some lunch. I made chicken salad. I've got to lose this baby weight. I didn't just eat for two; I ate for three."

Pastor Steve sat comfortably in the office chair in front of Michael's desk with one leg folded over the other. He often came into Michael's office to chat or discuss church matters. But this time he was there on a mission to encourage him.

"So how's it going? Anything new going on in your life?"

Michael rested his chin in his hands on the desk. "I don't know if you heard, but last week I got the papers saying the divorce is final. So I guess it's over, and maybe I need to move on."

"Are you considering seeing someone else?"

"You must have heard about Sophie, huh?" Michael blushed.

Pastor Steve raised his eyebrows. "No, what about her? She's the new girl helping out in the youth, right?"

Michael grinned sheepishly. *Me and my big mouth.*

"Yea. I was interested in her until God slammed the door shut in my face. He made it clear to both of us that we were not supposed to be anything more than friends. But I get so lonely, especially at night and on the weekends."

"And she's a beautiful girl. I get it. But you know you have to trust in whatever plan God has for your life."

"It's so hard when we can't see into the future. I wish I knew what His plan was. I believe He has made promises to me, but right now, I can't see how He is ever going to bring them to fruition in my life. I want to trust Him to restore my marriage, but I don't see how it can happen. It looks impossible. Especially now that we're officially divorced."

Pastor Steve pointed at the Bible on the desk to the left of Michael. "Open your Bible to Ephesians three." He waited as Michael found the passage. "Now read out loud verses twenty and twenty-one."

Michael read the scriptures out loud. "Now to Him, who is able to do exceedingly abundantly, above all that we ask or think, according to the power that works in us, to Him be glory in the church by Christ Jesus to all generations, forever and ever. Amen."

Pastor Steve pointed at the Bible once again. "Okay. So what does that scripture mean to you."

Michael meditated on the scripture before answering. "Whatever I ask or desire from God; He is able to do even greater, more magnificently and brilliantly than I can even imagine in my mind, if I'll just believe Him."

"That's right! And you don't have to figure it out or be able to see it with your natural eyes. You simply need to begin to see you and Zoe back together through your spiritual eyes. Begin to speak like you are back together. Begin to think about being back together. Thank God for that restoration, even when you can't see it. If God has promised it, He'll make it come to pass. Abraham called those things that were not as though they were, and he believed contrary to hope. With his natural eyes, he couldn't see how he could possibly become a father of many nations. His wife's womb was dead. But because God said He would do it, Abraham believed it as if it had already happened."

"You know, Pastor, I know all of that and could probably even preach it. It's just so difficult sometimes to live it."

"Keep your mind renewed in the word. The Holy Spirit is your strengthener. He'll help you as you take steps of faith and begin to line your thoughts and words up with God. God will make sure you can live it before you preach it to someone else. He wants you to pass this test more than you do so that you can help encourage others through your ministry. A word spoken from experiential faith is a whole lot more powerful than a word spoken from head knowledge."

Michael glanced out the window of his office. His mood matched the weather outside. The mild January weather had turned bitter cold, and the sky was dark and overcast. He turned back to his pastor. "Pastor, please pray for me that God would strengthen me. I want so much for Zoe to return to me. But sometimes, I want to give up."

Pastor Steve got up and walked around the desk to where Michael was now standing. He placed his hands on Michael's shoulders and began to pray.

"Father, I ask you to strengthen Your son. I thank You that he will not grow weary in doing well and that he will mount up with wings as the eagle. Undergird him with Your might and power. Give him a faith vision for his wife and eyes to see the complete restoration of his marriage. Prepare his heart for her return as You are even preparing her heart to return to him. We thank You that Your timing is perfect, and we trust in You. In Jesus's name, Amen!"

"Thanks, Pastor. I needed that today."

"We all need help every once in a while. That's why God calls us to walk in the body of Christ. So when one is weak, the other can lift him up. Marcie and I will continue to pray for you. Michael, the darkest night always comes before the dawn."

Pastor Steve walked out of the office leaving Michael staring out the window. *I don't care how bleak it looks outside. I choose to believe that it's going to be a good day.*

Zoe busied herself packing her bags. Her doctor visit that day revealed she'd already started dilating, though her due date was still weeks away. Catching a side glimpse of herself in the full-length mirror on her closet door, she didn't think she looked more than six months pregnant. From behind, no one would ever even know she was pregnant. She was proud of the fact that she'd only gained ten pounds and hoped she'd not have too big of a challenge getting her figure back into shape after the baby was born.

The doctor still felt like she was further along than she surmised. By her calculations, she still had at least ten weeks to go. However, since Emma had made an early entrance into the world, she'd decided, with much prompting from her dad, she'd move in with Amos and Barbara until after the birth. She packed one bag for her stay at their house while they waited on Amos Michael's arrival and one for the short stay at the hospital.

She was excited about moving in with her parents. She gave God all of the glory for the joy she'd shared with them as they spent their first family Christmas together since she'd married Michael and moved out of their house. Christmas and New Year's would have been unbearable had it not been for their love and constant support.

She'd begun to refer to Barbara as Mom. Barbara had been with her through all of the birthing classes and had toured the hospital with her. Amos said they were like two peas in a pod and playfully complained that between shopping, decorating, and talking about the baby, they didn't have any time left for him anymore.

She glanced around the bedroom one last time to make sure she wasn't forgetting anything before calling for Amos.

"Daddy, do you want to come get these suitcases. I tried to pack light, but you know me."

Amos entered her room and lifted the two suitcases. "You call this packing light?"

Zoe laughed. "Hey, you're the one who wanted me to move in so don't complain."

She went into the nursery for one more glance before leaving the apartment. Barbara was sitting in the rocking chair holding a blue blanket she'd knitted for little Amos. Tears were streaming down her cheeks.

"What's wrong?" Zoe walked over to her step-mom.

"Nothing's wrong. I'm going to be a grandma! It just hit me. I'm so thankful to God for turning my life around. Thank you for forgiving me, Zoe, and allowing me to be a part of Amos Michael's life."

"He's the one who'll be blessed to have you as his grandma. Between you and Daddy, I think he'll be one spoiled little boy. Thanks for helping me with everything. I love you so much. Thanks for being my mom."

Barbara sprung up from the rocker, and the two embraced.

Amos had returned from putting the bags in the car and watched quietly from the doorway as tears of joy filled his eyes. He looked up toward heaven. "Praise God!"

Michael was in line at Starbucks when he saw her enter. When he realized the beautiful pregnant woman walking toward him was Zoe, his knees almost buckled underneath him. *Oh, God, she's pregnant.* Though the weather outside was chilly, he could feel beads of perspiration breaking out on his forehead.

She hadn't noticed him until it was his turn at the register. She stepped out of line and made a beeline toward the door.

"Zoe, wait!" He handed money to the woman at the register before lunging after Zoe. "Keep the change."

He grabbed Zoe's arm just as she was about to exit the store. "Zoe, wait! I just wanted to say hi and see how you're doing."

She felt uncomfortable with him seeing her, much less talking to her.

"Did you and Zach get married?" He held his breath in expectation of her answer.

Zoe looked horrified. She wanted to run and hide. "No, Zach and I are not married." Her response was quick. "How are you, Michael? You look great." Though her voice had softened somewhat, she still appeared to be aloof.

"I'm okay. It's great to see you." He felt awkward. "Umm…there's an elephant in the room." Embarrassed, he turned beet red. "Ugh…I wasn't referring to how you look…you look radiant, very beautiful. I meant…you're pregnant. Why don't you come sit down and talk with me?"

"I can't. I was just coming in to get me a tea and a coffee for Daddy before going to work. You know how impatient he is. He wasn't about to wait in the drive-through. He has a client meeting this morning and doesn't want to be late." She rolled her eyes as if he understood exactly what she meant.

"Well then, could I come take you to lunch? Zoe, I want to know what's going on with you. Who's baby are you carrying?"

Her heart hurt for him as she witnessed the desperation in his eyes. "How about tomorrow? I can go to lunch tomorrow. I have a doctor's appointment today. They have me going every week now. Do you want to meet me at the office tomorrow?"

"Yea. I'd like that."

"Okay, I'll see you then." She turned and walked out the door without even ordering her drinks.

Michael couldn't believe he'd run into her. He wasn't sure if it was a curse or a blessing. *Is God trying to show me it's impossible for us to get back together?* A part of him was furious with her. *How could she go and get herself pregnant with another man's child? And how many guys had she slept with?* Questions swam around in his head. But another part of him felt grateful that she was willing to meet with him and talk to him. Confusing thoughts entered his mind. *Maybe God isn't going to restore her to me after all. Perhaps it's too late.*

"What in the world took you so long? I could have gone through the drive-through three times." Amos, seeing that Zoe was visibly shaken, tried to sound playfully perturbed. "Where's my coffee?"

"Daddy, I ran into Michael. He was at the register paying when I walked in."

"Well, what's wrong with that? You two are over and done with. The divorce is final now." Amos kept his eyes steady on the road but could tell his daughter was getting emotional.

"I think it broke his heart to see me pregnant like this. He didn't know about it. I felt so bad for him. I didn't know what to say."

Amos reached over and held her hand. "Life has a way of working itself out. Don't worry about it."

Zoe sat in silence the rest of their drive to work, and Amos didn't even bother trying to carry on a conversation with her. He was grateful for the silence since he didn't know what to say.

I forgot how unbelievably good-looking he is. Her heart had melted when he'd flashed a dimpled grin at her. Questions drifted in and out of her mind like the icy winter breeze that was blowing outside. *How could I have possibly been so stupid? And why did I agree to have lunch with him? How am I going to explain this to him?*

Dr. Fields peeled off the latex gloves he'd worn during the examination.

"Well, Ms. Zoe, it looks like you don't have much longer to wait to meet this boy of yours. You can sit up now. I'd say he could come any day now. Though the last ultrasound shows him to be pretty tiny, I think his lungs look to be developed enough that he'll be fine. You haven't dilated any further, but he's in position and ready. He could still choose to take his time, but I think he's going to be early."

Barbara helped Zoe sit up on the examining table. "We certainly are ready to meet him." She smiled at Zoe who had been unusually quiet since she'd picked her up for the midmorning appointment. It was as though her mind was a million miles away.

Once they were in the car, she turned in her seat to face Zoe. "Honey, are you all right? You seem very preoccupied today."

Zoe looked at her with sad eyes. "I'm still in love with Michael. I ran into him this morning at Starbucks. Mom, he was shocked, to say the least. He didn't know I was pregnant, and of course, how could he? He tried to be sweet but seeing my pregnant belly shook him up. I can understand how he would be. But…what do I do? How could he ever love me when I'm having another man's child?"

"Why don't you just try talking to him and telling him what happened? Give him the option to be a part of your life. If he decides he can't handle it, then that's that. But at least explain everything to him. I know how very much he loved you."

"Oh, Mom, I've made such a mess of my life." Zoe covered her face with her hands.

"Honey, our God does His best work fixing our messes. You just wait and see. I know He'll take care of you and little Amos. I'll be praying for you."

"Man, she's pregnant." Michael leaned his head against the steering wheel as he spoke to Brad over the phone. "I was shocked. I mean, we are divorced and everything, so she has a right to do whatever she wants. But I don't know… how could God ever put us back together now?"

"I know it looks bad, Michael. But go and talk with her. Hey, I think it's progress that she's even agreed to meet with you. She's always shut you out before."

"Yea, but I think she probably just wants to explain herself to me and make sure, once again, that I know it's definitely over. But hey, maybe I need to hear that so I can move on with my life."

"What if God still wants to put it all back together. Could you raise another man's child? That would be a question you need to ask yourself. I know I'd probably have a hard time with that one."

Michael thought for a moment before answering. "I don't know. I just don't know how she could have done this. I would never in a million years have guessed that this was going to happen. I can't stand the thought of her with another guy, much less the fact that she's pregnant with his child."

"Can you forgive her? Could you forget all that's happened and pick up the pieces of your lives and move on together with God, if she were willing to do that?"

Michael felt the question hit him like a bucket of frigid water being poured over his head. "I know I still love her. But I also wonder if I'm holding on to what used to be, the Zoe I used to know."

"Only you can answer that, Michael. Pray about it. I'll be praying too. We all make mistakes, and we're all in need of God's mercy. Mercy triumphs over judgment. Maybe Zoe needs to see the mercy of God coming from you. It might be what draws her back to Christ. No matter what she decides to do, she still needs mercy."

Michael hung up the phone and did just that. He prayed as if his life depended on it. He prayed for guidance and direction and to know the will of God. He asked questions and waited for answers.

Deuel watched as his charge earnestly sought the will of God. He knew Michael was struggling and wanted desperately to intervene and comfort his soul. However, he knew his assignment was to guard his charge against further enemy attack while the Holy Spirit ministered to him. Michael had to walk by faith and trust implicitly that the Almighty was leading his every step.

Deuel understood that sometimes life didn't make sense to humans, often leaving them with more questions than answers. His experience had taught him that in these difficult times, some gave up on their faith, while the testing and trials only made others stronger and more determined to seek the Almighty with all of their heart.

Michael fell into the latter category. For him, trials were like a stepping stool, each one taking him increasingly higher with God.

Deuel smiled. His charge would overcome and continue to go from glory to glory.

32

Be anxious for nothing, but in everything by prayer and supplication,
with thanksgiving, let your requests be made known to God; and the peace of God,
which surpasses all understanding, will guard your hearts
and minds through Christ Jesus.

—Philippians 4:6–7

Zoe woke up with a sharp pain in her back. She sat up and swung her legs over to the side of the bed. Just as she was about to stand up, a gush of water poured out from between her legs. She was panic-stricken. *Oh no. My water broke.*

She quickly grabbed her cell phone and called Barbara. They'd agreed that if Zoe went into labor during the night, Barbara would keep her phone beside her on the nightstand so that Zoe wouldn't have to walk all the way to the other side of the house to their bedroom. Her hands shook as she pressed the speed dial.

"Hello." Barbara bolted up into a sitting position on the bed, suddenly wide-awake. "Oh my, Zoe, is that you? I'm on my way." She hung up the phone without giving Zoe a chance to respond.

She shook Amos, who was still sound asleep beside her. "Amos, wake up. I think Zoe is going into labor." Quickly tossing the covers off of her, she slipped on her robe and house shoes and ran to Zoe's room.

"Are you having contractions?" She knelt over Zoe with one hand on her shoulder.

"I think so. My water broke. I feel bad. I think I ruined your mattress and the carpet." Zoe was half standing, half seated on the edge of the bed. "I'm having sharp pains in my lower back, and they seem to be coming every five minutes or so."

"Okay, let me help you get dressed, and then I'll go throw some clothes on." She walked Zoe into the bathroom. "What do you want to wear?"

"I think I can do this. You go get dressed. I think we have a little time. I want to take a quick shower."

Barbara raised her eyebrows; her face betrayed the anxiety she was feeling. "What? A shower! You need to get dressed so we can get going."

"I'll be fine. You go get dressed and get Daddy up. I promise; I'll just take a quick shower. I have to look good when I meet my son." She smiled weakly as she grabbed her swollen belly. A contraction moved from the small of her back around to her abdomen, causing her to pause briefly before moving toward the shower.

"Zoe!" Barbara ran to her side.

"Go, I'll be fine. I promise."

Zoe showered and dressed and was french-braiding her long wet hair when Barbara knocked on her bathroom door. "You can come in."

"Are you ready yet?" Barbara peeked around the door. "You have on makeup?"

"Just a little. I'll be ready in a second." She finished her hair and placed her makeup and blow dryer into an overnight bag. "Okay, I'm ready. Ouch." She bent over holding onto the cabinet as a contraction seized her body again. "These contractions are starting to get stronger."

"Your dad has the car warming. Let's go. I'll get the bags." Barbara hovered over Zoe like a mother hen.

Zoe glanced around the room. "I hope I haven't forgotten anything."

"Zoe, let's go! As excited as I am to meet my grandson, I don't want to be the one to deliver him."

"Okay, I'm coming."

They made their way to the garage where Amos was waiting in the car. "He has to decide to come at four o'clock in the morning. I haven't even had a cup of coffee yet." Though he tried to sound gruff, both women knew it was just a front. Amos was beside himself with excitement over meeting his new grandson.

Michael walked into the offices of Pointer, Richards and Brighten Law Associates, expecting to see Zoe at the front desk. Instead, another woman sat in her place.

"Hello, sir, can I help you?"

"I'm looking for Zoe Davis. Is she here today? We were supposed to have lunch." Michael assumed Zoe had probably decided to skip today so that she wouldn't have to meet with him.

"Zoe…ugh…Ms. Davis is having her baby today. So I don't expect she'll be back for at least six to eight weeks. Would you like to leave her a message?"

"Do you know what hospital she's in?"

"No, sir, but even if I did, I couldn't just give out that information."

"I'm her husband…or at least her ex-husband." He was disappointed in himself for sounding so harsh with the woman.

At that moment a tall, well-built man stuck his head around the corner. "Excuse me, did I hear you inquiring as to what hospital Ms. Davis is in?" He didn't give Michael a chance to respond or the woman at the desk a chance to protest. "She's in Texas Women's Hospital in the Medical Center. You'll find her in room 1086." He then disappeared around the corner as quickly as he'd appeared.

"Excuse me." The woman got out of her chair and poked her head around the corner, obviously ready to scold the man for giving out Zoe's personal information. But he was nowhere to be seen down the long hallway leading back into the law offices. "How could he have gotten down the hall so fast?" She looked back at Michael, though he wasn't listening. He was busy inputting the room number into the notes app in his phone.

"I've never seen that man here before." The woman appeared to be puzzled and upset that the stranger had given the information to Michael.

"Tell him thank you when you see him." He turned and bolted toward the door.

As he waited for the elevator, he pondered on what he should do. He wanted to go to the hospital, but what if the baby's father was there. *Of course, he'd be there. He'd be a complete jerk if he weren't.*

Once again, he felt hopeless. He got in his car with every intention of heading back to the church and sending Zoe flowers when, instead, he found himself turning out of the parking garage and into the direction of the medical center. He picked up his phone and called his pastor, but the phone went directly to voice mail. He left a message, knowing Pastor Steve would understand once he had an opportunity to explain the situation to him.

"Pastor Steve, I'm not going to make it back in today. I'll explain it all to you later."

He didn't know what he'd do once he got to the hospital or if he'd even have the chance to see Zoe, but he felt compelled to go. Sensing he was following the leading of the Holy Spirit, he assumed God would direct him once he arrived there.

Deuel, as well as several other angels that had been assigned by the Almighty, worked their plan to reunite Zoe and Michael. At all cost, he knew he had to get Michael to the hospital. So, though they didn't do it unless absolutely necessary, he'd appeared as a human to give Michael the information he needed to locate her.

Other angels went before him to clear traffic and change lights so that Michael could get there at the right moment. The Almighty's timing was always perfect.

Ramiah had his part to play in the matter as well. He was working on Zoe. The whole operation was like a giant jigsaw puzzle. Each piece had to fit perfectly in place at just the right moment. But the end result would be a beautiful masterpiece, well pleasing to the Almighty.

Deuel smiled as Michael made the turn heading toward the hospital.

Zoe held her son in her arms as Barbara and Amos looked on. She opened up the blue blanket the nurse had swaddled him in so that she could get a good look at his little body.

"He's perfectly beautiful." Barbara gently held his tiny hand.

Zoe barely heard Barbara's comments. She was transfixed, studying every feature of little Amos's face. He had the cutest, deepest dimples she'd ever seen on a baby. She didn't have dimples, and Zach didn't have them either. There was only one person she knew of who had such deep indentions in his cheeks. *Michael! Emma had been blessed with them also, though not as deep as little Amos's. How could it be?* She tried to think back to the last time she and Michael had been intimate, but it was so long ago, and her mind was fuzzy from the pain medication they'd given her after giving birth.

"Zoe, he looks just like Emma did when she was born." Amos beamed down at his daughter. "He even has her dimples."

"I know. I was thinking the same thing." Zoe stroked the baby's tiny face. "I think I made a mistake."

"What do you mean, you made a mistake?" Barbara looked at her with a puzzled expression.

"I think Michael is Amos's father. I know it sounds crazy, but Michael is the only person I know with dimples like this. He's the only one. Emma got her dimples from her daddy, not me." Tears filled her eyes as she glanced from Amos to Barbara, hoping for agreement. "Do you think I could be right? I've tried thinking back, and it has been just a little under nine months since we've been together."

"Well…" Amos was speechless. Barbara had told him of their conversation the day before. Was she trying to see something that wasn't there? He didn't want to get her hopes up. "Why don't you get some rest? We can worry about all that later. You're tired and…"

"Daddy, I need to see Michael. I just remembered we were going to have lunch today. Can you get me my cell phone? I need to call him."

"Zoe, I think you should give it some time before you call him. I'm sure if he went to the office, they would have told him you're having the baby. I don't think you should call him and spring on him that you think he's the father of your son. What if you're wrong?" He turned to face his wife. "What do you think?"

"What if she's right? Michael would certainly need to know."

A nurse came into the room and interrupted their conversation. "Excuse me, Ms. Davis, there is a Michael Davis here to see you. He said he's your husband, but your chart says you're single. Would you like for me to let him in?" The nurse looked skeptical.

"Yes!" She was overcome with joy. *Surely, it's a sign from God. It can't be a coincidence that Michael is showing up here at this very moment.*

The nurse disappeared behind the door. It was only seconds before Michael walked into the room looking like her knight in shining armor.

Barbara nudged Amos after greeting Michael. "We'll leave you two alone. Come on, Amos, let's grab a bite to eat downstairs. I'm starving."

They left her alone with Michael and her new son.

"Michael, how did you know I was here?" Zoe was amazed that he was standing before her.

"When I went to pick you up for lunch, a man told me that you were here and gave me your room number."

Zoe cocked her eyebrows in bewilderment. "That's weird. I just got to this room. I don't know how anyone would have known my room number."

Michael walked toward the bed carrying a beautiful arrangement of pink roses. "I brought these for you." He placed the flowers on the nightstand beside her bed.

"Thanks, they're gorgeous. I'm sure I look a mess. I wasn't expecting anyone except Daddy and Barbara."

"You look beautiful, as always. I can't believe, looking at you that you just had a baby. Can I see him?" Michael reached out to take the baby into his arms.

"Michael…" Zoe pondered what she should say as she placed the sleeping child into his arms.

"Who's the lucky guy?" Michael asked as he positioned the baby in his arms.

"His name is Amos Michael." She smiled up at him.

"No, I mean, who is the father?" Michael wasn't sure he wanted to hear the answer.

"I don't know for certain." It was a truthful answer. "I think that you might be his daddy." Her face felt flushed.

Michael stared at her in disbelief. "What? How could that be? We haven't been together in…" He tried to count the months backward since Emma's death. "Almost nine months. Emma's been gone almost nine months now!"

"Michael, look at his little face." Amos looked a lot like Emma when she was born. He had the same blond curly hair, blue eyes, and those deep dimples that had given Emma the appearance of a porcelain doll.

"He looks just like Emma, doesn't he? And he has your dimples. I don't know anyone who has such pronounced dimples as you do. I'd like to do a paternity test if you are willing."

Michael looked at her with a hint of anger in his eyes. "Well, how many other guys are in the running?" He knew as soon as the words came out of his mouth he shouldn't have said it. He saw the hurt look on her face.

"I'm sorry. I shouldn't have said that. But I mean…I'd think you would know who the father of your child is. Ya know…I'm sorry…I'm just confused and surprised."

"Michael, I've made a lot of mistakes. I'm mortified to say that there is a possibility that it could be one of two other men. You have every right to turn and walk out that door, but I'm praying you will stay." Tears fell down her flushed cheeks.

He handed the baby back to her and pulled up a chair. "I think I need to sit down. I just wasn't expecting to hear this. I mean… I'd be so grateful to God if he were mine. But…"

"I know it's a lot to take in. I was going to try and tell you today at lunch about Zach. I found out that he was married. Honestly, I thought this baby was his."

"So you slept with Zach right after you left me? Our life together meant that little to you?" He wrestled with feelings of anger and jealousy. The thought of her making love to another man made him sick to his stomach. "The only reason you're not with him is that he was married, right? I mean if he'd been single, you'd still be together?"

"Michael, I don't know. I just know God has been working in my life. I'm asking you to forgive me for hurting you. I know I've hurt you beyond words."

Suddenly overwhelmed with emotion he stood up. "I think I need to take a walk. I feel like I've been hit by a ton of bricks. I just wasn't…expecting…this is just too much at one time." He turned and walked out the door, leaving Zoe sobbing as she held her son close to her chest.

She'd never seen him so upset. Even when Emma died, he'd been the strong one. Fear settled in the pit of her stomach. "Oh, God…please help!"

A nurse walked into the room. Zoe noticed the name on her badge, Angelina. Glancing at the white erase board on the wall, she noted that her nurse for the day was supposed to be Deborah.

"Honey, is everything all right? Is there something I can do for you?" Nurse Angelina asked while walking toward the bed.

"No. I'm fine." Zoe sniffled. "Are you here to draw blood or something?"

"Oh no, honey, I just heard you crying, and I wanted to see if I could be of service to you. That is my job, to serve you." The woman's choice of words was odd, but she was touched by the tender compassion in her voice.

"Oh, thank you. I'll be fine. Just a disagreement with… my…a friend. It doesn't help that I'm like a bunch of hormones on steroids." Zoe wasn't ready to share her life history with this stranger.

"Well, don't worry, sweetie. God has a way of working everything out. The Almighty says in His written word, 'Be anxious for nothing, but in everything by prayer and supplication, with thanksgiving, let your requests be made known to God; and the peace of God, which surpasses all understanding, will guard your hearts and minds through Christ Jesus.' Pray to the Almighty. He hears your cries and knows your heart. He loves you beyond words."

The baby in Zoe's arms squirmed and let out a little cry. She looked down to comfort her son, but when she looked up, the nurse was gone. *That's odd. She left so quickly. I didn't even get to thank her.*

33

For though we walk in the flesh, we do not war according to the flesh.
For the weapons of our warfare are not carnal
but mighty in God for pulling down strongholds,
casting down arguments and every high thing
that exalts itself against the knowledge of God,
bringing every thought into captivity to the obedience of Christ...
—2 Corinthians 10:3–5

"So what do you think? Do you think Michael could be the baby's father?" Amos questioned Barbara while stuffing a bite of roast beef on rye into his mouth.

They were seated in the busy hospital cafeteria. People of every nationality filled the room. Some were patients, others were family members or friends, and some were hospital staff. The room buzzed with noise and activity.

Barbara took a sip of coffee before answering. "I don't know. I'd never considered the possibility. Zoe seemed so sure that Zach was the father. I guess anything is possible."

Amos searched Barbara's face for answers. "What do you think is going on up there? Do you think they'll get back together? I just want my baby girl to be happy. She's been through so much.

"I know, Amos. We can pray. There is no power on earth like the power of prayer. Why don't you finish your sandwich and let's go to the chapel and pray for them? After all, it doesn't matter what we want or what we think is best. It matters what God wants to do in their life. We need to ask that His will be done."

"You're not only beautiful, but you're smart. I knew there was a reason why I married you." Amos winked at her from across the tiny lunch table.

"Yea, well don't you ever forget how blessed you are, Mr. Richards." Barbara smiled at him.

After clearing their table, they walked hand in hand out of the cafeteria in search of the hospital chapel.

Michael sat in his car. He turned the heater on for warmth, grabbed his phone and dialed Brad's number.

"Hey, bud, what's up?"

"I need someone to talk to. You got a minute?"

Brad could hear the pain in his friend's voice. He'd been eating lunch with a friend and motioned that he was going to step outside for privacy. "Hold on, man, let me step outside. It's loud in here. I'm at lunch."

"Oh, sorry. You want to call me later?" Michael hoped his friend would take the time to talk to him.

"No, it's cool. I just stepped outside. Whatcha need?" Brad unlocked the door to his pickup truck and hopped inside the cab to escape the bone-chilling winter air.

"Brad…you know I ran into Zoe in Starbucks yesterday and found out that she was pregnant."

"Yea!"

"Yea, well that's not all. We were supposed to have lunch today. When I went to pick her up, I found out that she was at the hospital having the baby. I don't know why, but I just felt like I needed to see her. And you'll never guess what happened. She told me that she thinks the baby, it's a boy, is mine."

"What? That's crazy. How could that be? You two haven't been together since May." He silently began to count backward from January 31st to the middle of May.

"Well, I counted back to when Emma died. We would have had to have sex right before Emma's death. I don't remember if we did or not. But she also thought it could have been Zach's baby, the guy she'd been seeing—which is what threw me for a loop—'cuz that would mean she had sex with him right after we separated, which she didn't deny. I'm having a hard time wrapping my head around that. And I don't think he was the only guy she had sex with. I'm just…I don't know…I'm hurt, and I'm angry, and I would like to go kill the guy."

"So what does Zoe want? Child support? To get back together? Does she want you to be a part of the child's life?"

"I'm not sure. She said something about doing a paternity test. I left her room because I was afraid of what I might say. It was a lot to take in at one time. I'm not sure what she wanted. If we hadn't run into each other at Starbucks, I wouldn't have even known she was pregnant. I don't think she's with Zach anymore, but there might be someone else. She said there was another guy that she'd been with."

Brad silently prayed for wisdom as he listened to Michael talk. "Michael, you need to decide what is important here. I know you're hurt that she was with someone else, but that may be something you'll just need to get over. Are you still at the hospital?"

"Yes, I'm in my car in the garage."

"Okay, maybe you need to spend a few moments in prayer and then go back in there and talk to her. See what she wants. Maybe God has put it in her heart to get back together with you. She was gonna meet you for lunch, right? You've been praying and believing to get back together with her. What if that baby is your son? Man, God may be getting ready to turn your sorrow into joy, and you're sitting in your car angry because Zoe made a mistake. Isn't that why she left you? Because you made a mistake? I think you're going to have to man up and forgive her. She was going through a tragic time in her life, and she messed up. Remember, we talked about extending mercy?"

"I know, but don't you see? I think she'd have to have been communicating with him before Emma's death to hook up with him so quick or else she ran right to him for comfort." Michael winced as images of Zoe in Zachary's arms tormented his mind.

Brad prayed in the Spirit. "I understand. But do you want to hold onto the unforgiveness and pain, or do you want to be restored to your wife? You have to choose. I think you need to think about it. If you want reconciliation, you need to pray and ask God to help you to overlook those things that are hurtful and forgive Zoe."

Brad reached into the console of his truck and pulled out a well-worn pocket New Testament. He located a familiar scripture. "Let me read you a scripture. 'For though we walk in the flesh, we do not war according to the flesh. For the weapons of our warfare are not carnal but mighty in God for pulling down strongholds, casting down arguments and every high thing that exalts itself against the knowledge of God, bringing every thought into captivity to the obedience of Christ.'"

"Bro, I know that you know you have a real enemy. He hates you, and he hates the institution of marriage because it mirrors the relationship we are to have with Christ. I think he's doing a number on your mind trying to get you to focus on what Zoe did and your anger toward this Zach dude. You need to take those thoughts captive. You need to walk in forgiveness and get back up to that room and try to get your wife back. That's where your focus should be. Getting her back and determining whether or not that's your son."

"Is that what you'd do?"

"It doesn't matter what I'd do. It matters what Christ would do. He forgave you and put your past exactly where it should be, in the past. I don't mean to sound harsh but…"

"No, it's okay. It's what I needed to hear, and that's why I called you. I knew you'd speak truth to me, and you wouldn't cater to my feelings. Thanks. Sorry, I disturbed your lunch." Michael chuckled. "Man, I can't believe you'd leave your lunch on the table for me. I'm feeling some love."

Brad laughed. "I know dude. Right? Call me and let me know how everything goes."

"Yea, I will. Thanks again." Michael hung up the phone and immediately bowed his head to pray. "Father, forgive me for my anger toward Zoe and Zach. Help me to forgive and forget Zoe's past. It's the only way we can move forward. Cleanse me from the spirit of anger. Help me to accept Your plan for our lives. I don't know if this baby boy is mine, but I think I could raise him even if he isn't. I want my wife back. It's what I've always wanted. I pray Your will be done. Go before me Holy Spirit and help me to know what to say to Zoe. I ask for Your peace in this situation. In Jesus' name. Amen!"

Zoe was nursing her baby when Michael walked back into the room.

"Can we start over?" He sat on the side of her hospital bed stroking the baby's head as he suckled at her breast. "He really is a beautiful little boy."

"He is. I can't believe God has given me a second chance to be a mom after turning my back on Him. I'm so grateful." She reached out and put her hand on top of his. "Michael, I'm glad you came back. I know I've made awful mistakes. I turned against you and God. I blamed you for Emma's death. I'm so sorry. I wish I could redo the past, but I can't. I've been missing you and thinking about you lately. I couldn't believe it when I ran into you yesterday. Part of me was so excited to see you, but I was also so ashamed of what I'd done."

"I'm sorry I ran out on you. I'm just overwhelmed. Zoe, I have been praying and standing for our marriage all this time. I've never stopped loving you. I'd like to try to work it out. It doesn't matter to me if the baby is mine or not. I'd take you back in a heartbeat. I prayed about it, and I know I could raise Amos as my son."

"I know now that I set myself up for failure even before Emma died. God showed me that I was depending on your faith because you were the spiritual leader of our home. At least, you were when I'd let you. I was materialistic and fought you over money when you were just trying to be responsible and keep us out of debt. I've learned a lot. My biggest problem was my hatred toward Barbara. It gave the enemy entrance into my life. I've asked for her forgiveness, and we're closer now than ever. She was in the room with me when Amos was born. I wasted years of not having a mom because of my rebellion. The saddest thing of all is that I never let her be a grandma to Emma."

Michael's heart was filled with love for his wife. "I think to move forward we have to let the past go. We have to learn from our mistakes, and hopefully, God will use us to help others one day."

"I know your desire is to pastor someday. I want you to know I'd proudly stand by your side in ministry. I listened to your sermon on the Internet. I didn't come to church that day because I didn't want you to know I was pregnant. I was so proud of you."

Michael grabbed both of her hands and held them in his. "So, Zoe Michelle Davis, will you marry me again? Can we put the past behind us and move forward into all that God has for us?"

"Yes!" Tears of joy escaped her eyes. "Michael, you are the most wonderful godly man I've ever known. I think sometimes we have to lose something in order to discover how blessed we truly are. I'd love to be your wife. And this time I mean it when I say till death do us part."

Michael gently embraced Zoe and the baby. Nurse Angelina walked into the room.

"Well, I was just checking in to be sure you were doing better. It looks like the Almighty has worked everything out for your good." She winked at Zoe and smiled at Michael before exiting the room. She vanished as she took a step across the threshold of the door.

Skandalon Study Questions

WEEK 1 (Chapters 1-4)

1. Before reading the book and participating in this study, what was your understanding of the role of angels in your life?

2. Read the bottom section of the book beginning on page 19. How had God tried to warn Michael of impending danger? What was the result of ignoring God's warning signs?

3. Read the middle section of the book beginning on page 20 and ending on page 21. What can we do to enable the angels to work on our behalf?

4. Based on Chapters 1 – 4, as well as our study this past week, can you think of any doors Zoe opened to allow the enemy entrance into her life?

5. Read the section beginning on page 24 and ending on page 25. We see the spirit of lust inform Ramiah that he has a legitimate right to attack Zoe. What gave him that right?

6. Read the middle section beginning on page 28 and ending on page 29. In this section, we see that the enemy is able to keep Michael from entering into the worship service as well as receiving from the message being preached. Why was the enemy effectively able to attack Michael?

7. Read the section beginning on page 31 and ending on page 32. Zoe's Grandma Abby is led to pray for her granddaughter. How did the Lord prompt this need or desire within her to intercede?

8. Read about Michael's encounter with Brad beginning on page 34 and ending on page 36. Brad encourages Michael to make sure his motives are right when praying for Zoe. How can we pray with wrong motives? Give examples from your life if possible.

9. Read the middle section of the book beginning on page 51 and ending on page 52. Why do you think it is precious in the sight of the Lord when a saint dies? How comforting is it to know that when a child of God dies they are accompanied to heaven by an angelic escort?

10. After Emma's death, the Lord had three people to interact in the situation. The 911 operator, the police officer, and Pastor Steve. How did they represent the love of Christ to Michael?

Skandalon Study Questions

WEEK 2 (Chapters 5-8)

1. Read the middle section on page 65. Looking at the passage, what is God's response when we experience tragedy? How did He respond to Zoe's anger? Does our anger affect His love for us?

2. Read the middle section beginning on page 67. How do Grief and Despair overcome their victims? How did Zoe open her heart to their assault? Read 1 Thessalonians 4:13. What do you think it means to sorrow as those who have no hope?

3. Read the middle section beginning on page 70 all the way through to the end of the chapter. 'Where was God' is a question that is often asked by those who experience tragic circumstances. Read Hebrews 13:5. What is God's promise to every believer?

4. According to this passage in the book, what was God's response when asked by Michael, "Lord, where were you? Why didn't you warn me?"

5. Based on the above passage from the book, how did the enemy try to use the tragedy against the believers in our story?

6. Read the middle section beginning on page 76 and ending on page 77, what did Zoe do to allow the enemy the ability to keep her in his snare?

7. Based on the above passage in the book, how did the spirit of Divorce work to ensure the success of the kingdom of darkness?

8. Read the middle section on page 81 and ending on page 82. Does it bring comfort to you to know that God is able to keep those who belong to Him? Why?

9. Read the section that begins on page 88 and the following section that

begins on page 89. How was Michael able to overcome the spirit of Depression? What part did Deuel and the angels play to bring peace into the situation?

10. Read the bottom section beginning on pages 96 and ending on page 99. How can our words affect our hope? What do you think it means to have a dead womb experience? How would you react to such an experience?

Skandalon Study Questions

WEEK 3 (Chapters 9-12)

1. Read the middle section beginning on page 107 and ending on page 108. What do you think it means to be a surrendered, sold-out believer as opposed to being a Christian in word but not in deed?

2. Read the middle section beginning on page 113 and ending on page 115. What brought freedom for Barbara? What does the Bible have to say about truth? Read Psalm 51:6, John 8:32, John 16:13 and Ephesians 4:15.

3. Based on the section that begins at the bottom of page 118 and ends on page 119, how do you think it is possible to be influenced or manipulated by a demonic spirit? What did Zoe do to allow herself to be put in such an easy position to be influenced?

4. Looking at the same passage, what was the open door in Zach's life that gave entrance to the enemy?

5. Read the section beginning on page 120. What was Ramiah waiting for in order to take down Zoe's enemies?

6. Read the section beginning on page 138 and ending on page 140. Michael felt like he'd done something to cause God to abandon and punish him. What was Shara's response to her son?

7. On page 139, Shara gives possible reasons as to why Emma died. What were some of them? What does the word "ensnare" mean in Hebrews 12:1? According to Shara, how do we give the enemy authority to ensnare us?

8. Based on the last paragraph on page 139, how can we forfeit the authority that God has given us over our enemy?

9   Based on the last paragraph on page 139, what was the open door for the enemy in Michael's life?

10. Read the middle section on page 144. In this passage of the book, we see Ramiah doing a specific function on Zoe's behalf. What was it?

Skandalon Study Questions

WEEK 4 (Chapters 13-16)

1. Read the section beginning on page 155 and ending on page 157. How did Michael use the Word of God to bring peace into his situation? How was the Scripture passage revealed to him?

2. Based on the passage beginning in the middle of page 157 and ending on page 158, how was God able to use Michael's trial for good?

3. Read the section beginning on page 165 and ending on page 166. When faced with disappointment, what did Michael do in order to find God's peace?

4. Read the middle section beginning on page 170 through to page 172. Based on this passage, what does it mean to surrender your situation over to God? Share something (a situation, a loved one, a trial) that you need to surrender over to God.

5. Read the middle section beginning on page 175 and ending on page 176. According to this passage, what empowered Ramiah's sword?

6. Read the section beginning on page 184 and ending on page 185. What does Michael have to say about the importance of prayer? Think of a time in your life when the prayers of others affected your situation.

7. Based on the same passage, how did the Lord comfort Michael as he grieved over Emma? What were the angels doing?

8. Read the middle section beginning on page 191 and ending on page 196. How did Kira receive the word for Michael? What specifically do you notice about the word? Do you believe the Lord could and would give you a word for someone else?

9. Based on the above passage, can you think of a time when God has given you a word of encouragement from another believer? Was it based on Scripture? How did it affect your life?

10. Read the section beginning on page 194 and ending on page 196. When we surrender our situation over to the Lord, what is it demonstrating to Him? What advice did Brad give Michael about God's timing?

Skandalon Discussion Questions

1. Read the section beginning on page 201 and ending on page 203. Zoe is having a discussion with her grandma. Grandma Abby talks to Zoe about holding onto grudges...nurturing hatred and being unwilling to forgive. How do you think Zoe's attitude toward her stepmom affected her attitude toward Michael?

2. Read the middle section on page 204 as well as the section following from page 204 to 207. We see in these passages an importance on planting seeds in the life of individuals. What seed did Grandma Abby plant while on her phone call with Zoe? How did Carol water the seeds planted by Grandma Abby? What seed did Carol's neighbor plant in Carol's life after the loss of her son? Read 1 Corinthians 3:5-10. What does this passage say about the importance of planting and watering seed in the lives of individuals?

3. Read the middle section beginning on page 207 and ending on page 208. What does Zoe try to use to mask her pain to get Carol's story off of her mind and forget all of her cares?

4. Read the section beginning on page 208 and ending on page 209. How did Pastor Steve respond to Donovan's sin? How did he ask the church to treat Donovan?

5. Based on this same passage, what do you think Pastor Steve meant by the following sentence? "Are we going to help them back up and pray for their restoration, or are we going to throw stones?" Read John 8:3-12.

6. Read the bottom section beginning on page 209 and ending on page 210. How did one man's sin affect the entire church? How can your sin affect the lives of others?

7. Read the middle section beginning on page 214 and ending on page 216. How did the enemy try to discourage Michael from taking the youth pastor position?

8. Based on the above passage, what did Michael do to counter the attack?

9. Read the middle section beginning on page 231. Has it ever occurred to you that Jesus makes intercession for you? Read Romans 8:34 and Hebrews 7:25. What do these Scriptures tell us? How comforting is it for you to know that Jesus intercedes for you?

10. Read the middle section beginning on page 238 and ending on page 239. In this passage we see anger rising up in Michael after he receives divorce papers. How does Michael counter this attack? What Scripture did God speak into Michael's spirit? Read Matthew 5:44. How does Jesus tell us to respond to our enemies? How did Michael pray for Zach?

Skandalon Discussion Questions

1. Read the third paragraph on page 250. Why did Grandma Abby's spirit never taste death? Read 2 Corinthians 5:8 to help you answer this question.

2. Read the fifth paragraph beginning on page 250. How can we live a life without the fear of death as Grandma Abby did in this story? Read John 11:25-26 and John 3:16.

3. Read the middle section beginning on page 255 and ending on page 256. In this passage we begin to see Zoe's heart softening and the realization that her life is a mess. Thankfully, she cries out to the Lord for forgiveness. What kept her from receiving the Scripture that the Lord spoke into her spirit? Has it ever been difficult for you to receive the Lord's love, His promise or His forgiveness because of guilt and condemnation? If so, please share.

4. Read the bottom section beginning on page 256 and ending on page 257. Where do we see the Lord as Zoe prays for forgiveness? What is His proclamation over Zoe which gave the angels reason to rejoice? How does this give you hope when you cry out to God?

5. Based on the above passage, what happened as soon as Zoe cried out to the Lord?

6. Read the middle section beginning on page 261 and ending on page 262. What was the name of the chief power over the downtown abortion clinic? What was the name of his accomplice? What were they skilled at accomplishing?

7. Read Leviticus 18:21, Leviticus 20:2-5, and Jeremiah 32:35. Based on these passages, how did the Israelites demonstrate their worship to the

false god, Molech? What was to be the punishment for the one who sacrificed their children to the false god? How can we relate this to modern day abortion?

8. What does Romans 8:1 have to say to the one who has had an abortion but sought God for His forgiveness?

9. Read the middle section beginning on page 267. How was the spirit of Gossip able to coax people to gossip about Zoe?

10. Read the middle section beginning on page 286 and ending on page 288. What happened in the spiritual realm as soon as Zoe cried out to the Lord for help in forgiving Barbara?

Skandalon Discussion Questions

WEEK 7 (Chapters 25-28)

1. Read the middle section on page on 296. How was Dekar planning on using Shame and Disgrace to attack Zoe?

2. Read Psalm 103:12, Isaiah 43:25, Hebrews 8:12, and Isaiah 38:17. What happens when we ask for forgiveness of our sins?

3. Read Philippians 3:12-14. What does this Scripture tell us we are to do regarding our sinful past?

4. Read the middle section beginning on page 298 and ending on page 299. What happened to Michael when Zoe texted him that she couldn't come to listen to him preach his first sermon at New Zion Church?

5. What about you? Have you ever grown weary while waiting on God to answer your prayers or bring His promise to pass in your life? How did God encourage Michael to hang on?

6. Read the section beginning on page 309 and ending on page 312. According to the second paragraph on page 310, what does the word Skandalon mean? Can you think of a time when Satan has snared you with something that looked innocent and tempting?

7. How did Michael relate the word Skandalon in relation to Jesus and Peter? Read Matthew 16:21-23. Can you think of ways that the enemy could use you to set a trap for others?

8. Looking at the second paragraph on page 311, what common trap of the enemy does Michael address? How does he relate it to his own life? Read 1 John 4:18. How can perfect love cast out fear?

9. Read the top section beginning on page 325. How was Satan using

Sophie to entice Michael into a trap? How had Sophie unknowingly been used as bait for the trap?

10. Read the bottom section beginning on page 327 and ending on page 329. Look at the first paragraph on page 328. According to the paragraph, why are we able to love like Christ? Read Romans 5:5, 1 John 4:7-8, and 1 John 4:15-16.

Skandalon Discussion Questions

1. Read the bottom section beginning on page 333 and ending on page 335. Look at the prayer Carol's husband prayed after the birth of their premature twins. It is on page 334. How does this prayer demonstrate his complete trust in the Father for the life of his babies? Read Habakkuk 3:17-18. What does this Scripture speak to you about rejoicing in the Lord in the midst of trials?

2. Read the section beginning on page 337 and ending on page 339. How did Michael come to realize that it was not God's will for him to have a relationship with Sophie? (You might want to refer back to the dream he had on page 321-322 and the section beginning on page 335 and ending on page 336.)

3. On page 338 in this same section, God spoke to Michael about the television shows he was watching. What was God's warning to Michael? Do you believe that you can open yourself up to demonic activity by the forms of entertainment you choose to watch or listen to? Read Psalm 1:1-2 and Psalm 101:3. What do these two Scriptures have to say about guarding our eyes?

4. Read the bottom section beginning on page 342 and ending at the top of page 344. Zoe discovers that Carol and John lost one of their babies. How does she respond?

5. Based on the same section, how did God respond to Zoe?

6. How did John respond to the questions Zoe raised as to why God would allow the death of his son? Read Romans 8:28. How does this Scripture prove what John says about God turning this tragedy into something for His glory?

7. Read the section beginning at the top of page 347. Why were Gloom and Depression so upset? Read 2 Corinthians 10:5. What does this Scripture tell us to do with negative thoughts sent from the enemy?

8. Read the bottom section beginning on page 353 and ending on page 355. In this passage, we see that Michael is discouraged and unable to see how God can put his marriage back together since their divorce has become finalized. How does his pastor encourage him?

9. Look at the middle section beginning on page 372 and ending on page 374. Michael is upset and confused. Look at the last paragraph on page 373. What question does Brad pose to Michael?

10. How has the story of Skandalon changed your life, your perspective on the spiritual realm and how you pray?

Note from the author:

Thank you so very much for taking the time to read this novel. I hope you enjoyed Skandalon. I'd love to hear what you thought about the book. You can leave a comment on my website: sftjm.com or visit Amazon and leave a comment on my author page.

You can also connect with me on Facebook at Strength for the Journey Ministry

Determined to Soar,

Cindy

www.ingramcontent.com/pod-product-compliance
Lightning Source LLC
Chambersburg PA
CBHW060811030726
47503CB00002B/446